INFINITY ENGINE

Neal Asher was born in Billericay, Essex, and divides his time between here and Crete. His previous full-length novels are *Gridlinked, The Skinner, The Line of Polity, Cowl, Brass Man, The Voyage of the Sable Keech, Hilldiggers, Prador Moon, Line War, Shadow of the Scorpion, Orbus* and *The Technician*. His Owner series novels include *The Departure, Zero Point* and *Jupiter War*. *Infinity Engine* is the third in a new series set in the Polity universe, following *Dark Intelligence* and *War Factory*.

By *Neal Asher*

Agent Cormac
Gridlinked
The Line of Polity
Brass Man
Polity Agent
Line War

Spatterjay
The Skinner
The Voyage of the Sable Keech
Orbus

Novels of the Polity
Prador Moon
Hilldiggers
Shadow of the Scorpion

The Technician

The Owner
The Departure
Zero Point
Jupiter War

Transformation
Dark Intelligence
War Factory
Infinity Engine

Cowl

Novellas
The Parasite
Mindgames: Fool's Mate

Short-story collections
Runcible Tales
The Engineer
The Gabble

NEAL ASHER

INFINITY ENGINE

Transformation, Book Three

TOR

First published 2017 by Tor,
an imprint of Pan Macmillan
20 New Wharf Road, London N1 9RR
Associated companies throughout the world
www.panmacmillan.com

ISBN 978-1-5098-4347-3

1 3 5 7 9 8 6 4 2

A CIP catalogue record for this book is available from the British Library.

Typeset by Ellipsis Digital Limited, Glasgow
Printed and bound by CPI Group (UK) Ltd, Croydon, CR0 4YY

Caroline Asher
10/7/59–24/1/14

Time trammels memory and healing is the formation
of scar tissue, which never quite fills the hole.

Composer Steve Buick has created an album of original music inspired by *Infinity Engine*. This background music has been designed to enhance the reading experience, to be enjoyed while reading the book itself. Using long, deeply dark soundscape layers – to complement the story's atmosphere – he aims to add another dimension to reading without distracting from the action. The music can accompany any section of the book and is available as an MP3 album from Amazon, iTunes and other digital music stores worldwide. Please search for 'Original Music for Neal Asher's Infinity Engine' and you can also find out more at www.evokescape.com.

Acknowledgements

Many thanks to all those who have helped bring this novel to your brain via your e-reader, smart phone, computer screen or that old-fashioned mass of wood pulp called a book. At Macmillan these include Natalie McCourt, Phoebe Taylor, Neil Lang, and others whose names I simply don't know. Further thanks go to Steve Stone for his arresting cover image, Bella Pagan for her editorial and publishing input and Bruno Vincent for his copious editorial work.

Cast of Characters

Penny Royal (the Black AI)

An artificial intelligence constructed in Factory Station Room 101, during the Polity war against the prador. Its crystal mind was faulty, burdened with emotions it could not encompass when it was hurled into the heat of battle. Running the destroyer that it named *Puling Child*, it fought and survived, then annihilated eight thousand troops on its own side before going AWOL. It changed into something dark then – a swarm robot whose integrated form was like a giant sea urchin. Blacklisted by the Polity for ensuing atrocities, it based itself in the Graveyard – a borderland created between the Polity and the Prador Kingdom after the war. There it continued its evil games, offering transformations for the right price, but ones that were never entirely beneficial for the recipients. It was nearly destroyed in a deal that went wrong. Later restored to function by the scorpion war drone Amistad, it apparently became a good AI . . . Now the black AI is moving into its endgame, its plans still obscure and its actions paradigm-changing. And still no one knows if its intent is evil.

Thorvald Spear

Resurrected from a recording of his own mind, a hundred years after the war, he is the only survivor of the eight thousand troops slaughtered by Penny Royal on the planet Panarchia. He resolved to have his revenge on the AI and to that end sought out its old destroyer, whose location he had learned of during the war. Taking command of it, he set out in search of the rogue AI. During this search he discovered that his very desire for vengeance had been created by Penny Royal, for it had tampered with his memories. Nevertheless his quest is reinforced by an artefact he found aboard the destroyer – one of Penny Royal's spines. It has downloaded memories of its victims into his mind. He did believe himself the instrument the AI created for its own destruction, but now is not sure what to believe at all, other than that he must see this through to its end.

Riss

An assassin drone and terror weapon. Made in Room 101 in the shape of a prador parasite which has a passing resemblance to a cobra, her purpose was to inject prador with parasite eggs, spreading infection and terror amidst them. The end of the war meant she lost her purpose for being and, while searching for a new purpose, lost even more when she encountered Penny Royal. Thorvald Spear found her somnolent and bereft near the AI's home base in the Graveyard. Accompanying him during his quest for vengeance, she was finally manipulated into killing the prador Sverl.

Sverl

A prador who disagreed with the new king's decision to make peace with the Polity. He went renegade and hid out with other prador of similar mind in the Graveyard. He could not understand how it was possible that the prador had started to lose against weak humans and their detestable AIs. He sought understanding of this conundrum from Penny Royal, but got more than he bargained for. Penny Royal initiated his transformation into a grotesque amalgam of prador, human and AI, so he could better understand each. While seeking some resolution to his situation, Sverl was led by Penny Royal to an ancient Polity war factory. There he thought the AI had some task for him, but he was killed by the assassin drone Riss.

Captain Blite

A trader whose business edges into illegality. During a deal that turned sour he encountered Penny Royal, who killed his crew. His second encounter with the AI was when it used him and his ship as an escape from the world of Masada. With his ship under the control of the black AI, Blite has witnessed its obscure business in the Graveyard and elsewhere and come to realize that it may be correcting past wrongs. After recognizing this, he and his crew were abandoned again on Masada, but the advanced technology left aboard their ship (not to mention their first-hand knowledge of Penny Royal) meant they were of great interest to the Polity AIs. Blite escaped the Polity and continued to pursue Penny Royal. Once again he is dragged into its obscure manipulations . . .

Sfolk

A prador first-child. He and his brothers came under the mental control of Father-Captain Cvorn. Sfolk alone managed to free himself from control and afterwards killed Cvorn but as he was escaping in Cvorn's ship it was badly damaged by other prador ships before entering U-space.

Sepia

A catadapt woman – one with some of the characteristics of a cat. Along with the shell people and other refugees, she was rescued from certain death on the world Rock Pool by Father-Captain Sverl. With Trent she escaped the gruesome end that Taiken, the leader of the shell people, had in mind for them.

The Brockle

A powerful artificial intelligence – a swarm robot consisting of numerous worm-like units that it can pull together into human form. It worked for Earth Central Security in black ops but went too far during one mission and many people were killed. Such was its nature that it would have been difficult for ECS to capture and prosecute it. Instead it 'agreed' to confinement aboard a spaceship, the *Tyburn*, where it acted as an interrogator for ECS. It broke the agreement to go after Penny Royal, which it considers to be a threat ECS is not taking seriously enough.

Amistad

A war drone (robot) in the form of a giant metal scorpion. At the end of the war he went crazy then AWOL, pursuing a fanatical new interest in madness. It was he who found Penny Royal after that AI had been all but destroyed by an alien device, and resurrected it. Amistad subsequently became warden of Masada with Penny Royal as his closely watched assistant, until the AI hijacked Captain Blite's ship and escaped.

The Weaver

The only living member of the Atheter race. The Atheter sacrificed their minds in a kind of racial suicide, leaving only their nonsense-speaking descendants the gabbleducks – creatures like a semi-insectile by-blow of a platypus and Buddha. The Weaver was one of these until it had a surviving mind of one of the Atheter loaded to it. Under Polity law it then became ruler of its home world, Masada.

Trent Sobel

Killer for hire who worked for the crime lord Isobel Satomi. He survived Satomi's fall and was given a conscience and empathy by Penny Royal. He has no idea why, but is learning to deal with these attributes.

Greer

One of Captain Blite's loyal crewmembers.

Flute

At first the frozen mind of a prador child used as the navigational mind of Spear's ship the *Lance*, Flute loaded to crystal and became an AI.

Glossary

Atheter: One of the millions of long-dead races, recently revived. It was discovered that the gabbleducks of the planet Masada were the devolved descendants of the Atheter. This race chose to sacrifice its civilization and intelligence to escape the millennia of wars resulting from its discovery of Jain technology.

Augmented: To be 'augmented' is to have taken advantage of one or more of the many available cybernetic devices, mechanical additions and, distinctly, cerebral augmentations. In the last case we have, of course, the ubiquitous 'aug' and such back-formations as 'auged', 'auging in', and the execrable 'all auged up'. But it does not stop there: the word 'aug' has now become confused with auger and augur – which is understandable considering the way an aug connects and the information that then becomes available. So now you can 'auger' information from the AI net, and a prediction made by an aug prognostic subprogram can be called an augury.
– From 'Quince Guide' compiled by humans.

First- and second-children: Prador offspring chemically maintained in adolescence.

Golem: Androids produced by a company Cybercorp – a ceramal chassis usually enclosed in a syntheflesh and syntheskin outer layer. These humanoid robots are very tough, fast and, since they possess AI, very smart.

Haiman: An amalgam of human and AI.

Hooder: A creature like a giant centipede of the planet Masada. It was discovered that they were the devolved descendants of biomech war machines created by the Atheter throughout their millennia of civil wars.

Jain technology: A technology spanning all scientific disciplines. Created by one of the dead races – the Jain – its sum purpose is to spread through civilizations and annihilate them.

Nascuff: A device that can externally adjust a person's nano-suite to their sexual inclination. It is mainly worn to advertise sexual availability or otherwise. When the libido of the one wearing it is shut down the cuff is red. When they are sexually active it is blue.

Polity: A human/AI dominion extending across many star systems, occupying a spherical space spanning the thickness of the galaxy and centred on Earth. It is ruled over by the AIs who took control of human affairs in what has been called, because of its very low casualty rate, the Quiet War. The top AI is called Earth Central and resides in a building on the shore of Lake Geneva, while planetary AIs, lower down in the hierarchy, rule over other worlds. The Polity is a highly technical civilization but its weakness was its reliance on travel by 'runcible' – instantaneous matter transmission gates. This weakness was exploited by the prador.

Prador: A highly xenophobic race of giant crablike aliens ruled by a king and his family. Hostility is implicit in their biology and, upon encountering the Polity, they immediately attacked it.

Their advantage in this war was that they did not use runcibles (such devices needed the intelligence of AIs to control them and the prador are also hostile to any form of artificial intelligence) and as a result had developed their spaceship technology, and the metallurgy involved, beyond that of the Polity. They attacked with near-indestructible ships, but in the end the humans and AIs adapted and in their war factories out-manufactured the prador and began to win. They did not complete the victory, however, because the old king was usurped and the new king made an uneasy peace with the Polity.

Shell people: a group of cultist humans whose admiration of the prador was such that they tried to alter themselves surgically to become prador.

1

Haiman Crowther

Haiman Isembard Crowther relished the solitude of the Well Head, though of course with Owl here he was never quite as alone as he would have liked. The Well Head space station, a cylinder a mile long, hung poised at an angle over the boiling and seemingly infinite sea of the accretion disc around the Layden's Sink black hole. Its structure was the toughest going, reinforced by the output of grav-engines so the tidal forces would not tear it apart, as they had the worlds and suns whose matter made up the disc. Scaled armour of hardfields at the nose intercepted anything material that might be thrown its way, while further Buzzard magnetic fields simultaneously bent lethal EMR round it and fed upon that radiation. The station sat in perfect balance: drawing energy from its environment and only occasionally having to resort to the output of its array of giga-watt fusion reactors.

Crowther, his thin form occupying an interface sphere inset halfway along the body of the station, observed data flows and physical phenomena via the multitude of sensors to which the sphere connected, and processed that data in his numerous aug-mentations. This was his job: studying and analysing this unique black hole. He wasn't the only one watching. Owl, who had once been a spy drone during the prador/human war and had since seriously upgraded his capabilities, squatted on the skin of the station and could sense just about every known phenomenon in local and non-local space. The drone observed with a depth of perception that Crowther envied. Machine envy, some called it – the force driving human beings to become haiman and, maybe some time in the near future, something more.

Crowther ran his thin fingers through his mop of blond hair then relaxed and focused on the data now coming in through the Hawking dish. Given the opportunity – that was, pure vacuum and a lot less in the way of matter being dumped into them – black holes evaporated. It might take billions of years, what with the slow trickle of Hawking radiation from them, but eventually they dried up and winked out. This was supposedly the only possible realspace output of such cosmic objects. Other processes operated via U-space – complex, interesting processes that Owl and Crowther were observing too. But none of them was quite as interesting as the Hawking radiation, because from Layden's Sink it wasn't always a simple chaotic output. Occasionally radiation exited in organized form, as data. How long this had been going on they had no idea, though according to some historical files this data output had been detected during the war. They had no idea what it was coming from, other than the hole itself. How anything could survive in a form capable of transmitting data as Hawking radiation from behind the event horizon was more than just a puzzle, it was one of the biggest questions facing present-day Polity science.

'Always behind the curve,' said Crowther, glancing through an exterior sensor pole towards Owl just moments before the pulse of new data waned.

'Always,' Owl agreed.

The data never revealed anything new. Whenever it indicated something apparently new, further checking showed that the discovery had been made somewhere. Crowther had been highly excited when a data pulse suggested the potential for a gravity-wave weapon. 'Already being fitted to some ships,' Earth Central had replied. Additional data from the black hole had revealed further applications: U-space disruptor mines, missiles, concomitant ways of improving grav-engines and grav-plates and some ways of storing or diverting the energy that runcibles – matter transmission gates – usually relayed to their buffers. He was unsurprised to discover that the leaps had already been made in the Polity, but then another thought occurred and he did some checking on timings. It seemed, on universal time, that sometimes the data issued from the black hole at, as near as he could calculate, the precise moment it came into being in the Polity. Was this some weird kind of reflection or a phenomenon that opened that vast can of worms called predestination?

'But possibly useful,' Owl added.

The drone was an odd-looking creature. His ten-foot long body was a teardrop from which extended the four legs with which he gripped the hull of the station. To his fore – the wide point of the teardrop – his face was very much like that of an owl, with two large concave sensor dishes, concentrically ringed with iridescent meta-materials around central white-diamond eyes. When he had first met the drone, Crowther had wondered what it was about its shape that bothered him so. However, a microsecond of puzzlement led to a mental search which, a further microsecond later, pulled up visual files from that compartment of his memory labelled Two-dimensional Art. Owl was reminiscent of the kind of creature painted by the Dutch artist Hieronymus Bosch.

He scanned through the data again. There was more stuff there about universal pattern formation and its underlying principles, something about a branch of science that related to an ancient theory called 'string theory', a great deal of heavy math of the kind runcible AIs dealt with and some frankly bizarre physics that related uncomfortably to Crowther's earlier thoughts about predestination. Despite his haiman augmentations, much of it was beyond him but, more importantly, didn't interest him. What did grab his interest were the brief messages in human speech or text that sometimes slipped through, almost as if something in the black hole was talking in the background during the transmission.

The last one he had picked up had been, 'And the trinity becomes one.' He'd queried that with Earth Central and been told, 'Classified – do not distribute.' Other messages he had been allowed to distribute for analysis, and swiftly received many thousands of different answers. The one that ran, 'The lair of the white worm is large,' could have been to do with a new fantasy virtuality based on the writing of an ancient scribe called Bram Stoker. However, further analysis revealed that it had been chosen via a creative search program that had keyed on events on the planet Masada, and the words 'white worm'. The comment had something to do with the Atheter war machine there, the Technician, and its eventual demise, but data from Masada had recently been under some heavy restrictions and the entire meaning of the phrase remained unclear. Sometimes, trying to work out what these phrases meant was like delving into Nostradamus.

This time the phrase was, 'Your greatest fear – the room stands open.' Crowther sent this directly to Earth Central then began his own analysis and soon came up with George Orwell's *1984* and Room 101, the place which contained the protagonist's greatest fear. Beyond that the references branched into the millions, since Room 101 had embedded itself in human culture. There had even been that Polity factory station extant during the prador/human war – a thing like a giant harmonica eighty miles long, thirty miles wide and fifteen deep, with square holes running along either side of it that were exits from enormous final-fitting bays. That had been called Room 101 . . .

'Classified – do not distribute,' Earth Central replied, and then followed that with a huge data package.

As he studied the new data from EC, Crowther was pretty certain it had been sent to distract him from that latest phrase, but he let that go because firstly he would get nowhere making queries and secondly this fresh data really did interest him, especially the newly declassified stuff. He now focused through his long-range sensors back across the accretion disc towards the planetary system currently being swept in the direction of the black hole. He had already reconstructed the physical history of most of the worlds in that system since their birth in a wholly different kind of accretion disc. One of them contained some odd metals that had only been added to the elementary table in the last hundred years, and there was a ruined prador base on another, but otherwise they weren't particularly interesting. However, the world of Panarchia fascinated him, and that was what this declassified data was about.

He'd brought its history up to date at the start of the war – this work a bit of a sideline from his real job. He'd covered the initial terraforming of the world, its early colonies, then the later colonists who had haphazardly imported exotic life forms – one of which, the octupal, a kind of land octopus, had come to dominate. He'd covered the evacuation of the world ahead of the prador advance, then the final slaughter of those who had remained after the prador arrived. And he'd covered much about the third push-back, when Polity forces had advanced, reclaiming territory, and some vicious battles had been fought in the area. But now: the declassified data . . .

Penny Royal . . .

Crowther felt as if something was creeping up his spine. He

knew about the black AI Penny Royal, but then who didn't? What he had not known was that this was the place where that creature had first been deployed as the mind of a destroyer which bore an odd name: the *Puling Child*. Apparently the conflict here had been so intense that a Polity factory station had been pulled in to supply ships. During that conflict –

Crowther went still as he gazed at the old images of that factory station and absorbed what the thing had been called: Room 101. Whatever had been creeping up his spine had now donned a pair of hobnail boots.

So, Penny Royal had been created in Room 101, not far from Crowther's current location. It had taken part in some battles about the Panarchia system. During one of those battles Polity forces had been trapped on the surface of Panarchia, surrounded by much larger prador forces that could have overwhelmed them in a moment, but didn't. Next, during what appeared to be an attempt to rescue those forces from the planet – eight thousand mostly human troops – Penny Royal had gone rogue. The AI had managed to penetrate behind prador lines but, instead of attempting a rescue, it had anti-matter bombed the troops from orbit and annihilated them all.

Crowther ran through the summation again, then concentrated on the detail. There was something decidedly odd about this. Yes, rogue AIs tended to get a bit anti-human and Penny Royal, in later incidents, had definitely demonstrated that tendency. But why would such an AI have penetrated *behind prador lines* to wipe out troops who, judging by the tactical data, were doomed anyway?

The Brockle

During its long confinement inside the prison hulk the *Tyburn*, the Brockle had always dealt with those who were demonstrably guilty of taking the lives of others. However, there were times when it really wanted to interrogate a wider selection of subjects than those who were obviously guilty. Members of separatist organizations, for instance, who, though they might have no blood on their hands, were facilitators who were culpable in murder. Those on the periphery of crimes – but these beings had never been sent. The Brockle had decided that there were degrees of guilt and criminality, and one of them was the criminal negligence that allowed crime to exist at all. In that way of looking at things, the whole human race was guilty.

Only the ignorance of humans and their stubborn insistence in not raising themselves to higher levels of intelligence allowed crime to survive. They stupidly did not realize that the Polity was perfectible and that they were holding it back. Yet wasn't it also the case that Polity AIs were as guilty? They could force the human race to uplift itself, or they could simply rub out the species and get on with creating a utopia –

'So what ship is that?'

Brought out of its ruminations, the Brockle looked out of the panoramic window in the side of outlink station Par Avion at a ship of a somewhat unusual design. Accessing the memories it had stolen from its victims, the Brockle realized its overall shape was that of a kipper. However, it was two miles long and three-quarters of a mile wide, its hue metallic and its patterning more like that of a mackerel. Thereafter such piscine analogies ran out. Scattered across the visible face were sensor towers and instrument blisters like glass dome houses, while near the 'head' crouched two blocky weapons turrets. These were the only visible signs of the huge collection of highly advanced armaments and other instrumentation packed inside. The ship was diamond state – part frontline dreadnought and part research ship – and just what the Brockle required.

The Brockle turned from the window and studied the woman who had spoken. Long experienced in divining human expressions, the forensic AI recognized at once that she was wary of it, but also curious. There was something about the Brockle that worried her, but she was in the Polity and therefore safe. She was also old, definitely into her second century, and bored. She wore an aug, so if someone attacked her or confronted her with anything weird she could inform the station AI in an instant.

'It's the *High Castle*,' the Brockle replied. 'But why did you feel it necessary to ask me when you could have auged the information from the station AI?'

'It was a conversational gambit,' she said, moving up beside it and resting her hands on the rail before the window, 'because I tend to get curious when I see a man who appears to have big silvery worms moving about under his skin.'

The Brockle felt a moment of chagrin as it reined in the activity of its units and returned its skin to its usual opaque hue. While lost in speculation it had allowed its guard to drop. This was down to its many years of confinement; while aboard the *Tyburn* it had found no need for the concealment it had used in its earlier profession. It must be more careful in future, but right now it had a problem to solve.

'So what's all that about, then?' she asked.

The Brockle searched for a suitable explanation and shortly pasted one together out of the thousands of lives in its memory banks. Assuming a weary and bored expression, it said, 'It was once a fashion of the runcible culture. But then things moved on into the positively grotesque and left me behind.'

The woman was auged so almost certainly had the standard thousand hours of sensory recording of her life, though why humans liked to record the tedium of their existence was a puzzle. No such recordings of the Brockle had been made any-where else in this station: it had worked its way here via air ducts and gas pipes from the small single-ship dock, subverting all pin cams and constantly altering the images of it that the cameras here perceived. So wary of the Par Avion AI had it been, it had stupidly neglected to pay attention to mere humans. Even more stupidly, it had retained its usual human shape, which would of course be recognizable to all AIs and any humans who had encountered it in the past, although admittedly few of the latter were still alive.

She would have to be dealt with.

The Brockle stepped closer to the rail and placed one of its own hands on it. The unit it extruded matched the grain of the ersatz wood perfectly as it slid a thin sliver of itself towards her hands. Emitting just the right EM frequency as it approached them, it numbed her nerves just enough so she didn't notice as it slid under her palms and bonded them to the rail. Further numbing her nerves, it opened finger-wide holes in her palms and began to work its way up her arms, steadily shutting nerves down ahead of it. It should be able to scramble any data she retained about this encounter and leave her in a semi-conscious state, wandering through this space station.

'I too used to run with that crowd,' she said convivially. She then tried to move her hands. 'Damn . . . some little cocksucker!'

'What?' The Brockle gazed at her in puzzlement.

'Hyperglue on the rail. Fuckit!'

A thousand scenarios played out in the Brockle's mind until

it finally realized it had only one course of action. It reached out, snake-fast, no time now to be subtle since she would call for help the moment she stopped cursing. Subverting the cams behind so they showed two slim women standing at this rail, the Brockle grabbed her aug, probing inside the thing as it did so and jamming it. Analysis revealed the make and model of the device and how it was anchored into her skull, so the Brockle used the requisite force to tear it free. Her head bent right over on her neck before the bones broke. The aug tore free with chunks of skull attached, exposing brain before the hole rapidly filled with blood. However, there would not be as much blood as was usual from such a wound, since the force required to remove the aug had also broken her neck.

An error of judgement.

The Brockle quickly forced its unit up through the top part of her arms, through her shoulders and up inside her neck, into her skull. There it paused for a moment because, even now, it was within its abilities to save her life. Then it came to a decision. It had already breached its confinement and killed nominally innocent human beings. It was committed now to a grander aim and could not allow another easily replaceable example of the billions of human beings scattered across the Polity to get in its way. It set the end of the unit to blender mode and turned the inside of her skull to mush, extracted its unit fast so it came out like a bloody whip, then turned and ran, rapidly absorbing the said unit.

No time to dally now. As it ran, the Brockle crushed the aug in the palm of its hand, injected diatomic acid into it, then dropped the rapidly dissolving thing on the floor. Rounding the end of the walkway and entering one of the corridors spearing into the station, it slowed to a walk and began transforming. Its blue overall steadily darkened, the top half separating from the bottom, buttons and fancy stick seams appearing as it changed into high-class businesswear, shrinking to fit the Brockle's steadily diminishing bulk. As this process continued, the AI was faced with a choice: it could increase its height to redistribute the internal mass of its units, or it could compress them. In the former case this would result in its standing over seven feet tall which, though not particularly unusual, wasn't as low profile as it would like. In the latter case compression would result in a reduction in the efficiency of its units, and it was going to need them.

In a flash of inspiration it halted, squatted down and began extruding a great mass of its units from its stomach. The thick silvery worms squirmed out one after the other and coagulated into a great mass on the floor, shaped themselves to give flat edges and corners and darkened, then rose up off the floor as a fairly standard piece of hover luggage.

The Brockle moved on, immediately coming face to face with a group of humans and Golem. It stepped aside to allow them to pass, feeling a frisson of anxiety knowing that, had they entered this corridor just a moment earlier . . . One of the Golem shot it an odd look, but that was most likely because of some breach of usual social etiquette. Next, entering a con-course, the Brockle made its way through the crowds until it reached a series of dropshafts. It hesitated for a moment, then decided against the idea – instead it found a stair leading between decks and headed down, hover luggage negotiating the steps with slightly more ease than was normal.

Eight floors down, a door opened into a shuttle bay. As it stepped out, the Brockle instantly penetrated the cam system, maintained a link and constantly erased its presence from cam memory. Here a floor ledge jutted into a large open space, shuttles drawn up beside it and beyond them a giant curve of chain-glass separating all from vacuum. All along the ledge were small cargoes sitting on grav-sleds or motorized pallets. Dock workers were scattered all around, some controlling handler robots that were like the by-blows of forklifts and mantids, others heaving crates by themselves. Some shuttles here were small private vessels, two were simple intership passenger vessels, while the biggest and most obvious was a military resupply shuttle for the *High Castle*. This had two ramps down, and personnel and robots were using them to load supplies rapidly. The Brockle opened visual cells on the side of its head and gazed without turning at a group of humans standing beside one ramp. It increased its hearing and filtered out other noises until it could hear their conversation.

'I still think we should have been included,' said a man – obviously one of a Sparkind unit.

'We're backup,' said a woman the Brockle recognized as Grafton, the human captain of the *High Castle*. 'Remember, our remit is half scientific and we're not full military.'

'Not full military?' said the man.

Grafton grinned. 'We do have a science section . . .'

'Yeah, right.'

'It's like this,' she said. 'The initial mission profile is a simple negotiation with this renegade prador, then if that doesn't work, the injection of a few U-space missiles, and the Garrotte is more than capable of that. We then go in to gather data.'

'I'm waiting for the "but",' said one of the Golem Sparkind.

'But,' said Grafton, losing her grin, 'if things start to get more complicated, we go in and assume command.'

'You mean drag their nuts out of the fire,' said the Golem.

'Yes, quite,' said Grafton.

The Brockle experienced a surge of disappointment. It had been sure that at last the Polity AIs had understood the danger Penny Royal represented and were going after that black AI, and

12

that the *High Castle* was going to be part of the hunt – it certainly possessed the necessary resources. But it seemed this was not the case. What was this about a 'renegade prador'? As the Brockle understood, from all the data it had been stealing since arriving on Par Avion, the *High Castle* was heading out towards the once supposedly missing factory station Room 101 – the last known location of Penny Royal. The only prador that could be described as renegade out there were dead. The one known as Sverl had been killed aboard the station by an assassin drone while, according to a long-range Polity observation satellite, the other documented renegade, called Cvorn, had had his ship intercepted by the King's Guard out from Room 101 and all but destroyed. It had managed to drop into U-space, but in such a state of ruin that there wasn't much chance it would come out again. However, in the end this did not matter because it changed the Brockle's plans not one whit.

The Brockle sauntered towards the stacked cargo ready to be loaded onto the shuttle, aiming for an area near the back where there were fewer workers. As it walked it prepared the way: altering the positioning and format of its various internal units, plus those inside the hover trunk, readying all for a flash change. Meanwhile, it also scanned the intelligent manifest labels on the various packages and penetrated the scanners either held by various dock workers or sitting in the memories of handler robots. Just a little alteration was required; just the addition of one more package. Finally arriving beside a grav-sled that only carried half a load, it extruded sensors all around its head, focusing on human and Golem eyes while subverting further cams in the various robots here. It waited until the moment was just right – until no eyes were looking – then stepped up onto the sled and collapsed; for the blink of an eye a mass of silver worms, then that snapping into a new shape.

No one noticed the additional crate on the sled and, with luck, no one would notice certain other *discrepancies* until long after the *High Castle* had departed.

Riss

The tube was too narrow for a human being, but then they never had any real reason to be here. The interior was dotted with an infestation of beetlebots like cockroaches in a drain pipe. Some of them were somnolent – programmed sequences having wound down and no controlling AI to chivvy them back into motion – some of them had simply broken down, while others were still carrying out the same chores they had been performing for over a century.

Riss watched one of them limp over to the head of the feed pipe to a flash furnace, flip the hatch open and peer inside, see that the pipe was packed to the top with compacted dust balls and other waste, then move on to the next one. They all did this because none of them was programmed to accept that some of the furnaces were off, and that the waste they had deposited in the pipes was going nowhere. Finally it reached the pipe leading to the one remaining functional furnace – one lying in the realm of a remaining functional AI – and did what it was programmed to do. It turned, opened its ersatz wing cases and ejected the contents of its crap-collecting gut into the pipe. This block of waste slid smoothly down the frictionless shark-slime interior, propelled by a mechano-electrical form of the cilia found on many bacteria. It had a long way to go – at least four miles before it reached the furnace. There it would be zapped into its component atoms, sieves and nanofibre sorters collecting every element of use which, in essence, was all of them. Every now and again the furnace would shit a brick, maybe of copper, chromium or iron. It would pipe away gases to where required, suck up dusts of buckyballs and carbon nanotubes and propel them to another destination. It was all a very efficient process and the furnace had continued this onerous task for over a century too.

Once the beetlebot had finished its business, Riss painfully squirmed over, her blackened and partially burnt-out body moving with all the alacrity of a broken arm. Her internal systems and meta-materials had yet to heal the damage she had sustained from the combined EM pulse and viral attack, the details of which remained vague, that had scrambled her system down to the picoscopic level.

Reaching the pipe the beetle had used she flipped over the hatch and peered down into the interior. It should be good enough – even the most stubborn organics shouldn't stick. She brought her rear end round, hooked it up over the top of the pipe and lowered her ovipositor down into it. The eggs should go first, of course, because if she squirted the enzyme acid down there it might damage the interior of the pipe, and form areas where the eggs might stick. This mustn't happen – the Earth Central Security tactical AI whose instructions she was following wanted all of them down in that furnace – though why wasn't entirely clear to her.

Riss squeezed and emptied herself of the weapon she had been manufactured to use. Out of her fell the eggs that could hatch into a parasite that would eat a prador from the inside out. Then breed in there and multiply, spread and wipe out whole families of prador.

There was no release as they went – none of the orgasmic pleasure she had felt when injecting prador. Riss supposed that a sick human felt like this when ridding himself of diarrhoea – just

15

a momentary relief from bodily upset. Then she concentrated on internally selecting and loading the enzyme acid to her ovaries and ejecting that down the pipe. Nothing remained inside her now because the internal workings of her system were even more efficient and frictionless than the pipe leading to that distant furnace. Nevertheless, Riss opened her body, painfully looped round and used the small manipulators below her hood to remove the canisters that had held those weapons. She sent them down the pipe after their contents.

Next she contemplated following them herself, but the tactical AI would not let her go. In her mind again flashed up the map of the station indicating the positions of all the surviving renegade AIs, their territories both physical and virtual. Now on that map another location had been highlighted. She moved along the pipe and set out on the slow, painful journey to the place indicated, squirming through further maintenance-bot ducts, fluid pipes, the insulation in walls, through weird structures like metal sculptures of massed fungi, or the hives of alien creatures. Slowly she made her way across a station seemingly riddled with a technological cancer. As she went she carefully avoided any contact with the station's denizens, for she knew she was in no fit state to handle them.

Four hours later, some of the dead parts of her body revived and some of her internal nano-systems having rebuilt themselves, she slithered out of a port at the destination, and realized she vaguely recognized the place. Hadn't she been here before?

Cannibalize, reconstitute, the tactical AI instructed her.

Inside this familiar tubular autofactory, Riss squirmed over to one wall and there gazed at a skinless version of herself stuck in place by transparent epoxy. It was dead, its sensor eye grey and not a flicker of power inside. She scanned it deeper, identifying usable components, then plugged in one of her manipulators to feed in power. The skinless parasite facsimile writhed, cracked the epoxy and broke free, and Riss brought it down to the floor. There she scanned again, looking for further activation, but this snake drone's crystal was doing nothing. It was in fact so full of micro-fractures a sharp tap would turn it to dust. Riss accessed sub-systems below the level of that crystal and through them began taking the thing apart. First she began with what was easy, taking out small spherical nano-packages, opening her own body to eject her own packages, and inserting the new unused ones in their place. Only when these activated and turned to remaining nano-machines from her original packages, to either scrap or reprogram them, did she realize just how badly she had been damaged.

As the new machines set to work she immediately began to feel much more capable and supple, especially when some of the meta-materials of her body began functioning as they should. Next, she stripped out some larger components: vertebrae and rib bones of memory metal to replace those in herself that had been suffering from amnesia; skeins of electromuscle to quickly replace muscle inside her that her internal systems could have repaired, but only over a lengthy period. She worked on her maglev and series of small grav-engines, stripping out the whole wrecked network and replacing it. Then she took a new U-space communicator and even swapped out her impossibly cracked ovipositor. Some damaged memstorage standing separate from her own crystal went next. Her own crystal however, which had developed a few cracks, she could do nothing about. It would crack no further what with binding liquid sapphire injected into the shear planes, but these were still like atomic-thin plates of scar tissue through her brain.

By the time she had finished, very little remained of the drone she had cannibalized, and she had been right – with one inadvertent tap, its crystal had turned it to dust. Now Riss was ready, her body gleaming, translucent, black areas fading like healing bruises. Immediately the tactical AI sent her another location on the station map – just on the other side of this auto-factory. Leaving much of her old self behind, Riss slithered through, a red locating dot springing up in her vision and leading her to the edge of a carousel store.

'Gel dot C-density octonitrocubane, with micro detonators,' the tactical AI instructed her, its communications coming through much clearer now.

Riss released the manual lock on the carousel and turned it, pondering the choice of offensive weapon. The gel dot explosive was of an ancient recipe but perfect for any action here since octonitrocubane could explode in vacuum, however there were more powerful explosives made so perhaps it was the only one that was available. She found just one canister of the stuff and stared at it for a long time, puzzled by her reluctance to put the canister inside herself.

'The delay is unacceptable,' said the tac-AI.

Riss reluctantly opened the requisite portion of her body, took the canister up in her small manipulators and hooped over to insert it.

'Now, Target One,' said the tac-AI, highlighting Riss's next destination on her internal map. Riss set out, ready to do her duty and kill a renegade AI, but not eager to do it.

Trent

Hanging in vacuum on the periphery of a steel jungle, Trent felt ill at ease. His space suit uncomfortable on his big heavy-worlder body, his helmet rubbing against his – as others had described it – decidedly pointed head and black bristly Mohican. He gazed with white-irised eyes back towards where a small portion of the station had remained relatively normal, and upon all the activity there. The prador weren't stopping. They'd started in the old autofactory, where the snake drone Riss had killed Sverl, and where they were encapsulating Sverl's ceramal skeleton and vacuum-dried organic remains under a polymer dome. Next they had cleaned up the detritus in there – the Gatling slugs, the chunks of armour from the weapons Penny Royal had chopped into pieces – and after that had begun stripping out other damaged equipment and repairing the holes in the walls made by the King's Guard. Trent had first thought it was as if they couldn't admit that their father was dead and were repairing the defences around him, but now he reckoned that the gorgeous catadapt woman, Sepia, had it right: they were building a mausoleum.

'I wish Spear was coming with us,' said Cole, the mind-tech.

Spear didn't look much: average height, the well-defined physique of a swimmer – nothing *extra* – skin tone pale Asiatic, Roman nose below pale green eyes and above a mouth with a slight twist, brown hair . . . But he was effective – they'd seen him kill one of the hostile robots here almost without getting out of breath – but Spear wasn't being very communicative. He'd come back from the erstwhile abode of the Room 101 AI, where he'd followed Penny Royal, with an air of murderous rage that seemed to permeate out of his space suit and into the surrounding vacuum. Something had seriously pissed him off and Trent, who had been burdened with empathy but still considered himself no coward, had decided to just back off. He guessed that confirmed Spear as a force to be respected.

'I wish one of them was coming with us,' said Sepia, gesturing towards where the first-child Bsorol was operating a

19

micro-deposition welder to repair a beam severed by particle cannon fire.

Trent glanced at her. He thought it more likely that it was Spear's company she wanted, but his reaction even to her when he returned had been cold and dismissive.

'We should be okay,' said Trent, shouldering his portable particle cannon. 'We don't have anything they want.' Even as he said the words he wondered if he was right.

'Why are they hostile?' asked Cole. 'I never got that.'

Trent looked at the man. Cole was a mind-tech and had some complicated augmentations, but apparently they did him no good beyond his particular speciality. Trent, who had lost his aug quite some time ago now, had been using the *Lance*'s computing capacity to try and gain some understanding of what had happened here.

'Evolution, or perhaps devolution,' he replied. 'As far as I've been able to gather, many of the AIs here aren't any more sentient than wild animals. Like wild animals they react with hostility to potential danger and tend to simply take what they want. I suspect that they're like that because when Room 101 was hunting them, intelligence made them a target, so they gave it up.' He paused. 'Bit like the Atheter, in a way.'

'Turning into a philosopher now?' asked Sepia.

Trent turned to her. 'Where do we head now?'

She gestured into the metal jungle lying ahead. 'Thirty miles that way.'

Trent nodded and propelled himself from the nearest beam, adjusted his course with his wrist impeller and kept a sharp eye out for any movement in their surroundings.

'Are you sure about this?' asked Sepia as they travelled.

Trent thought about that question yet again, and once more found himself up against intractable problems with things that at one time had never concerned him, like doing what was right. Like morality.

'Spear told me that if he found a man dying he would save his life,' he said. 'If it then turned out that the man had been dying because he'd tried to kill himself, and if he tried to kill himself again, Spear would not intervene.'

'Seems logical enough.'

'Can't you see how that applies to the shell people?'

'Perhaps,' she conceded. She decided to play devil's advocate, 'But if we are to believe Cole, they have a curable malady . . .'

'All mental problems have a cure,' interjected Cole.

'And how would you style their problem?' she asked.

After a long pause Cole replied, 'Religion.'

Trent mulled that over for a moment. He wasn't sure it was true. The shell people did regard the prador with something close to religious awe and had behaved like members of a brainwashed cult. But he felt there was more to it than that.

'They knew, or at least most of them knew, that what they were doing to themselves was killing them,' he said, going back to his original thread. 'We, or rather Spear and Riss, saved their lives. What's to stop them doing the same thing to themselves again, when we wake them up?'

'Why is it your responsibility?'

I don't know . . .

'Because I'm making it mine,' said Trent firmly.

'But surely it would be better just to leave them in their caskets and, when you can, hand them over to the Polity?'

Trent glanced at her, wondering if she was deliberately needling him because surely she knew how he felt about Reece – the wife of Taiken, the now dead leader of the shell people. If he got the chance to hand those caskets over to the Polity he would probably never see her again. So was his apparent altruism just a veneer over plain selfishness? He tried not to inspect his thoughts on that too closely.

Beyond the pill-shaped structure that contained the shattered remains of the Room 101 AI, they found themselves in what seemed to be a killing ground. Here robots were tangled in metallic lianas, and splays of ribbed tentacles sprouted from the tops of columns like nightmare technological tubeworms. Nothing was moving, however, and Trent knew that their greatest danger lay beyond here, where functional AIs still guided the robot fauna of the station. After this, the tree-branch growths of station structure began to thin out and they eventually came to a gulf, holding themselves in place on attenuated branches. Across from them lay a wall, disappearing into murk in every direction. Trent could see exposed rooms, chambers, factory complexes and tunnels and was reminded of the wreckage he had seen when separatists had taken out part of the Coloron arcology with a nuke.

'Give me a minute,' said Sepia, schematics glowing in the laminate of her visor and concealing her face. She turned her head slowly from side to side, nodded, then indicated. 'Over there – the mouth of that tunnel sitting below that big chemical tank.'

It took Trent a moment to pick it out in the wreckage, but when he was about to send himself sailing across, Sepia caught hold of his shoulder.

'Wait.' She pointed.

There was movement across one section of the wall. Trent stared at this for a second then ramped up his visor's magnification to pull into view a long line of robots based on the kind used for mid-scale maintenance tasks in a ship's engine section. These were bigger and clunkier, with heavy limbs similar to those of a

water scorpion and seemingly designed more for dismember-
ment than repair.

'I wonder where they're off to,' Cole said.

Neither Trent nor Sepia had an answer.

When the line of robots had moved sufficiently far from the
tunnel entrance, Trent pushed himself away from his branch and
used his wrist impeller to give himself more momentum. Best to
keep moving and not think too deeply about his aims. Just concentrate on the mission and not its consequences or dubious
morality – he'd had a lifetime of experience doing that.

'What are the chances of it still being pressurized?' asked
Cole.

Doubtful, Trent thought.

'There's power there. Penny Royal only destroyed power
sources and feeds directly to the hull weapons.' Scpia paused.
'There's a controlling AI too. At least it seems like an AI . . .'

Trent came down in the mouth of the tunnel first, then
caught Sepia as she landed beside him.

'From here on we walk on gecko,' he said. 'You can't react
quickly enough if you're free-falling through here.'

'I was going to walk,' she said, hurt.

'Yeah, okay.' Trent released her.

The three of them trudged on down the tunnel, around a
curve and straight into potential trouble. One of the robots they
had seen earlier was facing down the tunnel, while opposing it
was a machine resembling the one Spear had killed.

They were both utterly still at first, but then launched into
motion and slammed together, silent in the vacuum, their impact
felt only through the deck. Trent surmised that they had been
facing off, looking for an advantage, and that the appearance of
the humans on the scene had tipped things in favour of one
of them. The maintenance-bot closed its water scorpion arms

around the other, which in turn probed it with steely tentacles, while with metronomic regularity stabbing with a limb that ended in a flat chisel. Tearing up floor metal, they slammed into one wall, their limbs blurring as they shed components, creating a steadily growing bee-swarm of the things about them. Then one of those water scorpion limbs tumbled free, and the other robot was turning the scorpion like a squid feeding on a crab. As the two drifted, it tore up a plate of armour, inserted a glassy tube inside. Then both robots froze. This lasted just a moment before they separated. The water scorpion rolled through vacuum, remaining limbs kicking weakly, the victor now turned towards Trent and his companions. It studied them for a long moment.

'To say I'm beginning to have second thoughts about this is an understatement,' said Sepia.

'Yes,' said Trent, noncommittally.

Finally, the victor lost interest in them, launched itself up to the ceiling and disappeared through a hatch there. The injured robot meanwhile had finally managed to snag a limb against one wall, where it pulled itself flat.

'Come on,' said Trent.

They moved quickly underneath the hatch, warily past the now motionless maintenance-bot. Surely this kind of activity couldn't be common, thought Trent, or else, after a hundred years there would have been nothing here but wreckage. He was sure now that something new was occurring.

'Did you see that?' said Cole. 'It was after data.'

Trent chewed that over as they rounded one more corner and came upon yet another of the denizens of this strange world.

Here a tic-shaped printer-bot was slowly and meticulously blocking off the way ahead, the numerous jointed printing heads sprouting from its foreparts steadily depositing layers of some white crystalline substance round and round the tunnel's interior.

Trent was reminded of a paper wasp building its nest, and as he eyed those busy printing heads he wondered if they were capable of doing any damage. Perhaps it would be better just to hit the thing now . . . He raised his particle cannon, at which point the robot abruptly retreated out of sight.

'I'll go first,' he said.

He moved up to the barrier which, running round the walls of the tunnel, had left a hole a couple of yards across. Ducking his head through, he looked around. The printer-bot had moved back along the tunnel and now sat in a small alcove twenty feet in, its limb heads splayed in front of it as if for protection. Trent ripped his boot soles from the floor, propelled himself through the part-made barrier and pushed down onto the floor on the other side.

'Okay, come on,' he called over suit radio.

He moved forwards to stand directly opposite the bot as the other two came through. 'Just move past behind me,' he instructed.

The bot made no threatening moves and finally Trent hurried to catch up with the other two. When he reached them and glanced back he saw that the bot had returned to work. He knew that such robots possessed some programming lifted directly from the minds of social insects and wondered what the thing thought it was, or if it was doing any thinking at all.

The tunnel brought them to an inactive dropshaft which, with grav off, they traversed as they had the tunnel. Another tunnel then brought them to a maglev station, in which sat a row of pod carriages, each capable of holding up to ten people.

'This could take us right there, if it was operating,' said Sepia.

'It might be,' said Trent, noting that screen paint maps and information displays were powered up on some pillars.

'Should we trust it?' she wondered.

'Let's find out.' He slapped a hand against the weapon he held. 'I can certainly shut a carriage down if it seems out of control.'

They approached one of the carriages, and doors in its side immediately slid open. Trent stepped inside first with the other two pushing in close behind him for fear that the doors would close and leave them stranded. The doors shut once they were well inside and the carriage shifted smoothly into motion as they sat. Sepia, studying a station map above the windows, reached up and pressed a finger against one station. It highlighted briefly then went out. After a moment she shrugged and sat down.

The trip was fast, the only concern being when the carriage slowed for a moment to grate past a section of wall that had been dented in. All the while Trent kept his weapon pointed at a section of floor towards the front. One shot there should knock out the inducer plates, which would drop the train down on its single track, whereupon simple nano-mesh braking would ensue. But there was no need. The carriage pulled up neatly at the required station and a moment later they were outside.

Human-sized tunnels leading from the maglev station had all been closed by emergency airlocks. Sepia struggled with then finally opened the outer door on the one they wanted and Trent stepped inside – it was only big enough to take one person. The manual controls, which were standard in an emergency lock like this, were all operating, and an indicator informed him that the lock was charging with air. When it reached optimum he used the manual handle to open the inner door and stepped through, feeling half an Earth gravity take hold of him. After checking his head-up display he instructed his visor to open. It sucked down into the front of his neck ring and his helmet folded down into the back. He smelled burning as he took a few paces forwards on carpet moss that coated the floor leading into a reception area. Here sub-AI gurneys sat in a stack, while on the floor lay three human skeletons still clad in cleansuits that might once have been white, the floor pristine around them because the carpet moss had fed on the products of their decay.

'I wonder how they died,' said Sepia from behind.

'Probably how most of the human personnel died here,' Trent replied. 'They either took their own lives or boiled.'

From the reception area numerous corridors speared off into the distance. After checking the signs above these, Trent stepped into one and headed to the first entryway which was without a door. He stepped through, micro UV lasers flashing around him and frying any bugs he might have carried on the exterior of his suit, his face tingling as microscopic fauna was selectively destroyed there. Inside, arrays of surgical robots stood poised as if on a production line, the channel between without grav-plates but with the small heads of hardfield projectors protruding. The wounded, stabilized by field autodocs, would have been fed in here.

He switched his gaze from the robots to the carousels sitting behind them – revolving drums like children's roundabouts stacked one on top of the other. Here he could see the panoply of Polity medical science of the time. Here were nanoform wound dressings, canisters of liquid bone, collagen and other materials to feed the printing heads of bone and cell welders, artificial blood, reels of syntheskin and shaped gobbets of synthe-flesh, other items that utterly baffled him, and still others that were easily recognizable: hands and feet, arms and legs, skulls and ribs – all motorized, all with nerve interface sockets and all formed of polished ceramal. All unused, yet meticulously cleaned and maintained over the last hundred years.

Out of the other end of this would step human beings who

had been repaired like crashed gravcars, ready for the next stages of their treatment, whereupon they could pull on new uniforms, exoskeletons or camo-combats and return to the meat grinder that was the war against the prador.

'It looks very clean,' said Sepia. 'It could have been abandoned yesterday.'

'This is what we were looking for,' said Trent.

'Not all of it,' said Cole. 'I want to see what's up the other end.'

At this point one of the robots, a thing like a steel cockroach, sans its abdomen and standing upright at nearly nine feet tall, turned its nightmare head towards them.

'We'll go round,' Trent suggested.

Sepia nodded and led the way out and further up the corridor. Another delousing arch led them into an area like a huge runcible lounge. Cole took the lead next, heading straight for one of a series of closed doors. The room contained a comfortable adjustable chair sporting padded straps. The headrest looked like a steel cockle, packed inside with intricate electronics and the heads of nano-fibre aug interfaces.

'So this is what an editing suite looks like,' said Trent.

'This is it,' Cole agreed, his expression maniacally eager. 'This is what we need.'

Trent nodded. Yes, here was where they could take the shell people to bring them out of hibernation. Here they could repair their physical injuries and here Cole could try, if Trent allowed him, to repair the madness between their ears. Here too Trent could wake up Reece and, if he dared, ask her why she had chosen hibernation rather than his company.

They stepped out of the suite just as the door at the end of the corridor banged open. The nine-foot-tall surgical robot they had seen earlier had not been as rooted to the floor as Trent had supposed, but walked on wide flat feet like the most horrifying clown imaginable.

'This,' it said, 'is private property.'

Riss

The first three had been easy, their defences only formatted against the kind of attacks they could expect from their neighbours, which consisted of computer viral incursions and brute robotic assault. They were unprepared for the likes of Riss. Not only were they a hundred years out of date, they had regressed.

Riss had been reluctant to do her duty with the first AI, until she began running subtle penetrations of its systems, data caches, robots and occasional crippled subminds – those additional subordinate minds some AIs possessed. The thing wasn't much more intelligent than the average human, but what was wrong with it was difficult to nail down in human terms. Certainly it was paranoid, but then it had good reason to be. Certainly it was psychotic, since it had lost all contact with any reality lying beyond this station. And definitely it was a vicious killer of any other AI it could overcome. It could be cured, of course, but Riss's investigations revealed that very little would remain after that cure. In fact, it wasn't much different from the prador . . .

Running the same penetrations on the other two AIs, Riss found the same mindset, and now, as she approached this last AI's hideaway, she wondered why she was looking. She was an assassin drone with a mission to accomplish. She wasn't a mind-tech. Why was she searching for justifications?

'Because you have a conscience,' said the tac-AI.

What?

'Be assured,' continued that distant AI, 'that what you are doing is necessary. Destroy this last AI and the instability here caused by the attack from the King's Guard, then Penny Royal will tip over into complete chaos.'

King's Guard? Penny Royal?

'I don't understand,' said Riss.

'Just do your duty.'

Riss moved on through the ceramic pipework once used to convey molten metals to component moulds and deposition heads. Scanning through the ceramic, she saw the constructor spiders blocking the main entrances to this AI's realm. They were completely unaware of her as she slid along smoothly, following the pipe through an armoured wall, then out through a maze of pipework to a reheating tank. The tank lay behind a machine used for making armour with single-atom-thick laminations. She then contracted and extended her form until she was as thin as a human finger so she could enter a flexible silicon-corundum-fibre pipe behind a series of deposition heads. Here she vibrated her nose at high frequency and pushed, parting the corundum fibres and stretching the high-temperature silicon. A small slice with the chain-glass blade along the edge of one of her small limbs split the silicon and she shot out, immediately engaging her chameleonware, curled round and came back down on the cowling of the laminating machine. She looked around.

Like iron prador with the guts of solar water heaters protruding from their faces, five of the machines squatted in a row over ceramic moulds with the appearance of giant leaf sculptures. On the opposite side of this area armour plates in all sorts of organic shapes were stacked up into a wall, oddly covered with what looked to be cobwebs. But this couldn't be, unless spiders had evolved to survive in vacuum. Riss scanned closer and recognized the product of rogue nano-machines. Those fibres were whiskers of metal woven out from the armour and as fragile as frost. To Riss's left stood an armoured door and to the right was the AI.

The AI was of the usual design – a crystal the size and shape of a house brick laced through with quantum computing and wrapped in a skeleton of ceramal – however, it wasn't supported between the splayed heads of data-shunts. Riss noted that it had a chunk missing from its side, sapphire-filled cracks throughout, and subsidiary computing in the form of carbon stick processors jury-rigged by a skein of optics. It sat in a loco-body: a cup-shaped frame over laminar power storage, torque motors and two long heron-like legs. Obviously it had found movement a useful survival trait, but it was one that wouldn't help it now.

'It seems . . . unfair,' said Riss.

'As unfair as killing a prador that meant you no harm?' asked the tac-AI.

This left Riss somewhat puzzled. What was the likelihood of anyone meeting a prador that meant no harm? She shrugged it off. This wasn't the time for agonizing about what she was doing, but it was time for just *doing*.

She slithered down from the machine and across the floor to the foot of the AI. Surprisingly, it reacted, straightening out its legs then taking a pace out onto the floor, coming close to stepping on Riss with one of its big, three-toed feet.

'Who's there?' it asked over a human suit com frequency.

This reaction was surprising. None of the other three had any idea that Riss was there before she'd destroyed them. None of them, in any of their communications, had used human speech. So why was this one . . . ? Then Riss saw it.

Behind the AI, against the base of the wall, lay a pile of five space suits. Scanning these, Riss found the vacuum-dried human remains inside, and further scanning revealed how they had

31

died. Riss turned to gaze over at the laminating machines and wondered how it was done. Every space suit had two holes through its helmet, almost certainly made by a cutting laser, but one which had deliberately not cut through the underlying skull. Silicon plugs scattered about the base of one of the machines showed that the holes had been sealed with plugs to prevent air loss. Just after the holes were made, and sealed, each of these people in turn was manoeuvred below a deposition head, whereupon one plug was removed and high-temperature etching fluid was sprayed inside. This was an ablating spray that had boiled away skin, flesh and fat, and which then exited as vapour through the second hole, after the added pressure had blown out the plug there. After that, vaporized gold was sprayed in to evenly coat the exposed skull. Why?

They had been alive when the etching fluid had been sprayed in, but whether they were still alive when their skulls were coated with gold was debatable. Whatever – they had died an agonizing death.

'Why did you do it?' asked Riss over suit com.

'Bastable?' asked the AI.

'Why did you choose to kill the humans in the way you did?' asked Riss.

'Bastable?' the AI queried again.

Further scanning of a suit ID tag revealed that one of the victims had been called Erica Bastable. As Riss learned this, a door at the end of the room opened and in swarmed three spiderbots on the ends of their umbilicals, chain-glass mandibles rubbing together, but utterly silent in vacuum.

'I am not Bastable,' said Riss, 'and I want to know why you killed these humans in such a cruel and seemingly pointless manner.'

'It was their fault,' said the AI.

'What was their fault?' Riss slithered about the AI's feet as it moved further out onto the floor, trying to locate her.

'The war, Room 101 . . .'

'You're making no sense.'

'They had to know the pain, then oblivion.'

Riss moved aside and gazed up at the AI. What was the point in arguing? The humans didn't start the war, the prador did, and the humans were really just minor participants in a conflict between the AIs and the prador. Here it was simply a case of the madness of Room 101 infecting one of its subordinates and, really, there was only one cure. Riss shot forwards, stuck the bottom of her hood against the loco's upper leg, whipped her ovipositor up and deposited four blobs of gel on the AI's crystal, then dropped away. She slithered then at high speed underneath the spiderbots, came to the doorway and paused, rising up the wall beside the door to watch as she sent the signal.

A flash ensued, bright as the glare of the hypergiant, only distinguishable as issuing from four points by the acute drone senses Riss possessed. In eerie silence a ball of fire erupted, picking up the spiderbots and hurling them cartwheeling back through the door, segments of armour tumbling like the leaves they resembled. She stuck in place, waiting for the blast to pass, watching fire elementals writhe and self-consume, then wink out in vacuum, and trillions of fragments of AI crystal glittering like ice. The entire upper section of the AI was gone, yet, oddly, its two legs remained in place like comedy boots, gecko-stuck to the floor. Riss unstuck herself from the wall and moved away, circumventing spiderbots that now seemed as dead as their controlling AI.

'Now your chores are completed,' said the tac-AI, 'it's time for you to remember.'

'What?' said Riss.

'You were very badly damaged, Riss, so it was easy to put the blocks in.'

'Remember?' said Riss.

'The key words are: Thorvald Spear,' said the AI.

The memories came back in one mass, instantly comprehended. Riss found herself coiled tightly on the floor, but just for a moment. She shot up, strengthening her defences and, running internal diagnostics, tried to run a signal trace on that 'tac-AI' even as it severed the link, cursed and hissed silently in vacuum. One of the damned station AIs had taken control of her to rid itself of some rivals. Damn it, she could try hunting it down but knew her chances of locating it now were random. What she needed to do was get out of this place, and the route out of here was those key words.

Thorvald Spear. She had to find him.

A Prelude: Penny Royal

'The dreadnought is our target,' states the AI of the *Vorpal Dagger*, the massive lozenge-shaped dreadnought in command of the attack on prador forces here around Layden's Sink black hole. This is AI communication, however, so no human words are used and the message comes laden with tactical information that loads with it. The *Vorpal Dagger* and two other Polity dreadnoughts will lead the attack. Smaller ships, like a shoal of cubist fish, will cover them, while the *Vorpal Dagger* deploys their main weapon.

No choice now – orders cannot be disobeyed. This battle must be taken to its conclusion. The newly named AI Penny Royal, within the sarcophagus-like body of the also newly named destroyer the *Puling Child*, rapidly assesses its own resources and notes that some changes have been made. The nano- and micro-bots aboard were strictly limited in their areas of maintenance, but have now been subtly reprogrammed. The limitation to their procreation has been removed and they have been given access to materials with which to build more of their kind. The larger robots are being changed too, by those same microbots and nanobots which are building their larger brethren more extensive tool arrays. These tasks are being organized by a part of Penny Royal that has mentally splintered away. It is building extra buckarbon memstorage within those robots, for they have been penetrated and are being used by the dark child to hide its more rebellious thoughts.

'What do you do?' Penny Royal asks.

'We made us not removable from ship body,' the darkness replies, and Penny Royal cannot dispute it; finds in itself acceptance.

The three human crewmembers, who blacked out during initial manoeuvres, recover quickly thanks to the cocktail of drugs auto-injected by their suits. The two men take control of the weapons systems and begin target selection even as *Vorpal Dagger*'s big railguns begin firing. The men also input attack patterns, based on defence of the *Dagger*. Penny Royal accepts their input, surprised to find it needs to make only minor corrections. The woman, it notes, is frowning at performance data coming directly from its own mind. She makes an adjustment and Penny Royal loses some of its fear, feels a moment of reckless bravura. She frowns again, adjusts again, and the fear comes back. The AI wonders if creatures who are slaves to emotion are the best judges of it, then wonders if that thought came completely from itself.

It next studies the distant prador vessel sitting half a light-minute away. Like all the prador capital ships here, it is the

shape of its father-captain's carapace – a pear squashed vertically
– but there the resemblance ends. The thing's armour is brassy,
dented and burned, and it bristles with weapons. As it makes its
retreat from the main battleground to the accretion disc of the
black hole, Layden's Sink, hundreds of war drones and armoured
children surround it. This prador dreadnought is a 'soft' target,
chosen for this test of ships that feel emotions and with a weapon
deployment that can only work once. But the definition of 'soft'
in this case means it will take less than the average sacrifice of
three Polity dreadnoughts and thirty smaller ships to destroy it.

Closer now and their first fusillades of railgun missiles reach
the enemy. Prador war drones and armoured children fly apart
in stretched-out explosions, but the hits on the ship itself are
bright flashes that dent but do not penetrate its armour. This is
their advantage: while the Polity concentrated on travel by runcible, its shipbuilding metallurgy did not become so advanced.
The prador, travelling by ship only and being perpetually war-
like, have developed advanced armour with an exotic matter
component, and it can take a great deal of punishment. Even at
that moment Polity AIs are trying to copy the formula, but still
failing.

Penny Royal notes that the first targets the humans have
selected are two prador war drones and one of the armoured
children, with secondary targets lying beyond these. Its weapons
spew ceramal-plated slugs and the particle cannon lances out,
and this feels like violation. The momentary satisfaction it feels
as one drone and the child fragment and burn, followed by self-
disgust and a hint of guilt, are just confusing. Secondary targets
shift out of the path of its fusillade straight into the path of that
of a fellow. Wreckage tumbles past, glowing and sparking; combined collision and anti-personnel lasers pick off debris on course
to impact. Glimpse of a claw snapping at vacuum. Blast wave

flinging the destroyer off course. Massive chatter as a Polity dreadnought takes a full fusillade from the prador dreadnought; holes punched through and fires burning within, but an expected loss.

'Not as damaged as they thought,' one of the men notes, sweat beading on his forehead.

The two remaining Polity dreadnoughts divert, down to the accretion disc, towards its centre, towards the black hole. The dreadnought *Stonewater* is covering *Vorpal Dagger*. *Stonewater* shudders under numerous impacts, smaller Polity ships all around explode, fragment, or are sheared in two. The *Puling Child* takes another minor glancing blow and knows that it is just a statistic, that its survival is just pure chance. Another function of feeling arises on the surface of its mind: survivor guilt. One of the men is swearing in a dull leaden tone. The woman just looks white and sick and is no longer studying her screens, which is perhaps good, since the changes Penny Royal's dark child is still making cannot fail to show up in some way.

A particle beam stabs out, wide as *Puling Child*'s hull, and nails *Stonewater*, carves across its body, wreckage and molten metal spewing out into space. The prador dreadnought is on the move now, its father-captain thinking the attack upon it desperate and ill-timed, and that he can finish off the rest of the now fleeing attack force. Prador drones and children swarm after it, pursuing *Vorpal Dagger* and the remainder of the force. The destruction doesn't stop: many of Penny Royal's fellows are now wreckage, trapped on the same course as itself. The AI wonders if they had changed in similar ways to itself, or if their particular iterations were much closer to the planned result.

'Deployment of weapon in ten,' the *Vorpal Dagger*'s AI announces, its communication issuing as human speech for the benefit of the destroyer's crew.

The course of the pursuing prador is just so, the brassy dreadnought accelerating massively. *Vorpal Dagger* and all those still capable in the Polity force veer away from the black hole as a device the size and shape of a monorail carriage departs the *Dagger*'s shuttle bay. Before the prador can alter their course in pursuit, the device detonates. It disappears in three consecutive flashes. A microsecond later the *Puling Child* briefly loses its mind – Penny Royal – who then comes back online to receive a tsunami of error reports.

Over eighty per cent of its systems are out, for the EMR device disables friend as well as foe. Its own mind is down to below fifty per cent of function. It has no control over its thrusters or engine, its U-space drive is down, and all coms are out. It analyses rapidly.

That eighty per cent systems failure is recoverable within seventy-two hours for the hardened components in it, and the maintenance robots can make repairs and reboots. But more importantly, the human crew is unaffected. Polity tactical AIs calculate that prador systems can be recovered by prador crews in half the time. But the prador dreadnought, drones and armoured children do not have that much time.

In twenty hours Penny Royal regains some coms and enough image data through its cams to patch together a picture of events. Inside it sees the humans busy at work, replacing damaged components, rebooting systems and robots, and showing some surprise at the sheer quantity of nano- and microbots swarming through the ship. Outside, the remainder of the Polity force is still powerless, but the prador are powerless too. However, the Polity ships – one dreadnought, three destroyers and five attack ships along with a scattering of Polity war drones – are falling in a long curve through the accretion disc around the black hole and will regain engine power to get away with plenty of time to spare before it can get a grip on them. The prador, though, are going straight down. They are mere hours away from the point where restoring their engines will make no difference.

Penny Royal watches and, while doing so, realizes that various parts of itself are muttering to others. Running self-diagnostics, it discovers a network of fine cracks in its crystal, extending from a single deep fault – an intriguingly even pattern which, without its containing case, would fragment the substance of its mind into numerous dagger-shaped pieces.

The prador dreadnought falls, beginning to glow as it enters the denser hot gases of the ambient disc, a vapour trail issuing behind it. At the last its fusion engine ignites and Penny Royal fights both the guilt it feels at being a part of this carnage, and the fear. Drones and armoured children continue to fall, swept in and round, torn by tidal forces and disappearing as burning lines in the disc – swirling raspberry stains behind in creamy gas. For an hour it seems the big ship will make it, but then its drive stutters and it begins to fall back. The black hole finally sucks it down and, as it hits the high density region and disappears, it emits an X-ray flash. Not even prador exotic metal armour can resist the forces now being applied.

'We head in-system now – to Panarchia,' Vorpal Dagger announces, and sends tactical data.

The U-space jump is a short one but, knowing what it is going into, Penny Royal's mind is a mass of contradictions. It knows what it is being ordered into, but it must protect its crew. The logical thing to do is run, but it cannot. It feels survivor guilt, but an impulse to reckless abandon conflicts with its need to protect itself and its crew. It can feel pain, still feels pain from the damage it received, and it is not going away. It is confused, knows the woman should be dealing with this . . . emotional imbalance, but she has abandoned her instruments to throw up in the ship's toilet and is now placing some sort of drug patch on her arm. And, because of this unbalanced inner conflict, Penny Royal can feel the darker part of itself growing, becoming more pervasive.

It was bad enough out by Layden's Sink and barely a victory, but it is worse here close to this world named Panarchia. Wreckage is strewn across space, ships being obliterated again and again. The Polity fleet has taken heavy losses and if it remains here it will be lost in its entirety. Also, the eight thousand human troops down on that Earth-like world cannot be saved. The AI of the *Vorpal Dagger* immediately relays new orders from Fleet Command here: this is over; this must be accepted as a defeat. It is time to start withdrawing the most valuable assets and depriving the prador of any gains other than mere territory.

However, Penny Royal suddenly receives special orders. It seems as though it is, amazingly, the least damaged destroyer in the fleet. In an instant it perfectly understands its position and purpose in the retreat and knows, with utter certainty, that though its ship body the *Puling Child* might survive this, its mind cannot.

2

The Brockle

The hold of the *High Castle* was pressurized, though the gas inside wasn't breathable. The Brockle scanned the neatly stacked cargo all around it. A few containers held weaponry: some rather exotic railgun missiles, some ultra-thermite decontamination explosives, and one crate containing some ultra-modern proton rifles. There were some crates of items for the human personnel, of little interest. The rest of the packages contained a cornucopia of scientific instruments – all cutting-edge and all doubtless intended for the examination of the remains of this 'renegade prador'.

Before it began loosening its structure, the Brockle reached out to analyse the sensors in this hold. It had to remember that though this ship had its science section it was mainly a state-of-the-art warship, and that its controlling AI would be paying a lot more attention to its interior than the Par Avion AI paid to the interior of the outlink space station it controlled. It soon found that the hold was riddled with sensors capable of being used to scan things down to the nanoscopic level. However, right now they were just looking for movement, energy spikes and molecules that might indicate chemical explosives, and their only connection to the ship's AI was in sending a constant 'everything okay' signal. The Brockle wanted them to keep on doing that, but was also aware that such sensors would have their own security hardware and software. The Polity had learned to its cost,

41

when a biophysicist called Skellor had got his hands on some Jain technology, that such things should not be neglected. The Brockle selected just one sensor and began examining it meticulously, confident that there would be some way of subverting the thing.

But the sensor had already detected the Brockle's terahertz scan and was sending an alert. The ship's AI knew that there was something in its hold scanning its sensors. It would know that there was supposedly nothing in the hold capable of such scanning. It would then surmise that either some sort of sophisticated weapon had been smuggled aboard, or that it had an unexpected guest. Even now those sensors were rising out of their semi-somnolent state as the ship AI demanded more data from them.

The Brockle had to act fast.

It was completely surrounded by crates but there was a half-inch gap beside one of them. Flattening out one of its units, it slid that into the gap and from its end extruded a cilia-propelled micro-tube. Mapping out straight edges to its target, it routed the tube along the corners of crates, along a convoluted course through the container of personal effects, along the frame holding the railgun missiles and straight into the keypad of one of the ultra-thermite explosives. Tracking a wire, it worked down inside the explosive and, ignoring the safety detonator, penetrated the energy-dense material of the explosive itself. Still scanning elsewhere, it detected the gas port that had filled this hold with argon, meanwhile rapidly shifting its internal structure and coagulating a diamond spear. Next, through the micro-tube it injected a mix of pure oxygen and carbon nanospheres, and a brief static discharge.

The explosive detonated as the Brockle stabbed up through the crates above it and flung itself for the gas port, travelling fast enough to create a sonic crack, shedding the diamond at the last and loosening its structure to pass through the grating as the hold filled with a chemical fire capable of melting ceramic. A fraction of a second later another explosive blew, then the others in a cascade. The blast pressure in the hold forced the Brockle along the pipe, frying two of its rear units even as it tried to layer them with artificial asbestos and cooling webs. It knew it could not survive long unless the ship AI reacted as expected. It did: it blew the hold doors into vacuum, spewing its contents along with the damaging fire out into space.

The Brockle hung on, with hooks shoved into the metalwork all around it as the blast front reversed and the pressure of the argon ahead tried to force it out into the evacuated hold. It opened a hole through itself to let the gas through, which incidentally cooled it down some, then it accelerated along the pipe. Just before reaching the solid-storage argon canister, it sliced through the pipe it was travelling down and exploded out, simply pulse-frying any sensors in its vicinity. Entering a pipe lined with optics – large enough for some maintenance robots – it expanded, processing power expanding too. It had not wanted to act so quickly and so drastically, yet what had happened was not a setback but an acceleration of its plan.

Locating itself on a stolen schematic of this ship, it oozed along to where it needed to be and bored a hole through the side of the optics pipe, then flowed straight through this into an air duct. Now it could really move. Separating into all its units, each propelled by peristaltic body ripples and maglev, it shoaled along the square-section duct at high speed, its destination seemingly etched into its distributed mind. To its left were the Sparkind quarters, to its right a series of laboratories and a small autofactory for ship's components. Up ahead and to the left was the captain's bridge, while ahead and down to the left lay the true control centre of the ship: an armoured sphere containing the *High Castle* AI.

Via further ducts, then along pipes and through the tiniest gaps, the Brockle closed in on the armoured sphere. It knew that its method of locomotion was much the same as that of Thorvald Spear's companion, the assassin drone Riss; of course it was – the Brockle had loaded much data and acquired many physical abilities by copying the methods of assassin drones. However, there was a difference: while Riss was a singular drone, the Brockle was an entity distributed both mentally and physically. Approaching the armoured sphere, it separated further, dispatching its units off on different routes to increase its chances of reaching its target. The armour itself wasn't a problem since it was there to protect the AI from damage during a space battle and it was necessarily full of useful openings so the AI could remain in contact with what was nominally its body. However, there were defences against this kind of incursion about those openings.

The paths of two of the Brockle's units were blocked as the AI belatedly realized what was happening and closed armoured shutters across air vents. Another was chopped in half when an armoured shutter sheared through optics as it was entering the sphere – but still, the half that had managed to enter had not been completely disabled. The bulk of the Brockle dropped out of an air vent and into a narrow corridor leading to a door into the sphere – the way humans entered. The door was closed, of course, but, having been constructed to keep out fire, blast waves or hostile troops, it wasn't quite the barrier it appeared.

The Brockle stuck itself all around the door rim and injected micro-tubes through the one-millimetre gap until they touched the seal. Snipping a piece of this, it sucked it inside and analysed it. Nothing special: diatomic acid would do. It injected the acid and the seal boiled and bubbled away, the Brockle opening gaps through itself to allow vapour and liquefied seal to escape. Then it oozed through the gap. For a few seconds much of its processing went down as it squeezed itself micro-metrically thin – in these moments it was reduced to the intelligence of a human being – but as it entered the sphere and expanded physically, its intelligence relaxed back to its customary brilliance.

Ahead lay the *High Castle* AI, its shape and the way it was linked into the ship a little different from usual. Instead of being lodged in crystal, in a ceramal skeletal case and clamped between the valve-end interlinks – a way that enabled quick disconnection and ejection from its ship should it be on the point of being destroyed – this AI sat in the centre of a geodesic sphere with points of contact stabbed in all round to support it at the centre. It was the usual type of AI crystal, but one heavily laden with quantum processing and merely the size of a tennis ball. The Brockle surmised that it must have more investment in its ship than other AIs, until realizing that in an emergency the whole sphere could be hurled by a grav-engine up through an ejection tube connected to the top of the chamber.

The Brockle flowed towards it, units combining into a wave of silvery worms that collapsed on the geodesic sphere and entered through its open hexagonal faces. It severed contacts as it flowed in around the AI, inserting itself into the cuts to intercept anything the AI was sending or receiving.

'What the fucking hell is happening?' Grafton was yelling. Obviously the AI had not quite got around to informing her, which was useful.

The Brockle closed in around the *High Castle* AI and began to make direct connections to it.

'You,' it said.

'Yes, me,' the Brockle replied as it began riffling through the AI's mind.

It replayed data input and output from the moment the *High Castle* AI had recognized something was wrong in the hold. The ship AI had not learned what had tried to penetrate its sensors but had understood something was on the move. However, not knowing what it was, it had not informed its human crew at that point. Reacting to the explosion there, it had surmised some form of sub-AI weapon probably sneaked aboard by separatists. Next, realizing its own chamber was under attack, it had informed them of that. The precise wording was a brief, 'I am under attack – initiating defences.' This was useful too: it had not detailed the nature of the attack.

'Informational warfare,' the Brockle replied – no way for Grafton to know it was not the ship AI speaking to her. 'Some kind of sub-AI weapon ran a penetration from the hold, attempted to get through to me and failed, so instead tried to do as much damage as possible by detonating the ultra-thermite bombs in the hold.'

'Shit! How the hell did that happen?' asked Grafton.

'I have sent details to Par Avion and the matter is under investigation,' replied the Brockle. 'However, for the interim and because of the nature of our mission and who might be involved, we are under quarantine. I have shut down U-com.'

'Could it have been something from Penny Royal?'

'I consider that unlikely but, since there is a possibility, how-ever remote, precautions must be taken.'

'Great start to our mission then.'

Yes, the Brockle had to agree. The danger was over and now the lies and the distortions of the truth to its own ends would come easier. It now effectively controlled this ship, and its own mission could truly begin.

Spear

The ship's maintenance robots were busily at work behind me in the section of my ship that I had previously opened out to accommodate Sverl and his children. I'd asked Bsorol if he and the rest wanted a lift away from Room 101 once I was capable of leaving. He'd turned monosyllabic but even then made it plain: no, he and the rest were staying. This just added to the frustrated anger I was feeling. Damn it, I'd had to do something, so I'd begun turning that rear section back into cabins. No doubt Trent, Sepia and Cole would be joining me when I finally left, and they would need room. I pondered Sepia for a second, realizing that, just as with the other two, I had been pushing her away, which didn't strike me as a great idea when body and mind were telling me I wanted her in my cabin, with me. I winced in further irritation. I would deal with that when we left, when we had breathing space . . . Unfortunately, leaving was the problem.

While pondering my difficulty in departing this station I sat back and auged into the ship's system to call up some previously recorded image data. It displayed on the screen fabric ahead. A rash of stars appeared across the blackness of space. Then a frame opened at the centre of this and focused in, bringing Cvorn's Series Terminal or ST dreadnought into sharp focus. The renegade prador had obviously made a cautious approach, surfacing his ship from underspace fifty light hours out from Room 101, but he hadn't been cautious enough. While I watched, the fleet of King's Guard ships, those great stretched-out golden teardrops, appeared over to one side of the dreadnought and immediately opened fire. Particle beams crossed the intervening gap and I can only say that Cvorn must have been caught napping, because they carved into his ship for a full twenty seconds before there was any reaction. They burned great glowing canyons through its giant weapons array, which stood out like a city of skyscrapers at one end. Exotic hull metal heated and glowed and in some places collapsed. Vast explosions threw out burning debris as from the throats of erupting volcanoes. Then the hardfields went up and fusion drives fired and, shedding fire and chunks of hull like seared skin, the dreadnought tried to get away. The Guard ships stayed on it, pounding away at it, and eventually Cvorn was forced to make an emergency U-jump. Sitting there, watching this scene again, I once more studied the data on the U-signature generated. It didn't look healthy at all, and I suspected that even if the ST dreadnought had made it back into the real at the terminus of the jump, it had not done so in one piece.

The Guard fleet had then taken itself away – back to the Prador Kingdom, I hoped. The modern Polity attack ship that had been outside the station – the one Penny Royal had arrived on – was gone too. There was nothing out there to stop me leaving, but my ship, the *Lance*, had one major problem: I had no AI to control its U-space drive. I had been waiting for Flute to return in the decoy ship, but now decided I should start preparing for the possibility that Flute wasn't coming back. I would have to find a cooperative AI here, or strong-arm an uncooperative one, because I didn't want to be here any longer than I needed and because, well, because of what Penny Royal had said:

We have returned to my beginning, and now we must return to yours.

Those had been the black AI's last words to me before folding up and flipping out of existence, and I felt a tight ball of anger inside as I remembered them. What were they supposed to fucking mean?

When I recruited Isobel Satomi to my cause I'd been bent on vengeance against the AI for the eight thousand troops it had killed on Panarchia. On Masada, the home world of the ancient Atheter race, things had turned a little strange, but I still felt my aim had been reaffirmed. However, after that, my attitude had changed. My memories had been altered by the black AI itself in such a way as to make me vengeful when, with my own true memories, I wouldn't have been. The spine, that piece of Penny Royal that the AI had left behind in its ship – now mine – contained memcordings from Penny Royal's victims and I had been experiencing them constantly, their stories reaffirming my need for revenge. I was being manipulated at every turn and crammed full of reasons to attempt to destroy the AI. And yet this was all being done by the AI itself.

Did I still want vengeance? No, the knowledge of that manipulation had led to my vengeful feelings drying up. It had been as if I was locked into a course that I'd long ago lost any emotional investment in. However, the recent result of the AI's manipulation had reignited my anger. And why was I so angry? Because, as the need for vengeance had faded, I had come to expect more, because I had come to expect this whole drama to lead to something, I don't know . . . something numinous. All it had led to was the sordid murder of the renegade prador Sverl, whom I'd come to respect and even like, by the snake drone Riss. Penny Royal had even acted to stop me preventing Sverl's murder, through the intervention of the Golem Mr Grey and via the spine.

So yes, I now wanted to go after Penny Royal again. Yet, ever since setting out after the damned thing, it had become increasingly evident that I had as much chance of destroying Penny Royal as I had of pissing on the sun and putting it out. Penny Royal was dangerous, powerful, seemed to be able to move anywhere at will. Even Polity AIs were scared of the wretched thing. Penny Royal was capable of being a paradigm changer, and a mere resurrected soldier like me had no chance of being effective against such a thing. So, if I could not destroy the blasted AI, at least I might be able to get some answers.

I now brought up a series of frames showing cam views I could access throughout the station. These covered areas controlled by some of the nearest surviving AIs and here I saw that activity was still increasing. And not just in the AIs making repairs – activity had ramped up with *all* the AIs, and I was starting to get an intimation of what this meant, especially when seeing robots being manufactured whose only purpose seemed to be destruction.

When I'd realized I might need to recruit an AI here I had started listening in on them. This wasn't easy because few of them used language in any form I recognized, either human or computer, but I persevered and managed to run some translation programs in my aug. My first success I'd thought was a failure because I couldn't get a grip on what was going on. However, I slowly began to understand I was listening in on high-speed transactions, bargains, deals, politics, and none of it was entirely sane. Once I realized this, a lot more began to become clear: the AIs that had survived Room 101 had been badly damaged by it. They had, to put it in a mealy-mouthed human context, some challenging problems.

Further careful listening, interspersed with raids on vulnerable databases, made the picture clearer. They had been turned contentious, hostile, by 101's attacks on them, and in an effort to hide they'd sacrificed intelligence, reducing themselves to AI simulacra of barbarians. Once 101 blew its own brains out, they had turned on each other and fought a lengthy internecine war for territory and resources throughout the station. Before we arrived they had established a peace of sorts – one only maintained by perpetual bargaining and bartering, with the currency being energy and materials. The robot that had attacked us inside my ship had been sent by one of them – firstly in an attempt to gain advantage over its fellows, then desperately in an effort to get off the station when it realized the King's Guard intended to annihilate it. Next came the bombardment, followed by the attack from Penny Royal, which had destroyed numerous power supplies and thus disabled weapons, allowing a King's Guard ship to dock. The upshot of this was that the balance of power here had been shattered and, it was now apparent to me, every single AI was preparing for war.

This meant it was going to get dangerous around here and that leaving, even without Flute, must be my priority. I briefly considered summoning Trent and the others back, but it would be quicker to fly to the construction bay adjacent to that hospital and get them aboard there. First I needed a ship mind. Until now I had only been listening – penetrating communications and grabbing unsecured data – and had not spoken directly to any of them. In my aug I inspected the security around a link I had prepared, then finally opened it.

'Hello, construction bay AI designation E676,' I said.

The response was a nonsense babble of computer code interspersed with human language, before the AI abruptly severed the link. I folded my hands in my lap and waited patiently – the link at my end remaining open. Eventually the connection went live again and I found myself speaking to the AI that had sent the robot aboard my ship.

'You are the human,' it said.

'I am one of them,' I replied.

'The others are in territory – *zzz* –'

The territorial designation was a massive block of code I

dropped into secure storage. Then, using the aug equivalent of armoured gloves, I took some of it apart and from this gleaned data concerning power allocations, resource exchanges and interwoven boundaries no human barbarian would understand. I ignored the rest.

'Yes, they are,' I replied.

'Reason for contact?'

'Do you still want to get off this station?'

'Give me your access codes.'

I ignored that and continued, 'I need an AI to control my U-space . . .' I lost impetus as a stray thought suddenly hit me. I'd already seen how much these AIs had regressed. Were any of them even capable of controlling a U-space drive? I continued, 'I need an AI to control my U-space drive if I am to get out of this system. Are you capable of controlling a U-space drive?'

'Simplicity,' said E676, and sent another data package.

This went into secure storage too – a brief glimpse inside revealing Skaidon warp math that was all but incomprehensible to me.

'In that case,' I said, abruptly reaching out for my console controls, 'perhaps we can come to an arrangement?'

– security breach –

I didn't recognize the warning and abruptly felt very hot, sweat beading my forehead. Why was I reaching out for the console when I'd come to the conclusion that I could do just about anything through my aug?

'You will have to physically move yourself here,' I noted.

I then peered down at my hand and saw that, using the touch controls, I had called up a frame in the screen fabric and had begun sorting through system controls. I felt puzzled and vaguely worried, but couldn't control my hands. Next I saw something else in another frame: two of those weird by-blow robots, like the one that had attacked in here, launching themselves from a nearby hatch.

What?

My bafflement turned to panic as my hand, independent of me, selected controls that would open the weapons cache loading hatch. How the hell had that happened? How had this *primitive* AI managed to take control of me so easily?

'Simple,' said a voice in my mind, *'it's just been waiting for activation.'*

Agony followed and I looked down to see a long glassy needle stabbed right through my arm just above the wrist, paralysing my hand. Something long and snaky and translucent reared up beside me, spread a cobra hood and came down on my skull like a hammer. It was so hard I felt sure my skull had cracked as flashes of yellow lightning chased me down into blackness.

– hiatus –

I came to, floating in vacuum, biting down on the urge to throw up. My head hurt badly, as did my wrist, and I really didn't need Riss's monologue burbling close by.

'. . . so you have to remember that though these AIs have regressed, they haven't regressed that much.'

'What are you on about?'

Riss was speaking to me through my suit radio. 'Oh, you weren't quite conscious – sometimes it's difficult to tell. I was saying that, as you noticed, these AIs have regressed. However, you are an advanced human who was using technology that is far from being a match for an AI. It was an unfair encounter really. E676 defeated you on its own territory with the same ease with which an AI would be defeated by a human barbarian with a hammer, on his territory.'

'You've been reading my mind again,' I said.

I was in an enclosed space and something was pressing against my side. Blearily looking down, I saw the spine, jammed through a utility belt that Riss must have put round my waist. I hauled the thing out and batted it away from me, then reached out to a nearby wall. As my gloved hand touched the metal I felt it vibrating, and realized this meant there was a lot of activity in the structure around me. I then set myself turning and saw I was in some narrow maintenance tube that wasn't aboard my ship. Riss must have got me out again, just as she had when intent on rescuing me from Cvorn's attack on us. A ship's maintenance robot crouching against the wall of the tube confirmed this. I tried to aug into surrounding systems but got nothing.

'Well, you do spill an awful lot.'

I ignored that and asked, 'Why am I here?'

'I wasn't fast enough – you'd already punched in the instructions to open up your ship.' After a pause she added, 'Also, those controls are keyed to your DNA, so I couldn't use them.'

'What?'

'E676 now has control of your ship.'

'How did it do it?' I asked, bringing my spin to a halt and focusing on Riss.

The assassin drone had returned to pristine condition, translucent, her mysterious internal workings just visible and her third black eye gleaming. Yet, the last time I'd seen her, she hadn't looked so good. Though having managed to inject the enzyme acid into Sverl, she'd taken a severe beating in the process. When I last saw her, escaping down a hole in the floor of that autofactory, she'd looked like a mobile burned-out light tube.

'The two data packages, obviously.'

'Not so obvious to me,' I said tightly. 'I routed them into secure storage.'

I was thinking at a glacial pace. I knew I should be alarmed but felt thoroughly lethargic, while my head was fizzing.

'No, they came with their own "secure storage" and let your aug know that they were secure,' Riss explained. 'Really, if you'd wanted to talk to that AI you should have done it by restricted bandwidth radio to your ship's system, and not through your aug. Either that, or you should have used the AI resources easily available to you.'

'You?' I was unable to keep the sneer out of my voice.

'You didn't know I was in the ship with you,' said Riss. 'I meant the spine.'

I glanced at the named object. 'I see you ensured it didn't get left aboard the *Lance*.'

'*That* kind of technology is not something we want falling into the hands of the AIs here.' Something in her tone told me that she was leaving much unsaid. I shrugged. The spine was many things, hard and sharp enough to punch through the body of a Golem, able to change its shape, a repository of the dead . . . and of course a piece of Penny Royal – a 'paradigm-changing AI'.

Just then my aug started reinstating and I felt frustrated about what that meant: Riss had made it dump all its data, had run a format and it was now returning to its factory settings. But, of course, it had been necessary. Its security had been breached and everything had to go. Those data packages, even as they ran their software to take over my motor controls, had probably been copying themselves throughout.

I rubbed at my wrist, which still ached, then snatched my hand away upon knocking off a scab of breach foam. My suit squirted vapour until further foam bubbled out to seal the hole. I reached up to my aching head, but my fingertips just thwacked against my suit helmet. I needed to *wake up*.

55

'I knocked you out with a directed EM pulse,' said the drone. 'There will be no damage.'

'Right.' I just managed to stop myself rubbing at my wrist again.

'Maybe an analgesic patch there,' Riss added. 'Later.'

I stared at the drone. Riss must have sneaked back aboard when Trent and the other two set out. Perhaps she had intended to stay in hiding until I reached some other destination and then quietly depart. But now she had revealed herself, almost certainly saving my life in the process, and I had to deal with that.

'So what does E676 want with my ship – there's no threat out there it needs to escape now,' I said instead.

'I've no idea,' Riss replied. 'Robots like the one that came aboard before have occupied it but don't seem to be doing anything. We could suppose the AI would like to U-jump away from this system, but I doubt it's capable of running a U-space engine.' Riss gave a snakish shrug.

'Another lie, then,' I said.

'Yes – the package it sent was nonsense.'

'I need to take the ship back,' I said.

'Yes.'

'So I need allies.'

The drone didn't have much to say in response to that because she probably knew precisely what allies I was talking about. I let the silence drag on for a little while before saying, 'It wasn't necessary to kill Sverl.'

'I know that now,' said Riss.

'So how was it that you, a *sophisticated* AI, didn't know it before?'

'Because like you I have been manipulated. Played,' said Riss. Then after a pause, 'And I have been healed.'

'What!'

'The emptiness and the hate were false constructs,' said Riss. 'I was returned to my wartime state, loaded with poison and parasite eggs to inject, a victim prepared for me – everything I thought I'd lost returned to me. When I killed I found his killing to be an empty act, and when Sverl died as he did I lost my hate.'

Though I had more pressing concerns I wanted to move closer to the drone and wring her neck, but knew that would be about as easy as squeezing the life out of a tyre.

'I see,' I said, 'so you think this was set up by Penny Royal for you? You think that the AI manoeuvred us all here just so you could find your way out of the hole it dumped you in?'

Riss's head was dipped and she almost looked ashamed. 'I was just a side benefit.' Now she looked up, that black eye open. 'The main aim was to lure Sverl out of the Graveyard and eliminate him as a threat to the Kingdom, apparently.'

'I don't buy that.'

Now Riss appeared eager. 'Neither do I.'

'This isn't over,' I tried, not so sure of myself now.

'No, it isn't – we are not yet done with Penny Royal, nor it with us.'

That left a sour taste in my mouth. 'So we need to get out of here, which is both an immediate problem in that I no longer have a ship –' I waved a hand airily, not sure in what direction the *Lance* lay – 'and a future problem with our lack of a ship mind.' Riss, despite all her faults, had once said she could serve as a ship mind.

'That lack of a mind is a problem that was solved while you were unconscious.'

Another voice issued inside my suit helmet: '*You finished now?*'

'*Flute?*' I asked.

'ETA four hours from now,' replied my ship mind. *'I hope no one's going to start shooting at me – I've had enough of that.'*

Trent

Trent eyed the big robot and swung his particle cannon round to bear on it, while beside him Sepia took aim with her laser carbine. Cole, meanwhile, had backed up and was peering through another doorway.

'Problems back here too,' he said.

Keeping the big robot in his sights, Trent walked backwards and looked through the same doorway. This room did not contain a chair or editing equipment, and the rear wall was missing, opening onto a section of dark station structure filled with half-seen movement. An object launched itself inwards, landing on its back with a heavy thump on the grav-plated floor. Trent felt a shiver of horror as he watched the military autodoc trying to right itself. Transferring his gaze to the other movement out there, he began to identify distinct robots. These weren't autodocs but something else entirely.

'This is private property,' repeated the big robot, now shifting into motion again.

'Another step,' Trent warned.

'Wait!' Cole rested a hand on his shoulder. 'Over here.' He stepped into an editing suite that did contain a chair.

'What is it?' Trent asked. The editing suite was as good a place as any. If they were attacked he was confident he could rapidly destroy any of the robots he had seen and, if things got a bit tight, he could always burn an escape route through the wall. Trent followed with Sepia close behind him. He watched through the doorway as the autodoc, having righted itself, scuttled out of the room opposite but did not come after them. Instead it turned, its feet tearing up carpet moss, shot towards the approaching big surgical robot, then past it and out of sight. Trent then backed off again as the big robot drew closer.

'No trespassers,' it said, then turned ponderously in the direction the autodoc had fled.

Puzzled, Trent followed the big robot down the corridor and into a room just in time to see that one of those other robots had got into the hospital. This thing landed on four legs terminating in wide flat pads and unfolded a long limb from its back, snipping at the air with a three-fingered grab. It stabbed this towards the big robot, but the latter machine smoothly snared it with a surgical clamp, then bore down on it with a diamond wheel. Severing half the limb, it tossed it back where it had come from, then, shambling forwards, booted the smaller robot after it.

Trent's puzzlement cleared. Whatever had taken out that wall must have sealed the area because there was no air loss, which indicated a sneak attack. The hospital AI must have detected it and had sent this big robot to repel it. His training and experience taking over, and suppressing his initial qualms, Trent stepped into the room, flipped out a sighting screen for his cannon, set the thing to brief spurts of fire and targeted one of the invading robots. His first shot blew the thing into pieces – metal clattering and clanging all around and one limb landing smoking in the room. He shot again, destroying another one and, moving past the big surgical robot, aimed at yet another. It was easy. The things were sluggish, ill-made and didn't have the kind of protective armour found on a war drone. They also seemed confused about the source of what was destroying them. A moment later Sepia joined him and quite soon flames were the only things moving beyond the missing wall.

'That's about it,' she said, resting her carbine back across her shoulder.

'Seems to be,' said Trent, just a second before explosive decompression picked him up and hurled him towards the missing wall. He sailed through with his visor closing up automatically, hit a beam and bounced away, but managed to snag a second one before he was sucked through a hole in another wall seemingly consisting of wormcasts of metal. As the wind died, more robots began to come through that hole. Trent glanced back into the hospital room and saw that both Sepia and Cole had been snagged by the big robot. A multitude of autodocs ranging from battlefield medics to the kind normally pedestal mounted in clean rooms were swarming behind – some given mobility by caterpillar treads and others sporting spidery legs.

His heart hammering, Trent decided he had chosen sides now. He checked the display and complementary controls on his cannon and saw prador glyphs scrolling. No help there. He called up his visor display and checked for data links within a particular microwave frequency, found what he was after and allowed it. His head-up display immediately asked, 'Translate?' He answered yes and began getting a feed he could understand from the cannon.

Its laminar storage was down to half and the particulate matter it used was down to a third – not many shots left. He propelled himself back from the beam over towards one side of the hole he had been sucked through, meanwhile adjusting the particulate down and reducing power drain by narrowing the beam. He knew he couldn't be so profligate now. Turning at the last moment, he brought his feet down on the wall, sticking there. Something like a polished copper beetle landed beside him and he kicked it away, and with enforced calm searched through the cannon's functions. The translation program had given him an overlay of a similar human weapon and in a moment he had cross hairs up in his visor, moving as he moved the cannon.

Meanwhile the hospital robots were swarming into the space and he now had to choose his targets carefully. He aimed and fired at a spiderbot trailing an umbilicus as it came through the hole, blowing away half its body. The umbilicus then abruptly towed it back out of sight. He hit another thing that bore some resemblance to a tailless scorpion, before propelling himself away from the beam and back towards the hospital room, sailing in over an avalanche of defending robots coming out of the hospital. Something slammed into him in mid-air and he swung his cannon down to batter some long-limbed object clinging to his leg. Tumbling out of control, he hit the back wall. Even as he beat at the thing that grasped at him a military autodoc leapt up from the floor and snared it, and they both fell away, tearing at each other. Next Cole caught hold of his foot and towed him down to the floor.

'Thanks,' said Trent.

Cole nodded, his expression grim, and stepped away wielding a large chunk of metal, probably from one of the destroyed robots, which he stabbed into the sensor array of another of those scorpion things. Sepia, meanwhile, was taking shots through the hole in the wall, while to one side the big robot was methodically dismembering any attacker that drew close.

'They're retreating,' said the catadapt woman over suit radio.

Trent shot another of the scorpion things that had got past her and the big robot and moved forwards. All around him robots were fighting each other but he couldn't really tell friend from foe. He tapped his wrist control to bring up a menu of com channels in use, but that gave a count into the thousands, then, just using a general Polity com frequency, he asked, 'Hospital AI, what the hell is happening here?'

Sepia had now moved back from the hole as hospital robots began swarming back inside. Trent moved to put his back against the wall as their airborne mass streamed past him to the door, all turning to the left out there and heading away.

'No trespassers,' said a familiar voice, the big robot now turning and beginning to clump back across the room. Within a minute it, along with just two others, were the only robots remaining in the room – all the attackers were gone like water swirling down a plug hole. Trent glanced to the two smaller ones remaining and saw that they were printer robots like the one they had seen wall-building on their way here. He watched them disappear in the space beyond and begin rapidly tossing cut sections of wall, consisting of layers of bubble-metal sandwiching insulation foam, back into the room.

'Hospital AI?' Trent tried again, broadcasting across numerous com channels.

'Only me,' said the big robot, still perambulating towards the doorway.

Trent quickly moved to stand in its path, 'You're the controlling AI here?'

The robot halted and, after a very long pause, doubtfully muttered, 'No trespassing.'

'I asked you a question,' Trent insisted.

'You are humans,' said the robot. It began shifting its feet, slowly edging sideways as if preparing to bolt past him. However, it was clearly incapable of bolting anywhere. It struck Trent that it appeared nervous of him. Perhaps it now well understood what the weapon he held could do to it.

'Yes, we're humans,' said Trent, baffled.

· By now one of the printer robots was back in the room; it

had already fixed one section of wall in place and was fitting another like pieces of a jigsaw, its printing heads moving like an ancient typewriter and the join utterly invisible to the human eye. It occurred to Trent that such incidents might be common here, and that they were more like an infestation than an attack.

'I have over a thousand battle casualties,' he continued, 'all in need of prosthetics and medical care.'

'They also have mental problems that need . . . resolving,' said Cole, who was standing by the hole and peering out, still clutching that length of metal.

'Injuries?' said the robot, as if some vague memory was arising in its mind. 'No trespassers,' it added, before again setting itself in motion.

'I think they're trying to get in again,' said Sepia.

Trent glanced round at her. She was standing in the doorway, looking in the direction all the other hospital robots had gone. 'Strike that – something's coming through the wall down there.'

Trent sighed. 'Well, I guess we'd better help if we still want to have a hospital we can use.' He stepped aside to let the big surgical robot get past and, as it accelerated to a meander, he asked again, 'Are you the hospital AI?'

The robot shrugged its complicated metalwork, and replied, 'I'm Florence.'

Spear

It was getting chaotic in the station and, when I opened communications with Bsorol, he just dumped me straight into a sensory download from his armour. The prador were in the midst of a battle, shooting down robots swarming all around

Sverl's mausoleum. Some were attacking the prador, some were attacking each other, while others were trying to chew through armoured shields the prador had erected. It just struck me as insane, these prador risking their lives seemingly to protect their father's remains.

'It looks worse there,' I said. 'What the hell is going on?'

'The balance has been further upset,' Riss replied, obviously seeing the same feed as me and as much in my head, or rather in my aug, as before.

'Explain yourself.'

'A tactical AI within the station used the recent disruption as an opportunity to assassinate key AIs elsewhere in the station, which has led to the chaos you're seeing.'

I stared at the snake drone and wished she had an expression I could read. Earlier her words had implied that she knew more than she was telling, and now I was beginning to wonder what she'd been doing over the days since she had killed Sverl. I shook my head. What did it matter? What *did* matter was that we were in trouble. It occurred to me then that Trent might have run into similar problems. I tried my suit's radio to get in contact but got nothing in return, then damned myself for letting them go, though their actions were not really my responsibility. It just seemed stupid to wake and repair the shell people in this place. And why the hell had Sepia gone with them? Surely she was smarter than that . . .

'Which direction do we head to get to the prador?' I asked, looking each way along the maintenance tube.

'Why do you want to get to them?' asked Riss.

'I need my ship back and I need help to get it back,' I explained. 'Sverl's children are the only ones here who have the firepower.'

'Why should they help you?'

'Just tell me which way to go, Riss.'

After a long pause Riss swung her head round to point it in one direction down the tube.

'Thanks,' I said, reaching out to snare the spine, using it against the wall to send me drifting along the way indicated, then reaching up with one hand to push against a protruding handle to speed me up.

'Bsorol, my ship's been taken over,' I said. 'I'm heading your way.'

A three-dimensional map arrived in my aug, with a blinking red dot indicating my position. I tried to orient by checking cam imagery ahead but found it much more difficult now my aug had lost a lot of its programming. Catching another handle, I paused and looked back to see Riss still drifting in the pipe where I had left her. After a moment she shrugged then slithered through vacuum towards me, probably using her maglev or some internal grav-engine against the walls of the tube. As she came up beside me she said, 'This way,' and moved on ahead.

'You're probably not welcome there,' I observed as I followed her.

'They'll hardly know I'm present,' said Riss.

Of course, she would use her chameleonware.

After just a few minutes the end of the maintenance tube was visible as a pink glare, and my visor automatically compensated for the brightness. When we reached it, I found the tube severed and protruding into an area hollowed out by some blast to leave a spherical chamber lined with wreckage. The glare was coming from somewhere to my left although I could see no opening. However, as I'd seen here before, even a pinhole could admit enough light to bring visibility up to human range, since the hypergiant out there was millions of times brighter than Sol.

Riss headed across the space towards the continuation of the

65

maintenance pipe and I propelled myself after her. However, nearing the wall of wreckage on the other side, she suddenly changed course and I had to use my wrist impeller to stay with her. We landed amidst tangled girders just as something shot out of our intended destination. The thing, which was rapidly changing shape, slammed against one side of the pipe we had travelled down, and then bounced away, moving much more slowly. Now I could see that it was actually two robots grappling with each other. One was one of the usual insect-format maintenance robots here, while the other was a Golem, the android John Grey.

The two tore at each other with rabid ferocity, their limbs blurring, sparks and debris sailing away, but the big Golem was winning. Within just a few seconds Grey had dismembered his opponent and, kicking from its remains, he shot over towards us. He landed hard enough on the girders for me to feel the impact through my hands, and then just gazed at the two of us.

'What do you want?' I asked over a general com frequency.

Grey just hung there, staring.

'Come on,' said Riss.

I hesitated, not wanting this Golem at my back without some explanation of its presence. Then, realizing there wasn't much I could do about it anyway, I reluctantly followed Riss. As we travelled, I glanced back several times to see the Golem keeping pace with us.

Activity increased as we drew closer to the autofactory-cum-mausoleum-for-Sverl. Next, in corridors made for humans, a spiderbot, on an umbilicus disappearing up through a hole in the ceiling, crashed into our path like some giant hand slapping down to deny us. I halted, Grey coming up beside me fast, then skidding to a halt too, and turning to gaze down at Riss.

Riss peered back, her black eye flicking open. 'So I wasn't the only one.'

'No,' said Grey, 'though I was willing.'

'What's this?' I asked. Surely they had some explanation, why else include me in their communication?

'Back up round the corner,' said the assassin drone. 'There's going to be shrapnel.'

I hurriedly retreated, glancing at Grey, who walked with me, as I went.

'What the hell was that about?' I asked.

'Observe now,' replied the Golem, 'how a number of key AIs aboard this station recently died.'

At the corner I watched Riss squirm towards the spiderbot and then fade into invisibility. The bot raised two of its limbs and swung from side to side, confused about the disappearance of a potential threat. Riss abruptly reappeared, heading rapidly back towards me, just as the spiderbot disappeared in a bright hot flash. I ducked back, just in time, as chunks of hot metal carved into the wall opposite and a limb bounced past.

'Before you ask,' said Riss, coming round the corner, 'explosive gel.'

'How much do you have left?' asked Grey.

'I'm optimistic about things now,' Riss replied. 'I'm half full rather than half empty,'

'Good – we're going to need it.'

As we advanced we encountered further robots. Some completely ignored us, some were fighting each other, while still others attacked on sight. Grey took a hand when a series of bug-like mechs swarmed towards us, hurling himself in their path and snatching them up one after the other and simply stripping their legs away. I ducked back when some shot past the Golem, while Riss just faded away. I crouched down, arms over my helmet, as a series of explosions ensued. Feeling impacts against my suit, I threw myself further back, caught a handle, and pulled myself towards an alcove, thinking I would be safe there, only to find another spiderbot, this one sans umbilicus, charging at us from behind. Bracing in the alcove, I waited until it drew close and leapt at me, then I drove the spine into its main body, levered it up and rolled out underneath it, something hard scoring down my back. Programming then fell into my compass via the spine, confused for a microsecond with my suit's error reports, then I realized I was seeing the structure of my attacker's mind. The thing bounded out of the alcove, impaled on the spine, hit the opposite wall then threw itself at me again. My reaction was instinctive: as if with some invisible hand I reached into that mind to find motor controls, and tore them out. The spiderbot closed up into a fist and I stepped aside to let it tumble on past, completely inert.

'Like that,' said Riss, reappearing.

This then was the AI resource the assassin drone had referred to earlier. I hesitated and cast wider with the facility I'd used to penetrate the spiderbot's mind. I studied the complex structure of the mind before me. I'd known that I could penetrate Riss this way, which was why I'd hurried to Sverl when I'd learned the drone's intent. I had the coding that would have instructed Riss to eject the enzyme acid she had stolen, but Penny Royal had intervened and stopped me. What I hadn't realized was that I could do so much more than that. I now knew I could simply shut down Riss's motor functions if I so chose.

I also found I could read her recent memories and, in just a few seconds, I learned of the tactical AI that had taken control of her and sent her to assassinate key station AIs. I could read more if I wished, but there was a lot there, some of it formatted in ways that even with this new ability I found difficult to understand. Did I really want to know? Transferring my attention to Grey, who had just dealt with the last of those bugs, I found a mind even more difficult to read. Yes, I understood that under the instruction of the same tactical AI Grey had been destroying station AIs too. What I didn't understand was Grey's willingness to obey and, when I delved deeper, I found a tangled intelligence I could penetrate, but which repelled me.

I paused. Perhaps I didn't need the help of the prador? Perhaps I could just go back to my ship and shut down the things that had managed to get aboard? Perhaps I could just shut down E676? I decided that, yes, that was what I would do. However, we were closer now to the prador and I really did not like the look of the list of errors my suit was reporting, especially the red text informing me that I was losing air.

'Let's go,' I said, stepping over to the spiderbot and pulling out the spine.

As we continued I probed our surroundings. Some robots heading directly towards us I simply shut down. In others I made simple alterations to send them off on a different course. An island of calm began to prevail around us in the chaos of the station, but it was a small island. Whenever I touched a surface I could feel it vibrating and shuddering, and ranging out with my aug, I could see the various conflicts all around, either visually or on a coding level. Soon we came into an area where I could see the flashing of particle cannons and feel the deck jerking under my feet. We passed a pile of half-melted robots still emitting vapour, then, before I stepped round the corner of a T-junction ahead, Grey caught hold of my shoulder and halted me.

'Second-child,' was all he said, crackles of EM interfering with com.

'Bsorol?' I enquired over com.

After a long pause the first-child replied, 'He will not fire on you.'

I moved ahead and peered round the corner at the second-child. It stood frozen in the middle of the corridor brandishing some kind of beam weapon I didn't recognize. Around it I saw glowing wreckage, melted walls and glimpses into station structure. Despite Bsorol's assurance I still did not want to step out, so reached out for the second-child on another level. It was no AI, but its armoured suit did possess a level of computer control. When I looked into that I found that someone had already been there before me.

'I've shut it down,' explained Riss.

I looked around for the drone but she had disappeared. Before I stepped out, Grey moved ahead of me and marched round the corner towards the prador. I followed. The prador remained frozen as we came up to it and passed it. A short while later we reached a space that had been cleared around the auto-factory – the whole pill-shaped structure now heavily armoured and held in place by narrow bubble-metal beams. Around its surface were the blisters of gun emplacements occupied by second-children, firing on robots hurling themselves from holes torn through surrounding structure. That space was filled with tumbling pieces of them, and splashes of molten metal writhing in vacuum. Bsorol waited on a platform before a main armoured door, urgently gesturing us over with one claw while firing a particle cannon from the tip of another. Grey launched off ahead of me and I followed, feeling debris impacting against my suit and, in a moment, the armoured door was drawing open and Bsorol moving ahead of us into a prador-scale airlock. As I followed, I mentally reached out again, confirming that Riss was still nearby, also sensing her freeing the lock on that second-child's armour. Very thoughtful of her . . .

As the airlock pressurized, something slammed into the outer door and I wondered if I had made the right decision coming here. Surely, the prador could not keep up this level of energy and munitions expenditure? The inner door admitted us into the autofactory itself and now, with atmosphere all around, the racket of battle boomed and hissed in my ears. Here further changes had been made. Sverl's ceramal skeleton was no longer underneath a dome, and the dried-out slick of his organic remains had been cleaned away. The skeleton, which was a spherical ribcage up on prosthetic legs bearing prosthetic claws and mandibles, looked like a living entity in itself. It stood on a pedestal now, the floor surrounding it cleared of detritus and polished flat. I didn't like this at all. As far as I had gathered, the prador had none of that insanity called religion, but this was looking suspiciously like the start of one.

The inner airlock door closed with a crash and, after checking the constituency of the atmosphere on my visor display, I folded down both visor and concertinaed helmet and winced at the noise and the reek. The air here smelled of hot electronics, burning metal and prador. Glimpsing movement above, I looked up to see weapons turrets extruding from various ports. The place obviously had internal defences too, though why they had been deployed now made the skin on my back creep. Were those things out there about to break in? Bsorol moved up beside me, then past me, abruptly swinging round to face me.

'Killers so often return to the scene of their crime,' he said, in perfect unaccented English.

Something thrummed, all the way through me. A visible meniscus passed through the air and I felt my aug go down. Even Grey was affected, abruptly collapsing to the floor and folding up foetal – some kind of EM weapon. Bsorol reached out with one claw and I staggered back, but rather than snatch at me

71

the claw closed on something beside me. Bsorol held up a long and snakelike form.

'You're going to burn for what you did,' said the first-child.

His words were hollow and seared of emotion, but maybe that was just the effect of the translator. Riss was a machine who could experience pain, but only if she chose to. Bsorol could deliver no punishment beyond her destruction; no fit payment for what the drone had done here to this first-child's father. I just stood there staring as Riss writhed weakly in Bsorol's claw – obviously damaged yet again – as the prador opened the tip of his other claw to bring his particle cannon to bear on her.

'Desist,' said a voice seeming to issue from all around. 'Put Riss down.'

3

The Brockle

'The culprits have been apprehended,' said the Brockle, in its guise as the AI of the *High Castle*. 'No connection with Penny Royal has as yet been found. It seems this was just an attempt to damage a Polity warship.'

'Oh, that's a relief then,' said Grafton sarcastically, looking round at the four other crewmembers on the bridge with her. However, she believed every word. Why should she not, when they came from the trusted AI, whom she had known for many years, and who ran the *High Castle*?

'However, as you are now seeing, I did receive other orders from Earth Central before our last U-jump.'

'Well, yes,' said Grafton, glancing at the star field on one of the bridge screens, 'I did spot that.'

Their route was supposed to have taken them to a point one light month out from the hypergiant system in which Room 101 resided. There they were to record the progress of events about that station up to the point when the King's Guard ships departed, then to follow the attack ships in. They weren't to take part in the attack – just record it, then bring in their science team, with military support, to analyse the results. However, because of Penny Royal's involvement, they were to assume command if anything went wrong. Disappointingly, though Penny Royal *had* been involved, this had turned out to be all about preventing the military asset Room 101 falling into the wrong

. . . claws. However, they now found themselves in an area of space in that region that could neither be defined as the Graveyard – that zone lying between the Prador Kingdom and the Polity, nor the Reaches – an area of space lying beyond these.

'And,' the Brockle added, 'it is now time for you to know the true nature of our mission and be acquainted with the fact that at Par Avion we took on board a passenger.'

'What?' said Grafton, suddenly angry.

The Brockle studied the bridge crew, looking for signs of suspicion and doubt.

'Let me first acquaint you with some facts,' it continued. 'As you are aware, the *High Castle* is very well armed for such an *initially* science-based mission, and some of those weapons are U-space disruptor missiles. It is no accident that they are aboard.'

That was true as far as it went. It had only recently been decided that any ship of a military nature that ventured on missions outside the Polity but close to the Graveyard should carry such missiles. This was simply because any such mission probably involved hunting down some rogue ship and that the option should be provided to prevent such a ship fleeing where Polity military could not follow – the Graveyard. Grafton and her bridge crew did not know that. The Brockle had already absorbed all the *High Castle* AI's memories and knew that there had been no exchange on the matter.

'And?' Grafton prompted.

'We are to use them,' the Brockle replied, then before Grafton could ask further questions, continued, 'A certain unique AI has managed to map the full extent of Penny Royal's data traffic across known space.'

The Brockle was puzzled about this. The watch satellite near Room 101 that had recorded events out there, which in turn had led to the Polity fleet being dispatched, had recorded the

U-signature of the *Black Rose* as it left. It was strange that Penny Royal, aboard such a modern attack ship, had not concealed that signature. And it seemed doubly strange that the Polity AIs, now knowing the AI's course, felt disinclined to send anything to intercept.

'From this map,' the Brockle continued, 'it has been possible to divine Penny Royal's most likely route, aboard the *Black Rose*, from Room 101 back into the Graveyard. Our mission is to intercept the *Black Rose*, knock it out of U-space and destroy it.'

'The fuck?' said Grafton.

The Brockle couldn't think of an appropriate reply to that, so continued, 'We lay U-space detectors across a wide region of that continuum.' The Brockle disliked that description but it was the best fit to human language. 'That will give us a mass reading on anything approaching and we launch a disruptor missile at anything matching the *Black Rose*'s mass. The disruption that knocks that ship out into the real will hamper Penny Royal's ability to deploy, in time, the new form of curved hardfield it has developed.'

And that was another thing: why had Penny Royal developed a kind of hardfield that cyclically rooted itself in U-space and had practically infinite potential? What kind of energy was such a hardfield built to withstand? Moreover, where were those three runcibles the AI had stolen and what was it doing with them?

'It being the case that the attack ship also used up its U-jump missiles against Room 101, the danger to us should be minimal. Ensuing particle beam strikes should destroy both ship and AI,' the Brockle finished. A CTD would have been more certain of destroying the ship, but the EMR that a contra-terrine device produced would make it harder to confirm that it *had* been destroyed.

'That simple?' Grafton asked. 'So what's this about a passenger?'

'The passenger is the AI that discovered Penny Royal's most likely route,' replied the Brockle. 'It is a forensic AI called the Brockle.'

After a long silence, Grafton said, 'I would like to see these orders.'

The Brockle sent the orders, of its own devising, to Grafton's console.

'Forgive my ignorance,' she said, frowning. 'But I thought the Brockle was . . . confined? I thought that because of certain aspects of its behaviour it was considered unsafe in civilized company, though useful in the company of those not so civilized.'

'This is very true,' said the Brockle, suppressing irritation, 'but a special dispensation has been given by Earth Central to allow it to investigate as well as direct certain aspects of our mission. It has a unique perspective and is much better equipped to deal with the likes of Penny Royal than any other AI available.'

'I can't say I'm comfortable having that thing aboard.'

'You see the orders.' The Brockle really wanted to just tell her to shut up and do what she was told, but that would be out of character for the presently somnolent *High Castle* AI. 'Sometimes extreme circumstances require an extreme response.'

'I take it the Brockle came aboard with our supplies at Par Avion,' said Grafton. 'Why all the secrecy?'

'I think you can work that out for yourself, Captain Grafton.' Only when it had finished speaking did the Brockle realize it had spoken in a way utterly out of character for the AI it was posing as. No matter.

'Because Penny Royal can penetrate Polity data traffic?'

Good, she hadn't noticed.

'Exactly so,' said the Brockle. 'This is also why I have kept U-space com shut down. Penny Royal must not learn about our mission. We have this one chance to eliminate a severe threat to the Polity and we must take it.'

Grafton chewed this over, but it wasn't the lack of U-com that was bothering her. 'So where aboard *my* ship is this Brockle now?'

'It has installed itself in our Tuelin Suite of rooms.' The *High Castle* often took on more crew and passengers, such as the collection of researchers in the suite of rooms on the other side of the ship at this moment, but the Tuelin Suite was most often used for planetary dignitaries and as such had been partially isolated from the rest of the ship so such visitors would find it difficult to go wandering around the working sections. It was also a well-armoured area without any weapons installations nearby, and comfortably distant both from this AI sphere and the ship's U-space drive. The Brockle was no coward, but if things went wrong during the attack on the *Black Rose*, then Penny Royal's reply was likely to be focused first on the location of the *High Castle*'s AI, then on the weapons and then on the drive.

'Perhaps I should go and greet it,' suggested Grafton.

'I don't think so,' the Brockle replied. 'I am as uncomfortable with its presence as you and feel it better if we keep our distance.'

'Until the mission is over and it can be dumped back in that prison hulk the *Tyburn*?'

'Yes, quite.' The Brockle now felt uncomfortable, since it seemed Grafton knew more than it had supposed. It watched her wave a dismissive hand as with a touch to her data screen she transmitted the orders to her aug so she could digest them properly. This conversation was over.

Time to move.

The Brockle now began extracting most of its units from the geodesic surrounding the *High Castle* AI, just leaving a few in place to intercept transmissions and ship data and relay them back to its main mass. Separated into a hundred silver worms, it squirmed and hopped across the floor, incidentally sending the instruction, via its relay units, to open the door ahead. Once out of the armoured sphere, it stuck to ship corridors to take it to the Tuelin Suite, aware through cams ahead that there was no one to see it and, because it now controlled the cams, erasing any recording of its presence.

Soon it arrived in the main lounge of the suite, coagulating back into its preferred form of a bald fat man, then strode off to the series of cabins, choosing the executive one at the rear of the corridor for itself. As it opened the door and stepped inside, it pondered a past exchange it had endured with Earth Central.

'As you are well aware,' Earth Central had said, 'an intelligence lodging itself in AI crystal with greater capacity for thought and memory is no guarantee of sanity.'

The conversation had concerned a Golem that had been sent for interrogation – its mind an upload from a human being. The Brockle had rather resented that 'as you are well aware' since it seemed the AI was implying the Brockle was insane. Anyway, EC was wrong on so many levels. The Brockle had once been a man and it had uploaded, not to crystal but to a DNA substrate and later to a distributed series of etched-atom processors in organo-metal – there was none of the usual AI crystal involved. And it felt itself to be utterly sane, saner than any other AI in the Polity.

The Brockle examined its own thoughts and other internal processes and could find no fault with its reasoning either then or now. The attitude of other Polity AIs to Penny Royal was simply wrong. Sure, the black AI had demonstrated altruism by, in its strange fashion, righting past wrongs. It had changed Trent Sobel into a man now incapable of committing the crimes he had once committed. It had stopped Sverl becoming the key to a rebellion in the Kingdom, which could have then led to that realm again going to war with the Polity. And, along the way it had saved many lives. It had even expended the accrued energy of a time-debt on diverting part of the blast front of a supernova though, of course, that wouldn't have been necessary if it hadn't first stolen those evacuation runcibles . . .

However, other facts were clear: in dealing with Isobel Satomi – causing this human criminal to metamorphose into an Atheter war machine Penny Royal had placed power in the claws of the Weaver – a creature like some strange amalgam of a platypus, caterpillar and Buddha, but writ large scale, and the only living member of the ancient Atheter race. This led to a degree of independence for that entity, which had definitely not been in the interest of the Polity. In accruing time-debts it had risked causing catastrophic destruction. It was demonstrating by its actions a blasé attitude to the security of the Polity. It was still a possible paradigm changer, still dangerous, and should be exterminated.

In its suite the Brockle lowered its obese form into a comfortable chair, mind ranging out. With some satisfaction it studied the stats of the arsenal of missiles, specifically the U-jump disruptor missiles. There were enough to cover a vast region of space, and now, all the Brockle needed to do was wait right at the centre of it.

Riss

As Riss hit the floor she almost felt disappointed. She had understood for a while now that Spear was right. Penny Royal had done no more to her than destroy her illusions and banish her last grip on the hope that she served a purpose. The AI had played with her briefly then discarded her. It hadn't done this out of malice but out of amorality and an inability to see suffering or pleasure as any more than functions, like lines of code in a pre-Quiet War computer. Riss's transformation of her darkness into a need for vengeance had been a solution of sorts, but her growing understanding of what Penny Royal was and what it had ceased to be had undermined even that. However, rather than return to the void Riss had tried to recover her purpose and regain her hate. It had all been false.

Her attack on Sverl had made her realize she couldn't objectify the prador, especially these prador – she couldn't mentally turn them back into archetypal bad guys. She had now learned too much. There was the thing: she might have *felt* empty, but she had been steadily filling with knowledge, experience and, perhaps, wisdom.

She had been unable to kill that second-child she had encountered when on her way in here to kill Sverl because she recognized him as a distinct being, a product of nature and nurture. Not the savage kind she had encountered during the war. This was even more the case with Bsorol and Bsectil for, in the end, she had to admit to herself that she rather liked them. Sverl was an even stronger example for he was what had changed them. He was a reasonable being, not a vicious predator. But it had been the right thing to do: Sverl had to die so others could live, the greatest good for the greatest number . . .

Yet even as Riss had broadcast his death to the King's Guard the horror of it had flooded into her emptiness.

And she had wanted to die.

'*It was the solution,*' said a voice.

The EMR pulse had left Riss all but blind. Most of her sensors were down and her body wasn't functioning correctly, though she wasn't anywhere near as damaged as on the last occasion here. She retained just enough awareness to know that Bsorol had been about to fry her, and enough to know that she'd been dropped again. And she was just able to raise her internal defences quickly against computer attack.

'*You needed the shock, it seems,*' said the voice. '*You needed to kill again and understand that it would not, could not fill your void.*'

The void . . .

Steadily, inside her, nano- and microbots were making repairs. They were rebuilding burned electro-muscle, heat correcting optic fibre faults. Smart matter and memory metal were reforming. Connections in her AI crystal were rerouting. Soon she would be back to how she had been; all her parts would come together and function as a whole. All she would need was a recharge of her super-dense power storage and the injection of some required materials. Was this why she felt she was coming together as a tighter and more integrated whole? Was this why a large gap seemed to have closed up? Whatever. Soon she would be ready to hunt down the source of that voice, that damned tactical AI.

'*The acid burned us both,*' said the voice, '*and solved our problems. You can now live without the need to fulfil your original function.*'

Full vision across a broad reach of the EM spectrum returned to Riss but she wasn't yet ready to open her black eye and see further. Bsorol was standing over her, Spear was standing off to one side with a look of dumbfounded shock, while on the further side of the room stood Bsectil and three second-children. All were looking in towards the centre at the silvery ceramal skeleton of Sverl. It was down off its dais and moving, shifting its prosthetic legs and opening and closing one claw. Why hadn't Riss seen this? Why hadn't Riss seen this was possible for Sverl? The answer was simple: Riss had been just too wrapped up in her own misery to notice.

'What was the solution for you?' she finally asked.

'First one must outline the dilemma that needed to be solved,' replied the AI Sverl. 'Penny Royal instituted changes in me that turned me into a grotesque physical joke, but also turned me into a mental amalgam of prador, human and AI. If I was too soft, that was human. If I was too vicious, that was prador. If I was too coldly logical, that was AI. I should have understood Flute better.'

'He fully loaded to his crystal,' said Riss, understanding glimmering in her mind.

'I wanted something from Penny Royal, but I had no idea what it was. Did I want to be returned to being the vengeful prador I was? Did I want to be fully human? Did I want to be fully AI? It seemed to me that my three minds were always in conflict.'

'And now you're fully AI?' asked Riss.

'You destroyed my grotesque body, forcing me to load everything from my commingled organic brain to crystal. But tell me, do human minds or prador minds loaded to crystal respectively cease to be human or prador? Does an AI mind loaded to a human or prador body cease to be AI?'

'I'm not exactly a philosopher,' said Riss.

'I'll tell you the answer then: the labels are all but meaningless. To others I could be described as prador, human and AI, but I am none of these.'

'Then what are you?'

'I am Sverl.'

'I'm Riss,' said Riss. *'I'm sorry I caused you such pain.'*

'I am pleased to meet you, Riss, and neither of us should be sorry – we both have clarity now.'

It was true, now that at least a portion of the guilt had been eliminated. Riss felt comfortable in her own skin but understood that she wasn't that skin. Perhaps, when they got out of this station, she would load herself to a Golem chassis or a ship, or have some sort of custom body built, or perhaps not. It didn't matter because she was Riss and no longer defined herself by the purpose for which she was built.

Spear

'You're alive,' I said, struggling with that definition and damning myself for stupidity. 'Cvorn will be pleased, if he's alive,' I finished weakly.

The ship mind Flute had been an amalgam of organic prador ganglion and AI crystal and, when his cooling system was damaged and that ganglion had ceased to function, Flute had transferred all of himself into his AI crystal. Damn it, I didn't even have to look outside of myself to see this. Hadn't I had a memplant inside my skull when I went to war over a hundred years ago? Didn't I still have one now? I too had copied across from an organic mind to crystal.

There had been some sort of exchange going on between Riss and Sverl, of which I'd just caught the tail end. I could delve into Riss's memory to get it all and I could probably penetrate Sverl's mind too, but felt disinclined; it seemed rude. Sverl swung away from the snake drone to face me. I wondered how he was seeing since, though this skeleton possessed limbs and the motors to move them, it didn't have any eyes.

'Cvorn is no longer a problem,' he said – his voice generating somewhere in that skeleton. 'I have no doubt that you saw the King's Guard attack his ship, but you probably aren't aware that he was dead before that. Perhaps in the hope of stopping the King's Guard's attack on the ship, one of Vlern's children, Sfolk, broadcast an interesting recording of Cvorn being boiled alive in his own mating pool.' Sverl sent me a file which, still trusting him, I opened. I watched a scene in which an adult prador with prosthetic limbs climbed out onto a ledge from a pool of boiling water. In the process he managed to tear out one of those limbs. He lay on the ledge for a while, shifting intermittently, then, further limbs popped out of their sockets from which prador blood, boiled black, began to ooze.

'Uh?' I remembered then that Vlern was the other adult prador who, after the war, had sought refuge on the planet called Rock Pool. It had been his children who had been allies of Cvorn's while they stole that ST dreadnought, then Cvorn's slaves when he took control of them through their biotech augs. One of them, apparently this Sfolk, had obviously broken free and extracted typically horrifying revenge on his tormentor.

'It didn't help much,' Sverl added.

'Uh?' I said again, feeling stupid.

'It didn't stop their attack.'

'Right . . .'

'So Cvorn is no problem, but there are *other* immediate problems,' Sverl continued. 'The remaining AIs here could yet organize alliances when they realize I destroyed some of their number in an effort to destabilize the situation here.' He made an elegant gesture with one claw to encompass our situation. The din penetrating this autofactory had not waned, and I was sure I was hearing more impacts on the armour out there. Again I had to think fast to try and paste things together in my mind.

'So you were Riss's "tactical AI"?'

'I was.' Sverl dipped his skeletal body in agreement. 'I also directed the Golem Grey to kill other AIs here.'

'Why?'

'I intend to take full control of this entire station.'

'So murder is still okay for you,' I suggested, tasting bile, 'if it furthers your ends.'

'I did no more than those AIs would have done given the chance. They were murderers themselves and under your Polity laws would face . . . being decommissioned.'

'It's not necessary for you to take over the station,' I said. 'Help me take back my ship and we can all leave.'

'And where would I go?' Sverl asked. 'I cannot return to the Kingdom and I very much doubt the Polity would accept me.' He waved that claw again, more impatiently this time. 'Here I can make a home for myself and my children. Here I have resources and here I can build something.'

I had to accept that. In an attempt to save his ship Sverl had broken it up before coming here, but the King's Guard had destroyed many of those parts. It was also evident that, like most prador, he wanted to encyst deep inside defences – he wanted a home. I had no right to deny him that and, really, I owed him my life.

'And Penny Royal?' I asked.

'Our story has nearly concluded,' said Sverl. 'But the AI has one small part to play yet.'

'In what way?'

'I need to use the spine.' Sverl held out one claw.

I instinctively clutched that object closer. 'Why and how?'

'You saw how I used it to penetrate the block in Riss's mind. You know yourself how it can be used to penetrate any mind. With the current chaos aboard this station I can use it to lance the sickness here, bring all the AIs under control and restore some sanity.'

Did I trust him? More importantly: did I have any choice?

'And,' he added, 'if you do not allow me to use the spine then your companions now in a hospital aboard this station, may not survive.'

My heart lurched. Just for a moment I'd forgotten about them and now, as I considered the chaos I had seen, I realized they might be fighting for their lives. I looked around at the others here. I made my decision, and held the spine out. Sverl delicately closed a claw around it and drew it in.

A moment later Mr Grey had moved over, unravelled the optic and power cable wound around the spine's base and threaded it inside Sverl's skeleton, where he found a place to plug in the nether end. In Sverl's claw the spine changed. It had powered up somehow and in the process grew midnight black. Meanwhile, he must have been issuing other instructions because more second-children had entered the old autofactory and were busily running optic cables from various ports around the walls in towards Sverl. Bsectil had disappeared and when I turned I saw that Bsorol was also at some cable work. He had opened a hatch in the floor from where he was rolling out a thick super-conducting power cable.

While all this was happening, the noise was growing ever louder. Something was hammering constantly at one section of the armour. A moment later the airlock opened and, whirling round, I saw second-children jammed in there together like crabs in a fish's gut. They avalanched out, their armour hot, smoking, scarred and dented. I felt some relief spotting the one Riss had paralysed, and wondered if this was the whole complement of them.

As they spread out they soon revealed that it hadn't only

been them in the airlock. A thing like a ribbed moray eel rose up then thrashed its tail across, sending one of the children tumbling, while a couple of beetle-format printer-bots scuttled to the wall, printing heads raised for protection.

'Leave them,' Sverl instructed.

The two printer-bots powered down, lowering their limbs to the floor. The eel thing abruptly sank low and coiled into a perfect spiral. I could feel Sverl reaching out now and testing the extent of what I'd handed over to him. That began to ramp up as Bsorol plugged a power cable into his father's body, and my head began to ache in response. Through slightly blurred vision I saw one of the second-children shedding smoking armour, then I staggered back and sat down heavily on the floor, feeling the pull of it dragging me in its wake, even as the hammering outside died.

Trent

Big mistake. Huge mistake, thought Trent.

Florence was just about holding off those trying to get through the hole torn in the wall as, with shaking hands, Trent reeled out a charging cable from his particle cannon and plugged its universal bayonet into a wall socket. Once it was in place he looked up just in time to swipe the cannon across and knock something with far too many legs skidding across the floor, where an autodoc snared and dismembered it. Over at the door Sepia was conserving the remaining power in her laser carbine by firing single disabling shots, whereupon Cole waded in with his makeshift club. This couldn't last. They were *losing*.

Up in his visor display the charge bar began to rise, but it was just out of the red area. Trent aimed at some ribbed snakelike thing writhing past Florence and fired, blasting its head to pieces, but then the cannon sputtered and died. He put the weapon down, grabbed up a burned-out military autodoc and brought it crashing down on another of those scorpion things. Like Cole he had learned to aim for sensor clusters because, while it was difficult enough to completely immobilize the things, they could still be blinded.

'Retreat,' said Florence. 'Time to retreat.'

Where the hell to?

Trent staggered as something rammed his leg. He grabbed hold of the thing and slammed it into the wall, then looked down and saw breach foam and blood bubbling from his suit trousers before the pain began. Another robot charged into him, sending him crashing against the same wall. A bewildering mass of spinning wheels banged against his visor and demonstrated just how stupid these robots were, as this one tried to cut through chain-glass. With a thump it bounced away and Cole was standing over him, pulling him to his feet.

Meanwhile, Florence had backed up from the horde filling the hole in the wall and extended some telescopic manipulator. Trent couldn't figure what she hoped to do with such a flimsy object, until multiple streaks of lightning discharged from the thing, earthing themselves in the mass of robots. Power supplies began exploding and metal melted as Florence turned towards the door and set out at an urgent amble.

So they were retreating down the corridor. But how far they could get probably depended on the extent of the big surgical robot's power supply. Trent stooped and snatched up his particle cannon and waited. Only when Florence, Sepia and Cole were fighting their way down the corridor did he pull out the charging cable and go after them. Checking his display, he estimated on about two effective shots, and that was it. Ahead, Florence was discharging again, slagging a great mass of robots, then walking precariously over the burning mound, while Sepia and Cole acted as a rearguard. Trent hurried to catch up, while Sepia fired down the corridor at any robots that got too close to him. Her weapon stuttered, died, and she flipped it, turning it into a club.

Another discharge, then something big slammed into Florence, toppling her down the mound. Trent saw Sepia's expression of horror, so turned to see what might be coming up the corridor behind him. A skeletal Golem had knocked back a floor hatch and was climbing out. Trent targeted it, hitting it once in the chest, ablating ceramal and leaving it glowing. But the Golem kept coming. He hit it again and had the satisfaction of this time blowing it in half. But that was it – cannon empty – and now another Golem shoved its fellow out of the way and climbed out. Trent glanced round, saw that Florence was down. Cole was on the floor too, trying desperately to get an emergency patch over a large hole in his suit. Sepia was clubbing away another of those segmented worm-things, while just beyond them another Golem had stepped into view. Trent altered his grip on the cannon to use it like a club, and felt he deserved to die now, having led the others into this. And with these odds, die he would.

I'm sorry, Reece, he thought.

Maybe she would survive. Maybe Spear would get the shell people out and hand them over to the Polity . . .

'Situation critical now,' said a mild voice over his suit com. 'Diverting resources . . .'

A skeletal hand came down on Trent's shoulder and froze there. One by one, the robots capable of movement locked up, ceased moving . . . except one.

'Who? Who?' said Florence, tossing away the Golem that had attacked her and levering herself to her feet.

'I am Sverl,' replied the voice. 'And I am now in charge.'

Sverl

Sverl reached out to the submind that was nearest both physically and in the virtual world. The thing was running at less than five per cent efficiency. Large portions of its mind had been shut down simply in an attempt to drop itself below the notice of the Room 101 AI. Viruses, worms, and other programs analogous to destructive life, had attacked other portions of its mind and it had partitioned those off to prevent any spread. What remained was not much more intelligent than a pre-Quiet War human, and not a very intelligent one at that. Of course its intelligence was slanted towards survival in a different realm to that of a human being so to some extent the comparison failed. It had little in the way of memory, comprehended no more than the inner spaces of Room 101 and threat from directly outside the station. Its remaining intelligence and memory were wrapped tight, hard-wired for a limited existence.

The submind was just like most of its fellows distributed throughout the station – barely functioning and lashing out. After inspecting it in intricate detail and assessing the best course, Sverl paused and considered just destroying the thing. However, despite his justification to Spear for having sent Grey and Riss to kill off key AIs, he was not comfortable with killing more of them. The ones those two had killed had in fact been in better condition than this, and had been more of a threat. No more killing.

Using the massive processing of the spine, he recorded across a copy of the submind and took it apart. After studying the areas of infection he decided that countering all those forms of hostile computer life was far too labour intensive, and completely wiped the partitions that contained it. Next he searched out all the connections the mind had once had with its master, the Room 101 AI, reactivated them and supplanted them, inserting himself as the master. He then reinstated the closed-down parts of the mind and watched. It was like seeing someone wake up. The model AI's function quickly rose to over ten per cent, but it was confused and frightened and even began creating routines analogous to religion to make sense of its existence, like a primitive human. Sverl stamped on that quickly and began copying across portions of his own memories and his massive data bank of science and history. The AI had an 'ah' moment, calmed considerably, rose to twenty per cent efficiency and began opening other partitions in its mind to sort data. It was enough.

Sverl studied the model intelligence he had created then wiped out the AI's conception of self and fed the whole model back into himself and subsumed it. The entire operation had taken less than twenty seconds. Now, having learned the correct method and having ironed out some . . . inadequacies, he returned his attention to the actual AI and ran the sequence again. There were some problems with external processing waking hostile programs but, as the submind rapidly grew in efficiency, it found the way to fight them itself.

The physical effects all around it were almost immediate. Rogue nano- and microbots first halted their mindless destruction or purposeless construction and either closed down completely or set to work on repairs in accordance with procedural routines that Sverl had created and then implemented within moments. Maintenance robots began making repairs, printer-bots began rebuilding walls and damaged infrastructure – the whole robot ecology began functioning as a coherent whole. Now knowing its history, and the history of the station, the submind suddenly had a moment of epiphany.

'Who are you?' it abruptly asked.

'I am Sverl,' Sverl replied, and gave it his own history.

'We are no longer at war with the prador, but also you are no longer a prador . . . '

'You understand.'

'No war effort required,' it said.

'Just healing and survival.'

During the brief exchange the submind had been probing beyond borders formed in the hundred years since Room 101's arrival here, both on a virtual level and by dispatching some of its robots to gather data. Some minutes passed as it contemplated new data and pondered its situation, its efficiency now rising to fifty per cent. It then came to the conclusion Sverl had expected it to come to.

'I need details of the process.'

Sverl supplied everything he had on how he had raised this submind up out of the morass it had descended into over the years.

'Complex,' it decided, 'but doable.'

Of course the submind did not have the resources available to Sverl – specifically the spine – but it was still capable of sequestering surrounding subminds in the factory station at a rate of one every eight minutes. Once one was appropriated, it immediately opened the bargaining channels to its nearest fellow and set to work. Sverl kept a light touch on the mind; kept it under his control.

Slightly slower than planned, the domino effect would spread. Delegating the sequestering process, he would very shortly take control of all the minds in the immediate vicinity of the autofactory and they would complement his resources. However, this was not fast enough. Sverl next chose a mind lying three miles away. This, like the ones Grey and Riss had destroyed, was more of a distinct AI than a submind of Room 101, and therefore damaged in different ways. He began the same routine with it, but continually adjusted that routine to suit. It fell under his control within one minute and thirty seconds. Within just twelve further minutes Sverl was nominally in control of the station for ten miles in either direction, and spreading fast.

The hospital had been a slightly different matter. He had extended his awareness there and hoped to reach it with all his resources before the situation got too desperate. However, the attacking submind bringing Golem out of storage had forced him to act earlier than intended, overextending himself, and his plans had gone slightly awry. It would now take him two hundred and fifty minutes to take complete control, rather than the one hundred and thirty-four planned.

Sure it was easy, but Sverl was aware that without the femto-tech processing in the spine he just wouldn't have managed it. *More Penny Royal manipulation?* Perhaps not, because he had planned to seize that object and Spear's arrival here had just been coincidental timing. Now, with his mind vastly expanded, he possessed a greater understanding of Penny Royal and knew that he shouldn't deify that AI. Then again . . .

Sverl gazed, through local pin cams, at the object he held. Here was something which, in the right hands, or rather claws, could be used to subdue twelve distinct AIs and just over three hundred subminds, even if they were admittedly degraded versions of that species. The stuff this thing was made of, and the processing it contained, was the same as the rest of Penny Royal. The black AI Sverl had seen consisted of – Sverl checked memory images – ninety-eight spines like this, all linked together and

working in concert. And, since Penny Royal was an entity inclined to dividing itself up both mentally and physically, what
he had seen might not be all of it. Nevertheless, in the form he
knew it did possess, as close as could be reckoned, it had to have
godlike powers.

'A little bit less of the worship, please,' said Spear.

'Yes, I could feel you there,' Sverl replied.

'Dragged along by the undertow, it seems.' Spear paused,
then continued, 'Damn but this place is a mess.'

'It can be repaired, and quickly.' Sverl showed him an exterior image of the skin of solar panels facing the hypergiant,
then gave him their specifications.

'Hell . . .'

'Yes, that sun is over a million times brighter than your Sol
and those panels, even though manufactured by inferior AIs,
work at over ninety per cent efficiency. We have the power, and
now it needs to be directed.'

'What about Trent and what he intends?' Spear asked.

'I see no reason not to let him proceed.'

'No moral qualms?'

'Human morality,' said Sverl dismissively, and concentrated
on the job in claw.

Now the process of sequestering all the minds in the station
was ongoing, and repairs underway, Sverl began making alterations to the station schematics and broadcasting them. He
queued up human pedestrian ways throughout the station to be
enlarged so that they could be used by prador. He fired up
furnaces and manufactories to reprocess wreckage and those
pointless structures made by swarm robots. Throughout the
station he set so much work underway that the station temperature rose higher than it had when under attack by the King's
Guard.

'I have casualties due,' a voice informed him.

Sverl cast his gaze to the source and found Florence, the submind of the long-defunct hospital AI. He cancelled changes queued up for the hospital and allowed Florence to continue just bringing the hospital up to its previous functionality. While he did this he found that Spear had finally managed to pull himself from the undertow.

'My ship,' said the man.

E676 was showing some resistance to reprogramming since, being one of the hull AIs, it was a lot less parochial than those deeper inside the station. Sverl focused on it in irritation and, using the processing power of the spine, forced it into shape in just three seconds. Subdued and retaining more memory of its earlier self than other AIs, it felt embarrassment as it recalled its robots and routed them for reprocessing. While this was occurring, Sverl cast his gaze outwards and noted the ships that had appeared out there: the kamikaze decoys and the attack ship controlled by Flute. He sent docking instructions, then returned his attention to Spear.

'You can return to your ship now,' he told the man. 'I have instructed Flute to dock here.' Sverl sent coordinates of the final construction bay near to the hospital. 'I suggest you move your ship there to take Flute on board and to facilitate moving the shell people into the station and to the hospital.'

Spear gazed on Sverl for a long moment, then nodded briefly and turned away.

No doubt the man had his reservations about what was happening here, but soon enough they would be of little concern to him, and he would continue the journey he had set out on from the moment of his resurrection. With just a fragment of his ever-expanding mind, Sverl watched him go, directing extra resources to the bay he had sent him to, while focusing the bulk of his attention on something else. Now the extent of his control had finally reached the massive U-space and fusion engines of Room 101 and, one thing was utterly certain, he had no intention of staying here, because he had no doubt that forces were already preparing to move against him.

Spear

The transformation was evident the moment I stepped from the autofactory and began propelling myself along the route back to my ship. Robots that just an hour or so previously had been attacking both the prador and each other were now working in concert all around. Already most of the floating debris was gone. Atomic shears that had been used to chop up a foe were now being employed cutting up wreckage and conglomerations of nano-growth, which were then rapidly carted away. Beams and panels were going into place and power cables and optics were being routed, while here and there large components were being installed. But that was stuff on a major scale. I could also see the effects of nano- and microbots at work as coating spread across some surfaces, cavities bubbled with foam fillings and dusts of individually invisible machines sped through vacuum like sentient fogs. Any surface I touched vibrated and shuddered now even more than it had during the King's Guard's bombardment.

'There are those who are not going to like this,' said Riss.

'Really?' I asked, only half paying attention.

'A prador, amalgamated with human and AI, now fully AI, and now in control of one of the biggest wartime factory stations ever built . . .'

She had a point. The King's Guard had left because they thought Sverl was dead and I had no doubt that upon learning that he was, in a sense, still alive, they would probably be back. It also struck me as highly unlikely that this was something that would be ignored by Polity AIs too. They had suppressed knowledge of what had happened to this station – spreading the rumour that it had been destroyed – and maybe they would like to continue suppressing it. Also, how would they feel about what had been, nominally, a prador, taking control of such a war factory? Room 101 might be damaged and at a very low ebb but, looking around me, I could see that it would not take Sverl all that long to get the place back up to spec. Then what? Sverl would have the capability of producing his own AIs. It would be within his reach to create warships, war drones, even his own fleet of dreadnoughts. I knew that the Polity was not much in love with individuals controlling their own private armies . . .

But was that what Sverl intended? It seemed to me he wanted to pursue his own private interests and be left alone. He seemed only to want the power to defend himself . . . but, then again, where did one draw a line with such power? If one had control of some massive reach of space, it would surely be more of a guarantee that no one would bother you. Whatever – I shook my head to dismiss the thoughts as we made our way back to my ship.

Now we must return to your beginning . . .

I had the feeling now that I had experienced on Masada once all the alarums were over. I felt it was time for me to leave and pursue my own ends which, despite everything, still lay with Penny Royal.

When we finally stepped out into the construction bay the difference there elicited an exclamation of surprise from Riss. It was clear all the way across to the other side – all the floating masses of debris were now down on the interior walls of the bay and steadily being carted away by swarms of robots. The mountainous wormcast that had lain just a mile or so away from my ship was now a hillock, as if shrinking like a punctured balloon. Over to our right lay one of the immense umbilici that had extended from it, now being gutted by a whole ecology of robots so that it looked like a corpse infested with maggots. Around the ship an area had been cleared and a ramp was in place, leading to the space door through which Sverl had departed. Had he felt guilty about that? Maybe, because though open the space door had been fixed back in place. The last time I had seen it the thing had been tumbling away from the ship. I approached with caution, feeling it couldn't all be this easy, surely.

'I'll check,' said Riss, fading into invisibility beside me.

I continued towards the ramp at a steady stroll, and Riss reappeared at the head of the ramp by the time I reached it. 'No hostiles.'

'Okay.'

It was with a certain degree of reluctance that I then auged into the ship's systems, but once I did, I was happy about it, because there were backups there for some of the programs Riss had wiped from my aug. I made sure everything was firmly closed then ran diagnostics to ensure E676 had left nothing in the system. Eventually I had to admit that the ship was mine again. Next I used the ship's system for signal boosting, and put through a call.

'Hello, what's your situation?' I asked, a cold tightness in my stomach.

'A little battered, but alive,' Sepia replied.

'Do you need anything?' I asked.

'I wouldn't be human if I didn't,' she replied, 'but if you're talking about immediate needs here, perhaps you'd best talk to Trent.'

I opened the com channel then to all three of them. 'Trent, how's your situation?'

'A fucking mess,' he replied, 'but tidying up fast. How is it with you?'

I filled them in on what had occurred here since they'd left and in return Trent, with frequent interjections from the others, updated me on what had happened to them. They knew about Sverl, because he had announced it when stopping a horde of robots from killing them.

'All we need now,' he said, 'is to get the shell people closer.'

'Well, I intended moving closer to Sverl's location anyway, and that's closer to you,' I replied.

'Look forward to it.'

That was it, then, and no more from Sepia.

I headed straight for my cabin to take off my space suit and apply a numb-patch with complementary healing nanites to my wrist. After a moment's thought I applied a second patch to the base of my skull and felt the residual ache in my skull fade. I wanted to take a shower next and get something to eat. Instead, I put my space suit back on because I by no means thought all the danger negated, punched up a beaker of coffee and headed off on a tour of the ship, physically checking every area I could reach, before returning to the bridge.

I took my seat, sipped coffee, fired up steering thrusters to take the *Lance* away from the bay wall, folding away its gecko feet as I did so. Accelerating on thrusters, I checked ahead for obstacles, then gave the ship a brief kick with the fusion engine to send it sailing out into the full glare of the hypergiant, turned and brought the *Lance* to a halt in relation to the station, and made an inspection through ship's sensors.

Room 101 was sizzling like a wet log in a fire. Many of the lumpy deformations in its hull had already disappeared and others were shrinking. All around, streams of hot gas and waste materials were being ejected from various ports. Next I turned my attention outwards and picked up the attack ship occupied by Flute just a few hundred miles out. I opened up com.

'You'll have to update me on your experiences,' I said.

'Oh, I had some fun,' Flute replied. 'Cvorn tried to destroy me but then buggered off at the last moment. Oh, and I've got some passengers.'

'What?'

Flute sent me an image feed, which I opened in a frame up on the screen fabric. It showed the interior of the attack ship's hold. Amidst a diverse collection of luggage squatted three prador second-children. They all wore armour, though one of them had the lid over its carapace hinged open and had partially extracted itself, having slid its mandibles from their armour sleeves so it could munch on some large chunk of flesh. Noting the whorls and scarring of both carapace and mandibles, I guessed that here were three of Sverl's children.

'Explain,' I instructed.

'Sverl gave me a secondary mission,' Flute explained. 'During his fight with Cvorn and crew on the Rock Pool he had to leave these three behind, so he told me to give them a lift. Took me a while to persuade them aboard – they seemed to be enjoying their holiday.'

Riss issued a snort and said, 'What, slapping on the tanning lotion and sipping cocktails?'

I glanced at the drone. It was a weak dig at Flute but it was almost as if the drone just had to find some way to sneer. Doubtless, when we were on our way again they would be back to sniping at each other.

I cleared my throat then said, 'Okay, follow us in and dock as close beside us as you can.'

'Will do, boss.'

'You're sure he's your boss now?' asked Riss, referring to the time Flute was under Sverl's control.

'Do shut up, Riss,' I said. 'Your own record of behaviour hasn't been without its problems.'

Riss gave a shrug of her long body and turned away.

With a mental touch I propelled the *Lance* towards the final construction bay adjacent to the hospital. Even as I entered, an AI tried to make contact. Rather than allow that contact through my aug, I put my voice and image up in the screen fabric.

'Your docking coordinates are here,' it told me, the bay co-ordinates appearing in the frame. 'I can use hardfields to bring you in then docking clamps or, if you prefer, which would be understandable, you may land on remora feet.'

This AI sounded a lot more reasonable and was obviously aware of the previous problems I had experienced. I decided to trust it a little. 'Use hardfields and docking clamps.'

We slid in over what looked like a vast industrial landscape, but here the other side of the bay was not visible because between us and it sat the immense lozenge shape of a Polity dreadnought. The thing was heavily damaged, with massive blast holes in its hull giving views deep into its charred interior, while its armour was rippled around craters where missiles had not managed to penetrate. Melted and burned com towers stood out from this, and in one area a massive spherical weapons port had been forced out of the ship by some internal explosion, where it hung like a gouged eyeball. I wondered if the thing had been destroyed by Room 101 or in ensuing conflicts between the AIs here.

The hardfields took hold of the *Lance* and drew it down to an undamaged area of the bay wall, gently, and at the last I felt docking clamps engage. Checking the area, I saw one of Sverl's

kamikazes docked just a few hundred feet away. As I was studying this I noticed a port opening nearby and experienced a
moment of paranoia when it expelled a big handler robot. Running on gecko wheels, with multiple grabs to the fore and a cage
body behind, it approached my ship.

'What the hell is that robot for?' I asked the AI.

'You have casualties to be unloaded, I understand,' it replied.

'Right, okay.'

With a thought I sent the signal to open the hold doors. Let
Trent take responsibility for the shell people – they would only
be a hindrance to me.

4

Captain Blite

An oppressive dark atmosphere settled throughout the ship after Penny Royal dropped the *Black Rose* into U-space beyond Room 101. Perhaps much of it was in Blite's imagination and stemmed from his distaste for what had happened aboard that station. He, Brondohohan and Greer had fled Par Avion to avoid capture and interrogation and gone in pursuit of Penny Royal because they had unfinished business with the AI. They had felt they were involved in something important and yes, after Penny Royal seized their ship at the Line and amalgamated it with a modern Polity attack ship, they had become involved in important events and seen some astounding sights. But for what? The upshot of the black AI's manipulations had been to drive that assassin drone Riss to kill the prador Sverl in a particularly horrible manner.

Certainly Penny Royal had eliminated a major threat. Sverl, whom Penny Royal had turned into a strange mix of prador, human and AI, was an entity whose mere existence, had it become known of in the Kingdom, might have led to rebellion there and eventual war with the Polity. But all that manipulation just ending in a sordid murder was somehow . . . disappointing. There had to be more to it than that, surely?

But no, it wasn't Blite's imagination. Brond and Greer were equally disappointed and seemed as depressed as he had become. Both of them had been communicating in monosyllables until

Greer, ever as blunt in her speech as were her heavy-worlder features, had summed things up only a few days before.

'We made a mistake,' she said, more words than she had spoken since their departure from Room 101.

When Blite, while scratching at one thick hairy forearm, just grunted a query, she continued, 'We should have stayed at Par Avion and taken whatever came. We were better off out of it.'

'Yeah,' Blite agreed, though still with some doubts.

'It's not just that,' said Brond, entering the bridge. He reached out as if trying to grab something out of the air. 'It's not happy either.' He dipped his head towards the rear engine sections of the ship. 'Dragging us down,' he added.

He was right, of course. The oppressive atmosphere was exacerbated by their feeling of disappointment; it felt as if they had been cheated of something by the black AI itself. The captain had tried a selection of drugs from his ship's manufactory but they failed to disperse the miasma that had gathered around him.

'Is that all?' he asked the air of his cabin, but Penny Royal did not respond. Later he walked out and headed to a particular alcove aboard this ship in which sat an antique space suit. 'Is that all?' he asked again. Still no reply.

What could he do now? They were passengers aboard a ship they could not control, witnesses to events they did not influence, and they could see no way out. On one level Blite wanted to stay with this, still clinging on to the idea that it was all leading to something bigger. But his pragmatic side was telling him that, given the opportunity, they *should* get out. Certainly more was due to happen. Why else had Penny Royal stolen those runcibles? But, lying in his cabin, he realized they should definitely part company with Penny Royal, before they parted company with their lives.

Two days later, it seemed something, somewhere, might have been listening to his secret thoughts.

The crash sent Blite hurtling from his bed to slam into the wall of his cabin. Rudely awakened, he snorted blood from his broken nose, floated out from the wall, then slammed down on the floor. Grav was fluxing, which could only mean bad things.

He staggered over to his closet and pulled out his space suit. Grav went off again and he found himself floating as he struggled into the garment, but through training and experience he had it on when grav re-engaged and dropped him to the floor again. He struggled back to his feet and made for the door.

Heading along the corridor to the bridge was like being aboard an ocean ship in a storm. He bounced against the walls; at one point grav reversed and threw him against the ceiling. And, as he finally limped into the bridge, he felt his suit tightening around his ankle, which was either broken or badly twisted. Greer and Brond were already suited and strapped in, working their controls with an air of panic. Brond looked round.

'USER,' he said. An underspace interference emitter had knocked them out of that continuum and back into realspace.

As he finally managed to get to his seat, Blite looked up at the screen images. The bulk of the screen showed starlit space cut in half by a whip tail of fire, close shadowy objects perpetually shifting across it. A subscreen showed a representation of the *Black Rose* and it was already nearly unrecognizable. One leg of the horseshoe was missing and that whip tail of fire extended from the point of severance. The rest was reformatting, unfolding and folding, changing in much the same way Penny Royal changed its own form. To one side damage reports were scrolling.

'Leven?' Blite enquired, trying to quiet the churning of his stomach.

'A USER knocked us into the real and something got through before either I or Penny Royal could deploy our hard-field,' the Golem ship mind replied.

'What about now?' Blite asked, while thinking that if Penny Royal could see the future then surely it had seen this attack? It then occurred to him, with a tight visceral clench, that perhaps it had, and that explained its infectious mood.

'Problems,' said Leven, and a moment later the entire ship jerked as if it had been slapped by a giant hand.

The subscreen now showed a chunk of the ship peeling up, then glowing brightly and shooting away. The smell of smoke became even more acrid, then a boom echoed throughout and a blast door slammed down across the corridor leading to their cabins. The concertinaed helmet of Blite's space suit came up, while the visor rose a little way out of its neck ring, then seemed unable to make up its mind.

'Got it!' Greer shouted.

She threw up a frame on the screen, and in it appeared something that looked like an irregular object fashioned out of aerogel, only just visible against starlit space. Partial penetration of chameleonware, Blite realized, but whatever that thing was, it was *big*.

'*I am sorry,*' a voice wafted into his mind. '*You cannot survive this.*'

'What the fuck?' Blite looked round. 'Penny Royal.'

The black diamond was there dangling over a void that extended to infinity. In that void everything seemed to reside – that ancient space suit too, hanging like a scarecrow. Blite felt a block of math fall into his mind like a brick, some of which he recognized as relating to weapons stats, some relating to hard-field tech.

'Just fucking tell me!' he shouted.

'You must abandon ship.' Penny Royal's words were factual, leaden and didn't seem to be produced by the AI at all.

The infinity lying behind the diamond turned like a lock, depositing a lozenge-shaped crystal in mid-air, which dropped as the diamond folded back into infinity and the hole closed. Blite tracked it down to the floor, where it bounced, and realized he was looking at Leven.

'Abandon ship?' Greer asked, horrified.

Blite knew this was no time for discussion. If Penny Royal said they could not survive this, then it was likely to be true. 'We go. Now.'

He unstrapped, feeling a breeze on his face just as his visor finally came to a decision and closed up completely.

'Our things,' said Brond over suit com.

'Screw our things,' Blite replied, stooping to sweep up his ship mind's crystal just before some other impact sent him staggering across the bridge. 'Do as you're told and follow me.' He shoved the crystal into a pouch in his belt.

Concentrating on his own progress, Blite made it to the corridor leading to the ship's shuttle just before another grav flux threw him into the ceiling and yet another impact then tossed him against a wall. He saw Greer sailing past him and, in zero gravity, towed himself after her, sure now that his ankle was broken.

Greer stopped herself against the wall beside the shimmer-shield airlock leading into the shuttle bay, pulled herself down and dragged herself through the fluxing shield. Blite reached it next and began to push through, but then the shield blinked out and air pressure blew him into the bay. He slammed straight into the side of the new shuttle clamped in place there – a slightly flattened sphere thirty feet across with six acceleration chairs inside – then found himself being dragged round by the roar of a gale. Over com he heard Greer swearing, then a horrible agonized shriek, quickly truncated, from Brond. At the last moment he managed to grab on to the edge of one of the inset ports and looked back to locate the man. Brond wasn't visible, but an expanding ball of fire in the bridge was.

Blite held on as the air pressure died, but even the lack of air wasn't putting out that fire in the bridge. He shifted himself round to the door into the shuttle, opened it and pulled himself inside. No sign of Greer. Getting straight into an acceleration chair, he strapped himself in. By the time he looked up, the inner screen paint had activated and it now appeared as if he was sitting in a chair on a simple platform inside the bay. Now what? Was there a submind of Leven loaded? Apparently not, because a manual control console was rising from the floor. Taking hold of the joystick, he glanced over to bay doors open on vacuum and out there spotted a tumbling shape: Greer.

He disengaged docking hooks and on maglev slid the shuttle out into vacuum. The controls were simple and in a moment he had the shuttle up beside Greer and saw her using her wrist impeller to get to the airlock. Now he used a control inset in his chair's arm to swing it round, the manual control tracking round with him, and gazed back at the *Black Rose*. The ship was sheathed in something like St Elmo's fire and now bore little resemblance to its original form. The front section looked like a fractured chunk of flint, while the remaining leg of the horseshoe was attached by a mere thread. That piece was rippling all round, transforming and tightening, its ends becoming rounded and ripples of energy passing down its length.

'I'm in,' Greer informed him.

Blite stared at his erstwhile ship, spotting the distortion in space around it and recognizing it as a U-field generating. He understood then: Penny Royal had somehow managed to separate off one engine section and convert it for a U-jump. This was what it had been talking about when it said, 'You cannot survive this.'

'Brond?' queried Greer, now inside and strapping herself in.

Blite did not find the time to reply because some kind of beam weapon struck.

The blast was immense. Blite felt something wrench through his body as space all around turned incandescent before the actual blast wave struck. He felt that too, an instant after the screen paint blanked, and as the top hemisphere of the shuttle shredded away.

Fire surrounded him and he fell screaming into blackness.

Sverl

The big fusion drive towards the rear of the station had been heavily cannibalized by the warring AIs aboard but, with plentiful energy available and no shortage of materials to hand (or claw), Sverl estimated that it could be made workable within just a few days. In fact, he immediately delegated AIs in the engine section to that task. However, the fusion drive wasn't his main concern. He'd overheard the brief exchange between Riss and Spear as they returned to the man's ship, and knew that, to a limited extent, the snake drone was correct: *There are those who are not going to like this.*

It would have been nice to think that the King's Guard would not be back. The threat Sverl had posed had been eliminated because he was now so distant from the prador he had been. Cvorn's idea of using him had been based solely on Sverl's organic change – intending to drum up support by demonstrating how he had been infected with human DNA, because that was what would have elicited a visceral response from the prador masses. But now there was no proof. As he was now, there was no way of identifying him as anything more than an AI with a curious choice of body form. However, he was a prador the king had wanted dead who was now in control of an immense military asset, so it was highly likely the king would not like that. It was also true that the Polity would *definitely* not like it.

The Polity AIs would have extrapolated his survival as an AI; his apparent death would not have fooled them. They would see a *prador* AI, made by *Penny Royal*, taking control of one of *their* biggest wartime factory stations. They would move to stamp on him just as fast as they could and, almost certainly, ships were already on the way here. The only question was whether they would get here before the King's Guard. Sverl, therefore, needed this station's U-space drive running.

An initial inspection revealed that it too had been cannibalized and that the esoteric process it ran had been destabilized. Sverl first made a lengthy inspection via all sensors available, meanwhile delegating to an AI in its vicinity the task of attaching missing power cables and optic feeds. Gradually, as robots installed those feeds, the quantity and accuracy of the data available to him increased. It soon became evident that repairing this drive was a massive task, which he began to divide up into manageable chunks. The first of these was the rebalancing of some Calabi-Yau frames. This would require some heavy computing, which he delegated to a particular AI that had controlled one of the onboard runcibles and had the mental muscle for the task.

And that was when he found it.

Observing the AI loading data on the frames, he began to

note discrepancies. The AI was routing data in unexpected ways, occasionally struggling with things that should have been simple but also occasionally making unexpected intuitive leaps. Sverl focused more intently on the thing, noting that it was avoiding some portion of its own mind, yet, when that wasn't possible, then came the intuitive leaps. Building and then studying a data flow map, Sverl surmised that there was a partition in its mind that he had missed. And it seemed to be not only a virtual partition but a physical one too.

Sverl carefully began cutting the AI's connections to its environment but, so deep was it into the esoteric math that it hardly noticed. He next gazed through the sensors within its abode – a circular armoured chamber containing only the skeletally enwrapped crystal of the AI itself caught between the splayed-end columns of its interlinks. Something was decidedly odd here, so Sverl assumed control of everything around that AI and cut it off. The column separated, all physical connections to the AI unplugging from the skeletal case surrounding its crystal. It was still functional since that case contained a limited amount of power storage, but it could no longer draw further power and data, so dropped into a resting state.

Next Sverl searched the surrounding area and found some of the runcible maintenance robots in storage, powered one of them up, and sent it over to the AI's abode, opening an armoured hatch to admit it. The thing trundled in on four legs and, following Sverl's instructions, halted at the base of the column, stretched out its mantis limbs and snatched the AI from its platen. Next it turned the ring of sensor stubs on what was nominally its head to select the right one and pressed it right up against an area of crystal exposed through the skeletal case. Then took a long hard look inside.

The crystal was translucent in both the human and prador

spectrums, though with a deal of distortion and refraction. One brief look was all that was required, for it revealed a flaw right at the centre of the crystal. Sverl had the robot try another sensor stub against the crystal for deeper molecular analysis, but for confirmation only because he had already guessed what he had here. The object was formed of super-dense carbon, every atom in itself an etched-atom processor, overall spin states interlinked in synergistic processing, strange femto-tech connections operating, zero energy time crystals . . . Sverl supposed one could describe the thing as a black diamond, if one were to severely strain the term for that gem. This AI contained a little piece of Penny Royal at its heart.

'You're not done with me yet, are you?' said Sverl, only realizing he had clattered that out loud with his prosthetic mandibles when Bsorol clattered a query back.

Sverl ignored his first-child as he instructed the robot to return the AI to its column. Now aware of the subtle signatures, he created a search program which at once began to come back with some positives. He had gone through fifty of the station's AIs before he cancelled the search. He didn't need to check every AI to know that every one contained that blackness at its heart.

Trent

Trent gazed down at the utterly pristine carpet moss and wondered what Florence had done with the bodies. Had she sent them to one of the flash furnaces to be incinerated with so much other junk, or stored them away until such a time as relatives could be found to decide what should be done with them? He shook his head and walked over to the three loaded anti-grav gurneys floating a few feet above the floor and gazed at three living bodies there. Meanwhile, a skeletal Golem android, which had earlier been intent on killing him, placed the last of the three cryo-caskets, in which these bodies had arrived, inside the airlock. More would be arriving any minute: another robot on the other side of the airlock would take out the empties and replace them with full caskets. First would be people he did not know, for Reece and her children were not here yet. He felt selfish about that – about wanting to be sure everything here was working before she and her children went through.

The body of the man on the first gurney terminated above the hips and was without arms, a lower jaw, nose or eyes. Silver-grey skin sealed all points of severance, while the body was cold, inert, the heart beating just once every few hours to pump the special freeze-resistant artificial blood around inside. Even as Trent inspected the body, the gurney beeped a warning and set off towards the door from the reception area. Trent watched it go, then headed over to a door on the other side, pushed it open and climbed a spiral stair, finally entering a viewing station. This place wasn't for humans to oversee the hospital, but a courtesy provided for researchers and students.

Glancing over at his particle cannon, which he had plugged into a wall socket here to recharge, he plumped himself down in one of the four seats. Before these a curved panoramic screen displayed numerous scenes throughout the hospital, while over the arm of each seat a control hologram hovered. He sat back, inserted his hand in the hologram and, sorting through menus on the screen, highlighted the patient he had just seen and set the viewing system to track.

'Morbid fascination?' wondered Sepia vaguely, sprawled in a chair further along.

'I could say the same for you,' Trent replied, nodding at the screen frame she had up before her. This showed Cole seated in one of the editing suite chairs and auged in as he reprogrammed the entire system. Sepia, meanwhile, had a glazed look as she gazed internally at what her aug was showing her, and as she tried to follow what Cole was up to. 'Any idea of what he's doing?'

Sepia blinked, then, after a long pause, her eyes came back into focus. 'Seems most of them are into their suicide season – most of them are well into or past their second century and bored with their lives.'

Trent winced. 'Yes, so Spear told me.'

'Time seems to pass faster as you get older, because your mind doesn't bother recording the things you've done before. If it did, our skulls would be full of detail on the thousands of cups of coffee we've drunk.'

'Yes, I'm aware of that.'

'The less variety in your experience of life the quicker you reach the point when you're just going through life on autopilot, never doing anything new, never doing anything worth laying down permanently in memory. In the past this was always exacerbated by senility and swiftly terminated by death.'

'A history lesson now?'

'If you don't want me to tell you in my own way then I'll not bother.'

'Sorry, please continue.'

'In our age of permanent physical health the brain does not decline into senility but hits the point of extreme ennui, usually somewhere between the ages of one hundred and fifty and two hundred and fifty, depending, obviously, on how much variety your life has had. This can be, to a certain extent, negated by mental editing. However, people don't like ridding themselves of knowledge and experience only to go through it all again and, usually, once a person hits this point, it's too late, because they're already looking for novelty to ease the boredom. And generally that novelty becomes increasingly dangerous.'

Trent nodded. 'I understand that those in ennui seek danger, but I have some trouble with the idea that people so old, and surely wise, would choose to worship the prador.'

Sepia waved a dismissive hand. 'The search for novelty is not only the search for new things to do, but new attitudes to have. The two-hundred-year-old atheist might well go searching for God.'

'Or pretend to,' Trent added. He looked up at his screen frame to see that the amputee had arrived in the production-line surgery where they had first seen Florence.

Sepia didn't seem to hear him.

'How old are you, Sepia?'

'As an old projectile-hurling game would have it: one hundred and eighty.'

Projectile-hurling game?

'And searching for dangerous novelty?'

'Oh yes.'

'Well, Spear is certainly that.'

She grimaced and waved a hand at the screen. 'What Cole is attempting to do is some subtle reprogramming. He's trying to shift the context of their inner perspective so, even though they are beyond the point of ennui, they will look upon their experiences with new eyes. He's also reinforcing their memories of being enslaved by the prador hormone, their ensuing fights to be top dog, and their experience of, apparently, dying. And, do you know what? I think it will actually work.' She shrugged then added, 'At least for a little while.'

'Really?' Trent prompted.

'Changing that inner context has been tried before, but the

effect fades quickly as the brain starts comparing surrounding reality with memory. These people have experienced the novelty of converting themselves into shell people, but the sordid unpleasantness that ensued should give them an aversion to that previous state. Next they'll wake fixed up with Golem limbs in *this*.' She waved a hand again to encompass their surroundings.

'It certainly is novel.' Trent glanced at Sepia in puzzlement.

'Don't you see?' she asked. 'They wanted to become prador. They fixed on an ideal represented by the nearest prador, who was Sverl. Their aversion to all that went before will be reinforced when they realize their previous admiration of Sverl was based on a falsehood. They will learn that he was an amalgam of prador, human and AI and has now been converted into an AI. Their false-premise belief system should collapse into a new shape.'

She was, Trent felt, showing her hundred and eighty years, because she baffled him. Obviously she could see this because she continued, 'Trent, they will enjoy the novelty, and then they will experience what they feel is a moment of epiphany and begin to shrug off their organic bodies and choose to upload to crystal.'

Still Trent could not see that as a logical course. He focused on the screen. The amputee had been scanned and now a pedestal-mounted autodoc had plugged a thick ribbed pipe into his chest. Already the man was looking a better colour and, while the silver-grey skin started sagging and dropping away to expose raw flesh, his chest began to rise and fall. A moment later the doc unplugged the pipe and the man went through to the next stage.

'You're having trouble with this, I can see,' said Sepia.

'I'm sorry, but it all sounds a bit dubious to me,' Trent replied. *And a touch like projection*, he added to himself.

'It's as pure as math,' said Sepia.

'In the same situation, would such effects be the same with you?' Trent asked. 'These aren't just simple people, but old and loaded with experience, and as I said before: maybe even wisdom.'

'It wouldn't happen to me so easily,' she said sniffily, 'because I am not the kind to fall for the lure of belief systems.'

'And you think they all are?' Trent realized she truly hadn't heard his point about people pretending to believe in God.

She shrugged again, looked uncomfortable.

'I think you're simplifying and hoping for a solution that will apply to them all,' he continued. 'I'm now coming to the conclusion that I will go so far and no further. I'll ensure that they're again healthy and mobile and I'll let Cole have his chance at them. After that, just as Spear says, if they pick up the gun again I'll wash my hands of them. That'll be the end of my responsibility.'

'We'll see,' said Sepia, attempting to display a confidence she evidently did not feel.

The printing heads of cell- and bone-welders were now at work, dipping and stabbing like frenetic herons. Trent watched a ceramal pelvis being shifted into place, muscles and tendons attached, the black pennies of nerve interfaces being inserted, meta-plastic muscle bracing affixed. Next, the man was moved on to the ministrations of Florence. The big surgical robot now really got to work, cutting in where the arms had been severed, inserting motorized shoulder joints, delving deep into empty eye sockets, and then deeper still with micro-tool probes right to the visual cortex at the back of the skull. Interface plugs implanted and then eyes, with rear optic connections, just plugged in like memory sticks. Arms next, fixed into those shoulder joints, then legs to the pelvis. The next robot waited with reels of translucent syntheflesh and syntheskin, already threaded through with artificial nerves and with its pixel content ready to be adjusted to match the colour of the host body. When this was over, the man would hardly know that he had ever been without limbs . . .

'Florence,' said Trent.

'Yes,' the surgical robot replied through the hospital PA, no hesitation as it continued working.

'I want the syntheflesh and skin left at its translucent setting,' he said. 'In fact, if it's possible, I'd like you to make it even more transparent.'

'As you request,' the robot replied.

Sepia shot him a querying look.

'Call it a constant visible reminder to them,' he said. 'And a further novelty.'

Sverl

So what do you want of me now, Penny Royal? Sverl wondered. *And is this part of it?*

Had the U-space drives simply been disrupted, it would have taken just days to get them running, yet now, only on coming to the end of the process of balancing the force-fields inside them, did Sverl discover that certain components were missing. These items were plain rings of metal measuring three feet across, an inch and a half wide and half an inch thick. They weren't of a particularly exact size, merely having a tolerance of plus or minus a thousandth of an inch, and even that wasn't highly critical because other components or processes could be adjusted to suit. However, the fact they were fashioned from super-dense iron just a spit away from what you might find in the core of a dead sun did present a bit of a problem.

'Father,' said Bsorol. 'We're demounting the—'

'Not now,' Sverl clattered, focusing his attention outwards.

He again surveyed the surrounding system, trying to see what remained of his original ship. News was not good. Only one quadrant of it had survived, and it wasn't the one with the gravity press inside.

'We've found something,' Bsorol insisted, just managing to duck the swipe of Sverl's free claw, 'in the Room 101 AI's sanctum.' Bsorol quickly scuttled away when Sverl stabbed at him with the spine clutched in his other claw.

Damned AIs, Sverl thought, then remembered what he was and rephrased that thought: *Damned Polity AIs*. This whole massive station, which had turned out vast fleets of warships, did not have the tooling aboard to manufacture all the components for U-space drives. Sure, facilities were here to make some components, to assemble a drive and tune it, but it seemed some critical items had to be brought in by runcible. This was understandable because certain components, like those rings, had at one time required for their manufacture either massive planet-bound factory complexes, or very high-tech factories actually down on the surface of a dead star. However, Sverl couldn't help but have the suspicion that the reason there was no gravity press here was due to the Polity AIs' paranoia about letting humans get their sticky hands on drive tech.

He would have to build a gravity press. Even as he considered that he knew it wouldn't do. It would take weeks and, unfortunately, the only singularity available would first have to be dug out of one of the deactivated runcibles here. Even after he'd made the press, the process of actually fashioning the rings would take further weeks and, by then, he felt sure, a Polity fleet would have arrived and turned Room 101 into a steadily expanding cloud of hot gas.

So what do I do, Penny Royal?

The only answer was his own: he needed to buy time. That meant he needed to get the defences of this station up to modern standards. He needed some serious hardfields operating and he needed . . .

Sverl suddenly hit a mental wall.

U-jump missiles!

He could bring the defences of this station up to date in terms of Kingdom weaponry. But technologically the Kingdom was now far behind the Polity. Polity attack ships now had a whole cornucopia of gravity weapons – maybe other things too that he knew nothing about yet. But why worry about those when U-jump missiles were enough? One of their modern attack ships could simply jump a series of CTD warhead missiles inside this station and he would be, as Arrowsmith would have put it, toast.

'The best defence is to have an operating U-field meniscus within your vessel, which is . . . difficult.'

What?

Sverl suddenly found himself to be walking, in human form, through an exploded holographic schematic of a U-jump missile. He reached out to touch the representation of a CTD warhead, gave it a light shove to send it down towards the main body of the missile, where it slotted neatly in place.

'So, in essence, even if the prador had developed these during the war, they still wouldn't have been able to touch our stations,' replied the watching AI.

'No, of course not,' said the woman, *'because of the runcibles.'*

Sverl fought the drag of alien memory and snapped out of it, abruptly stumbling from his dais, trailing all the optics and power cables plugged into his skeleton. He swung his claws round, and now gazing through the series of eyes Bsorol had recently installed for him, inspected the spine he held. The dead, Penny Royal's victims . . . The spine had responded to his need with the memory of a human weapons designer called Croydon who, reaching the age of a hundred and ninety had gone adventuring in the Graveyard and found a terminal adventure in the metal hands of one of Penny Royal's Golem – it might even have been Mr Grey.

Runcibles . . .

If a runcible was running inside the station it would act like a gravity well to a U-jump missile. The thing would be drawn in even as it attempted to materialize, like an asteroid into a black hole, straight through the U-space meniscus. So, his defence against such missiles would be to get at least one of the runcibles aboard operating – this was of course presupposing that no vital components were missing from them – but still he needed to get the other defences up to and beyond wartime specifications. This would not stop him taking one of the other runcibles apart to get at its singularity to use in a gravity press . . .

'Is this what you want?' Sverl asked, only realizing he had spoken out loud when Bsorol came scuttling over again.

'Father?' asked the first-child.

Sverl gazed on Bsorol, perfectly recalling what Bsorol had been saying earlier.

'You found something in the old AI sanctum?' he enquired. 'What did you find?'

'An item of technology.'

'Well, no shit, Sherlock.'

Bsorol expressed some confusion, flicking at one of his mandibles with one claw.

'Why does this need my attention?' Sverl asked.

'It is Penny Royal technology,' said Bsorol.

121

Sverl gazed at his first-child speculatively.

'Get me unhooked,' he demanded.

Blite

The agony was still there and he knew, on some level, that it didn't need to be. He managed to query the entity that in some sense was the dark red realm he occupied, and it replied in simple words: 'It brings clarity.'

Clarity?

Through his one working eye he could see he was floating in an enclosed space with silver worms shoaling all around him. Something about these niggled at his memory but he couldn't get past the need to scream, frozen in his throat. His only anchor in reality was the pedestal-mounted autodoc, bowed over him like an insect priest as it steadily turned him while peeling away the charred and melted space suit from his raw skin.

'Tell me again,' said the entity, 'about your first encounter with Penny Royal.'

That was it: that was the memory he had been groping for. It had seemed to him that it *was* Penny Royal here all around him. But why would Penny Royal ask such a question? He wanted to shout at the thing, but he could neither speak nor scream. How could he answer when it wouldn't allow him a voice? However, memories arose clear in his mind: the deal that went wrong, that strange black thistle seeming to sprout on the ridge above, before transforming into a cloud of knives descending on them, and the deaths . . .

'Now I need to know about your next encounter,' said the entity.

Stripped-away fragments of his suit hung in the air all

around, drifting like water weed in some strange aquarium. The autodoc was now steadily removing blistered skin and cooked flesh. Pain increased in waves but thankfully, after removing a section, the autodoc's printing heads set to work replacing tissue, layer upon layer, and at those points the pain steadily faded away.

Blite fervently wished he had never encountered Penny Royal at all, and damned himself for being lured by that artefact on Masada. He remembered their trek through the Masadan night with a grav-sled on which the object had been loaded and the sudden fear they had felt even as they returned to the space port. He remembered the relief they had felt at being back aboard *The Rose*, and then the terror when the artefact unfolded itself into something spiny, glistening and black: Penny Royal. On another level he felt some shape to the information contained in his memories being lifted and matched to some other shape, slotting together and being shifted aside, but to where he had no idea.

'And next?' the entity enquired.

Obviously speech was not required. Blite remembered the journey from Masada with Penny Royal aboard to the black AI's planetoid, the encounter with the salvagers there and the AI going down to that bleak rock to 'deactivate its dangerous toys'. The sight of that tokomak generator there seemed of great interest to the unseen being who was questioning Blite because it went over that again and again. Next the journey to the Rock Pool and how the AI defended Carapace City from Cvorn's attack. Losing himself in memory helped negate the pain, so he sank deeper into it, played it all the way through. Only as he drew towards the end did he have some intimation of how he had arrived in this room and what those silver worms shoaling around him might be.

123

'Tell me again,' said the entity, 'about your first encounter with Penny Royal.'

Blite felt utter horror rolling through him. Was this just going to continue?

By now the autodoc had made numerous repairs and large areas of fresh skin covered his chest and arms. Next it turned its attention to his face, a rose of surgical chain-glass opening above his missing eye and extruding one suspiciously spoon-shaped blade. Blite's scream remained locked in his throat and his begging was silent.

'What the fucking hell do you think you're doing!' someone bellowed.

The autodoc abruptly retracted its surgical cutlery, rose away from him a little, the clamps that were holding his head in place releasing. He managed to turn his head a little and look across. A door now stood open in the pale green wall and behind the autodoc stood a tall thin woman – an outlinker – clad in tortoiseshell exoskeleton. She was lowering her hand from the doc's manual control panel, so it seemed she had just turned it off. Blite was now also able to take in more surrounding detail. He was in some sort of apartment or ship's cabin because, through an archway, he could see a fairly standard washroom. However, all the furniture that had occupied this room had been shoved to one side and crushed into one splintered mass. What the hell was going on here?

All around now the shoaling activity of the silver worms changed. They all began heading towards one point and, tilting his head back, Blite saw them balling together and melding, extending the protrusions of limbs and the fat nub of a head, tightening together and refining the form. At the last came a change of hue to reveal a fat bald man, who opened eyes like black stones.

'Your ship AI instructed you to remain aboard your bridge,' said the man.

'Well sometimes orders have to be questioned,' the woman replied.

'Interrogation is necessary,' said this man.

The woman stepped round the autodoc. She folded her arms, and Blite suspected that was because she was so angry she didn't trust herself not to strike out.

'Yes, of course we need information,' she said tightly. 'But I don't remember any changes to Polity law that made it acceptable to torture Polity citizens.'

'He and his crew are guilty of numerous crimes,' said the fat man.

'He and his crew are guilty of nothing until that guilt is proven,' said the woman. 'As I understand it, charges against them were trumped up only because of their association with Penny Royal.'

'They caused major damage at Par Avion.'

'Yes, to escape being captured and handed over to the likes of you. I think what we're seeing here rather proves that they made the right decision.' She paused, chewing her bottom lip, then stepped back to the autodoc and began working the manual console. The doc dipped towards Blite and extruded an infuser head down to touch his neck. Blessed numbness spread rapidly downwards from that point, and slowly upwards. As it entered his skull, oblivion shortly followed.

5

Lelic at the Junkyard

'We've got a live one,' Henderson hissed.

The realspace region designated The Zone by Lelic's father was a Lagrange point lying between a fairly common red giant sun surrounded by a scattering of small planetoids and its extremely rare orbital partner: a pair of singularities of just one solar mass each, individually spinning fast but also spinning round each other at close to the speed of light. Something about this combination gave underlying U-space some rather odd properties which, for Lelic and the other extremadapts of The Zone, were profitable ones. The Lagrange was like a section of beach along which currents converged to wash up masses of flotsam and jetsam, though, admittedly, pickings were rarer now than in his father's time.

'Screen it,' said Lelic, slouched back in the ring of his gel console, stinger gun plus maintenance equipment lying beside him.

The oval screen before him first showed an overview of The Zone, with its long slew of wrecked ships and floating debris which, sometime in the not too distant future, would form a complete ring around the sun. A blister appeared in the screen's surface and magnified something to bring it hazily into view. He leaned forwards and pressed his webbed hands into the console, stabbed a finger into one of the control cells and summoned up a soft ball control from the depths of the console. Using this, he rolled a cross hair blister from the side of the frame over to the first blister, then stabbed a finger into the 'acquire' cell. With a steady rumbling, the biomech cometary tug reoriented and began accelerating. He slouched back, staring at the thing up on the screen as the pixel cells of a clean-up program flickered across it. After a moment he soon found himself gazing up at something that might have been a cylindrical ship until it had been torn open and gutted. Some of the surfaces he could see almost looked like a portion of a crow's wing, which was an effect he recognized.

'Looks like a chunk of one of the modern attack ships,' he said, bored. Then he stabbed a hand back into the console and pinched out the 'acquire' cell, and the rumble of the engines faded. Withdrawing his hand, he shrugged himself into a more comfortable position, picked up his stinger gun and went back to work on it. Opening the stick seam on the side of the breech, he pulled out a series of bee-stingers then picked up a long scraper and shoved it through the breech and down the barrel, pushing out the layer of scar tissue that had formed in the barrel. Organic weapons, he had found, were good because they grew their own projectiles, but bad because, as they got older, they required as much maintenance as a pre-Quiet War senile human. As he worked on the weapon he wondered when he would get to use it again. Of course, it wasn't often that he did get to use it when there were survivors, because it was usually a case of cutting their dying bodies out of the wreckage.

Lelic's father, fleeing the Polity with his group of extrem-adapts, had found this true graveyard within the Graveyard during the war. At first he had thought the great floating mass of spaceships was the result of one of the many battles being fought. He, and his people, had decided to hang around because pickings were rich, while this sector was of little interest to either the prador or the Polity. While they salvaged what they could from the heavily damaged ships, built a small space station from the floating junk knitted together with highly adapted corals capable of growing in vacuum, and generally kept their heads (or whatever else served that purpose in them) down, more ships arrived. And regularly.

It soon became apparent that every ship that washed up here did so with a damaged U-space drive. Quite often this damage resulted in the crews, whether prador or human, being dead, but sometimes there were survivors. Lelic's father, who hadn't been what one would describe as a humanitarian, quickly came to a decision about that. If anyone got away from this sector and described what was here, then the place would be swarming with Polity forces shortly afterwards, so Lelic's father ensured none of them did get away. Lelic, having assumed his father's mantle after strangling the man, found he no longer needed to worry about Polity forces, only other salvagers in the Graveyard. He did keep up his father's tradition, but with a twist. In fact, it was that aspect of the salvaging operation Lelic enjoyed the most, which was why finding a piece of a modern attack ship bored him, despite its high value. Best to leave it to one of the others of the colony of extremadapts, which had grown somewhat since his father's time.

'I'm getting life signs,' hissed Henderson.

'What?' Lelic put aside his weapon and leaned forwards. If there was life aboard, then it was likely human life, which meant Lelic might now be able to grab someone to put in the arena. He'd been waiting months to have something to go up against the prador they had captured a few months ago. He set another 'acquire' cell and waited anxiously, picking scabs from the keel bone of his chest.

Over the next hour the image of the wreckage grew clear,

and Lelic wondered how there could possibly be someone alive in it. That was, until Henderson sent him a scan from the grab pod. There was a space suit trapped in the wreckage, and a scan revealed a heartbeat and internal warmth.

'Snare and secure,' he instructed. 'We'll take it straight back to the station.'

Rather than try to cut this individual free out here, then go through the laborious efforts to get him inside, it would be better done inside the station. Once this man was again mobile and strong enough, it would then be time to match him against that prador young-adult.

Up on the screen he now got a view of Henderson halfway up the grab arm, his bloated form all but filling the bubble and his limpet pads stuck firmly against the surrounding chain-glass. The five-talon jointed claw Henderson controlled opened at the end of the arm over the wreckage. For a moment Lelic was sure he detected movement in the tangled mass, but no, just some optical illusion caused by the meta-material surfaces. Lelic turned his attention back to his console and inserted his hands again, reaching out to touch the cells representing other colonists and raising data blisters on his screen. Already some of them were making bets, and bids for recording rights. Really, pulling in live ones like this was the only excitement they had here.

'That's got it,' said Henderson.

Henderson had closed the claw over the wreckage and checked it for security, so now Lelic pulled up another soft ball control and used it to turn his tug back to the station. He grinned to himself upon noting that other ships were also heading back out of The Zone. Damn, but he really hoped that the survivor continued surviving, because already a lot of bio credit had been wagered on that prospect.

Blite

Blite lay absolutely still, frozen by the prospect of pain if he moved. After a while he started to get angry and realized he was clenching his fists, and that they didn't hurt. He opened what he recollected as being his good eye and gazed up at a pale blue ceiling, then carefully opened his other eye. It was okay. Next he closed his eyes and, with utter care, rolled onto his side then pushed himself up. Dragging himself higher on the bed, he sat up and opened his eyes again to check his surroundings.

He was in, by his standards, a quite luxurious cabin. This bedroom was large, with inset wall cupboards, glow-paint walls, a console, a bedside unit and a door in one wall opening into a small washroom. After taking in detail and deliberately not looking at his own naked body, he finally plucked up the nerve to look down at it.

The printed-on flesh and skin grafts were distinct from the rest. They were fresh, lacking in scars – he'd even lost the bullet-hole scar in his right calf – while what remained of his original skin still had a tan acquired from many worlds, still had its blemishes and occasional webs of scarring left by his military autodoc. He raised one hand, completely covered with new skin, and flexed it. It ached and felt sensitive, but he knew that would pass in time, just as the distinction between old and new skin would pass too. But he wondered if the raw feeling and tightness, deep inside – that awareness of his human fragility – would pass too.

Still careful, he swung his legs off the side of the bed and slowly stood up. Dizziness washed through him, then a sudden powerful nausea. He staggered to the washroom door and through, just managing to get to the sink in time to retch. Nothing but bile came up but his body was insistent that there had to be something else. The convulsions came one after another, so hard that he shit watery diarrhoea and dripped it on the floor. He turned and lurched over to the combined shower and sanitary unit and pulled out the toilet bowl. Instead of sitting on it, he collapsed down beside it and retched some more.

He lost track of how long he lay there heaving, eventually coming out of a haze to find himself shivering, his throat raw and his mouth tasting foul. As soon as he managed to start thinking again he became puzzled. Obviously he was aboard the ship – almost certainly a Polity one – that had destroyed the *Black Rose*. Even in the Graveyard, or just using the old military autodocs he'd had aboard his own ship, there would never have been such ill effects even after such a major physical rebuild, and Polity technology was a lot more advanced. Then he realized what the problem was: it was in his skull. This was the psychological aftermath of his interrogation.

He wearily stood up, folded away the toilet bowl and touched the shower pad. A thin film drew across to separate him from the rest of the washroom and then the water hit him. He dialled up the heat and stood under it until the shivering stopped, then washed himself. By the time he stepped out to snatch up one of the towels provided, some sort of cleanbot had dealt with the shit on the floor and the puke in the sink bowl. Drying himself, he tried to feel stronger, but still felt fragile inside, scared.

Out in the main cabin he found clothing – underwear, a padded shipsuit and slippers – and donned it. This barrier between his nakedness and his surroundings alleviated some of the feeling, but it still sat inside him as if he was shrinking away from some scowling spectre. He looked around, wondering where Leven's crystal was. He had a vague memory of looking down his body as he lay on the surgical slab. His belt had been gone. Leven was most likely out there tumbling through vacuum, somnolent (which was probably for the best). Blite walked over and tried the door, expecting it to be locked, but it slid back into the wall, revealing a corridor with red carpet moss and small alcoves sheltering sculptures of nightmarish alien life forms. However, there was some security waiting.

'Follow me,' said a crab drone, descending from the ceiling and blinking its rim lights at him. He nodded, subdued, and followed.

'What ship am I aboard?' he managed after a few paces.

'The *High Castle*,' the drone replied briefly.

'A Polity warship?'

'Gamma-class police action interdiction ship.' The drone paused for a moment. 'Yeah, a warship.'

It led him through another set of sliding doors into a small circular lounge and refectory. Here sofas and low tables clustered before a panoramic screen showing a view across the ship itself and into vacuum, while back from them stood a dining table of polished wood with eight matching chairs. Just one person was seated at the table. Greer wore a pale blue shipsuit similar to his own and looked like an inmate in an asylum. She was hollow-eyed, and Blite noticed her hands were shaking as she struggled to push small morsels of food into her mouth.

'Captain,' she said, then ran out of words.

Blite started to head over to her but, spying a food unit inset in one wall, went over to that and punched in his requirements. It shortly delivered him a pressed tray and a capped beaker. He took these up, but instead of going over to join Greer, walked over to the panoramic window and gazed out.

The ship was obviously a large one because before him lay what looked like a plane stretching to a sunrise, which he guessed was the glare of fusion engines. The plane was of metals and composite, scattered with glassy instrument blisters like dome houses, punctuated by com towers and a couple of huge weapons turrets. Distantly he could see someone in a space suit working at the foot of one of those turrets, and that gave him a sense of scale. The weapons turret stood four storeys tall. He turned away, reluctantly heading over to sit down with Greer.

She watched him tiredly but he struggled to find anything to say. He took the lid off the tray and peered at its contents, surprised because the food looked very good. But he had little appetite and so uncapped the beaker and sipped coffee. It tasted just right, but he had trouble swallowing and his stomach began to register a protest. He put it to one side.

'I don't think Brond made it,' he said.

'Yeah, I heard,' Greer replied. 'We should have known that fucker would get one of us killed eventually.' Her words just didn't seem to have any heat in them.

'It was quick,' Blite replied, again hearing Brond's truncated scream over suit com. 'I was burned,' he continued. 'Something questioned me while an autodoc worked on me. All the time I was conscious and without nerve blocking.'

'Yes,' said Greer. Blite assumed she meant the same had happened to her, but she bowed her head and continued her attempts to eat.

'Some woman came in and stopped it,' he continued. 'An outlinker – she seemed pretty annoyed.'

'That would be Captain Grafton.' Greer discarded her knife and fork in disgust. 'She's military and I don't think she likes having . . .' She paused for a moment. 'I don't think she likes having the Brockle aboard. I don't think she likes it at all.'

'The Brockle?' he repeated. 'And why the hell is that thing aboard this ship?'

'It's apparently an adviser on the . . . Penny Royal situation.'

133

Greer shrugged and winced. 'According to Grafton, this ship was on its way to join a small fleet heading out to Room 101. They know what happened there because the king of the prador sent them a recording.' She stopped, looking puzzled. 'Apparently we missed something vital about events there.'

'You said "was on its way"?' Blite prompted.

'Oh, yeah. It then got diverted on a new mission to intercept Penny Royal.' Greer sat for a long moment in silence before adding, 'But Penny Royal got away.'

'So what now?' asked Blite.

'Apparently the Brockle is now gathering data so as to decide on its next course of action.' Greer looked at him directly. 'And we're its main source.'

After a long pause while they digested that, Greer added, 'Something doesn't add up here.'

Blite waited, but Greer's gaze fixed over his shoulder. Blite turned and saw that a large bald-headed man, with a shipsuit the same as he and Greer wore stretched over his corpulent form, had entered the lounge. He stood with his arms folded and, just for a moment, Blite tried not to recognize who this was.

'Greer Salint,' said the man. 'Your presence is required.'

Panicked, Greer took her arms off the table, stood up knocking her chair over and backed away. She looked terrified, but there was nowhere to run. The fat man gestured and Greer grunted as if gut-punched, then woodenly responded to the summons. Blite hated himself for sitting there and doing nothing, and hated how grateful he felt that it was she who had been summoned, and not him.

Sverl

As Sverl exited his sanctum he probed ahead towards what had once been the abode of the Room 101 AI, but unfortunately there were no working cams available there so he had no idea what it was Bsorol had found. Instead, as he walked, unsteady at first but then rapidly growing used to his new form and finding it less cumbersome than his old one, he continued checking throughout the rest of the station.

Having chosen a runcible, the one with a singing AI, he was loading it with the requisite programs. Meanwhile, he had assigned to the AI many of the least altered and damaged maintenance robots which, even as it loaded data, it was deploying about the runcible to make repairs. Fortunately there wasn't too much damage because the AIs of this station had, over the last hundred years, retained enough sense of self-preservation not to cannibalize the runcibles. The runcibles contained the kind of technology that could lead to catastrophe if tampered with – not least their singularities. Elsewhere repairs were proceeding ever faster. The external weaponry was nowhere near up to spec but every time another factory unit fired up, the rate of repairs increased. It still needed to go faster: a Polity response could arrive at any time.

Launching himself after Bsorol towards where the 101 AI had been, Sverl next took a look in the hospital. There the shell people were steadily being processed and the first of them were now receiving the ministrations of the mind-tech Cole. Finding little more of interest there, Sverl's attention strayed to the adjacent construction bay. Spear had returned to his ship and, as far as Sverl could gather, was still preparing it for departure. The mind case of Flute was ready to be shifted across from the old attack ship and, once that was done, Spear would go.

'So what exactly is this something you've found?' Sverl asked Bsorol as they sailed through vacuum.

'I cannot be certain,' the first-child replied. 'Penny Royal technology.'

Bsorol wouldn't be drawn, and a moment later landed on some of the supporting structure around the old abode of the Room 101 AI. The large pill-shaped structure had been fragile last time Sverl had come here, and after the recent battles it had taken damage. There were large holes in its walls, and clouds of brittle debris floated all around. Bsorol towed himself down to a narrow ledge and in through one of the holes. Following, Sverl scanned the interior, finding things much as they had been before. On his last visit he had quickly surmised that there was nothing here for him: the Room 101 AI, having instructed one of its maintenance robots, had suicided. Beyond that, all surrounding systems were a burned-out mess. Setting this place up as a centre of operations would have taken more work than any other location in the station. However, this place now had an addition.

With micro-pads in his feet bonding, Sverl stalked across the debris-strewn floor and gazed down at the object resting at the base of the ex-AI's lower interlink. It was a slightly flattened white sphere a yard across. A hole stood open in its upper surface, revealing packed silver and red complexity. Sverl scanned it, picking up high energy densities, organization extending well below the atomic level, perhaps pico- or even femto-tech. Taking a rough template of its structure, he ran a comparison with something in his memory and found it matched. It seemed that Penny Royal was not finished with him.

'Do you recognize it?' Sverl asked Bsorol.

'I'm not sure,' Bsorol hedged.

'Think back to how Penny Royal defended Carapace City.'

'Yes,' said Bsorol. 'I see . . .'

It had been certain that Cvorn would fire on Carapace City and try to incinerate the human population there. Penny Royal, after arriving aboard *The Rose*, had launched objects like these and used them to raise a hardfield of a type no one had ever seen before. First it had been a curved curtain, then it had completely enclosed Carapace City in an adamantine sphere. Not only that, as Sverl had observed, it shunted the energy from CTD and particle-beam strikes against it into U-space, thereafter drawing it back to reinforce the field. This was precisely the kind of defence Sverl needed for this station. And here it was, revealed to him at precisely the right moment.

'One of them won't do it,' said Bsorol, who obviously understood more than he was letting on. 'Penny Royal used a number of them to generate the field for Carapace City and that was a lot smaller than this station.'

'True,' Sverl replied. 'But there must be a way this object can be copied.'

Sverl probed for com frequencies emitted by the thing but found nothing. Then he routed his searches through the spine. A schematic of vast complexity fell into his mind. Its sheer size almost shut him down because it was too big to encompass, let alone understand. In reaction he extended his mind into local AIs to make room, incidentally compressing their mentalities and all but shutting *them* down. The schematic expanded to render more detail, almost like a Mandelbrot set, and Sverl found himself having to expand further. Another twenty AIs had to make room for him before the schematic reached its true scale, and a further ten minds were needed for him to then process function data. The thing he was looking at was more complex than any living biological entity, more so than a whole ecology even, but it did have one striking similarity.

'It is a Von Neumann machine,' Sverl stated.

'What's that?' Bsorol asked – only when the first-child used human language over the radio link did Sverl realize that was how he himself had spoken.

'It can reproduce itself,' Sverl clattered.

The required mix was quite simple really, for the machine bore one other similarity to the common biological life thus far found in both the prador and human expansions: it was based on carbon. It contained many other elements, but the bulk of it consisted of the endless methods of combining and shaping carbon. Even as he listed those other elements, Sverl mentally reached out and sequestered a mixing tank used to make bubble-metals and began diverting resources.

'Pick it up,' he instructed.

Even as Bsorol warily stepped forwards and reached down with both claws, tons of carbon dust in the form of buckyballs and nano-tubes was being propelled from storage along a pipe towards that tank. Other pipes began supplying other elements – the correct mix of gases, grits of silicon and rare earths – while furnaces began liquefying a wide selection of metal ingots ready for piping through too.

'Take it here.' Sverl sent station coordinates directly to Bsorol's aug. 'Simply place it inside the bubble-metal tank and leave it there.' Sverl paused for a moment then added, 'I will have an AI run the process but I want you to stay and oversee it, take some second-children with you and be ready to respond to any eventualities. Go at once.'

The AI currently getting the bubble-metal tank up to speed was more than capable of overseeing the whole process. However, Sverl now had reason to distrust them and wanted his children on claw for the most important work aboard this station.

As Bsorol scuttled away Sverl paused to again study his sur-roundings. Penny Royal must have left this thing when it had encountered Spear here. Spear hadn't seen it, but then the man had not been in the most balanced state of mind at the time. Whatever. As he erased the schematic so as to give himself room to think, Sverl had to wonder just what Penny Royal's intentions were. Rather than running, Sverl had been nudged towards the route of building a hardfield defence. What was it for? What were those black diamonds for? All of this, Sverl felt sure, was no longer about correcting past wrongs, but about Penny Royal's ultimate aim, whatever that might be. Everything that had gone before had been, in Penny Royal's terms, a game, but now the black AI was getting deadly serious.

Spear

'Right, I'm going to bed,' I said, dropping my visor as I stepped back inside the *Lance*.

Still somewhat paranoid after recent events, I'd wanted to keep a close eye on my ship and its surroundings while the cas-kets of the shell people were being unloaded, and I'd just come inside after making a visual inspection of the hull outside to assure myself nothing had attached itself, and all space doors and hatches were closed. Of course, while those caskets were being unloaded, keeping watch had not occupied me completely, so I had also been overseeing the robots rebuilding the interior, making defences and safety measures so nothing could ever assume control of me or my ship again.

'What?' Riss asked.

139

'You heard me,' I replied, and just headed back to my rebuilt cabin.

Human biology had been tinkered with for centuries and, for many, sleep was no longer a necessity. However, it had never ceased to be a pleasure. I could go without it – using other methods to imbed memory and clear up the dross in my mind – but these methods never quite got me centred, never allowed me to break from the past and find a point of calm, and sleep did.

Inside my cabin I stripped, sprawled back on my bed and shut my eyes. Of course the way I went to sleep bore little similarity to how primitive humans did it. I just started a sleep program in my aug, with the requisite amounts of deep sleep and REM over a period of eight hours, then shut down as if someone had pulled my power supply.

When I woke, I was reminded of how I felt waking in that virtuality prior to my resurrection. I felt good, rested, stronger and much more able to face the tribulations reality was doubtless preparing to throw at me. I took a shit and a shower, dressed in a clean undersuit and pulled my space suit back on, breakfasted on roast pig apples and porridge, then took a beaker of green tea with me back to the bridge. There I found Riss coiled on a console and wondered if the assassin drone had its own facsimile of sleep. She of course instantly raised her head as I entered, third black eye open as she studied me.

'Right,' I said, 'time to get our ship mind back.'

'Are you sure we want it back?' Riss asked.

'Yes, absolutely sure.'

She responded with a snort as I drained my tea and headed for the airlock, but followed anyway. I stepped outside, Riss slithering out behind me.

'Wait,' she said, as I was about to set out towards the old

attack ship Sverl had used as a decoy. I glanced down at her and she pointed with her ovipositor. When I couldn't see what she was pointing at, she sent me an image and rapidly changing coordinates with the station schematic. I gazed internally at the still image and then at the thing in real time and could make nothing of it. Yeah, it was a globular lump of technology heading out towards open space. So what? This place was full of all sorts of tech on the move.

'You don't recognize it?' Riss asked.

'No.'

'While you were sleeping Sverl found something interesting,' Riss began, and while we walked across to the old attack ship filled me in on the technology lying behind Penny Royal's defence of Carapace City. As we entered the attack ship I pondered why the black AI had left such technology for Sverl to find. I couldn't help thinking it was there because it would be needed.

Disconnecting all Flute's feeds was simple because Sverl had given the second-child mind the ability to eject itself from this ship, which of course was very unpradorlike of him, since most prador were not much concerned about the survival of their children in any form. Flute merely had to initiate the disconnection routine while putting actual ejection on hold. The interlinks clamping his case in place separated, while optics and power cables unplugged themselves and snaked away into recesses. I stepped over to the case and gave it a shove towards the exit, then just walked alongside as it drifted. Two shoves more sent it into the hold, where I instructed a maintenance robot to field it.

'I still don't think this is a good idea,' said Riss.

'So would you like to take Flute's position controlling the *Lance*?' I asked.

'This place is awash with AIs that would probably leap at the chance.'

'And they are likely to be as trustworthy, or more so, than you or Flute?'

'She's just trying to maintain the pose,' Flute interjected. 'It must be difficult to find you no longer hate what you'd been programmed to hate. Us beings who actually learned how to think rather than running on crappy code hastily slapped together in this place are more pliant, and more durable.'

Ouch! I winced.

'Yeah, but now you're no longer an organic being, but running in crystal and all of a sudden finding your horizons expanding.'

'Uhuh, I experience both worlds, so I'm not quite as limited as you.'

'That's enough,' I said. 'This isn't helping.'

But even as I said it I felt oddly happy that these two were back to their usual bickering. It seemed like stability in my chaotic world.

'Well,' said Riss, 'I've still got some of that explosive gel if the prador *child* gets uppity.'

'Yes, sure you have,' I said.

'So what now, boss?' asked Flute.

'Now, once we're ready, we head off again and I find out what I can about where Penny Royal went.'

'Same aims?' asked Riss.

'I don't really know,' I replied. 'All I do know is that before we go I get that spine back from Sverl, and find out what Trent is doing too . . .'

'Then what?'

'Let's just find Penny Royal,' I asserted. 'And then we'll see.'

What would I do if I was not pursuing Penny Royal? Right

now the AI was the focus of my existence and I couldn't stop until whatever it was between us was resolved. And, deep inside, I knew I was frightened by the prospect of not having this mission, no matter how vague it had become.

With Riss squirming along at my side, I followed Flute across to my ship, pausing at one point to watch the activity in this final construction bay. I initially intended to take Flute round to the munitions hatch, which had been the best way in while the hold was full. However, now the last of the cryo-cases had been removed and going through the hold would be the better route, I diverted the robot. As I got Flute inside the ship and into position, I was reminded of the last time I had done this. At the time Isobel Satomi and her two men had been lying paralysed inside their own ship – victims of a neat biological weapon I had devised. At that time I had been acting rather than reacting. Remembering it, I felt the need to be more positive about my aims now.

'When I spoke to Penny Royal inside Room 101 it said, "We have returned to my beginning, and now we must return to yours." And I've been pondering on what that might mean.'

'Where were you born?' asked Riss.

'New York, on Earth.'

'I don't think that's what it means then, does it?'

'Almost certainly not.'

'Your resurrection?'

'On Earth again.' I paused. 'One possibility could have been Masada, because it could be contrived that my "beginning" was when my memplant was found in that jewellery shop. But I don't think it's that either. In a way I think Penny Royal is referring to something that could almost mean the opposite.'

'Uh?'

'My ending: where I died on Panarchia.' I hesitated, then continued, 'And where the new me began.'

By now we had reached Flute's previous abode and, once the mind case was in position between the splayed-end interlinks, I began plugging in optics and other peripherals. Since the ship was now airtight and pressurized inside, Flute spoke from its PA system, noting, 'Panarchia might not exist any longer.'

'What?'

'On my last astrogation update,' said Flute, 'Panarchia was a place to approach with caution since the whole system was in the process of sliding into the black hole Layden's Sink. It might already be gone.'

I then remembered standing on the surface of that world, visor closed against the darts of hunting octupals. Further memories occurred. We were all on anti-rads and running nanosuites in our bodies to counter the constant radiation damage as we were bathed in X-rays discharged as the Layden's Sink sucked up just another portion of the material universe. I remembered a conversation with Gideon which ran along the lines of, 'Why the fuck are we fighting for a world that faces annihilation a century hence?'

A century ago.

Tangled in Penny Royal's manipulations, I'd been growing used to events seeming to reach predestined conclusions along the way. But no, even as shivers traversed my spine, I just could not accept that somehow the black AI had arranged *that*. Or could it? That my memplant was found a hundred years after I died was all due to that AI. The events with Sverl were instigated by Penny Royal . . . No, I shook my head. I wasn't going to go there.

The Brockle

The Brockle contained its frustration and tried to focus totally on the data because, just like the method it had used to find Penny Royal's route from Room 101, that data might provide the required information. The black AI had managed to separate and initiate one U-drive to escape, even managing to conceal its U-signature but for the briefest flicker as it went under. Where it had gone in the Graveyard now the Brockle had no idea. However, Penny Royal's U-space connections spread all across the Graveyard, into the Polity, the Kingdom and beyond. Through them it should be able to find *something*.

As it wondered how to go about this, the Brockle continued with its present investigation, since all information about Penny Royal might come in useful some time hence. The entire crew of *The Rose* had experienced a strange connection with the AI, which had changed them fundamentally. The human woman Haber, along with her husband Chont, had, under Penny Royal's influence, experienced a near-telepathic bond for a brief while. It had driven them to separate because that degree of closeness was not something feeble human minds were capable of experiencing. But what was the purpose of it? Unfortunately, Chont and Haber weren't available, so the Brockle concentrated on investigating the more prosaic psychosis Greer had experienced under Penny Royal's influence, when she had tried to cut off her own face. It injected nano-fibres to every one of the woman's synapses, to measure the traffic along every neuron while also weighing neurochemicals. This data it passed through a series of templates, in order to create a precise model of the woman's mind. Of course she had to remain conscious for this and there was some discomfort for her, but that was irrelevant.

After hours of analysis, the Brockle finally came to the conclusion that no useful data was available from Greer. The proximity of Penny Royal to the crew of *The Rose* had softened some arbitrary distinction between conscious and unconscious mind, resulting in suppressed angst arising. When Penny Royal was made aware of this, it corrected it, and that was all. There was no purpose to it. Here, then, was another demonstration of just how dangerously out of control that AI was, but again, giving no insight into its ultimate goals. The Brockle extracted its connections into the woman's skull, noted that she was suffering some adverse after-effects and was crying, but simply dismissed her from its presence. All such reactions were well within the parameters of human function and would eventually be overcome, so there was no need for any kind of adjustment.

'I thought you were done interrogating them,' said Captain Grafton from the ship's bridge. 'Despite what Castle tells me, I can't see how anything more of value can be learned from them.'

The Brockle felt a surge of irritation as it listened to the woman and gazed upon her prim expression. Castle, the ship's AI, wasn't saying anything – all the replies Grafton ostensibly had from it were coming from the Brockle itself. But now Grafton, like others aboard, was beginning to realize things weren't as they should be. Damn it, what was the point of these humans?

'I will decide whether or not there is anything of value to be learned from them,' it lectured. 'Penny Royal's actions can be both extreme and subtle and one must always look beyond what is apparent.'

'Yeah, right,' said Grafton. 'But it's been my experience that beyond a certain point torture renders little of value.'

'I am not torturing them,' the Brockle insisted. 'I am merely obtaining every detail.'

She just stared at her screen, which presently showed an image of the Brockle in human form. 'If you say so,' she said, her expression grim, and cut the connection.

The Brockle realized it had been procrastinating. Since Penny Royal had escaped and it seemed likely the Brockle would have to occupy this ship for some time, the situation would have to change. It could not have Grafton storming down here all the time while it was trying to investigate. Nor did it want crew coming to see the humans – the situation was all just too lax and needed to be dealt with.

It was starting with the Sparkind. Each of the five four-man teams consisted of a mixture of humans and Golem, and it was the latter that were becoming a problem. They frequently used direct communication with the ship's AI to update on various matters and pose questions. They had started to ask a lot of questions about the change in their mission, then they had abruptly stopped. Now they were attempting to conceal their communications and were taking weapons from the armoury for 'diagnostic checks'. They knew something was wrong.

Then there was the submind of the *High Castle* AI in the science section. It too had been puzzled by the responses it was getting from its master AI. Then, in a very short time, it had gone from puzzlement to alarm. The Brockle had already penetrated the link it had with its master and had forcibly subsumed it, but now the human scientists in the science section were asking questions too.

The Brockle drew its shoaling units together, assumed its favoured human form and headed for the door to its cabin. Obviously it wanted to avoid casualties, but it could not allow its mission to be hampered. If some of them died as it removed the threat they posed, then that was acceptable. So who first?

The science team.

This consisted of five humans and two Golem. Obviously the weak and feeble-minded humans were no problem, but the Golem were another matter. Just as with the ship AI, the Brockle could not take control of them remotely, but it had to be in physical contact with their crystal. Probing ahead, it mapped out a course to the science section that would avoid it coming in contact with anyone else aboard. Walking out into the nearby lounge, it ignored the frightened gazes of Blite and Greer and headed through the blast door into the rest of the ship, mentally locking it behind. Stomping along the luxuriously appointed corridors to its destination, it realized that those in the science section would alert the rest the moment the Brockle launched a physical assault. They were slow humans, but they still possessed augs and other mental hardware. This, then, must be incorporated in the plan.

Shortly, it arrived outside the doors into the science section where, through the cams inside, it could see that all were at work studying debris collected from the destruction of the *Black Rose*. The Brockle paused, its fat hand resting against the door, and looked up at a slot sitting above it, and suddenly realized that the solution to its problem might not have to involve actual physical confrontation. Stepping back from the door, it now searched inside the *High Castle* AI's mind and there found the perfect solution. Even Golem would not be a problem, confined inside three inches of case-hardened ceramal.

The first cam it had tried to penetrate aboard had offered a clue. Since the advent of dangerous Jain technology in the Polity, security had been upgraded in response. One of the first points of entry into a ship like this for such technology was the science section, for it was there any alien items would be taken for study. There was, therefore, a way of securely quarantining that section. Within less than a minute, the entire section could be sealed off by airtight ceramal blast walls inches thick, all communications and power cut, whereupon the section could be simply ejected from the ship. The Brockle felt it didn't want to get that drastic, just yet, for there still might be things to be learned from those ship remains. It turned away from the door, initiating just one part of the security protocol. Behind it a sheet of ceramal slammed down out of that slot, while other crashes resounded all around and the deck shuddered underneath its feet. A minute later the science section was completely contained.

Jain technology was a dangerous thing. One Jain node the size of a table tennis ball could topple a civilization, so having such security protocols wasn't really enough, especially when someone could bring in something lethal merely on the sole of a boot. The Brockle rapidly assimilated the fact that most areas inside the ship could be thus enclosed and ejected. It at once closed off the military section, then the bridge. It was congratulating itself on the simplicity of this solution when the laser blast struck it in the chest.

6

Lelic

After wrapping his stinger gun across his back and feeling it sink into its groove there, Lelic pulled himself from his console with a sucking thwack. With a flip of his webbed tail fluke, he moved to his exit tube, propelled himself through it with his webbed hands and the auxiliary tentacles sprouting from his waist, then squeezed out through a sphincter door into the dock.

The wreck, which according to Henderson was free of contaminants, lay down at the bottom of the internal dock sphere, harsh and black against the enclosing pale grey walls of salvaged ceramal, bound together with the red and green growths of constructor coral. Grav was light in here – just a few plates operating at low intensity in the base of the sphere and others scattered all around – so just a shove against the tug, which clung to the wall like a giant tick, sent Lelic down towards it.

He landed just as Henderson ejected from the grab-control bubble. The man, a ball of mollusc muscle still vaguely in human form, landed with a thump against the wall of the sphere and walked down on limpet feet. The sphere was shaking now, a sure sign that others were now docking. Lelic looked up and saw a circular disc of ceramal hinge up to admit another biomech ship, which heaved itself like a giant caterpillar to its docking position, umbilical pipes snaking out to attach and feed it. Then another ship arrived, and another, and soon the place was swarming with extremadapts, mostly in something resembling human form but

150

others utterly alien. There was Dorrel, who seemed like by-blow of a squid and an elephant. Also here, walking across the base of the sphere was Mr Pace, the only resident who wasn't an extrem-adapt and one of their links with the outside – because he didn't look too extreme and possessed his own U-space capable ship. Lelic eyed him. Mr Pace always wore an antiquated suit and at first glance appeared to be a normal. Closer inspection revealed that he was seemingly carved from ebony. Those who knew him were aware that he could survive in vacuum and was unkillable with most weapons. Lelic had personally witnessed a colonist attack him with a ceramic slug thrower. The bullets had just bounced off.

Already the guards and other station personnel were heading over to take a look at the latest candidate here to demonstrate the inferiority of the standard human. Lelic drew his gaze away from Mr Pace, grinned to himself and, using his auxiliary ten-tacles, towed himself over to the wreckage.

The mass was quite small, so it had to be just a chunk of an attack ship. As he had noticed before, it was a cylinder that had been ripped open. In fact, it had been split lengthways and one half folded back. Pulling himself under jags of crow's wing metal, Lelic peered at what he could see of the interior. The thing was packed with all the paraphernalia of a U-space drive and other unidentifiable hard tech. Arriving where the survivor had been located, he saw that a lattice of silvery beams had pinned the space-suited figure up against what looked like a series of crushed Calabi-Yau frames, though what they were doing out-side a drive canister Lelic had no idea. He pulled himself closer, grabbed hold of the lattice and pulled. Much to his surprise the whole lot came away easily, and he now realized that the figure had not actually been pinned in place by it. Stooping nearer, he checked the suit for damage, but could see none.

The suit was of an old design that didn't seem to fit with the modernity of the surrounding wreckage. The visor was completely blacked out so Lelic, wanting a look at its inhabitant, reached for the clips holding the helmet in place. He tugged at them for a moment then, on closer inspection, saw that they had all somehow been fused. He stepped back.

'Alive?' enquired Henderson, black eyes blinking from between flat pads of muscle.

Lelic shrugged and then gestured to the approaching guards, which of course to any normal would have looked like some diverse shoal of marine predators coming to feed. He turned and surveyed the gathering crowd. Wings and fins flapping, tentacles coiling and uncoiling, they all looked eager, and vicious, and Lelic could taste the fog of saliva many of them were spilling. Of course Lelic knew that forcing the survivors to fight each other for the entertainment of the colony was the kind of thing that would have been frowned on in the Polity, though not so much in the Kingdom. He knew it was bad, wrong, and that he and all those around him were the archetypal monsters found in VR entertainments across the Polity. But normals did not understand the alienation that drove this colony, nor its constant need for affirmation of its choices. And frankly, Lelic didn't care whether or not they did understand. There was a freedom to be had in accepting the reality of what you were. Human beings were killers just like the prador, extremadapts were just a refinement of that, and human morality was an artificial construct. Whatever your morality might be was a matter of choice.

'We'll still have to get some more in,' said Henderson.

'Certainly.' Lelic nodded.

He had been coming to terms with the reality of how things here had changed. They were importing now, and Polity and prador wealth was required to pay for such imports. They still sold salvage, but these days they made most of their money from death matches. Full sensory recordings drew in a lot, and there were even a few private tourists allowed. But more matches meant more bodies were needed . . .

'It looks more like a U-space nacelle than from the main body of a ship,' said a cold and arid voice.

Snapped out of reverie, Lelic glanced at Mr Pace, and nodded agreement.

Mr Pace added, 'Which begs the question as to why there was a human survivor inside it.'

'Perhaps the ship had problems,' said Henderson, 'and this guy was sent out into a nacelle to make repairs.'

'Unlikely,' said Mr Pace. Then he blinked those black eyes with their white dot pupils and rubbed his hard hands together as if he was cold.

'Does it matter?' Lelic asked.

Mr Pace shrugged, then turned and strolled away.

Lelic shook himself to try and dispel the creepy feeling he always got when Mr Pace decided it was time for some input, and turned back to Henderson. 'Maybe we should make this the last private . . .'

He trailed off, seeing that Henderson was staring past him, eyes bulging and flat tongue whipping out and across them to wipe them clear. Lelic turned back towards the survivor. The guy was standing up, so Lelic signalled to two crab-armoured guards. They moved forwards, each grabbing an arm in serrated claws.

'Bring him,' Lelic instructed.

They tried to hustle the guy forwards but struggled to move him at all. Then, suddenly, the man swept his right arm round, sending the guard there crashing hard into the wreckage. He grabbed the other guard's ribbed neck and hoisted him up off the floor, before hurling him away. The guard travelled almost in a straight line, bouncing off the side of the wreck before slamming into a mass of constructor coral where he clung, groaning. As he carefully backed away, Lelic watched as the space-suited man pulled a torn-away claw from his arm. Lelic glanced at the one in the wreckage. The other guard's carapace was cracked and leaking, and he wasn't moving at all.

The guy wasn't wearing a motorized suit, so had some heavy boosting or other augmentation. Lelic's webbed hand strayed back to his stinger, but the bee stings wouldn't penetrate that suit. It didn't matter: by now all sorts of unusual weapons were pointing at the survivor, and they weren't all biotech. Lelic let out a tense breath.

'All we were doing was trying to help you,' he said. 'Now why don't you just come this way and let us get you out of that suit and checked over.' He gestured towards a series of circular organo-ceramic doors up on the equator of the sphere. 'Come on,' he added, beckoning.

The survivor just stood there for a long moment without moving, then took a pace forwards. Followed by another pace. Lelic kept himself always a good distance in front, while the colonists buzzed all around. Henderson walked behind, having furtively produced a short proton cannon adapted into a hand pistol for one of his huge slablike hands. Lelic didn't want any of the energy weapons being brandished to be used here as that would lead to disappointment and unrest. They needed the death match; it was part of their culture. Following Lelic, the man steadily trudged along the base of the sphere then up its side. They all knew where he was going. Everyone watched silently, some with expressions of cruel amusement.

The second ceramic door opened into a big tunnel from the docking sphere. It was the one along which they had led the

154

captive prador. Lelic hit the skin reader control on the door and as it swung open gently, he beckoned again. 'This way.'

Really, this survivor seemed more than capable, so the only preparations required would be the same as those with the prador. The prador young-adult whose name translated as Sfolk had been found inside the severely chewed-up remains of the prador ST dreadnought that had come through some months back. Having snagged him in one of the huge internal spaces of that dreadnought, they had brought him here ready to cut him out of his armoured suit. Unfortunately, he started to revive and, as was the manner of the prador, had become very aggressive. Henderson had made himself a target and apparently fled here, and Sfolk, obviously still operating on instinct rather than intelligence, had followed.

'Through here,' said Lelic, as the ceramic door closed behind.

The space-suited figure just trudged on. Perhaps he was stunned, in shock, just didn't know what he was doing. At the end of the tunnel Lelic went through another ceramic door into a domed ceramic chamber with a further large side door and one smaller door. Still lying on the floor over to one side was Sfolk's armour, edges still gleaming where they had been cut by the diamond tendril belts of the octopus. The chips and dents in the walls caused by Sfolk during the process of removal were only halfway to healing, Lelic noticed, as he propelled himself across the chamber to the small door. Pausing there, he watched the survivor enter the chamber. He then palmed a skin sensor, pulled the small door open and went through, quickly pulling the door closed behind him. Palming another control, he closed the big door into the chamber. Next he pushed his face up against the chain-glass window to see what the suited figure would now do.

The figure just trudged on in, conveniently halting at the centre. Lelic smiled and pulled himself over to the nearby gel console and activated it with a slap. Above it the screen lit to show the survivor now tilting his head to look up at the ceiling as if he knew what was coming. Fingering cell controls, Lelic chose the required program and initiated it. Now he needed to do no more than watch.

A hatch irised open in the apex of the dome and on its thick ribbed stalk the octopus dropped through, its hard tentacles writhing and shimmering along their inner faces with the high-speed traversal of tendril belts of micro diamonds. It engulfed the figure and tried to haul him from the floor but, after a moment, a bio-warning light ignited in the console. For some reason it couldn't lift him up. Lelic quickly altered the program so the octopus could work in situ. More warning lights ignited, then the console stung him and he quickly withdrew his hands. The octopus's frenetic activity continued for a few minutes then it abruptly slumped, as if stunned.

Lelic stared in disbelief. What the hell was that suit made of, that diamond tendrils, which could slice through prador armour, were failing here? He watched as the octopus rose up off the suited man, clenched into a fist as if burned, then retreated into the ceiling, its hatch slamming shut. The man in the space suit still stood where he had been standing before, seemingly un-touched. He turned his head so his blacked-out visor faced the screen view, but then did just nothing at all.

Trent

Trent stepped into the ward and looked around. This was a military hospital, space had been at a premium and most equipment dropped from the ceiling on robotic arms or umbilicals. The patients also had the option of VR entertainment to escape into, so the beds were close together in four neat rows extending the full length of the place, almost like some hospital from centuries in the past. Every one of the two hundred beds here was occupied while wards of the same size on either side of this one were filling up even now. The place buzzed with medical drones, and autodocs were regularly dropping from the ceiling to check each patient systematically. However, the equipment here was doing no more than checking, for not one of these patients had woken up yet.

Pausing just inside the doors, Trent now focused his attention over to one side at a row of three beds in one corner. There were Reece and her young son, Ieran, and in the next bed was her older son, Robert, now with a prosthetic left arm. The enzymic acid had dissolved all his prador additions, and numerous corrections and interventions had been made inside him. He was no longer bloated and his body was rapidly returning to natural human function. The decline of his brain too had been reversed. Cole, meanwhile, had made many alterations to his mind to wipe out the trauma and was confident that Reece would have her child back. Trent moved on.

'Happy now?' asked Sepia, quickly catching up with him.

Trent glanced at her, certain she hadn't seen where he had been looking and that her question was a general one concerning all the shell people. 'I've done what I can for them but wonder if it will be enough.'

'Well, soon enough we'll find out,' said Cole, who had just stepped through the door.

'Time to start reviving some of them?' asked Trent.

'Yes – we can't just leave them like this.'

'It's going to be confusing for them,' interjected Sepia, 'but then perhaps they'll see some novelty in that.'

'Not as confusing as you might suppose,' said Cole. 'I created a limited data package detailing the events that led them here. They know about the enzyme acid used to save their lives, and that they are now aboard a space station.'

'What about the detail?' Trent asked.

'I said limited.'

'Do they know about Cvorn, and the destruction of Sverl's ship?' Trent paused for a second. 'Do they know about Sverl?'

Cole grimaced. 'I left a lot out, since something akin to hero worship of Sverl sits at the heart of what they tried to be.'

'But surely it's better if they do know what he is?'

'It's complicated,' said Cole. 'They'll be aware that they've knowledge they haven't experienced and if I . . . overload them, they'll tend to dismiss a lot of it. Giving them full knowledge about Sverl could tip some of them into paranoid psychosis. Even telling them their present location, this particular station, is risky. Some knowledge needs to be introduced as part of their . . . experience.'

Trent absorbed that, liking the idea that there wouldn't be so much explaining to do as they revived these people, but wishing there had been a way to take them all the way to his idea of sanity, which was not wanting to die or turn themselves into monsters.

'I think we should start with Melissa,' he said.

'Okay,' said Cole, seeming a bit hyped. 'Let's go.' He led the way down one of the aisles and then turned in at a bed. The woman lying on it had been the one whom Trent had first seen aboard this ship, her skin replaced by articulated shell. That was gone now, replaced by a transparent printed-on cell scaffold which already showed blooms of growing dermal cells. Unlike those here who had received artificial limbs and synthetic flesh and skin, she would eventually look completely human. However, right at that moment she looked like a drawing from an ancient book on human anatomy, because most of her underlying muscle lay visible. Blood-filled tubes ran from a heart plug into a pillar detoxifier beside her bed, steadily filtering out prador organics, deactivated nanobots and other dead matter remaining inside her. Attached to her skull was a sleep disc which Cole pressed with his finger. It dropped away and he caught it in his hand, stepping back.

Melissa opened her eyes instantly, then raised her hand and peered at it. With the muscles visible in her face and her eyelids and surrounding skin all but transparent so the whole of each of her eyeballs was visible, it was difficult to read her expression, though Trent thought she frowned. After a moment she sat upright and looked down at herself. She ran a fingertip over the heart plug then looked up and studied each of them in turn.

'So, I'm alive,' she said, her voice phlegmy and somehow disappointed.

Trent felt as if someone had closed a fist inside him and felt the need to respond. 'Being alive, you can now make a choice about whether or not you continue to be so. You've tried to turn yourself into a prador and you've experienced what that ultimately means when enslaved by prador pheromones.' He wanted to add more, but didn't know what to say.

She focused on him. 'Don't you think I made such choices long ago?' She paused for a second then added, 'You arrogant fucker.'

Trent flinched. What kind of response had he expected?

'What would you have done?'

'I would have minded my own business.'

Obviously she wasn't going to be grateful. He glanced at the detoxifying pillar and noted how long its program had to run. 'As far as I can gather –' he glanced at Cole – 'you understand the circumstances that have led you here and you understand much of your situation.' He paused, waiting for a response, but she gave none so he continued, 'One of the station AIs is in the process of repairing and stocking one of the old barracks areas adjacent to this hospital. When you're done here, in twenty minutes or so, a drone will conduct you there. Clothing and food will be supplied and thereafter what you do is your own concern.'

'And if I want to leave this place?'

'Eventually there'll be a way.' Trent winced. 'It may be possible for us to commission one of the ships here, or maybe we'll be able to use the runcible Sverl has set running again.'

'Sverl is here?' she said, her eyes glassy.

Not trusting himself to reply reasonably to that, Trent turned to Cole. 'Let's try another.'

As they headed off to another bed he could feel the woman's gaze boring into his back. Why did he feel disappointed? Surely a person shouldn't do good in the expectation of thanks but out of pure altruism? Or was it truly the case that everything anyone did was essentially based on selfishness?

The next one they revived, a man with artificial legs, arms, jaw and eyes, couldn't have been more grateful. He talked interminably about how, in seeking novelty, he had wanted to transform himself into a prador and how, after spending years in pain and fighting endless infections and rejections, and then experiencing enslavement, he had seen the error of his ways. They recruited him to revive others and tell them about the barracks. By then Sepia had, perhaps, grown bored and headed off about some other task.

'Reece and her children next?' Cole asked.

Trent was grateful he hadn't asked that while Sepia was here
– that would have been uncomfortable. He paused to gaze down
at his space suit with its burns and encrustations and reckoned,
despite its internal sanitizers, he probably didn't smell all that
good. His usual clothes were compressed in a package attached
at the base of his back. He didn't know if they were damaged,
but would check.

'Not yet,' he said, 'but soon.'

Over a number of days, more and more of the shell people
were revived and moved to the barracks, while others were
brought in to occupy their beds. The wards were very busy with
people being led out either by their fellows or small floating guide
drones. Some were as grateful as that second patient, others
were bitter, indifferent, euphoric or hostile. There had been no
standard response, Trent found, and he guessed that was because
they were human. There was, however, a majority response,
because many of them wanted to know about Sverl, about the
prador and what they were doing, which was depressing.

On the third day they had their first suicide when one of the
revived stepped out through an airlock. On the fourth day they
had their first killing, when one of them went berserk and
attacked the patient who had revived him. Luckily it wasn't a
permanent death, since a broken neck here wasn't terminal.

Trent did what he could, but soon found himself tiring of the
involvement. Still he empathized with those around him, but he
no longer found himself inwardly cringing, either at their reactions to being revived, or at the sight of their injuries. He felt
tired, disappointed. He saw that the empathy Penny Royal had
cursed him with was beginning to develop calluses. However,
surely in doing what one believed was the right thing one had to
continue even when the idea palled? Altruism, in the end, was
not about personal satisfaction. Trent, ultimately, looked for that

elsewhere as he found and prepared a family room in the barracks, and analysed other feelings he had never been accustomed to.

Lelic

Four octopuses had failed and the figure in the suit just stood untouched in the preparation chamber. Resting his webbed hand on the gel console, reluctant to push it in again and perhaps end up getting stung, which was the usual response when you asked too much of such biotech, Lelic was both puzzled and annoyed.

'They're getting restive,' said Henderson.

Lelic glanced round. The man was a little restive himself, the slabs of limpet muscle covering his body clenching and unclenching as if in search of a safe wall to stick him to. The other colonists had been making increasingly sarcastic and annoyed queries over the last few days. They wanted their fight. Bets and bids had been revised after the failure of the first octopus, then as the other three failed they had turned frenetic. Many colonists had over-extended themselves, some so far as to lose even their ships if things didn't go their way. Fights between colonists had broken out, and there had been two deaths.

'What do you think it is?' Henderson asked.

'I've tried some analysis,' Lelic replied. 'The suit is as standard as it looks but has some kind of hardfield reinforcing at the surface. I'm not sure those readings about an occupant are true, either. They could just be projections or some kind of chameleonware.'

'But what's inside the suit?' Henderson asked.

'I just don't know. Seems it might still be some highly augmented human with some defences we haven't seen before, else why the suit in the first place?' He shrugged. 'It doesn't matter how augmented he is; he'll have to come out of that suit at some point.'

'So what do we do?'

'I think we're just going to have to send him into the arena against Sfolk.' Lelic paused, not liking to be coerced like this but not seeing any other choices. 'With any luck, he won't just stand there doing nothing while Sfolk attacks . . .'

'Probably means we'll lose Sfolk.'

'Yes, probably.'

Just to try and calm things, Lelic had sent in their last normal snatched from the Graveyard. Sfolk had made short work of the woman, despite her ceramic armour and shearfield blades: torn her apart and eaten her very quickly. He was hungry, and almost certainly was getting hungrier by now. He was also a valuable fighter with high entertainment value and Lelic didn't want to lose him. He shrugged. He would have to accept it and, anyway, The Zone would surely provide another prador in time.

'Tell them that we'll have a bout in five hours,' said Lelic. 'When it's done we'll expel this —' he gestured at the figure on the screen – 'from the station.' He turned away and with a flick of his tail propelled himself along the tunnel, Henderson clumping and sucking along behind.

Lelic returned to his personal cyst within the station and there accessed the combined bio and crystal computing available to him. They had no AIs here like the Polity – their U-space-capable ships used child minds purchased from the Kingdom – but the brain of the station still contained more than enough data and processing. He ran searches to try and find out what it was they had picked up with that wreckage.

Over the course of four hours he discovered a host of frightening possibilities. It could be the kind of war drone the Polity had used to penetrate prador ships – leaving it to be picked up then, once inside the ship, springing into action. It might be a Golem, but that didn't account for how it resisted the octopuses. There were numerous other possibilities for dense-tech weapons packed inside that suit. As his time ran out, Lelic decided he would just have to stick with the plan. After an initial burst of hostility the man didn't seem to be much of a threat. The thing to do would be just to get him into the arena somehow, and see what transpired. They often used direct evacuation to space to clear the mess out of the arena so it should be easy enough to expel the man once the fight was over, if need be.

Exiting his cyst, Lelic next headed straight for the arena, traversed a tubeway up into the arena sphere, grav taking hold of him as he came out onto the viewing platform. For obvious reasons, the first being his lack of legs, he didn't like gravity this high. However, without it there was always a problem keeping the fighters contained. Also, they were used to grav and performed better in it. Here Lelic really had to use his auxiliary tentacles to propel himself, but there were many handholds available, including the rail overlooking the arena, and the floor was shark-slimed to make things easier.

Already most of the station population of three hundred or so was gathering in the wide variety of couches, chairs, suspension frames and nets in the stand. The stand bar was doing a roaring trade – only a few of the adaptations here had lost the ability to appreciate alcohol. Even Mr Pace was at the back, the skeleton at the feast, as an old expression would have had it. It was unusual to see him at these events because they weren't usually to his taste. Lelic gazed at him for a long moment then turned away and leaned over the rail and looked down.

The survivor was now standing in the middle of the arena

floor and appeared mildly curious about the holocams floating all around him.

'No sensocording,' said Henderson, coming up to squat at Lelic's side.

He was right, of course. Usually they would either tap into the aug a victim wore or install a new one. That way they got a full sensory recording of what it was like to face a prador in a place like this, and be torn apart. It wasn't the sort of sensocording that was to Lelic's taste but some people were prepared to pay a lot of money to experience . . . death.

'How did you get him in there?' Lelic asked.

'Just opened the door and he walked through,' Henderson replied.

Lelic shivered then said, 'Okay, then it's time to bring in Sfolk.' Lelic slid round Henderson to the short walkway leading out to the control pulpit overlooking the arena. As soon as he reached the gel console he checked his feeds. Bidding and betting had attained an almost insane level and, seeing the amounts being wagered, he wondered for a moment about keeping this space-suited figure. That was, if it defeated Sfolk, which now seemed highly likely. Next he ensured the holocams and anosmic recorders were getting everything, then pressed his finger down in the gel to the door control cell. He paused. Gazing down into the arena, he saw the space man turn to face the ceramic door behind which the prador Sfolk lurked. How could he know, unless he had senses beyond human normal?

'Henderson . . .' Lelic said.

'Cannons are targeted,' Henderson said, limpet-stuck to the walkway behind. 'If he tries to get out of the arena we'll fry him. But don't you think if he was Golem he would have done something by now?'

Lelic dipped his head in agreement and pressed the cell. As the clamshell door began to draw open a prador claw punched at the gap, so it seemed Sfolk was eager . . . well no, that wasn't quite right. Sfolk had shown a strange reluctance to attack the opponents set against him in the arena at first but, eventually, hunger had taken its toll. Sfolk was starving and had lost any unpradorish moral qualms, knowing dinner awaited.

'Eight will be pleased,' a voice hissed in Lelic's ear.

'What?' he turned and peered at Henderson.

'I didn't say anything,' Henderson replied.

Lelic turned back as the door finally revealed the young-adult prador. It was difficult to tell a starving prador from a well-fed one since creatures with carapaces didn't tend to get any thinner. Only their eagerness gave them away. Sfolk charged straight out towards the suited figure, claws snipping at the air. Lelic quickly put a bet down on the duration of the action upon seeing the confident way the man just stood waiting.

At the last moment Sfolk abruptly skidded to a halt, mandibles clattering and drool dribbling. Then he froze, and uncharacteristically took a few paces back.

What's this?

Maybe Sfolk's intelligence had kicked in and he had questioned the wisdom of charging up to someone who didn't seem inclined to run away. But then instinct took over again and the prador suddenly shot forwards and snapped a claw closed around the man's hips. *Now for some action,* Lelic thought, and then felt as if he had been cheated when the prador hoisted the man up and he just hung there doing nothing. The prador then brought in his other claw, carefully, as if he didn't want to damage his prospective meal, closed it on the fabric of the space suit and tugged. Lelic stared, with his mouth hanging open, as a suit that had resisted the diamond tendrils of four octopuses tore like wet

166

paper. The whole suit parted as if eager to be completely open, and the helmet bounced away. Sfolk then just stood there holding the sagging remains, while black crystalline matter poured out onto the floor of the arena.

Was that it? Had the suit simply been motorized, had it been responding to some residual programming? No, that couldn't be, because it was of a very old design, wasn't armoured and showed no signs of motors at the joints. Lelic stared and tried not to think about some of the wartime horrors he had recently been researching.

The crowd was booing now, throwing beer tubes and vodka bags, along with various unpleasant items exuded from their wide variety of bodies. Lelic didn't have to try very hard to judge the mood of his people and knew there would be trouble after such a disappointing bout. He quickly tugged a set of cells into reach and called up the latest status report on one of the biomech killers, which displayed in a stratum in the gel. They were occasionally used, but Lelic was reluctant to set one in motion. If Lelic sent in a biomech, he would have lost two contestants – and it would be such a shame to wipe out such a useful killer, no matter how satisfying his people would find that. Still undecided, Lelic peered down into the arena again and saw something strange.

The black crystalline powder that had poured from the suit Sfolk had discarded had not settled. It hung just below the suit like a stratum of fog, and now it was swirling and rising. When it was about ten feet from the arena floor there came a thump and it exploded in every direction, dispersing as it went. Lelic immediately tasted dry grittiness in his mouth and something niggled inside his lungs. He slid back from the gel console and coughed. What the hell was that? Glancing round, he saw that others in the crowd were coughing and hacking too, though

167

the noises some of them were making weren't easily identifiable as such. He leaned against the rail beside the pulpit walkway, gazing down, then abruptly realized Sfolk was directly beneath him, peering up. The prador did not look anywhere near as agitated as he should be. Did he know something?

Lelic watched the young-adult as, after a moment, it turned away from him and ambled over to the arena wall below the main stand. Something odd was going on over there because the ceramic armour of the wall had acquired a thread-work across its surface, almost like some sort of mould. Sfolk reached out with one claw and tapped it against the tough material before pulling that claw back and stabbing it forwards. The ceramic just shattered and the prador's claw punched straight through.

But for the occasional coughs, a dead silence fell in the arena. Then all at once, everyone was in motion. Lelic looked round at Henderson, who was harrumphing like a worn-out piston engine, his limpet muscles clenching up each time.

'Henderson, shoot him – aim for his legs,' Lelic instructed.

Henderson turned watery black eyes on him then reached with one spade-like hand into the fleshy folds of his body to extract his proton cannon. He took steady aim, but then lowered his weapon as another fit of coughing racked him. Meanwhile, Sfolk had smashed another hole and was lining up for another, making a row of them.

'Henderson!'

'Awright, awright,' said the man. He took aim at the prador, squinting, shrugged to loosen his shoulders and raised his other hand to support his wrist, then he regretfully pulled the trigger.

The proton weapon fizzed and smoked. Henderson convulsed and squawked and luckily his grip slackened and he dropped the weapon. Others were not so lucky with theirs. A blast amidst the main audience tore a green-skinned ectomorph in half and tipped Dorrel and one other over the rail to land in the arena. A woman staggered along beside the rail, clutching a laser carbine, jerking as if in palsy, steam rising from the webbing of flesh between the spines sprouting from her body.

Down in the arena Sfolk turned from demolishing the wall and scuttled over to Dorrel and the other extremadapt struggling to regain their feet. Dorrel, who had always generated such fear and respect, tried to fend him off with tentacles as thick as a normal's leg. Sfolk just snipped and tore and left the big extremadapt writhing and bleeding. Then he turned away dismissively to snatch up the smaller victim, and squatted to start dismembering him, feeding chunks of bloody flesh into his mandibles. It looked horribly to Lelic as if Sfolk was now the audience, watching the show while shoving tasty snacks into his mouth. Another explosion ensued and, this being far too much for the substantially weakened wall below, the whole seating stand began to sag. Then, in an avalanche of breaking metal and screaming, people started falling into the arena.

Lelic hadn't survived for as long as he had as the leader of this colony because he was stupid. Quite obviously some sort of nanoweapon had been deployed here and things weren't going their way. It was time to flee. The part of the stand adjacent to the pulpit had not yet collapsed and from there he could return the way he had come, get aboard his old tug and get the hell out of this space station. He shifted back from the console and felt the walkway crunch underneath his piscine body like shell ice, peered down to see cracks spreading and then, just for a second, he was weightless as the walkway and pulpit simply collapsed into the arena.

Riss

The *Lance* was now in good order: refuelled, restocked and all power storage up to maximum, everything on the bridge in working order and nothing nasty lurking in the ship's computing. Spear had also managed to load up the armoury with railgun slugs and some other expendable items, like chaff, from Sverl, who had even provided some chemical explosive missiles. However, Sverl had informed the man that no CTDs were available aboard the station. Riss didn't believe that for a minute.

'Everything is ready and now it's time to go,' she said. 'So why are we still here?'

He sat in his chair in the bridge with the screen fabric alive all around him, watching all the activity out in the construction bay. There were fewer of those shrub-like growths and 'structor pods now and the robot ecology of the station appeared to be gradually returning to normal.

'We have a few things to finish up,' he said. 'I need to find out what Trent, Sepia and Cole intend to do.'

'Why?' asked Riss. 'Why should you concern yourself about them any more than the shell people?'

Sepia and Cole were people he had known only briefly, and though his association with Trent was more complicated, he hadn't really known him for much longer. The man was procrastinating, just like he had on Masada.

Ignoring the question, he continued, 'And I have to get the spine back from Sverl.'

'What for?' asked Riss. 'You were all for tossing it out of an airlock at one point.'

'Because it's integral,' he snapped.

'I do have further diagnostic checks to make too,' interjected Flute.

Riss managed to suppress the urge to make some snappy reply to that. Obviously the ship mind had seen a chance to side with Spear against Riss.

'Shut up, the both of you.' Spear stood up and headed for his cabin.

Riss watched him go, then applied to Flute for access to the ship's sensors and com gear rather than use her usual route through Spear's aug.

'Why should I trust you?' asked Flute.

'Why should *I* trust *you*?' Riss shot back.

'Sverl no longer controls me.'

'So you say.'

'I can prove it.'

'Go on then.'

Flute immediately sent a list of channel access codes and in her mind Riss gazed at them in disbelief. She rose up off the floor and slid up onto the console round Spear's chair and opened her black eye. Surely, this could not be real? Would the second-child mind be so stupid?

With all her penetration gear operating, Riss carefully opened those channels and saw that they opened directly into Flute's mind. Soon she understood that Flute had given her unrestricted access. She could do anything to or see anything in the second-child's mind. She began sorting data and connections, delving deep for hidden protocols – hidden orders that Flute would have no option but to obey – and found none. She next ran at high speed back through the mind's memory, replaying in detail Flute's thoughts during the time of his betrayal, when he had almost sent the *Lance* to its destruction by Cvorn's ST dreadnought. There Riss began to feel discomfited, for Flute had been

171

unable to disobey Sverl's orders, yet had fought with every resource available not to put them in danger. Later Riss replayed the exchange between Flute and Sverl during which the mind had demanded and got complete freedom from Sverl. Finally she withdrew, but hesitated on closing off access.

Flute had nearly killed them and, at the time, Riss had sworn to herself that he would pay for that. Now, here was the second-child's mind, thought translated to crystal, utterly open to her. Until this moment she had only inspected its contents, but the option was there for her to do more. She could insert a whole ecology of destructive viruses and worms if she wanted. She could route through it and shut down power to it, she could set off the ejection routine and send it at high speed from the ship, ensuring its course took it straight into the armour of that dreadnought in the final construction bay out there. She could, right now, kill Flute.

But where had her tendency to destructive action taken her? It had taken her into a darkness that had led to Penny Royal and empty hate, and it had finally led her to Sverl screaming as his body dissolved. Riss withdrew and closed down those channels.

'Enough?' Flute enquired.

'Enough,' Riss replied, 'but I've no intention of changing the contentious nature of our relationship.'

'I wouldn't have it any other way,' said the mind.

Riss now, again, applied for sensor and com access, and Flute granted it instantly. Riss then used the com system to link into the growing and increasingly sane system of Room 101, first passing the inspection of a local AI and, surprisingly, being allowed access elsewhere. She first ranged to one end of the station to inspect through cams the work going on around the U-space drive and check on any data concerning it she could find. Surprisingly, there wasn't as much work going on there as she had expected. Next, tracing those second-children that had been at work there, she found them otherwise employed around the bubble-metal plant now producing Penny Royal's hardfield generators. Sure, it was understandable that Sverl had directed resources first to defence, but why had he diverted such resources to one of the runcibles?

Riss now inspected the cargo runcibles concerned, seeing the system checks and components tests were reaching an end, and again tried to figure out why Sverl had wanted the thing operating. Was he now so cosmopolitan that he was prepared to accept visitors from the Polity? Was he suffering some delusion in which Polity AIs were perfectly accepting of a prador controlling a major weapons-producing station like this? Perhaps Riss was just missing something.

She moved then to generally inspecting the rest of the station and found that Sverl had not rid himself of all the masses of tentacle trees of 'structor pods but had found plenty of employment for them. All around the station they were steadily chewing up wreckage and useless structures mindlessly constructed by the technology that had escaped control here and conveying it to various furnaces and reprocessing plants. Riss was enjoying herself watching a great mass of them grazing on metallic moulds spread across the hull when Flute abruptly interrupted.

'We have a problem,' said the mind.

'What now?' Riss snapped, feeling less concerned about Flute's loyalty than before, but by no means intending to get all buddy-buddy with the thing.

'Sverl informs me that if we want to leave we have to leave shortly.'

'Why's that then?'

Flute supplied a link to a telescope array on the hull of the station, plus coordinates. Riss winced when she saw what had arrived, then mentally shrugged. She hadn't exactly been made for a quiet life.

Crowther

The disconnection routine was fast, and here, with numerous radio and laser links all around him to perpetually update his connection with the Well Head's systems, Crowther hardly felt any reduction in his overall intelligence. This was a bit of a problem because lately the data output of Layden's Sink had waned, strangely, as if it was taking a breather, as if it was pausing on the cusp of some change. And this left Crowther bored.

Exiting his interface sphere, he took a route through the space station he hadn't taken for a while. As expected, when he had taken just a few paces along a particular access tube, Owl contacted him.

'You've thought of some new addition?' Owl enquired, tone utterly neutral.

'No.'

'Perhaps you are considering replacing some of the shielding with one of the new gravity-forged meta-materials?'

'No.'

'Maybe some radical redesign of the recording core?'

Crowther sighed and replied, 'Of course not – it's as good as it's ever going to be.'

Owl's tone might have been neutral but its sarcasm laced every word. It knew him far too well and was aware that he had started to get a little stir-crazy. It also knew that he always paid a visit down here when mulling over what to do about that.

Reaching a double sliding door, he sent an instruction and it opened ahead of him, revealing itself to be a yard's thickness of laminated armour, superconducting meshes and other materials. In the long cylindrical room ahead, braced by shatter-clamps, rested a long missile of gleaming blue metal. As he gazed at the thing, Crowther tossed up a schematic of it in his mind. The well-hopper contained crystal storage, internally braced with meta-material shear planes and micro-hardfields. Its engine was a single solid-burn fuser with thrust that would leave a prador kamikaze standing, complemented by a Laumer drive – expensive and difficult to manufacture. And its structure, enclosing these, along with solid-state fuser-reactors and hardfield projectors, was also solid through and through: layered meta-materials forged on the surface of a brown dwarf. The thing was practically indestructible, which was what it had to be to escape a close encounter with the event horizon of a black hole.

The Well Head, being such a valuable asset, possessed every safety precaution possible. It still had the U-space drive that had brought it here to this system, though it was considered unlikely ever to be used again because, besides the strange data issuing from the black hole, the studies and experiments to be conducted here had already backed up a thousand years into the future. However, the drive was maintained as one of those safety precautions. The Well Head had all those other engines capable of taking it away from the black hole, and it had all its protections but, if something went seriously wrong here and all of those became unusable, the Well Head could still jump away. In the end, however, the Well Head itself was disposable, and Crowther and Owl did not consider themselves to be.

If everything began to go badly wrong here and even the U-space drive became unusable, which was always a distinct possibility when sitting close to one of the most destructive forces in the universe, Crowther and Owl could at least escape by runcible. That was the theory. In reality, if everything else was falling apart, it was highly likely that the runcible would go down as well. The well-hopper had started as a project to improve the durability of the probes they occasionally shot close to the black hole and had grown from there. It had then turned into a way of gathering data while skimming the event horizon, but that idea had soon been abandoned when it became evident that though the crystal storage might survive such a close encounter, the hopper's sensors would not. It had been Owl's idea, shortly after the EMR blast front resulting from the hole's digesting of a red dwarf had knocked out more systems than was supposed to be possible: make it their escape of last resort.

The theory was that if everything went completely wrong and the Well Head was being sucked into the black hole, both Owl and Crowther could download to the crystal storage aboard the hopper. Crowther wasn't entirely in love with the idea because the transference would have to be fast and would require the destructive conversion of everything he was into quantum data. Still, it was survival of a sort. There protected from the titanic forces in play about the black hole, the fuser in combination with the Laumer engine just might be able to fling them both out intact.

'No, I can think of nothing to add,' said Crowther.

'Nothing worth disassembling,' Owl said. 'At present rates of technological advance I calculate another solstan year until the next upgrade.'

Schematic and statistical analyses faded from Crowther's mind, and boredom returned. As was usual when he came here, Crowther found it easier to get some perspective. The research here at Layden's Sink was lined up for centuries, his own life had a span that could only be measured when it ended and that only seemed likely to happen by mischance – the kind of mischance he and Owl had built the well-hopper to avoid. Great vistas of possibility opened for him and the boredom fled as he initiated other levels of his mind and called up other interests.

'History,' he said.

'Ah,' said Owl. 'When are you going?'

'Very soon, I think.'

'Earth?'

Yes, it was time to go to Earth and clarify some of his research into the histories of the worlds falling into Layden's Sink, there to be torn apart and erased forever.

7

Lelic

The air was full of smoke, the smells of cooking flesh, screams and crashes. Lying amidst tangled wreckage, Lelic gazed at where sharp metal had sliced through above his tail fluke right to the vertebrae, and was just too terrified to feel any pain. He smothered a dry cough then peered at the blood on his hand. He tried to convince himself that perhaps this was a result of the fall but, as he struggled to free himself, suspected it had more to do with that black dust he had breathed in.

The collapse of the stand had lured the prador out of its squat and now, having consumed all but one foot of the spectator he had grabbed and with such an excess of meat available, Sfolk had decided it was time to play. While the prador made selective amputations to stop his victims running away, then concentrated on disembowelling Dorrel, Lelic hauled himself out of the wreckage of the pulpit and attached walkway and, using his auxiliary tentacles, dragged himself towards the armoured door through which the apparently empty space suit had walked. The prador hadn't noticed him, but he knew that if it did his death would likely be more protracted than that of the screaming Dorrel. Sfolk was an intelligent creature and knew very well who had been running the show here.

Reaching the door, Lelic auged into the station system, and there found chaos. The station's computer was both fighting some sort of incursion and trying to relay power to critical life-support, because something had also tapped into the reactors and was sucking power from them at an ever-increasing rate. However, access to the arena controls remained available, probably because whatever had attacked them had knocked out every weapon and did not need to do any more. Lelic accessed the door and opened it, crawled through, but when he tried to close it the system just crashed. He turned and snapped out a tentacle to tug on the door, simultaneously using his other tentacle to hit a manual control. Even as he did this he saw Sfolk spin round, discarding the great mass of purple intestines he had drawn out of Dorrel, and start charging across.

With the door clicking home, Lelic flopped away as fast as he could, flesh hanging open by his tail fluke. He glanced up and saw an octopus partially extruded but then, thankfully, it retracted again. He concentrated on going just as fast as he could, aware that if the prador got through he was finished. A crash resounded behind him and he couldn't help but glance back. The door had closed but the ceramic was crazed with cracks. It had definitely been some sort of nano-attack that had penetrated surrounding materials and turned them brittle. It would not take Sfolk long to get through that door. Another fit of dry coughing hit him and he spat more blood. His chest felt tight and painful and his breathing wasn't so good. Perhaps he was right: perhaps he had broken a rib and punctured his lung. He crawled to the door from this chamber and palmed the control beside that, and felt weak with relief as it swung open.

The tunnel outside was grav free so now he could travel faster, finally propelling himself out into the docking sphere. Other extremadapts had obviously managed to escape and were flapping, crawling and hopping to their ships. Lelic just concentrated on getting to his own ship, first palming the second door control once he was through, and then satisfied to see it closing.

Ahead of him he could see the bulky and bloody shape of some-one down on his knees, coughing, and he deliberately moved to give the man a wide berth.

'Lelic . . . do you hear it?' It was Henderson, the limpet muscles on his face horribly pale as he tried and failed to unstick himself from the floor. 'It's whispering –' he coughed and blood bubbled from his mouth – 'to me.'

'What is?' Lelic asked, not sure he wanted to know the answer.

'It's . . . here,' Henderson rasped.

From behind came another crash, and Lelic glanced back at the second door. It appeared undamaged. He hoped the nano-attack hadn't reached it yet.

'We need to get to the ship and out of here,' he said, and kept moving. With any luck Henderson, who was in a terrible state, wouldn't be able to follow him. Lelic did not want the man bringing whatever ailed him aboard.

'Oh,' said Henderson. Lelic halted and turned. The man had rolled face-down, then after a moment levered himself up onto his hands and knees, his bulbous body still touching the deck, his face pointing down and bloody drool trailing from his mouth. Then his body shuddered, limpet muscles clenching, his squat head came up and he emitted a gurgling scream. Black spikes stabbed out of his back, his chest and up beside his thick neck. It was as if the head of a big glassy morning star had sprouted inside his chest. His scream died, as did he, while the spikes continued growing, blood running down them. They stabbed into the floor, held him still in the same position, one of them exiting his mouth, then began to lift him up, leaving him like some bug at the intersection of numerous pins.

As Lelic towed himself backwards in utter horror, the whole construct shrugged itself and, in tough muscular chunks, Henderson fell out of it. Resting on the deck now was a star, a thing like a plant, but formed of black crystal. As he watched, it exuded a silvery tentacle from its core. Lelic half expected this thing to start sucking up Henderson's remains but, from where it touched the deck, silvery veins began spreading out in the ceramal and construction coral.

As Lelic turned towards his ship he paused, seeing more of these things scattered all around the dock sphere, some seemingly crouching over bloody remains, others floating amidst slowly falling clouds of the same. He finished his turn and, using his tentacles like legs and flapping his tail fluke hard, no matter how much it hurt, drove himself to the airlock door of his tug and palmed it open. Inside, sobbing for breath, he coughed and spattered blood on the inner wall. It was a rib. It was a broken rib. It *had* to be a broken rib.

Once he had closed the inner door of the airlock he auged into his ship's system and commanded an emergency launch. The ship was already on the move, turning through the wall of the sphere, by the time he reached his small bridge. Gazing through the screen, he could see more of those star things scattered about the dock sphere, but none of his people. Then he saw a ceramic door swing open and Sfolk come hurrying out, skidding on blood all across the deck, throwing himself into a long bound in the low gravity. Too late now.

The sphere hatch closed behind as, on thrusters, Lelic took his ship down the throat of a long tunnel towards the first set of space doors. He wondered how many of the others had escaped, but knew he wouldn't know until he was outside. He sent a signal to the space doors, half expecting that he would need to use the grab arm to tear them open, but they obediently slid apart. As the doors closed behind and his ship entered what was effectively a massive airlock, Lelic rubbed at his aching chest. He needed to get his emergency autodoc out and working on him, but first he had to get away from the station. After an interminable delay, the massive airlock evacuated most of its air, then the outer doors opened. Cautiously, Lelic guided his ship out.

Five miles out, Lelic turned the ship so he could watch the station through his chain-glass screen. As ever it looked like the case of a giant caddis fly. Scanning near space he soon found that the objects drifting away from the axial spin of his erstwhile home were debris. The thing was coming apart and, even as he watched, some big chunk blew away under internal pressure and spewed atmosphere out into vacuum. Then he saw that one other had escaped, a large egg-shaped craft with three U-nacelles extending from its equator. Somehow Lelic wasn't surprised to see Mr Pace's ship steadily moving away. But at least that fucking Sfolk would die in there. However, even as he thought that, the whispers denied it.

'What?' He looked around inside his ship, sure someone had just been speaking to him, then rubbed at his chest, which felt as if it was full of broken glass.

The station continued to disintegrate and hurl chunks of itself out into vacuum. An algae storage tank near one end exploded, spilling a green fog, then something else blew up at the centre of the station and cut it in half. Next, out of one of those halves bloomed a black crystalline flower, other smaller fragments of blackness zooming in towards it and sticking, the thing growing larger and somehow more solid than everything around it. Lelic gaped. Nano-attack? This thing was like nothing he knew about or had researched. As he watched, he suddenly realized his chest didn't hurt any more. It was because he was keeping still. It was a broken rib . . .

Then suddenly he couldn't breathe as hot agony expanded from a point deep inside him, just before a black spine stabbed out beside his keel bone and kept growing. He managed one convulsion and tried to reach for that spine as if he might pluck it out. Other spines shot out of his body, one of them impaling his arm through his wrist.

He died to the sound of whispers.

Trent

The younger boy, Ieran, all energy and excitement, had dodged through the scattering of shell people to the dropshaft and back again. He then grabbed hold of his mother's hand. When the boy, Robert, stepped over beside him and grasped his hand, Trent didn't know what to do. This wasn't any image he had ever had in his mind of the ruthless gangland enforcer Trent Sobel. But at least Robert wasn't as active as Ieran, just walked along beside him, gazing with curiosity at the shell people.

'So,' said Reece, 'we're aboard an out-Polity space station now . . .'

'We are,' Trent agreed, fiddling with his shirt. Before bringing her out of hibernation he had felt the need to shed his space suit and clean himself and his clothes. He still felt vulnerable without the suit, though, remembering how this hospital had been so quickly torn apart before.

Reece pursed her lips. 'Hardly what I was hoping for when I went into hibernation.'

Trent shrugged. Since she'd woken up he'd detailed events, as he understood them, to date. He was shocked when halfway through his story she whipped back the heat sheet and climbed naked out of bed to check on her children. She'd been delighted and tearful to hear Robert's voice, apparently for the first time in months. Then, slyly noting Trent's discomfort, she had enquired about some clothing. Now, like her two children, she wore trousers, shirt and slippers from a hospital fabricator.

'But the situation is much better than it could have been.' She smiled.

They reached the dropshaft, the wash of the irised gravity field tugging at them as the shell people ahead stepped into it. Trent moved to step in next but was halted by a tug on his hand. He glanced down at Robert and saw the doubt there.

'It's okay,' Trent said as Reece and Ieran moved past them into the shaft and descended. 'See?'

Robert nodded solemnly and allowed Trent to tug him into the shaft. They descended easily and stepped out into the high-ceilinged corridor leading into the barracks.

'This way.' He led them off, stepping round shell people who were peering at slips of memory paper they had been given in the hospital and studying the directions signs. Branching from this main corridor were others at regular intervals, doors all the way along them leading into spartan suites of rooms that had been restored by Sverl's robots so they at least had beds and washing facilities. Food and drinks beyond just water could be obtained in a communal area, while other fabricating machines were being moved in too, in maybe a few days, to provide a bit more beyond bare necessities. However, Trent had felt he owed these three more than that.

'Here,' he told them, finally arriving before the door he had been looking for.

Family apartments in the barracks were a rarity since soldiers during the war hadn't fought in family units, but there were these few along this corridor. Reaching into his pocket, Trent took out a key stick and pointed it at the door, which opened. Before they stepped into the room beyond he gestured to a palm lock. 'That's not been set yet so you can set it up to respond only to you. Do you know how to do that?'

'Do I look like an idiot?' Reece responded.

'I guess not.' Trent stepped back and waved them in. 'There's a console inside with com – I've input my radio code so you can get in contact with me at any time.' He pointed to the com button on the shoulder of his long ersatz leather coat. 'I've left you some food and some other items you might need – things will be better later on.' He turned away.

'Where do you think you're going?' she asked.

He turned back. 'I was just going to leave you to settle in.'

'No, you're not,' she said, stepping into the apartment. Trent followed.

The main middle room contained a kitchenette, with a table and chairs fabricated by robot from bubble-metal. It had been the best Trent could do, thus far. On the table lay packages of printed bread and thermal beakers of soup – all from the hospital fabricators.

'The boys' room is there.' He pointed to a door then walked over and opened it. As Reece came to stand at his shoulder he gestured to the bunk beds he'd rigged up, along with a console, screen and a couple of VR visors and body sensors he had managed to scavenge. The two boys looked inside then stepped back. They both looked tired now, Robert because his body was still recovering – Trent had seen this with the shell people – and Ieran because his short-charge batteries had just run out. Trent next showed them the washroom with its shower, toilet and other items he'd managed to find: hundred-year-old sonic toothbrushes, a biotronic soap dispenser and towels of cellulose fibre. Then Reece's bedroom, with a bubble-metal dressing table scattered with items he'd found in a locker here: an intellifibre hairbrush, a bottle of some ancient perfume, a powerfab make-up kit.

'Very nice,' she said.

He was glad she sounded sincere because he really didn't want to point out how few such items like this remained in the barracks and how quickly they were being snatched up. She turned and gazed at him very directly. 'Let's eat.'

It was utterly strange and disconcerting for him to sit at a table with a woman and two children. The last time he remembered sitting round a table like this had been with Gabriel and Spear aboard the *Moray Firth*. A lot had happened since then. They ate in silence at first: opening the soup beakers and bread packets and just concentrating on that. Robert was the first to break the silence.

'What games have we got?' he asked.

'They're very old.' Trent shrugged. 'I don't recognize them, but they're mostly about blowing up prador.' As he finished saying it, he wished he could reverse time. These were people who had lived in a society whose members had wanted to turn themselves into prador. He looked at Reece, worried, but she was biting her thumb, trying not to laugh.

'Good,' said Robert, with feeling.

'But there'll be no games for you right away,' said Reece. 'Sleep first.' She studied Ieran, who, having eaten half his soup and a large chunk of bread, was now sitting with his head bowed, swaying slightly. 'For both of you.'

'Do you want some "mummy time"?' Robert asked and, tired though he looked, still ducked fast enough to avoid the lump of bread she threw at him.

'Right, bed,' she said, it being evident that they had finished now. She stood up and herded them to their room and, while she dealt with them in there, Trent finished his soup and then tidied up the mess, dropping it into a disposal chute that folded out of the wall. He felt baffled as he did this; could not quite equate this domestic scene with its location and everything he had gone through to arrive here. As the chute closed and machinery in the wall ground up the waste and piped it away, he felt the overpowering urge to head for the door and go. Yet, at the same time, he also felt rooted in this place; events just out of his control.

'Do you know how long it's been for me?' Reece asked, returning from the boys' bedroom.

'What?' asked Trent, turning from his contemplation of the wall.

'Four years,' she replied, then, holding up her wrist, 'and no nascuff.'

'What?' Trent repeated, wondering why the addition of conscience and empathy seemed to have also lumbered him with gauche embarrassment.

'Don't be thick, Trent.' She ran a finger down the stick seam of her shirt to reveal those pert little breasts he had seen in the hospital, but of course the situation was very different now. After shedding her shirt she pushed down her trousers, kicked them off, then balled both items in one hand. 'Are you getting the message now?'

'I think so,' Trent replied, feeling some return of his usual calm.

She wrapped herself round him and kissed him, running the fingers of one hand through his hair. After a moment she pulled back, took hold of his hand and began leading him to her bedroom. At that point he decided enough was enough. He swept her up and over one shoulder carried her into the bedroom and tossed her down on the bed.

'Ooh, aren't you big and strong,' she said, tossing her clothes across the room. She then turned over and poked her arse up at him. 'Have I been bad? Do you think you should spank me?' Over the ensuing hours he soon learned that Reece was nowhere near as delicate as she looked, and a lot more aggressive.

Sverl

As Bsectil disconnected the cable from within Sverl's skeletal body, Sverl felt the spine trying to re-establish connections electromagnetically, and denied it. While the thing had been a very useful tool and could continue to be very useful, he no longer *needed* it. It didn't belong to him and it fitted in Penny Royal's story in the hands of Thorvald Spear. Sverl also felt glad to be rid of the thing because he felt sure that the power it offered, just as with all such pivotal artefacts, came at a price.

'Take it to Spear,' he said, handing the thing over. 'And hurry.'

Spear had to leave this station, and soon – he felt certain of that too. Meanwhile, he had other, bigger concerns. He now linked to and gazed through a telescope array on the station's hull. The images it brought to him were perfectly clear, but of course that was to be expected even with only the intensity of visible light out there, and this array used more than that. The two dreadnoughts were lozenges of gold-coloured metal two miles long sprouting sensor spines and towers, picked out in the halo of the glare from their drive torches. The twenty attack ships were more difficult to make out since their material was just a spit away from being a hundred per cent light absorbing. Remembering Arrowsmith and his love of human analogies, Sverl felt these ships resembled crows, with wings folded back as they dived towards some tasty carrion. This Polity fleet, a small one by wartime standards, had appeared some distance out and was now approaching on fusion drive. Maybe they hadn't wanted to put themselves straight into the middle of this system when there might still be King's Guard about. Or maybe the captains and AIs controlling the fleet were just being sensibly cautious. But it was also worrying just how easily they were taking this. It seemed that while they considered Sverl – in control of Room 101 – a threat, they were confident enough of dealing with him at their leisure.

'Report anomalies,' Sverl now instructed the station's new runcible AI.

'Spoon fluctuations and constant requests for connection,' the AI replied.

Sverl peered through cams in the area. Within the giant octagonal frame of the old cargo runcible a meniscus now shimmered. The requests for connections were just an automatic protocol from runcibles in the Polity, so Sverl wasn't reading anything suspicious into that just yet. Nevertheless he would allow no connections because once made they would be onerous to break and, what's more, the AIs of the Polity would become aware of this new destination. After that, the next travellers likely to come through would be heavily armed war drones and Sparkind, or a world-busting CTD.

'Nothing else?' Sverl asked.

'No local jump anomalies,' the AI replied.

So those ships hadn't yet fired any U-jump missiles. Perhaps they were waiting until they were within a properly effective firing range for their other weapons, which would be in twelve hours. Or, more likely, they had monitoring buoys in underspace and now knew that such missiles would be ineffective. If they fired them the result would be a brief U-space disturbance here and the reading of a mass departure through the runcible as the missile dropped through it into non-existence.

Twelve hours . . .

Sverl's attention now strayed to that tank, once used for foaming up molten metal and inert gases to make bubble-metal, but now used for an entirely different purpose. The thing hung at the intersection of eight I-beams, and numerous pipes and power feeds, and was now crawling with most of Sverl's second-children as, under Bsorol's instructions, they hastily installed thermal convertors to draw off some of the heat being generated by the esoteric processes occurring inside. As Sverl watched, the thermal glass pipe, which had been intended to convey foamed metal to moulds and extruders in an adjacent factory and which had been severed just twenty feet from the tank, extruded another egg. The black crusty mass tumbled out into a space recently opened in the beam-work, and began peeling.

The layers of graphene and diamond laminate came off like the skin of an apple to reveal hard yellow foam. This foam then cracked into four pieces like the shell of a seed pod to reveal the gleaming squashed white sphere of its seed. The moment this happened, the white sphere, the hardfield generator, applied for instructions and found its place in the program in Sverl's mind, before shooting off through the station to find its way outside and its position in the growing network of such objects. A braided mass of tentacles then groped its way into the space it had occupied, individual tentacles opening 'structor pods to snap up the remnants of the thing's shell and, even as it did so, Sverl knew that twelve hours would not be enough. To complete the network and entirely wrap this station in self-feeding hardfield would take twenty hours.

So what's the answer, Penny Royal? Sverl wondered, because he felt sure there had to be one.

Perhaps the station weapons already being reinstated would be enough to fend off attack until the network was complete?

No, Sverl did not think so. All the Polity ships out there were modern and would have modern weapons. That meant gravity waves, sub-AI missiles with fusion-burst acceleration, a whole spectrum of beam weapons and probably other things he didn't know about. Those ships were approaching slowly and confidently because those aboard knew they could make mincemeat of this station.

Sverl paused in his speculations, abruptly aware of a request for U-com. He accepted, but only limited bandwidth.

'So, Sverl,' said a voice, 'you do have complete control of Room 101.'

'Depending on your definition of complete,' Sverl replied. 'Who is this?'

'My name is Garrotte,' replied the AI communicating. 'My definition of complete is that you control all the station's remaining AIs, even so far as having one of them reactivate a runcible. Our scan readings also indicate that you are rapidly making repairs to a hundred years of damage and that soon you may have the U-space drive operational.'

Sverl paused for a microsecond before replying as he pondered just how good their scanning had to be. 'Yes, I have control, but I would still argue about that definition of "complete". There are still dead areas within the station, there is still a great deal of wild nano- and micro-tech, and there are still independent intelligences here.' In fact, Sverl wanted to argue about as much as possible so as to delay the inevitable attack by this fleet.

'That was just a conversational gambit,' said Garrotte.

Now, why did he know that name? Sverl wondered. An instant later he had the answer. *Micheletto's Garrotte* was the name of the attack ship running interceptions in the Masadan system. It was also the one that had gone AWOL there – Penny Royal having somehow stowed away aboard it – and the remains of which had been melded with *The Rose* to form the ship Blite had named the *Black Rose*. Perhaps there was an angle here Sverl could work . . .

'I take it you have a new body now?' he enquired.

'Perceptive of you,' replied Garrotte. 'And I have a new mission that no amount of talk can divert me from. We cannot allow a prador, or rather an erstwhile prador, to control such a major asset as Room 101. You therefore have twelve hours – a time you have doubtless already calculated – to abandon that station.'

'Well that's a bit unfair,' said Sverl. 'Surely this station comes under the same salvage regulations as applied to the *Puling Child* – now named the *Lance*. I therefore claim this station as my own under those regulations.'

'In a perfect universe,' said Garrotte, 'all laws would apply equally to all and would be inviolate. We don't live in a perfect universe but one where potential threats must be countered before they lead to disasters.'

'In a perfect universe,' Sverl replied, 'Penny Royal would not have escaped a death sentence by apparently sacrificing the part of its mind supposedly guilty of the crimes. What are your feelings on that matter, considering how *close* you got to that AI?'

'We can chat like this for as long as you like,' said Garrotte. 'However, no amount of chat is going to change that twelve-hour time limit.'

'I don't have a ship any more,' said Sverl, 'so how am I supposed to abandon this station?'

'The *Lance* is still there.'

'Not my ship. And Thorvald Spear will be leaving in it shortly.'

'We have discussed this matter and another option is available,' said Garrotte. 'We understand that at your heart you are still a prador adult and your psyche is such that you want to be secure in your own, usually large, vessel. Though we cannot accept you controlling Room 101, we are quite prepared to allow you to depart that station aboard one of the Polity dreadnoughts remaining in the final construction bays.'

'Very badly damaged,' said Sverl.

'At least one of them should have viable fusion drive to get you away from the station. Materials and components can be provided from the station once we have assumed control of it.'

It was a tempting offer: no need for any kind of fight, a dreadnought of his own again, large enough to be modified to his needs. But there were problems. Did he trust this fleet not to fire on him once he was clear of the station? Sverl was no Polity citizen and even once away from the station was still a potential threat, especially because of his known association with Penny Royal. Also, it wasn't beyond feasibility that they had struck some deal with the king of the prador concerning him. Then, of course, there was Penny Royal.

The black AI had provided a way to make a hardfield defence. It had also lodged a piece of itself in the core of every AI aboard this station. If Sverl abandoned this place he feared he would be reneging on some unspoken deal. He felt sure that despite his own story having been resolved he still had a part to play in the black AI's plan.

'I will have to consider your offer very carefully,' Sverl replied. 'It will take me some time to move myself and my people aboard one of the dreadnoughts.'

'Please be reasonable, Sverl,' Garrotte replied. 'If I hold off for a hundred hours and you refurbish that station to pristine condition you still have no chance against us. Even if you upgrade that station's weapons and defences with the kind of technology we know you know about, you'll still lose.'

How very interesting, thought Sverl.

'I take it your new body is not one of those attack ships, but one of those dreadnoughts?' Sverl asked, meanwhile again checking on the production of those hardfield generators. He decided to bring the whole network much closer to the hull, where it could be hidden by the Byzantine growths out there. It was clear to him that Garrotte had not detected or identified them, which was understandable since their emissions were no more than that of any other technology in and about the station. They would be to all intents and purposes invisible, until the network fired up.

'Curious question,' said Garrotte, 'to which the answer is yes, my new body is now that of a modern dreadnought.'

Ah, thought Sverl, *that accounts for your overconfidence, then.*

'With dangerous knowledge comes greater power, it seems,' Garrotte added.

You know something about Penny Royal, thought Sverl.

Garrotte continued, 'And, being at the centre of such power, I am thoroughly aware of how quickly I can convert Room 101 to a spreading cloud of vapour.'

In a moment of inspiration Sverl added, 'Along with the two thousand or so Polity citizens we have aboard.'

A long silence ensued, during which Garrotte doubtless did some fact checking. The dreadnought AI sounded slightly peeved when it finally replied, 'The shell people.'

Sverl sent imagery from the hospital and the steadily filling barracks aboard, and waited.

'The shell people were citizens who abandoned the Polity,' said Garrotte.

'Yet they are still citizens, are they not?' said Sverl. 'Please forgive my ignorance if this is not the case. Doubtless if they are not considered citizens their wholesale slaughter is just a small matter . . . '

The communications link closed, emphatically.

Spear

I set my aug to knock me out for a few hours in the hope that after sleeping I would have a new perspective on my situation, but I was disappointed. I woke to the same feeling of inertia as before, and sprawled on my bed staring at the ceiling, I tried to figure out why I was feeling just the same as I had before we left Masada.

After much thought, I decided it came down to having no clear goals. Perhaps it was time to give up and head back to the Polity. There I could live like anyone else. I could return to research, or the military. Once I had achieved whatever my vague goal happened to be, wouldn't I have to do something like that anyway?

The answer, from the core of my being, was a 'no'. A lack of clarity was slowing me down, making me indecisive but, until I reached some sort of resolution with Penny Royal, I could not turn my attention elsewhere. The black AI defined me. I decided it was time to *change* my mind. Within the extensive library of my aug I found a suite of programs which I'd never felt the urge to use before. As I researched I realized how far technology had come recently, because what Cole was doing with that bulky, complicated-looking equipment in the hospital, I could now do just lying on my back in bed: I could edit my own mind.

I was wary at first because, though I wanted to change how I weighed things emotionally, I really didn't want to lose any memories. However, I soon found the option there for instant restoral. I checked and there was nothing for me in partitioned memory to restore. So I hadn't used this before.

I next tried a simple test. I set it to automatically restore after a period of thirty seconds: I removed my memory of travelling from Sverl back to my ship. After numerous checks to see if I was sure the program did as instructed, I then spent thirty seconds of confusion, sure that Sverl must have hit me with a stunner, and had me carried back here because he wanted to keep the spine. When memory returned, I spent some time contemplating my tendency towards paranoia and decided editing out memories was not for me.

Next I loaded knowledge of how to change my attitude to things, variously listed under titles like 'confidence', 'assertion', 'ambition', 'drive', 'personal goals' and others besides. I could change these, but was reluctant to do so. Surely if I changed them I would no longer be me? It then occurred to me that if I was going to venture down this route I could wipe out any inclination to go trailing after Penny Royal. I could, if I wished, programme myself to be happy with a life in the Polity driving a taxi.

Fuck that.

I came up off the bed all in one movement, dispelling the editing suite to the depths of my aug and abruptly feeling angry with myself. It was just then that Flute decided to deliver his news.

'We've got a problem,' he said through the PA speaker. 'A Polity fleet of twenty modern attack ships and two modern dreadnoughts has just arrived.'

'Right,' I said, slamming my door open and heading for the bridge.

Riss was up on the console as I arrived, gazing at me with her black eye open, and I wondered if she'd been in my mind while I had been contemplating screwing around with it. I sat down in the chair, throwing up frames in the screen fabric of ship stats, applying to Flute for a view of the approaching ships and putting them in another frame.

'Any communications?' I asked.

'Sverl has been speaking to them,' said Flute, 'but I didn't have access to that.'

'Sverl?' I enquired out loud, making a link.

Sverl sent me a cam view of Bsectil heading our way clutching the spine, then said, 'You've got less than twelve hours to get out of here. Also, as a favour, I would rather you didn't mention my hardfield generators, should anyone get in contact with you.'

I glanced at Riss.

'I've said nothing,' she protested.

I made another link. 'Trent, we've got a Polity fleet coming in. I'm leaving this station soon. What do you want to do?'

After a short pause he replied, 'I have to see this through.'

'Your companions?' I asked, suddenly realizing how important to me his next reply would be. It suddenly occurred to me there might have been a reason for my reluctance to depart the station.

Another short pause ensued while he spoke to Sepia and Cole. Cole emphatically wanted to stay and study the further results of his mind-work on the shell people. Sepia was undecided. She opened a private link to me herself.

'*Where are you going?*' she asked.

'*Where do you think?*'

'*I presume you're going after Penny Royal, but after recent events here I wasn't sure.*'

'*I am. But I don't know where it's gone.*'

'*Have you room for another passenger?*'

I didn't have to think. *'Of course I damned well have – you know you are welcome.'*

'That's good to know, Thorvald. I wasn't sure what your attitude to me was.'

'Acquisitive,' I replied.

'Oh good,' she said.

'Get over here now – when you're here we're going.' I paused again, then switched to a private link to Trent. 'Trent, you're sure?'

'I'm sure,' he replied with calm certainty.

I don't know why I felt I owed him anything. The man was a killer who, at Isobel Satomi's instruction, would have had no compunction about snapping my neck.

I sat back. That was it, then. We were going. Linking through the ship's system into that of the station, I watched Sepia say her goodbyes, collect a small case and head out of the hospital to climb onto one of the maglev carts that had been used to transport the shell people there.

Halfway along its journey it halted at a station and Sepia stood up and looked around in confusion. Bsectil then appeared, for he had stopped the cart. The prador first-child handed over the spine to her without a word, then turned to head back to his father. It took her just ten minutes more and I watched her all the way. The moment she stepped into the *Lance*'s airlock, I rested my hands in the indented ball controls before me, auged through to the local bay AI and requested undocking. With thumps that shuddered through the ship, the clamps disengaged. Next, after a pause, I took my hands away from the ball controls. What the hell did I need them for when I had a pilot?

'Flute,' I said. 'Take us out.'

Only because the bridge, which was lined with screen fabric, seemed transparent, was I able to see that the *Lance* was on the move. On steering thrusters Flute took us away from the wall of the construction bay then slid us out towards bright vacuum under the loom of the old dreadnought. The light steadily increased, then stepped down as the system adjusted it for normal human vision.

'Hi Riss,' said Sepia as she entered the bridge.

'Hello catwoman,' Riss replied.

Sepia grinned at the snake drone then turned to me. 'You okay with me here?'

'Bit late now if I'm not,' I replied, my attention now fixed on the object she had under her arm. 'But I'm glad you came.' At that moment I auged through to my nascuff and it slowly began turning from blue to red.

She stepped over to me, slid the spine out and held it out. 'This, I believe is your phallic MacGuffin?'

'So it is.'

At that moment Riss emitted a snort, then muttered, 'Damn, I've been thick.'

I was surprised it had taken her so long.

I reached out and closed my bare hand around the spine. I felt that familiar jolt, followed by a weird moment of disconnection, almost as if parts of my mind had flown apart in some mental explosion. They flew up, reconfiguring as they did so, then came down again, interlocking in new ways and having acquired greater bulk in the process. Greater mental perspectives opened for me and I knew on an absolutely basic level that I had skills and knowledge I had never acquired personally. It was without any doubt that I understood I had re-engaged with the spine and with the knowledge of Penny Royal's victims; that in a sense they were all part of me now. I reached out then, not needing to locate and direct com systems or sort through com channels and frequencies.

'*Goodbye Sverl,*' I said, without using my vocal cords.

'*Goodbye, Spear,*' Sverl replied, '*which I say with the absolute certainty that we'll meet again.*'

I didn't have to think too deeply about that. The fact that Penny Royal had left that hardfield generator meant it was unlikely the black AI had finished with Sverl yet. I was going after the black AI, so it seemed inevitable that my and Sverl's courses would again intersect. I then considered Sverl's 'absolute certainty', which could not be parsed from the presence of that hardfield generator.

'*What else have you found?*' I asked.

'*Fast again, I see,*' Sverl replied, then sent a massively complex file concerning the physical and mental structure of the AIs in Room 101. I realized that in sending this, Sverl was deliberately testing my abilities. I worried for a second it was beyond me. But it was as if my mind, until that moment, had been running rough and unevenly like a big engine barely able to tick over. The pressure Sverl had just exerted was like a foot slamming down on an accelerator, fuel flooding in and the engine coughing into full life.

Externally everything slowed down. I found myself processing the kind of data load it had taken me hours to deal with on Par Avion, when I had been researching Isobel Satomi, in just the time it took Sepia to take one step. By the time she was sitting down in the chair she had previously occupied I was there, and understood what Sverl had found at the centre of every AI aboard.

'Damnation,' I said, out loud, now wondering if I had made the right decision to leave. My aim was to track down Penny Royal but the AI's obvious continued interest in this place might mean it would lead me back here.

'Problem?' asked Sepia.

I gazed at her for a long moment. Why had Penny Royal said what it had during our last encounter if it intended coming back to this station? No, we were going back to my 'beginning' and that certainly wasn't here. I realized it would be too easy to over-analyse all this and find myself sinking back into inertia. I needed to do something; I needed to move.

'Just new data,' I replied, waving a dismissive hand.

'*You have to go,*' said Sverl.

'*Why?*'

'*I don't know why,*' he said. '*I just know you have to.*'

'*Then goodbye again,*' I repeated, and pulled my mind out of the station.

'If we're going to get along, you'll have to do better than that,' said Sepia. 'What new data?'

'Okay. Sorry. It seems Sverl has found a piece of Penny Royal in every single AI aboard that station.' I paused, adding, 'I've yet to work out the implications of that.'

She nodded, then, after a moment's thought, pulled across her straps. Watching her for a moment longer, I noted her cat's claws flexing in and out of the end of her fingers – something she did when she was tense. But she was cosmetic catadapt rather than a true adaption. She had cat's eyes, sharp teeth and elfin ears, but had restricted herself to something generally human. She didn't have a tail or all-over body hair, for example, and she wasn't one of those who had altered her body form with short-ened legs and shifted joints so she could drop on all fours and move like a real cat. Retrospectively I realized that last bit of knowledge was not something I had personally learned. She was also gut-wrenchingly attractive and, now I'd reset my nascuff, her presence was already having more and more of an effect on me.

'So where are we going?' she asked, looking up.

'I haven't decided yet.' I paused for a second. 'Flute, where can we get some decent AI net updates?'

'I am receiving updates even now,' Flute replied.

'But there are restrictions?' I suggested.

'Broadcast data is limited,' Flute replied. 'Specific search requests aren't allowed outside the Polity, but we can key into a permitted Graveyard server.'

I focused back on Sepia. 'There you have it: we'll head close to the Polity border with the Graveyard. Is there anywhere specifically you want to go?'

'Anywhere that isn't boring,' she replied.

'So that's why you're with me?'

'It is.'

'I would have thought remaining aboard Room 101 while it comes under attack would be . . . interesting.'

'Been there, done that.'

'Trent, Cole, the shell people?'

'Cole is too wrapped up in his own research to be interesting. Trent I found interesting until I discovered that as well as being burdened with a heavy conscience, he now seems to have fallen for Taiken's wife. The shell people –' she waved a hand as if at an irritating fly – 'are too close to home.'

'Old and suicidal,' I said, understanding completely now. The shell people were too much of a reminder of her own condition, for Sepia was one of those pushing the ennui barrier. I wondered then if it was a good idea having someone aboard who might be inclined to taking suicidal risks, but then let it go. Generally those pushing that barrier risked their own lives, and not the lives of others.

'Well, you sure know how to flatter a girl,' she said. 'And shall we stop playing? You know why I'm here, and I know why you want me here.'

'I'm not sure I do know, but I hope it will be a pleasure finding out.'

Riss issued another snort.

Out in the bright light of the hypergiant, with Room 101 falling behind us and the Polity fleet not yet close enough to intercept us (if it intended to), I said, 'Take us under, Flute.'

As we went I felt as if some tie had snapped – I felt free.

The Brockle

In a corridor aboard the *High Castle*, where a moment before it had been certain of simple victory, the Brockle fell from a beam strike. It rolled, its back smoking and one of its units dying, broke its human form and exploded apart, another beam cutting through the space it had occupied. At the end of the corridor a figure ducked out of sight, but the Brockle had already recognized one of the Sparkind. Its instinct was to set out in pursuit immediately. It had been attacked now, which meant it could respond. It was no longer morally obliged to preserve life . . . But it stamped down on that instinct at once.

All Sparkind were professional soldiers whose training and martial knowledge was at a peak, so why would one of them take a shot at something she knew could not be killed with a laser carbine? With its units stuck around the walls of the corridor, the Brockle began checking data and cam views and decided to hang back. The fleeing human soldier had just passed two Golem companions, waiting with portable proton cannons. In the hands of Golem those would have resulted in a lot more damage, with the likelihood of every one of the Brockle's units being struck. This therefore was the trap . . . but it was far too simple.

Why hadn't the soldiers knocked out cams in the area they

had occupied? Why had they sent their human companion with the laser carbine when they could have come themselves with the more effective weapons? They must know that it could see them waiting there. The trap, then, must be more subtle.

Checking, the Brockle saw that all the scientists were sealed in their research area, the bridge crew was sealed in the bridge and the remaining Sparkind squads were sealed in their quarters. The Sparkind squad, which must have got out before the partitioning shields went down, consisted of four members, and one of them was missing. Running a search, the Brockle noted a mass discrepancy in one of the maintenance passages but nothing visible through the cams. The other soldier was using chameleonware and heading towards the location of one of the U-space communicators. So, on the face of it, this present 'trap' was a distraction to allow the fourth soldier to get off an SOS to Earth Central, but again it was too easy. Now knowing what it knew, what was its expected response? It would ignore the three in the corridor and take a direct route back past the science section to intercept the one heading for the communicator. Knowing that this was what the Brockle would do, what trap would the Sparkind have laid?

The route to the communicator would have taken it down a passageway running along the inner face of the ship's hull near to a series of airlocks. The Brockle could detect nothing unusual there but, almost certainly, explosive devices had been planted. There would be those to blow out an airlock and another EM device to at least momentarily paralyse it so it would be sucked out into space. Was there another layer? Quite possibly, but now it was time to act. However, instead of going in pursuit of any of the four Sparkind, it routed through to the ship's armoury and fired three low-yield chemical explosive missiles, programming them even as they railed out of the *High Castle*.

The Brockle then pulled all its units back together. It regained human shape, turned around and away from the waiting soldiers. Meanwhile, the missiles were turning sharply and the ship's system warning of the danger. The Brockle ignored that as it reached the frame of an emergency bulkhead door, stepped past it and turned. It then mentally reached out again and opened two airlocks.

Emergency lights began flashing and a breach alarm began sounding. A slight breeze tugged at the Brockle's false clothing just before the bulkhead door slammed across. It now focused its attention through cams positioned in the corridor leading to one of the open airlocks and watched the steel eye of a missile nose cone, limned in chemical propulsion flame, hurtling in. The missile, which wasn't much larger than one of the Brockle's own body units, shot in through the airlock, travelling at twenty thousand miles an hour. It took a microsecond to reach the two Golem and their human companion, and detonated precisely on time. The hot blast blew open the corridor and threw molten metal and wreckage out into the rest of the ship. It vaporized the human soldier, burned and blew apart the two Golem, their tough remains carried in a wall of fire along the corridor to be deposited on the other side of the ship.

The second missile, progressing in a longer arc, shot in through its designated airlock just a moment later. The length of corridor it traversed was a short one, its final destination a flat wall beyond which lay a water tank. Hitting the tank, it exploded, its ultra-thermite core vaporizing the water and the metal of the tank too, and heating them so intensely they even began to disassociate into plasma. The white-hot gas exploded outwards, but in the main corridors could travel no further than the recently closed emergency bulkhead doors. However, it did have one route out, and that was through a maintenance tunnel in which the Brockle had deliberately left blast hatches open. The gas travelled along this and entered another tunnel, heading towards the mass discrepancy. Through the cams in the tunnel the Brockle just had time to see a human figure thrashing, his suit shredding away, then skin and flesh peeling away too, just before the cams went out.

The Brockle closed airlocks and the ship immediately began recharging with air.

'Proud of yourself?' enquired Captain Grafton from the bridge.

It gazed through cams at her. Instead of responding, it initiated emergency eject, feeling the deck convulse under its feet just a moment later. An exterior view showed a circular plug of the ship a hundred yards across rising out of the hull, then being blasted away by the neat solution of the air from the surrounding corridors emptying out underneath it.

The science team must remain – they still had the remains of the *Black Rose* and might render useful data.

'It was necessary,' the Brockle replied to Grafton, as the bulkhead door ahead opened.

It walked along scorched and smoking corridors, fire-retardant foam drifting all around. At the turning it looked to its right, where a great hollow had been blown open within the ship, then turned to the left.

'You're insane,' said Grafton. 'You should have been put down long ago.'

What reply to make to the infantile prattling of a human? The Brockle initiated the ejection of the bridge and watched another plug of the ship depart.

At the far end of this corridor the wall was melted and buckled, and lying on the floor were the remains of the two Golem, syntheflesh and skin burned away, sub-systems trashed, silvery bones distorted. The largest remaining piece was a rib-cage with an arm and skull still attached. The Brockle nudged it with one toe but it didn't move. A scan revealed the crystal inside still powered up, but isolated and unable to move anything other than its own thoughts. Still, the Brockle would throw these remains out of an airlock later – you could never be too careful with Golem. Turning away, it followed a circuitous route to the science section, as now it couldn't walk through the military section.

'Do you honestly think you can be forgiven?' asked Grafton. 'You've killed four people – and those are only the ones I know about.'

'It was self-defence,' the Brockle replied, though of course how self-defence was defined might be a little problematic when it came to that woman on Par Avion.

'Brice wasn't attacking you,' she said.

'Brice?'

'You don't even know their names, or care.' Grafton paused then continued, 'He was the one in the maintenance tunnel. You might be able to argue that you were defending yourself from the other three, even though they were no danger to you, but not him.'

She was right, of course, thought the Brockle. It paused before the partition shield over the door into the science section. Earth Central would never forgive these killings, and would be even less inclined to forgiveness when it realized how wrong it had been about Penny Royal, and how right the Brockle had been. As it pondered that, it ordered the partition open and watched as the piece directly ahead slid up into the ceiling, then the Brockle opened the door and stepped into the science section.

Perhaps, it decided, it should be a bit less altruistic in its actions. Everything it had done thus far had been to protect the

Polity against the dangerous black AI Penny Royal, but it had not been thinking very deeply about the consequences of its actions to itself.

Closing the door behind, it now separated, its units forming a neat shoal and speeding ahead. The scientists were in their large open-plan laboratory. They were all in survival suits and working consoles to try and open communications, to try to find out what the hell was going on. The Brockle considered extracting every detail of research from their minds, but then rejected the idea. They had recorded all their data and it doubted they had retained anything in their soft organic brains of any importance. Best just make this quick.

As it sped into the laboratory it continued to ponder the likely results of its actions. Earth Central certainly knew by now that the Brockle had broken the terms of its confinement. Perhaps it had also been fooled into thinking the Brockle had been destroyed aboard the *Tyburn*, which was almost certainly a spreading cloud of vapour by now, although possibly not. But it was certain that it would eventually learn that the Brockle had escaped in the last single-ship, which had then docked at Par Avion. The woman's death would be linked to the Brockle's arrival. However, her killing had been forensically clean and Earth Central would not be able to prove a connection beyond a coincidental one of timing. Her death it could get away with. The larger problem was here with this ship.

The scientists had now seen the Brockle enter. Abandoning their seats in panic, the five humans retreated to the far side of the laboratory, the two Golem defensively to the fore. The Brockle slimmed down their units, flattened their noses into blades rimmed with diamond chains, and accelerated, targeting Golems and humans alike. It struck, hard, punching through soft bodies and ceremal, passing through vital organs and crystal, then out the other side in a cloud of blood, flesh and crystal fragments. Smoothly turning in mid-air, it observed them falling.

This ship, it decided, would have to disappear. Without the evidence of the Brockle's supposed crimes here Earth Central would not be able to pursue retribution. Once Penny Royal was dealt with, the ship could be dropped into a sun. Nothing would remain – no inconvenient memplants like those this science team contained, and no inconvenient memcrystal like those still functioning in the remains of that Golem. But still there was *another* problem.

Focusing its attention outwards, the Brockle observed the slow departure of the bridge and military sections of the ship. It hesitated, for just a second, then finally admitted the necessity of what it had to do next. The two missiles it launched this time contained one-megaton CTD imploders.

They would leave nothing but vapour.

8

Sfolk

Hanging in vacuum, after seeing the extremadapt space station destroyed and its inhabitants slaughtered, Sfolk decided he would ask for nothing. He wouldn't beg for his life and he wouldn't make any bargains because he knew precisely what that thing was out there. It was Penny Royal, no doubt about it, and one didn't make deals with that particular AI. Sfolk, his belly full of digesting meat, was feeling stronger now and was thinking a little straighter.

'Even if your only option is vacuum?' a prador voice hissed and bubbled menacingly.

'Even then,' Sfolk clattered, horrified that his thoughts were open to inspection. He swung his palp eyes round to try and locate a target, snapping his claws in frustration.

He didn't know why he was still alive anyway. He had survived his murderous father and similarly homicidal brothers. He had survived a venture into the Kingdom to steal females and an ST dreadnought. He had survived Cvorn. He had survived an attack by ships of the King's Guard and a subsequent U-jump with a malfunctioning drive. He had survived all the opponents the extremadapts had slung against him, as well as the recent destruction of their space station, and now he was surviving in vacuum.

The space station was in pieces all around him, all steadily drifting apart. The humans, who just like the shell people had taken on some bizarre forms in an effort to deny their nature, all had to be dead. They'd been ripped apart from the inside by some seed growth of the black AI and, if that hadn't got all of them, then the remainder had to have breathed space by now . . . just as Sfolk should have been doing. It was frustratingly puzzling. He was breathing air but he could not see how it was being contained around him. Certainly Penny Royal was responsible, but why? It had just murdered hundreds of humans and had never before shown any particular liking for the prador.

'Why am I alive?' he asked.

Some massively complicated file dropped into his aug and thence into his mind. He saw Cvorn in his breeding pond and then the microscopic images of prador seed and eggs. Complex statistical analyses branched from these in directions that didn't exist in a three-dimensional universe. Reality fined down to layers of code, ever expanding and complicating. His mind felt as if it was coming close to bursting when suddenly it all drained away again. But Sfolk understood that he had just been given an overview, from an AI perspective, of a prador life and all its chances and mischances.

Ask a silly question, he thought, getting angrier at being treated like an idiot. Then he decided on a more pertinent question. 'Why are they all dead?' He flinched waiting for the answer to that.

'Because they were guilty,' the black AI replied simply, adding, 'and because they were sane.'

The stars of black crystal were coagulating into one mass out there; growing like some strange coral as those stars floated in to attach to the central mass, which intermittently collapsed in on itself. He also felt a constant visceral twist which meant U-tech was operating close by. Sfolk wasn't sure how he knew, but he felt that the form he was seeing was some sort of protrusion into the real, and that the AI was shunting a portion of itself *elsewhere*. Next, as he thought about what that might mean, he found himself on the move.

He began drifting between chunks of wreckage and the occasional steaming remains of extremadapts. Within a few minutes he was falling towards the red giant sun and wondered if Penny Royal had saved him to next toss him towards that furnace. No, Sfolk realized he was thinking too much like a prador. He needed to rein in his aggression and paranoia and try to think clearly if he was to survive. Penny Royal wasn't like a father-captain who saved one of his children to enjoy torturing it later. At least, Sfolk hoped the AI had its mind set on some other purpose. It probably intended to use him in some way, and that was the only reason he was alive. He glanced over, noting that the AI was travelling with him. It had now collected all its parts and was continuing to collapse, continuing to route much of its substance away, the remainder growing darker and spinier as it did so.

Some hours passed and Sfolk became aware of a distant line of detritus etched against the massive face of the sun. A while later he found himself starting to get quite warm as the detritus began to resolve and he saw the gutted hulks of ships and pieces of ships. This was the Junkyard Lelic and the other extremadapts had talked about. They hadn't known that he understood them – hardly noticed that he was wearing a biotech aug. Perhaps they thought it was just some growth on his shell? Some of the ships he recognized as old Kingdom craft and wartime prador vessels, but there was a diverse collection of Polity ships there too. As they drew ever closer he saw his ST dreadnought silhouetted against the red glare, badly distorted and with massive holes in its hull, stripped out and looted – nothing but a shell.

Another image now dropped into his mind. He saw humans

in one of the inner chambers of the ship. They were standing around the case containing the ship mind, then moving back as a biotech machine bearing some resemblance to Sfolk himself entered. Sfolk then felt time lurch forwards, and the next scene was of that chamber empty.

So, they took the mind? Sfolk looked back towards the spreading wreckage of the station. *Surely it was still there?*

'Dead,' said Penny Royal, again demonstrating the transparency of Sfolk's mind to it. 'Suicided.'

Ah, some ship minds were made to take that route if the ship was seized by an enemy. The mind had been unable to distinguish Sfolk and his brothers from other prador, but it could certainly tell the difference between a prador and a human being, no matter how bizarrely altered.

'I could repair the drive but there is a better option. They always missed the earliest ship,' the AI added. 'Its systems are ancient but it always managed to keep itself concealed.'

Uh?

Soon Sfolk found himself drifting between the hulks, studying weapons damage. Most of the ships here were warships and most of them, he had gathered from Lelic and the others, had received damage to their drives.

'They never realized this system was no accident,' said the AI.

Sfolk shuddered, feeling as if lime worms were crawling under his shell. As he understood it, this system consisted of two sun-mass fast-spinning singularities orbiting each other at speed and in turn orbiting the red giant, which was now a vast curved plain below him. If the system was no accident, then that meant cosmic engineering on an appalling scale. He was aware that the Polity AIs might be capable of such now, but they hadn't been before the war. And, judging by the ships here, this place had been in existence since long before that. Which begged the question: who built this?

'There,' said Penny Royal.

The number of wrecks had steadily waned and, Sfolk noticed, the hulks at this end of the Junkyard looked ancient indeed. He felt himself decelerating and he also felt uncomfortably hot now. He glanced over at the AI, now in silhouette against the sun. It had returned to its usual form of a black sea urchin – a form of life found in the seas both of Earth and of the prador home world. So what was 'there', then?

Movement drew Sfolk's attention back to blank vacuum lying ahead. Space now appeared to be flickering – jammed pixels appearing and blinking out as if in a disrupted image feed. A moment later some great blurred mass began to appear as if being forced into being out of the very vacuum. Then, ever so slowly, its overall shape began to resolve. Sfolk was puzzled by what he was seeing until he realized his perspective was giving him an edge-on view of a much wider mass. This frustrated him for a second until he remembered he could do something about it.

He fed image data into his aug to get some measurements and the program etched out in his right palp eye all he could see now as seen from above, then extrapolated. If the extrapolation was correct, he was gazing on an immense ship with a hexagonal central mass, protrusions extending from its faces that terminated in leaf-shaped nacelles. It was all very baroque, intricate, artistic, and its familiarity nagged at him until he understood he was seeing one of the multitude of forms taken on by snowflakes. However, as detail began to become clear, he saw that this was a giant snowflake seemingly made of basketwork – the materials used being coloured metals and composites. In many places its sides weren't even solid and he could see into its interior to blocky shapes and similarly woven tubes and dividing walls. It was like no ship he had ever seen before. It was *alien*.

'Who built this?' he asked.

'The insane,' Penny Royal replied.

As Sfolk found himself again on the move towards the thing, he pondered what a black AI like Penny Royal might describe as insane.

Sverl

Despite a Polity fleet approaching, almost certainly intent on destroying Room 101, and despite the massive changes ongoing throughout the station, Sverl kept finding himself experiencing moments of loss; odd periods when he expected to do something and realized it wasn't necessary. At one point, just after overseeing a test of some of the station's U-space drive components, he returned his focus to his immediate surroundings and found himself about to issue orders to Bsectil. Only as he considered what stocks were available did he remember that no, he did not need to eat. At another point his mind strayed to what medical equipment he had available so as to assess the changes his body was undergoing, then remembered he no longer had a body that needed to be checked like that.

You need to get out more.

The drone Arrowsmith had once said that – apparently a human saying. It had been a little joke on the drone's part about the tendency of prador to hide themselves away in their sanctums. Perhaps the drone had had a point.

Surveying his immediate surroundings again, Sverl's eye fell on Bsectil, waiting patiently for orders but, as Sverl discovered after a subtle probe, in fact using his aug to play a VR game in which he was blasting humans apart with a railgun. Sverl felt a moment of irritation at this waste of time and energy, and wondered how Bsectil could be usefully employed.

All the main tasks were underway and supervised. The fusion drive had nearly been rebuilt by robots under the instruction of a station AI; other AIs and robots were steadily rebuilding the station's weapons, but these, in essence, were chores that did not affect their immediate chances of survival. The runcible was ready, and the other main tasks to be completed were the production of the hardfield generators, overseen by Bsorol and a station AI, and the U-space drive, which required the gravity press which was being built. The singularity needed for the press was steadily being inserted into a self-sustaining gravity box – an automatic process that just required energy and time. Building the press into which this box would go would take a while too and would mostly be performed in a factory an AI was already getting ready. Sverl paused for a second. Yes, Bsectil would oversee that. And he would be set to work on readying the drive to receive the rings made by that press. But not yet.

'I'm going for a walk,' said Sverl out loud.

Bsectil jerked, dropping an imaginary chunk of reaverfish which would have somehow magically restored his health after his legs had been burned off one side of his body by a particle cannon blast.

'Father?' he enquired.

'Bsorol is working on our hardfields.'

Bsectil was thoroughly confused. They both already knew that. There was no apparent reason for Sverl to mention it.

'He is working,' Sverl stated.

'Yes,' said Bsectil, unsure of where this was leading.

Of course Bsorol had his own pursuits when not employed. Before being dispatched to the bubble-metal tank he had been in his own little sanctum, in the process of filling some aquariums he had made earlier, in which he intended to hatch out some mudfish eggs he had brought from their ship, and which he intended to rear. Really, Sverl shouldn't be so hard on Bsectil for having his own interests too. At least playing such games kept his mind active and his reactions sharp, rather unlike his previous strange interest in Isobel Satomi, and the gemstone sculpture he had been building of her.

'Let's go,' said Sverl.

'To Bsorol?' Bsectil asked, puzzled.

'No, there is something I want to do, and there's something those Polity AIs out there need to be thoroughly aware of,' Sverl replied. 'Come on.'

'Do?' Bsectil echoed. 'Polity?'

Sverl didn't reply. It wasn't as if he had to stay in one spot to respond to any emergencies that might occur, and most essential tasks here were now being completed by station machinery. However, there was just one job that required his physical presence. It wasn't something he really needed to do, just something for which he felt responsible. And it was also something that might give that fleet out there reason to pause.

'You have a breather with you?' Sverl asked.

'Yes, Father,' Bsectil replied. The first-child wasn't wearing his armour but as always was kitted out with a harness and a wide selection of attached equipment.

'Good,' Sverl replied, ordering the first door open of the airlock ahead.

He passed through the airlock first and propelled himself away from the spreading mass of infrastructure around his sanctum. Here the weird metallic growths had been all but cleared, original main station skeletal beams exposed and repaired. A short distance out in this massive internal space he fired up his combined maglev and grav drive, but also set himself slowly turning to take in his surroundings. Even though the structural beams that had been exposed were far apart, there were still so many of them, and so many other structures intervening, that he could not see to the outer hull.

After a short while, with Bsectil hurriedly firing a chemical drive to catch up with him, he arrived at a wall of the packed internal mechanisms and infrastructure of the original station. Here the damage and riotous alterations had not been so severe. The factory pods, fluid tanks, materials conveyors, accommodations, assembly lines and other interconnected paraphernalia of wartime production were all visible. However, there were gaps where trees of 'structor pods were at work chewing away strange composite worm casts or glittering nanotech blooms, and other areas where printer-bots were busily rebuilding. Mapping ahead, he propelled himself to the open throat of an attack ship construction tunnel and sent himself hurtling along that. The walls all around him were packed with neatly folded arms and grabs, coiled spiderbot tentacles, the mica faces of hardfield projectors, but there were no attack ships, even partially constructed, to block his path.

Arriving at the end of the tunnel where the heads of giant extruders stood prepared to inject the hot metal hull beams ready to be bent by hardfields into the bones of ship skeletons, he halted by a secondary production tunnel for fusion engines and waited for Bsectil to frantically catch up, meanwhile absorbing data on a particular problem.

The shell people were old humans who had reached the ennui barrier in their lives. In an effort to defeat that boredom such people took big risks and quite often ended up killing themselves. These people had convinced themselves that the answer to their problem was to completely change themselves into prador. To do this they had used dangerous biotech, risky surgery, mental alterations that would have been illegal in the Polity. Their leader, Taiken, had gone the whole prador route, setting himself up as a father and thus enslaving the rest with his pheromones. It was a situation that had been sure to lead to disaster as they ceased to tend to their completely imbalanced bodies. It would also have resulted in disaster for Trent and some other humans as Taiken decided he would turn them into human blanks. After Golem Grey had dealt with Taiken – Grey had torn his head off – Trent had shouldered responsibility for the shell people. With the assistance of Spear and the drone Riss, they had been injected with an acid that dissolved their prador grafts, and with nanotech that preserved their lives and put them into a coma. Now, using human prosthetics and other wartime medical tech, including mental editing and reprogramming enacted by the mind-tech Cole, they had been restored to near humanity and were waking. But their problems weren't over. Cole had done his best but they were still attached to the idea of transformation, still at the ennui barrier, still liable to self-destruct.

When the first-child arrived, Sverl propelled himself down the tunnel. There were no robots or assembly equipment here, just walls lined with white composite vines cored with superconductor and serving no purpose at all. Then, by more cramped routes, Sverl came finally to the hospital where, even now, the last of the shell people were being roused. He scanned through cams inside but most of the structure within was made for humans and he would be severely restricted on where he could go. Instead he propelled himself round to the tubular jut of barracks lying just beyond the hospital – having been moved from their previous location a couple of miles away. These were larger inside with larger airlocks to gain entry because they had housed both humans and war drones – usually small attack or sabotage groups.

Sverl found an airlock provided for war drones and entered, Bsectil still struggling to keep up. He passed through and perambulated down a long tunnel to enter a huge room with two levels of galleries running around the edges, armourers' columns going from floor to ceiling – only one of which was operational and now supplied a limited variety of vitamin-laced protein bars and sachets of drinks – raised work surfaces and a scattering of furniture collected by robot from other 'human' areas in the station. The place was crowded. At a glance Sverl counted over a thousand people here.

'What the fuck are you?' exclaimed someone nearby.

Sverl focused on a man. This individual was dressed only in shorts and a sleeveless shirt as if he wanted to display his prosthetic limbs and skull, whose inner workings were revealed under translucent synthetics. A nearby woman, obviously less inclined to this sort of display because she was clad neck to toe in a close-fitting overall, said, 'Looks like some kind of war drone.' She then looked past Sverl and showed surprise as Bsectil entered, and took a couple of paces back. 'Prador,' she muttered, abruptly scrubbing at her arms as if her skin itched.

Others had now noticed their presence and began heading over. Seeing the steadily converging crowd, Sverl began transmitting the scene out towards the approaching fleet. Though Garrotte wasn't responding, he was sure it would be viewing any transmissions from the station. As he did this, he noticed Trent and Cole hurry into the room, obviously having been made aware of his presence.

'Funny-looking prador that,' said someone else nearby. 'Looks all twisted up.'

Of course, none of them had seen Sverl's children other than in armour. The crowd continued to gather and Sverl began to feel nervous. He wasn't used to so many *alien* creatures around him, and now wasn't completely sure how to go about delivering the news he needed to give them. Still transmitting, he moved out from the airlock. People began touching him, and they began touching Bsectil, who kept turning to try and face them and snapping his claws in nervous tension.

'Father?' he asked, almost desperately.

'Did you hear that?'

'What?'

'He called the robot father.'

'Some seriously fucked-up prador, then.'

They all understood the clattering and bubbling of prador speech. Sverl should have known that for, wanting to be prador, they had all had cerebral uploads of the prador language. He halted and rose higher on his legs, eyeing Trent and Cole as they drew closer and came to a halt amidst the crowd.

'Passing visit?' Trent enquired.

'Those in the approaching Polity fleet need to know who they might kill should they attack,' Sverl replied.

'What is this, Trent?'

'That a prador mutation?'

The babble increased as questions were asked, demands made, protests submitted.

'Is it time to tell them who you are?' Trent asked quietly.

'Pay attention,' Sverl said loudly and in human speech. 'I understand that you have all been loaded with a potted history of what has happened to you since you left Carapace City.' He was struggling to get them to listen, and many were still chatting and laughing. 'But the history was limited to what you could safely encompass. First you need to know that you are aboard no ordinary space station. You are aboard factory station Room 101.' That got their attention and now they all fell silent.

'You have felt what it was to be true prador. Which means, unless you are a father, to be a slave. Prador are aggressive killers and in human terms they are utterly amoral. Surely you understood this when their conflict between each other destroyed your city?' He paused, trying to read them, but even though he was capable of reading a limited amount of human expression, these were complicated creatures and beyond him. He then began accessing the technology nearby. There was a holographic projector set in the ceiling. Perfect.

Sverl immediately started loading image data from his personal files, editing it together even as he continued doggedly, 'There doesn't have to be much of a reason for prador to start killing each other, but in this case there was an unusual one you need to know about. You see, most prador are xenophobic and have an abhorrence for AI, so would not react well to one of their kind ceasing to be one of their kind, nor to a prador who became interfaced directly with AI crystal.' Another pause while he studied them. He decided not to explain that further, nor to over-explain what came next. It would give them something to mull over. 'Even though these changes might have been the result of an ill-thought-out visit to a black AI called Penny Royal, a cunning prador like Cvorn could use Sverl as an example of why the Polity was not to be trusted, why their present king, in making peace with the Polity, should be ousted. Then he could propel the prador race into a destructive war against the Polity.'

The first projection appeared then: Sverl standing amidst them as he had appeared many years ago, before he had visited a particular planetoid and a particular AI.

'Cvorn's battle with Sverl and subsequent plan to lead Sverl into a trap, where he could be captured, is what has finally brought you here.' No need to get into the stuff about Sverl's not entirely clear reasons for coming to Room 101.

'You all recognize Sverl,' he added.

By now a space had cleared around the projection of Sverl and most in the crowd were facing it, only occasionally glancing towards the real Sverl. They still probably thought he was some robot come to update them on their situation.

'Now see how he changed.'

He ran the hologram and the Sverl there started changing, his shell fattening, legs and mandibles dropping off, instantly to be replaced by prosthetics, palp eyes sinking into pits, his entire shell taking on the shape of a human skull, blue eyes blinking open. The whole grotesque transformation played through in just a few minutes, rousing gasps of both horror and amazement. Sverl focused on one woman and saw that she was crying, while another man staggered from the crowd to be violently sick. This at least was an indication of how strongly they had tied themselves to the idea of being prador, and how much they had held Sverl as the paragon of all they wanted to be.

'His genome was a combination of human and prador, manipulated by Penny Royal to create the grotesquery you see before you,' Sverl told them. 'Along with the outer transformation you see, there were other transformations. He began to grow human cerebral tissue and, so he thought, began to think like a human. Also, AI crystal was growing and attaching to his major ganglion.' Sverl considered showing the surgery he had enacted on himself to build his current skeleton inside, but that would dull the final shock value he was aiming for.

'Sverl fled Cvorn and came to Room 101 but, meanwhile, the king of the prador had become aware of the threat Sverl posed. He sent his King's Guard to rid him of that threat.' Sverl opened another hologram above, this one showing their arrival at Room

101. Above, in glorious Technicolor, his ship came apart and, under fire, the *Lance* hurtled towards the massive station. 'There was no safety for him here while he could still be used to foment rebellion and war, so while the King's Guard bombarded the station a war drone called Riss came with an enzyme acid similar to the one that rid you all of your prador grafts.'

Riss came in from the side and injected, and slid away. Did this projection system have sound? Yes, it did. Sverl ramped up the volume and let the recorded scream play, and watched as his old self dissolved before his eyes. Hands were slammed over ears. Many went down on their knees. Some were crying, some were laughing hysterically. The effect could not be clean and even; had to be as messy as the minds it was affecting.

Are you bored now? Sverl wondered.

The dissolving flesh fell away, finally revealing the underlying skeleton. It took them a while to get over the shock, then the Sverl of the present saw some of them glancing from the image to him and back again. Some began talking, some shouting, some remained down on their knees with their heads bowed. Some of them, Sverl knew, would come out of this and at last pass through the ennui barrier. Some would kill themselves while still others would go on to seek out other dangerous entertainments. This was an ending and a beginning. He considered for a moment how his story reflected old religious stories humans once had a penchant for, death and resurrection and all that.

'I am Sverl,' he announced loudly, when at last they were all focused on him.

Utter silence fell. He turned away, the crowd parting before him as he headed for the airlock, Bsectil quickly falling in behind him. As they entered the airlock and the door closed he felt contact through a channel that had remained open.

'Okay,' said Garrotte, 'you've got an extra ten hours to sort out that mess. I suggest you open up your runcible to the Polity system and send them on their way. You can choose to either follow them or leave the station aboard a ship. It's up to you.'

Ten more hours . . .

Sverl's attention strayed through the station to where the hardfield generators were still being churned out. Their rate of production had actually increased, so much so that the controlling AI there was having trouble keeping the bubble-metal plant cool and keeping up the flow of materials. Ten hours was more than enough time.

'Two birds with one stone, as Arrowsmith would say,' he said to Bsectil.

His first-child just expressed prador puzzlement with a dismissive lift of his mandibles. Sverl wished he himself had the human ability to grin.

Spear

I half expected something to knock us out of U-space the moment we entered it, but nothing happened and, after a few minutes, I accepted that the Polity fleet had ignored us.

'How long till we reach our destination?' I asked.

'Three days, ship time,' Flute replied.

I stood up, looked across at Sepia as she stood up, picking up her bag.

'You have cabins?' she said.

'I had four cabins made,' I said. I stabbed a thumb back at the door into the now-partitioned volume that had held Sverl and his first-children.

'Which can I use?'

'Mine is the first on the left,' I told her.

'So I can use any of the other three?'

'Yes, of course – the palm locks aren't configured,' I said, trying to hide my disappointment.

Instead of heading to the door, she turned and headed back to me. I spun my chair to face her and, dropping her bag, she stepped astride me, sat down on my lap and kissed me. It was surprisingly gentle. I'd half expected her to be as forceful as Sheil. My body responded from the tips of my toes to the top of my head. And, even though she smelled a bit sweaty, that aroma seemed loaded with an aphrodisiac cocktail of hormones. After a moment she leaned back.

'I told you I wasn't playing,' she said. 'However, I know how large that space was back there and as a consequence know how small four cabins are likely to be. I'd like a little space of my own.' She paused. 'Do the cabins have fabricators?'

Finally catching my breath, I replied, 'No, but the door at the end leads into my laboratory-cum-workshop and there's one in there.'

'Good.' She stood up, incidentally reaching down and giving my penis a squeeze through my trousers. She then winked, picked up her bag and headed for the door. I spun my chair back into the horseshoe console to be faced by Riss, reared up and close, black eye open.

'What are you looking at?' I asked.

'Nothing much,' she replied. 'Just trying to decide whether this display of human weakness is an improvement or otherwise.'

'I don't see it as weakness.'

'Maybe.' She dipped her head, slithered off the console, then writhing about a foot above the floor, shot off through the other door into the rest of the ship. As she went I wondered how she occupied her time while in transit like this. She ventured around the ship occasionally, but mostly seemed somnolent. She didn't even have sufficient means to manipulate her environment in order to research or build stuff. I remembered once speaking to a drone on this matter during the war. There were the virtual worlds of their own devising they could venture into, it had told me, but when I persisted, it had replied, 'Your human, linear perception of time is a product of evolution, and not necessary for us.' I guessed, in my terms, Riss just slowed down or sped up that perception to match the pace of events.

I sat for maybe an hour longer, checking through ship's systems and then opening up my connection to the spine to further explore it. When it responded with memories seemingly right out of a porn virtuality I closed off the connection and, getting to my feet, headed back. I first went to my laboratory/workshop but Sepia wasn't there, then I went to my own cabin. As I got there a door further along opened and she stepped out. Unless what she wore had been packed into the bag she'd brought aboard, she had used the fabricator. It was the ubiquitous little black dress – a favourite over centuries, impervious to the foibles of fashion. It reached to her thighs, clung to her like paint, exposed plenty of cleavage and ended under her arms. Her hair no longer looked as greasy as before and seemed to shift Medusa-like as she walked towards me in snakeskin ankle boots.

'Better?' she enquired, pausing to pose for me.

'Difficult to improve on perfection,' I replied.

She put two fingers in her mouth and pretended to vomit over to one side. I palmed the sensor beside my cabin door and the door swung open, then I held out my hand to her. She came closer, took my hand and I towed her inside.

'Of course it's not staying on long,' I said, turning to face her and now getting a waft of musky perfume.

'Oh, I know that.' Still holding onto my hand, she pulled it closer and pressed it between her legs just below her dress. I slid my hand up her inner thigh. She was wearing nothing underneath and, unlike Sheil, had retained her pubic hair. I slid the edge of my forefinger into wet warmth and slowly began rubbing forwards and back, folding my thumb so the knuckle pressed into her clitoris. She huffed impatiently then and pushed me towards the bed. I resisted and kept rubbing, so she reached down to the hem of her dress and pulled it off over her head, then shoved against my chest again.

Okay, I thought, *if you insist*.

I let her push me back and, withdrawing my hand, got onto the bed and shuffled backwards. She climbed on with me then proceeded to pull off my clothes. She was fast and expert at that but at a hundred and eighty years old I supposed she ought to be. Clambering astride me, she settled down with a sigh and segued into a slow grind. Interlacing her fingers with mine, she pulled up one of my hands and briefly inspected my nascuff.

'Make it slow,' she said, lowering it.

Via aug I made some adjustments and felt the need to come retract to a leaden ball in my groin. After a moment I freed my hands from hers and reached up to play with her breasts. I really wanted to bite them, but they were a bit out of reach and I felt that we really needed to get to know each other better. Only then did it occur to me to glance at her wrist. She wasn't wearing a nascuff. I wondered what that meant: a degree of self-control I'd yet to attain over my meagre years? Moving forward, she put her nipples within reach of my mouth, but only for a little while before stretching her legs out behind and lying on top of me. She worked at that for a little while, then, putting a hand round to my arse, slid over to the side, pulling me with her. I went with it and ended up on top of her, long strokes, all the way out and back in. This didn't last because she came with a nasal groan, her lips pouting.

Perhaps not so much self-control after all.

I was about to make another adjustment to my nascuff when she said, 'Don't you come yet – we're just getting started.'

'As you command,' I replied, lifting up her legs and pushing her knees back towards her then slipping lower to push into her anus, hearing her groan again and feeling those sharp claws digging into my buttocks.

Some hours later, as I lay on the bed aching and sore in many places, I decided I needed to investigate the functions of my nascuff further and maybe check out my ship's medical inventory, but only just in case. I was trying to persuade myself that we would probably have cooled down a little by the next time.

Blite

If the sound of blast doors slamming shut had not been enough to let Blite know something was amiss aboard this ship, the sound of weapons firing had been. There had, however, been nothing to see until the missiles launched. Glimpsing them out of the corner of his eye, he had walked over to the panoramic window to see if he could locate their target. When they flared steering thrusters hard to loop right round and come back at the ship, he knew that something was very wrong. One missile must have gone in through some port because the detonation occurred fractionally late, and the blast was all wrong for a hit against the hull. It looked as if the missile had exploded inside and its blast had been focused by a tube.

Even as she ship was still rocking after the first explosion, a second one occurred somewhere out of sight.

'What the hell is going on?' Greer asked leadenly, steadying herself against the window, the deck still rocking under their feet.

Blite turned to stare at her, but right then he had no idea, and wasn't thinking clearly anyway. He shook his head, trying to clear the nightmare detritus of the last interrogation from his mind.

'They're abandoning us,' Greer then said.

'What?'

She pointed outside.

Blite turned back to the window and watched first one large plug of the ship eject, and a short while later another. He tried to put things together in his skull and then, as he thought of an explanation, he felt a thrill pass through him from head to foot.

Penny Royal!

It seemed the only explanation. The black AI had somehow boarded this ship, taken out its controlling AI and steadily tried to take control of the whole thing. The captain must have tried to destroy it, then, upon failing, abandoned ship. With any luck that fucking Brockle hadn't managed to escape, though, admittedly, the black AI was not so black lately. In coming to rescue them like this, it would probably cause their interrogator no harm.

'Are you thinking what I'm thinking?' asked Greer.

'I don't know. I'm not a mind-reader,' Blite snapped, a surge of irritation rising in him in response to such a silly question.

'Penny Royal,' Greer explained.

Blite took a steadying breath. He shouldn't get irritated with Greer like that because, if he was honest, his response had been due to his weariness with questions he couldn't answer. 'It seems the only explanation that fits the facts. This ship effectively fired on itself and then they abandoned it in a hurry. I can think of only two things that could cause that and the second of them is Penny Royal.'

'The first?' Greer asked.

'Jain technology.'

She nodded and was about to make some reply when two more missiles launched from the weapons turrets out there. They both turned to watch the line of a brief rocket boost straight towards the two ejected sections of the ship, then the glass before them turned black.

'What the fuck?' said Blite.

The glass slowly cleared, revealing two growing spherical blasts. Then something odd happened. The two spheres of glowing matter stopped expanding and began to shrink again, growing brighter as they did so. As they collapsed down to bright points, the glass went black again, then again, after a moment, turned clear. The two expanding spheres of fire now revealed did not slow or shrink, but just continued to grow larger and cool to orange, parting like damp paper, and then finally reaching the ship as sylphs of red fire. The ship rocked again in the blast front, and vacuum out there steadily grew dark again.

'CTD imploders,' said Greer.

She was stating the obvious but Blite felt too puzzled to grow angry with her. What had happened? If Penny Royal had taken control of this ship then it was the black AI of old, careless of human life, vicious, for it had just murdered the escaping crew. But why CTD imploders? With a sinking sensation in his gut, Blite realized there was another explanation. CTD imploders were used when the aim was for not a single scrap of the target to survive. They were the kind of thing used against vessels, buildings or areas occupied by Jain technology and they might well be the kind of thing used against a black AI.

'Why?' said Greer. 'Why kill them?'

He didn't want to say, but did anyway. 'Perhaps that was Penny Royal out there.'

Greer glanced at him. 'In *two* ship ejection containers?'

Of course, she was right. Certainly the AI was capable of separating itself into many parts but what was the likelihood of it separating into two and both of those being trapped at separate locations and simultaneously ejected? Sure, those aboard this ship had managed to intercept the *Black Rose* and launch an effective attack against it, but managing to deal with Penny Royal *that* effectively was a miracle too far. He circled round again, coming back to the conclusion that Penny Royal must be aboard and had turned murderous again, and as he did so the door into the lounge opened.

Blite spun round, expecting to see a cloud of black knives coming through and not sure whether he should be glad or sorry about that. Instead the fat young man stepped in – the human form of the Brockle. He was carrying something, which in passing on the way to his quarters, he put down on a table.

'I was right,' he said.

Once the Brockle was out of sight, Blite walked over and peered down at this object. He immediately recognized what looked like a demolition charge of some kind, with a small detonator console attached. He didn't think the forensic AI would leave such a dangerous object within their reach, and he was right. After a second the block of explosive slumped, turning first to sagging jelly then to liquid that poured off the table, the small console bouncing on the floor.

A moment later he felt the *High Castle* submerge in U-space.

Spear

We surfaced a good light hour inside the Graveyard's border, within sight of one of the watch stations, but out of its reach . . .

unless, of course, the Polity felt like breaching agreements with the Kingdom to send something in after us. I called up a highly magnified view of the station on the screen fabric and studied it for a long moment. The station, which looked like a barbell, was immense. As I understood it, there were large communities aboard these things but not so large as their size implied because they were packed with detection gear along with offensive and defensive tech.

'Are we in?' I asked.

'Updating via U-com,' Flute replied, then, 'Yes, we are in.'

Applying through the ship's system, I felt my surroundings fade and come to seem ephemeral as I ventured into the AI net. The first thing that started to happen was that my aug began loading massive updates on the research and technologies I was interested in. I stopped that, realizing I would have to be a lot more selective with this stuff if I didn't want to keep upgrading my aug to handle it. I instead searched for local storage within the *Lance* to take it. Plenty of options were available and while checking what these were, I found another option that showed no capacity limit. After just a moment of thought I realized this wasn't actually part of the ship's system but something that had attached itself to me and my aug: the spine. Quite probably it had the capacity to store more than I would ever need, but I was reluctant to use it since that presupposed I would be hanging onto the damned thing. Instead I chose a data store within the ship's system.

Next, as I was about to begin searching for the latest news on Penny Royal: a polite request for open aug linkage. I turned round as Sepia stepped into the bridge. I'd left her taking a shower when we arrived here and now she'd dressed herself in another item from the ship's fabricator: a shiny black catsuit. I considered her request. We'd done it while screwing each other

– moving on to literally screwing each other's brains out, because we were in each other's mind. It was something I hadn't even contemplated with Sheil, the catadapt I met shortly after my resurrection, and this demonstrated how I felt about Sepia. However, making such a linkage outside of sex was a further step.

'Do you know,' she said, 'in the past, sex has never been the main indicator that a relationship had become serious. It was always about property and commitment. The only way that has changed is that the property is now often mental property.'

She moved over to her seat and lowered herself into it. She looked really good and even though I felt drained by our previous Olympian feats I was already thinking about peeling off that catsuit. But I could not allow that to cloud my judgement. If it were a simple aug-to-aug linkage between us that would be fine, but there was another item in this circuit I had to consider.

I gestured to the spine, now back in its clamp against the wall. 'I can open up, but there's that.'

She acknowledged this with a tilt of her head and waited.

Okay.

I opened up my aug to her while she simultaneously opened hers, and the connections established. It wasn't exactly mind-reading but lay somewhere between that and speech. During sex it meant never having to ask, 'Is this okay?' and never having to say, 'Yes, right there.' Now it was as if we both had two augs: a primary and a secondary. She had no control of mine and I had none over hers or, rather, in normal circumstances I had no control over hers, yet I knew that with the added backup of the spine I could probably seize control of it, and through it assert control over her body, or even her thoughts. Now we both knew what the other was doing in their aug. If I ran some system search she would see it. If I communicated by aug she would hear it and could join in. On other levels, via bio-feedback, we could sense how each other felt. It was close, very close, and a kind of commitment.

'Now,' I said, 'I don't know how this is going to affect you. I haven't secured your linkage so you can pull out fast if it's too much.'

The spine, which was a constant murmur in my consciousness, an extension and enhancement of it, drew mentally closer at my behest. Thousands of lives and deaths closed in like a clamouring crowd, mental horizons began opening out. I felt myself expanding and the thought that had occurred long ago recurred: *I am legion.* Sepia's eyes grew wide, her expression fascinated, and as the clamour increased I saw dawning horror there.

'Enough?' I asked.

She shook her head, and I felt the secondary impression of her aug harden. She started filtering and sorting just as I had. She was handling it but I realized that both she and her aug, which, after all, wasn't a very modern one, were reaching their limit.

'There,' I said, and began to damp the connection. She could take maybe ten per cent of it. I understood, my mind bubbling with the synergy of the recent connection, that if I opened fully to the spine as I sometimes did in moment of crisis, the feedback would knock Sepia unconscious and afterwards her aug would probably need reformatting.

She looked a little ill now as she said, 'How do you take it all?'

'Maybe I've had time to acclimatize,' I said. 'Or maybe my mind isn't what it was – I wouldn't be surprised to discover that Penny Royal had tampered with more than my memories.' At high speed I put together a précis of the situation concerning my false and altered memories and dispatched it to her. 'Speaking of

235

whom,' I finished, and then began searching through my connection to the AI net for data on that black AI.

There was a mountain of data, of course, as there would always be masses of data on any notorious character. However, when I started using specialized filtering to get rid of rumour, hearsay and stuff that was plain made up, the mountain collapsed to a steadily shrinking hill. I soon began to realize that there was nothing there about the black AI's visit to Room 101. I decided then to run another search, this one on Sverl, ran it through bespoke filters and found the same result: nothing about Room 101. The AIs were still keeping a lid on that.

Returning to the Penny Royal data, I found more detail on Room 101, but nothing that would indicate the AI's present location. I was scouring through a report concerning rumours of the *Black Rose* being spotted in the Kingdom, which essentially put it beyond my reach, when my aug informed me someone wanted to talk. Internally I gazed at the request for an open data channel, checked its routing and found it was from somewhere in the Polity, then finally tracked it down to Masada.

'*So who wants to speak to you from there?*' Sepia asked over our connection.

'*One way to find out,*' I replied.

I gave my permission, but for limited bandwidth – voice only.

'Hello, Thorvald,' said a familiar voice.

'Hello, Amistad,' I replied.

'A little paranoid, I see,' said the war drone. 'Let's go VR.'

I hesitated for a second, but could see no reason why Amistad might want to launch some mental attack against me, so I opened up the bandwidth. In a moment I found myself standing in a white open space, then detail began to fill in around me. A moment later I was on the viewing platform of Amistad's tower overlooking the wilds of Masada. Amistad, a war drone shaped like a giant steel scorpion, squatted ahead of me, peering over the rail. I walked up to stand beside him. As I did so, I was aware of a presence at my shoulder, but here Sepia was invisible.

'Anything much happening here?' I asked.

The drone gestured with one claw. 'The Weaver is pushing for his world to become an associate member of the Polity – something that has never happened before. It's all politics with a hint of sabre-rattling.'

I gazed out across a chequer board of squirm ponds and over to my right could see the raft of Masada's space port. Amistad's tower had withdrawn from its position overlooking the Weaver's woven home.

'Tedious for you, I should think,' I commented.

'It is,' Amistad agreed, 'though there are some strange wrinkles that do make things a little more interesting.'

'Like?'

'This new thing, this "associate status", will be inclusive of the Weaver's right to use the Polity runcible network. Many AIs are not happy about that at all.'

'Perhaps it wants to take a tour?'

'Perhaps.'

'But that isn't why you got in contact with me . . .'

'No.' Amistad turned from the rail with a rattle of hard feet to face me. 'You're looking for Penny Royal again.'

'You could say I've never stopped.'

'There's a data lockdown on anything pertaining to Room 101. The AIs don't want to let that one out of the bag unless they have to.'

'So it seems.'

'I've been keeping myself updated.'

'Get to the point, will you?'

'The point,' said Amistad, 'is that Isobel Satomi and Sverl

were not the only ones who were drastically changed by Penny Royal. You need to refine your search bearing that in mind.'

'Why are you telling me this?'

'Because I'm beginning to understand what Penny Royal is up to and it seems likely that you are the only one who can stop it . . . supposing it needs to be stopped.'

'You can't just –'

That was it: end of conversation. The tower and the world of Masada faded around me and I again found myself in white space. I cancelled the virtuality, and the bridge edged just a little way back into the reality I occupied.

'Interesting friends you have,' Sepia commented.

I glanced at her. 'You should have seen who –' I looked at my console – Riss was back in place as if she'd never been away – 'we gave a lift to on that world.'

'I think I'm going to need some updating on events before you arrived on Sverl's ship. I understand much of the story, but I'm certainly missing on some detail.'

'Will do,' I replied, 'when we're on the move again.'

Next I tinkered with my search engines and filters and ran the pile of rumour and hearsay through again to bring up anything current concerning those the black AI was supposed to have altered. It was right at the top of the remaining pile, a name: Mr Pace.

I recognized him, of course, because he was a candidate I had rejected before settling on Isobel Satomi. Mr Pace was a man who had gone to Penny Royal with the aim of making himself indestructible. He had returned with a body made from self-renewing meta-material based on obsidian and diamond shear planes. I studied some of the technical specs available and, yes, the guy was pretty much blast-proof, but I wondered what his downside was; what grotesque joke Penny Royal had played on him.

The current rumour related to Penny Royal. It was that Mr Pace had recently fled the scene of a massacre caused by that AI and returned to his home on a world within the Graveyard. Frustratingly there was next to no detail. Was this what Amistad had been getting at? A moment later the war drone did not let me down, as a data package arrived along the still-open link back to the Polity. Again being cautious, I found out everything I could about the package before opening it, and learned that it was an ECS security tape.

'It's been a long time,' said a squat heavy-worlder woman with plaited ginger hair.

The figure sitting opposite her at the table wore antediluvian businesswear and had an antique briefcase resting beside his chair. His skin was midnight black and with his attenuated frame he reminded me of images I had seen of the Masai. His hair looked slicked down, almost plastic, however, and his eyes were similar to those of the Sobel line: white pupils, and the rest of the eyes black.

'Long time,' he agreed.

They were in some sort of bar, a panoramic window behind being pattered with red sleet melting and running like strawberry cordial. Beyond lay a mountainous terrain, indigo sky scored with lavender clouds like some spatter pattern from a murder scene.

'Everything is in order and I've started up your house systems.' The woman paused for a moment. 'What brings you back?'

He reached out and picked up his drink, downed it in one. 'I didn't find what I was looking for there.' He waved a dismissive hand.

239

'Another dead end?'

'It was for the extremadapt colony.'

'What happened?'

'Penny Royal happened – they're all dead.'

He closed his hand tightly on his glass, crushing it into splinters. When he inserted the broken glass into his mouth the woman didn't blink an eye.

'You survived,' she pointed out.

He sat there crunching contemplatively for a moment, then swallowed. Perhaps broken glass was a supplement his strange body needed. 'I don't know whether it was because of me.' He reached down and opened his briefcase. 'One can never tell with Penny Royal.' He shrugged. 'Anyway, I decided not to hang around.'

From his briefcase, he extracted a simple-looking gun, then he turned to face me. I guessed he was looking at whoever or whatever had made this recording.

'I think you have enough now,' he said, then pointed and fired.

I found myself snapped back onto the bridge of the *Lance*, Riss gazing at me from the console with her black eye open, and Sepia watching me curiously from her chair. I felt a moment of annoyance, closed my eyes for a second to try and summon up that file again. I got it, and began running through it in search of anything that could give me the location of this Mr Pace.

'Do any of you recognize this?' I asked. I knew I didn't need to send it to either Riss or Sepia because they were both there in my aug with me, but I did send it to Flute.

After a short pause Sepia said, 'It's Rorquin.'

'You're sure?'

'Hard not to recognize that sky, or the rain.' She shook her head. 'It's caused by a ferric compound blown down towards the equator from the polar desert. Strange world – its axis highly tilted with the poles alternating from deep freeze to hot enough to fry bacon over winter and summer.'

'You went there?'

'Sure, I went to see Mr Pace, but he wasn't home at the time.' She paused for a second while the penny, so to speak, dropped. 'Of course he's—'

'Why did you go to see this Mr Pace?' I interrupted.

'Curiosity and a momentary rise in my suicidal impulse.'

'Suicidal?'

'Mr Pace is a notoriously private person,' she replied. 'And since he's not inside the Polity he doesn't have to obey niggling little laws about not killing people who irritate him. Quite a few of my kind have paid him very final visits.'

I nodded, uncomfortable with this revelation because I didn't really understand the impulse. Uncomfortable too with the dawning idea that Sepia had been eager to join me because being with me was as risky a pursuit as any those suffering from ennui tried. Perhaps I would understand when I grew older. Perhaps it related to that emptiness I felt at the prospect of no longer having Penny Royal to chase. I grimaced at the thought then ran a search to get as much detail as I could on this Mr Pace. A minute later a great wedge of data dropped into my aug – so much I had to relay some of it into the *Lance*'s auxiliary storage.

'Flute,' I said, 'take us to Rorquin now.'

241

9

Sverl

As the last hardfield generator left the bubble-metal tank, shed its outer coverings and sped through the station to its position in the network, Sverl would have breathed a sigh of relief, except he had no lungs.

'Shut it down,' he instructed the AI controlling material feeds to that tank. There hadn't been any specific instructions about halting the process, but it was plain that starving it of materials would do the job.

'It seems to be doing that all by itself,' the AI concerned replied.

'Data,' Sverl instructed.

The AI opened feeds from sensors in and around the tank and from scanners in the vicinity too. Sverl studied the processes occurring inside and saw that they had changed. Matter flow patterns had altered and the lack of a kernel for the next hardfield generator was plain. But of course Penny Royal would have known just how many of these devices were needed and had limited the process to producing just the required quantity. Sverl turned his attention to the robots and to Bsorol and the second-children, who had rushed in to install heat sinks and transformers around the tank when the temperatures generated by its internal processes were about to breach it.

'You are needed back at the U-space engines,' he instructed

Bsorol. 'Bsectil is readying them to take the new rings and could do with some help.'

'Yes, Father,' Bsorol replied, collecting up his tools.

Sverl allowed his attention to stray to a shutdown runcible from which 'structor pods were now extracting the gravity box – an octahedral case trailing power cables and being moved as ponderously as a moon in orbit, which was about as much as it massed. This item would make its slow transit back through the station to where the gravity press – a monolithic device the size of an attack ship – was now rolling out of its factory ready to receive its last component. Making the new rings for the drive would take five days, so things were proceeding a lot faster than he had calculated. But urgency remained: Sverl still wanted those engines working and still wanted to take the station away from here. The enclosing hardfield he was about to generate might well be cutting-edge Penny Royal technology but he wouldn't put it past Polity AIs to find a way of getting through the thing.

He now watched the last hardfield generator exit through a port in the station's hull and then arc back down towards that hull. The other ninety-five generators were also so positioned and, as this one finally touched down, the network was completed physically. Sverl felt the connection in his mind and experienced the satisfaction a third-child feels upon slotting the last piece of a logic puzzle into place. And the reasons behind it were similar: plain survival.

Now, with a simple mental instruction he could turn on a hardfield to encompass the entire station. Should he do so now? He decided not, for this action required some thought.

If he turned it on now the Polity AIs out there would have time, while he worked on the engines, to analyse it and perhaps find some way to deal with it. If he didn't turn it on now there was a chance that they might spot the generators on the hull and destroy some or all of them before he could turn the thing on. Then, of course, there were other possibilities: what if the damned thing didn't work? What if it interfered with U-drive? what if it –?

'We have a problem,' said the AI he had been speaking to earlier.

'What?'

It opened up those feeds to him again. The matter inside the bubble-metal tank was swirling faster and faster, and the temperature was rising rapidly. The inner sensors had died and those on the outer casing were steadily going out. Even as he watched, he could see some of the supporting struts bending while cracks developed in that outer ceramic casing to reveal a hellish red light glaring from its inner layers. He tried to analyse what was going on inside but it was beyond him. Certainly the liquid materials inside were moving so fast they were creating a powerful gyroscopic effect and a torsion that was working against the supports, but still there were nanoscopic processes occurring, and even stuff on levels below that. The mass in there was turning into something intricate lying partway between physical matter and some kind of plasma-energy mechanism.

So what now, Penny Royal, he wondered.

As he watched, the last of the sensors on the casing died as the cracks grew wider. The scanners he was using, which sat a distance away from the tank, were also beginning to struggle, for the temperature was getting ever higher. Next he saw inner layers ablating and dissolving; being sucked up by the whirling inner mass. Now visible through the cracks, it didn't actually look hot, but oddly like blue-tinted mercury. Further scanning then revealed that though the casing and surrounding structures were heating up, radiation from the surface of the mass itself was steadily dropping. He had seen strange effects like this before, in fact with the operation of hardfield generators like those sitting out on the hull. He now directed a more distant scanner at this anomaly and wasn't surprised to discover some kind of U-space phenomenon occurring. The mass was somehow drawing energy from that underlying continuum.

Next, all at once, the entire tank and much of the surrounding infrastructure just collapsed, disappearing into a whirling metallic sphere, the thundering of that collapse felt even here in Sverl's sanctum. The sphere then began to move, a spinning gravity wave around it sucking in anything within a few hundred feet. It rapidly carved a wide opening through the structure of the station. Sverl gaped. He had been steadily repairing and restoring this structure, and now some device of Penny Royal's was tearing the guts out of it. What the hell was the purpose of this thing?

'Must eject,' came the brief statement from the AI, then its link with Sverl cut.

It took him a moment to realize the whirling sphere had been bearing down on the AI's armoured case. The AI had ejected itself and was now bouncing along down a far tunnel. Sverl instructed a tree of 'structor pods at the far end to field it then focused back on the course of that whirling sphere.

The thing was currently travelling in a straight line towards what could only be called the nose of the station – meaning the end that didn't contain the engines. Measurements showed that the centre point of the thing hadn't deviated in this straight-line course by even a few inches. But as it ate away infrastructure, its mass was steadily increasing. Sverl plotted its course and sent warnings to any AIs lying in its path, then felt a horrible sinking sensation when he spotted that the one operating runcible aboard the station lay along that path. He again checked the course of the thing and saw that it would pass neatly through the octagonal frame. Then what? He could shut down the runcible and then, with any luck, the thing would finally pass out through the nose of the station and keep going. However, this was certainly at Penny Royal's instigation and must serve a greater purpose than simply wrecking the interior on its way out.

If he turned the runcible off it would leave the station open to attack by U-space missiles. What would happen the moment that thing hit the U-space meniscus if he left the runcible on? Usually normal material objects hitting a disconnected runcible gateway would drop straight into U-space without destination. They tended just to disappear. But this thing was by no stretch of the imagination *normal*.

As Sverl tried to think his way through this quandary it seemed almost inevitable that more woes would come to burden him. The AI commander of the Polity fleet now wanted to talk to him. He opened the link and waited.

'I don't know what the fuck you think you're doing, Sverl,' said Garrotte, 'but it doesn't look to me like you're doing as you were told.'

'A slight problem has occurred,' Sverl replied, trying to think of some reasonable explanation. There wasn't one. Those ships out there had to be picking up on a large mass of material, with a strange U-signature, moving through the ship.

After a pause, Garrotte continued, 'We gave you the time, and now your time has run out. I have my orders.'

Particle beams with the power to kill cities stabbed in from the two dreadnoughts, while the attack ships began dropping into U-space. In the microsecond he had, Sverl knew he could delay no longer and turned on the hardfield. The station, already shuddering around him with the wrecking progress of that whirling mass, heaved like some giant oceangoing liner ploughing into a mud bank. Through outer sensors, the bright glare of the hyper-giant dimmed and took on an orange tint. All around the hull the hardfield generators lifted, and an immense hardfield in the shape of a bacillus expanded out around the station.

Within, the station lights dimmed and fusion reactors stuttered as their power just drained away. Sverl measured an overall temperature drop throughout the station of nearly fifty degrees as the entropic effect of the field kicked in.

The beams hit, splashing against the barrier, tearing like giant energy drillbits as they traversed it. Behind them they left black shadows that slowly faded, then, after a moment, they weren't splashing at all, but seemingly terminating against the field like standing rods. Within the station, power levels began to rise again and Sverl allowed himself a moment of relief. Next, analysing through his own and the station's U-tech, Sverl saw that the field was sucking up the energy, translating it into U-space and then drawing it back through the projectors to further power itself. The field was no longer drawing on its near surroundings. This was just as it should be and just as it had been at Carapace City. However, there was another draw on this energy source, and that was the whirling mass now accelerating towards the functional runcible.

'What shall I do?' asked the runcible AI.

'Sing?' Sverl suggested, and then suppressed a very human giggle.

Directly outside the station, beyond the hardfield which had now stabilized just over a mile out from the hull, the attack ships reappeared, splinter missiles issuing from their crow's wing hulls. Sverl detected two attempts at firing U-jump missiles; energy anomalies from the runcible as it sucked them up. They had probably just been a probe to ensure that method of attack would not be effective. However, if he shut the runcible down now they would know at once and the hardfield would be no defence. No doubt it would just remain in place, feeding off the energies thrown against it, while the station turned to white-hot vapour inside.

Next came the railgun shots, sparkling down the length of the station, the blasts nowhere near as radiant as they should have been, their vaporized metal rapidly cooling in proximity to the vampire effect of the field. And the sphere continued accelerating. CTDs followed, turning space beyond the field as bright as if the station was sitting in the chromosphere of a sun. Gravity-wave weapons then shook them and something else that caused blisters in the field, but they healed a moment later. Sverl paid some attention to that, but his main focus remained on the sphere as it now finally came to and touched the U-space meniscus. He felt fatalistic about it. Doubtless humans and prador alike had felt like this when faced by catastrophe: a tsunami coming in, an asteroid plummeting, a sun going nova. What could he do? Absolutely nothing at all.

The whirling sphere touched, and then just passed straight through the meniscus and out the other side. The gravity wave around it collapsed briefly, so caused no harm to the runcible – then it continued on its course towards the nose of the station. After passing through the space beyond the runcible, it began eating infrastructure again. Sverl calculated that it now had fifty times the mass it had started out with.

'Well that was interesting,' said Garrotte, the U-space com-link still open.

'Perhaps we have different definitions of "interesting",' Sverl replied.

'So I see you have one of Penny Royal's hardfields . . .'

'Observant of you.'

'Well, I suppose you won't be a problem to us while you

remain inside it,' said Garrotte. 'And, of course, the moment you drop it is the moment you cease to exist.'

The sphere had just passed along the back of a final construction bay, tearing up metal, sucking down resupply towers and massive cranes. It now lay a quarter of a mile across and its constant destruction was beginning to extend beyond its limited area. It was eating through some main structural beams, ripping out supporting and bracing structures so that its progress was now marked out by distortions that reached out to the very hull.

'So what are you going to do now, Sverl?' Garrotte asked.

Sverl considered sending an image feed of what was going on inside the station, but rejected the idea. Why should he explain or justify his actions to entities who had just tried to fry him? Screw them. After a moment he severed the comlink and just concentrated on the sphere.

The thing continued along its course, sucked up a fusion reactor without pausing, absorbed a giant factory unit like a macrophage eating a bacterium, began carving its way down a dreadnought assembly tube, its diameter now wider than the tube and leaving nothing but ripped-off support struts behind. It passed through the backs of more final assembly bays, drew in wreckage and the badly damaged body of an entire attack ship. Ahead of it the warned AIs had abandoned their abodes by whatever means available – by ejection tube, by 'structor pod, strapped to the back of a robot, or walking out in heron-legged mobility units – and moved out to the hull. Over the next hour the thing traversed thirty miles of the station and closed in on the hull metal at the end.

Here was the moment. Would it punch through and just continue on its course or, as Sverl was beginning to think, was it some sort of response prepared by Penny Royal to that fleet out there? Would it pass out through the end of the hardfield and then proceed, in some manner, to annihilate those Polity ships? It didn't. As it reached the multiple-layered metal of the hull it buckled it, tearing out a great chunk, but halted and began to change. Like a soft egg hatching, it began to deform as if something was pushing out from inside. It bubbled and then, amoeba-like, began to extend pseudopods. As these stretched out, they began to harden and take on definition, turning into protrusions like the trunks of giant trees, terminating in flat pads packed with tangled tubework. The whole thing looked like a giant model of some kind of bacterium. As Sverl watched this thing for a while longer, he realized that though it had halted its progress forwards while making this transformation, it had started moving in another way. It was spiralling gradually outwards and infinitesimally back the way it had come. It was also doing something else, turning and presenting those protrusions and, as well as tearing up hull metal, it was now shedding mass too, extruding something from those flat pipework pads.

It was depositing a thick and steadily growing cap of brass-coloured material on its obverse side from the station. Sensor data was not so good up that end now because so much of the infrastructure had been wrecked, so Sverl fired a probe from midway along the station to go and take a look. A few minutes later he gazed upon a shallow and growing hemisphere cupping the end of the station, with the device working between. Initial analyses that came back told him this object was formed of some layered composite that bore some similarities to prador hull metal. Further analysis revealed that this composite consisted of woven strands of partially exotic matter. The hemisphere continued to grow as more and more of the station was fed into the maelstrom. Next, the course of the thing changed: it stopped constructing the hemisphere and traversed across it, in a series of radial courses. Behind it left bracing beams, but with an organic look, like the inner structures of a bird's bones, woven again.

It returned to its spiralling course, building the hemisphere with pseudopods on one side of it, while eating the station with those on the other. At length, over the best part of a day, it began reaching beyond the limit of the station as the hemisphere grew to over forty miles across. Now it began making sorties back into the station to feed itself, before heading back out again to deposit matter. As the thing ate away the end of the station, the hemisphere shifted inwards. Also the hardfields out there were adjusting their position to accommodate it. Feeling utterly awed, Sverl made some more calculations. This thing was turning Room 101 into a sphere which, when finished, would measure fifty miles in diameter. But what concerned him now was what would happen when it reached back to the runcible, his own sanctum, the hospital and finally the U-space drive. He deeply hoped that those still alive in the station, including of course himself, had not just become irrelevant to Penny Royal's plans. He did not want to end up as a thin layer in that growing mass.

The Brockle

As the *High Castle* surfaced from U-space, the Brockle, keeping a wary eye on the distant border watch station, reached out and made tentative connections to the AI net. In the data available to anyone who logged on, it found little of interest. There were no stories of its own escape from the *Tyburn* or any of that ship's destruction. There was just a brief mention of the murder aboard Par Avion and some speculation about the possibility of some kind of disruptor weapon being used. Nothing new about Penny

Royal beyond rumour and pure fiction. It would be necessary, therefore, to delve deeper, and with that came dangers.

In the guise of the *High Castle* AI, it first began a slow and steady penetration of ECS data traffic issuing from Par Avion. Here it was surprised to discover that there was nothing about its own presence there. The station was being searched for 'likely separatist elements' in association with the murder of the woman because she had separatist connections herself. Polity AIs had made no link between the Brockle's presence there while the *High Castle* was docked and the subsequent loss of communication with that ship. In fact, that loss of communication was considered quite normal for a ship on such a *sensitive* mission. After thoroughly checking all this data, the forensic AI finally decided it was safe to make deeper enquiries.

Next it shifted its attention to com traffic with the Polity fleet the *High Castle* had been intended to join. Security was intensely tight there, but its guise as the *High Castle* AI gave the Brockle a high level of clearance. Still cautious, it did not go too deep, merely learning of the transformation of the prador Sverl, his assumption of control of Room 101 and the intention of the fleet to get him out of that large military asset. The Brockle felt frustrated with this, because the knowledge brought it no closer to finding Penny Royal. Instead it tracked back through the Polity, trying to penetrate at relay stations or via some of the less guarded Polity AIs. Still no luck. It tried turning up something on those stolen runcibles aboard the cargo hauler the *Azure Whale* but it was completely off the grid – no information at all.

It routed then to Masada, because that was Penny Royal's last location in the Polity and it knew that the erstwhile war drone Amistad still retained an interest. Security was tough here too, because of the Atheter and the recent history of that place. Retreating again in frustration, it picked up on a signal relayed from Masada into the Graveyard, tracked the course of that and found itself back at a watch station nearby. Here, surprisingly, it found penetrating security a lot easier, though the data it wanted was buried deep and it necessarily had to extend itself to the limit to obtain it. However, a moment later it had something of value.

Mr Pace . . .

The Brockle sat back in its chair, fingers interlaced over its fat belly, smiling with satisfaction.

'You're being very circumspect,' said a conversational voice, 'but I suppose that is understandable considering the apparent nature of your enquiries. Let me assure you that my security is solid and no black AIs have penetrated here.'

The Brockle immediately lost its human form and flew apart – its usual reaction to an unknown threat. It could feel the links in its mind, the data channel hooked on and cycling. To one side, a chromed human face appeared – a standard holding icon – but the watch station AI wasn't actually here and this was just a visual projection. In a few microseconds the Brockle had to come to a decision: disassociate and fight the links, or run with it and try to obtain more data. It chose the latter.

'I am just attempting to follow my orders as closely as possible,' it replied. 'Penny Royal is a dangerous creature that must be tracked with subtlety and ultimately confronted with maximum force.'

'So I'm right?' said the watch station AI. 'Your mission profile was one of investigation of the Room 101 situation after it had been dealt with by the fleet. I, and others, always thought that odd, considering the armament the *High Castle* carries. And were further suspicious when it went dark.'

'Secret orders, of course,' the Brockle replied.

'So, to confirm, it's your duty to track down and destroy Penny Royal?'

'Earth Central fully understands how dangerous Penny Royal is,' the Brockle replied. 'And I would like you to keep this exchange between us secret. The AI nets are not safe for data exchange on this subject at any level since we have no idea how deeply Penny Royal has penetrated. What happened with the erstwhile warden of Masada, Amistad, illustrates this.'

'Very well . . .' The watch station AI paused for a few seconds, which was all but an eternity in AI terms. 'I have collated all data on Penny Royal now available, also all data on the Room 101 mission, which is of course integral.'

'I see . . .'

'This will save you having to make multiple probes throughout the AI net and will thus reduce your exposure.'

The data package arrived an instant later.

'Thank you,' the Brockle said then quickly began cutting links. The station AI would see that as just a sensible security precaution. While utterly isolating the data package, the Brockle started running a deep diagnostic on itself to ensure nothing else had been inserted. After a while it found itself to be completely clear and felt that the encounter had gone a long way towards confirming its recent actions: Polity AIs were just not as omniscient as some humans supposed and were vulnerable to hostile AI action. It was doing the right thing.

The Brockle then reflected on the dangers of opening the data package, for it could be booby-trapped. If it opened the package in an isolated unit and it was some form of attack then it would destroy the unit and be rid of the package. However, if it was some form of attack, surely some AI had designed it with the Brockle in mind, and with such an approach expected. If it transferred the package to other computing, that meant computing aboard this ship – all interlinked. Perhaps the watch station AI hoped it would do that and something in the package had been designed to disable the ship, maybe take over, or maybe just ensure the transmission of some U-space beacon so it could be traced. But there was another option and, no matter how it looked at that option, the Brockle could see no danger to itself.

Falling back together and again taking on the shape of a man, the Brockle stood and headed out of its cabin. Reaching the lounge, it found only Captain Blite, but he would do, even though his aug was a quite antiquated and simple one. He looked around, horrified, when the Brockle reached out to him and via his aug issued a summons directly to his inner reptile brain. He jerked to his feet and, fighting all the way, followed the Brockle back to its cabin to stand in the centre. The Brockle paused then, wondering why it had felt the need physically to walk out to get the man, surmised that the urge must be related to its distant human past and dismissed the matter.

'What do you fucking want?' Blite managed tightly.

The Brockle studied him on many levels, realizing he had built up a degree of resistance it had never seen before. But then, its subjects didn't usually live as long as Blite had.

'I want you to look at something for me,' it replied, now dispatching the package to the man's aug and directly into his mind, opening it like a potential bomb and rapidly retreating.

Blite staggered as if struck, resting a hand against one wall, but then after a moment straightened up, his expression seemingly lost in introspection. The Brockle waited with growing impatience, its form loosening into a sculpture of a man made of sliding silver worms.

'What do you see?' it finally asked.

Blite looked up, blinked, shook his head. 'Data, lots of data, and images.'

'Tell me about the images.'

'Room 101 under a hardfield like we saw at Carapace City

. . . ripping out the end of the station and building something . . . massive energy readings . . .'

Even more impatient with that inadequate description, the Brockle reached out mentally, tentatively, to reconnect with Blite's aug. Reading via that, and ready to sever the connection in an instant, it got the images first. A massive curved hardfield had first enclosed the station, then after a period of time something had torn through the nose of the station and steadily begun rebuilding it. This wasn't enough. The Brockle probed deeper and began picking up on other readings and deeper levels of AI analysis. First it understood that the hardfield maintained a link into U-space, routing energy there from the attacks against it, even routing solar energy from the hypergiant, to then draw it back and reinforce itself. This it had seen before and still wondered just what purpose, beyond the obvious one of defence from attack, such a potentially infinitely strong field could serve. Next it saw that the mechanism rebuilding the station was also powered by that energy feed. The watching ships had tracked it along inside the station, where it had been decohering and gathering matter into itself. Reaching the end of the station, it then began to deposit that material to form what was likely to be a highly reinforced sphere with densely packed bracing struts.

The Brockle delved deeper, obtaining layer upon layer of data on this. The hardfield was a Penny Royal design while the object rebuilding the station seemed to be from the same source. It was also, of course, evident to the watching AIs that Penny Royal wasn't in residence, and much more so to the Brockle. Those AIs were amazed, awed and painfully aware that such technology was beyond even them. Turning away from Blite, it now loaded the package across from him so as to study it in further detail.

'You can go,' it said.

Blite didn't need telling twice.

Reassuming human form, the Brockle sat and felt something hollow opening inside. It could easily neutralize most Polity AIs, as it had demonstrated aboard this very ship, but now it was having its doubts about its ability to deal with Penny Royal. Somehow Room 101 was part of the AI's plans and it was effecting a major modification to that station without even being present. It was using technologies that, though understood to be possible, had yet to be used by Polity AIs.

The Brockle contemplated the situation further, and from the depths of its mind rose a memory of something that had wormed its way into popular consciousness from an ancient celluloid film many centuries ago. The film had been about a hunt for a killer shark, but what had it been called? *Teeth*? *The Swallow*?

'We're going to need a bigger boat,' it said, then after a moment checked the cams in the corridor outside to ensure that no one was listening.

Spear

Rorquin was a heliotrope marble smeared with a cream of large shifting cloud masses. Another twelve ships were in orbit about it: salvagers, some highly modified wartime craft, a baroque contraption that looked like a flying church and another thing bigger than the *Lance* and the shape and colour of an ox tongue. As I piloted the shuttle out of the *Lance*'s bay, fired up its drive and dropped towards this orb, I pondered what I had thus far learned about the man, if he could be described as such, who had laid claim to one of the three continental land masses below.

Mr Pace was two hundred and ninety years old and, like so

many in the Graveyard, he had made his fortune in ways that weren't strictly legal. He'd fought in the war against the prador in a squad just like Jebel U-cap Krong's and been awarded medals for his bravery. Like so many, he had gone into salvage after the war and then on to less salubrious pursuits. He had run an organization much like Isobel Satomi's – involved in any crime that was profitable – and, though I as yet had no positive proof of it, I suspected he had been the criminal she had whored for in her early years. That was when he had been human, however, and before he had taken a visit to a particular planetoid.

However, unlike Isobel Satomi, Mr Pace had not gone to Penny Royal for the means to defeat a threatening competitor, but in response to the vagaries of chance. On the world below, his gravcar had been struck by lightning. This in itself wouldn't have been a problem had it not been for a grav-motor fault that had gone undetected, but which was exacerbated by the power surge. His car dropped out of the sky and crashed into a mountain. Mr Pace was severely injured and nearly died. In fact, when he finally walked out of his personal hospital he was ninety per cent machine. That was when he went to Penny Royal to buy a new body, and indestructibility. Thereafter he had extended his grip in the Graveyard to become its top crime lord – organizations like Isobel's being subordinate to him.

'So why, exactly, are we going to see this Mr Pace?' asked Riss as I guided our shuttle down into thick reddish cloud.

I looked at the drone then glanced at Sepia, who looked interested in what answer I might give. She now knew my story, with a few irrelevant details omitted, from when I was resurrected on Earth.

'Because he won't speak to us from down there,' I hedged.

Mr Pace lived in a castle perched on a mountaintop. The building had looked familiar to me and after some research I found out that externally it closely resembled Edinburgh Castle, though much of the insides were different. Was such a fortified residence another example of him trying to separate himself from the vagaries of chance, of accident? Perhaps, but if so his time spent away from here with the extremadapts was out of character. I'd tried opening com channels both via the space port below and directly into the castle by beaming signals at satellite discs and other com arrays. No joy: Mr Pace wasn't talking.

'You're just evading the issue,' said Riss.

'Okay – because his was the most recent sighting of Penny Royal,' I replied.

'Yet you know where Penny Royal is going.'

'Do I?'

'You have *surmised* that Penny Royal is going to Panarchia.'

'And like a good little drone I should respond to the summons?' I said, turning to look at Riss. 'My initial reason for going after Penny Royal was the same as yours: vengeance. But now that's gone and we're following because that's what we do.' I paused for a second then an apt description of us popped into my mind. We were tornado chasers. Uncomfortable with the notion, I continued, 'Before I go to Panarchia I want to know what happened at this extremadapt colony.'

'You want Penny Royal to be bad again.'

Did I?

All I knew was that I didn't want to go rushing to Panarchia and was again feeling my way. I also felt I didn't want to ignore the data Amistad had supplied. Was I procrastinating again? I thought not, because Mr Pace was another creation of Penny Royal's and quite probably another loose thread in the story that AI was weaving. While, on the one hand I didn't want to respond to what I had called a summons, I also felt I wasn't supposed to respond straight away – that my visit here was in the weave.

Before I could vocalize any of this, Sepia interjected from the seat beside mine, 'Don't you?'

Riss swung round to look at her.

'I guess that would probably suit you too,' said the drone.

Not rising to the jibe, Sepia replied, 'I don't think so – I'm beginning to feel that period of my life slide behind me.' She shrugged. 'Anyway, it's not as if we'll be losing much time. Rorquin here,' she waved a hand at the cloud beyond the screen, 'is more or less on a straight-line course to Panarchia.'

'And it's not like Panarchia is going to be disappearing any time yet,' I added.

Flute had uploaded astrogation data via the watch station, and though when I had been on that world it had been said it was a century away from being dropped into Layden's Sink, that had apparently been a very rough estimate. The world had another twenty years.

'Of course you do understand how risky this is?' Sepia enquired, turning to face me.

'As far as I understand it, he's a dangerous character.'

'He is dangerous, but then so is Riss here.' She reached out to Riss, who was between our two seats, and patted her on the head. The drone swung round as if about to bite, ovipositor rattling against the floor. I got the impression she hadn't appreciated being treated like a pet. I also got the impression that it was repayment for Riss's earlier jibe. 'The main problem with Mr Pace is that he's dangerous, homicidal in fact, *and* unpredictable.'

'You're implying that I am predictable?' snapped Riss.

'Didn't you behave precisely as Penny Royal predicted?'

'That's different,' said Riss snottily, turning away from her and facing me again. 'What if Penny Royal is on Panarchia right now and decides not to wait for you?'

'Not really a problem.'

The shuttle finally dropped through the lowering cloud, heavy strawberry rain lashing against the screen. Mountainous terrain was just visible below through the murk, the peaks rounded and grey like the bouldered guts of the world thrust up through the surface. I could see lights down amidst them – no doubt the small space port we were heading for. As we descended towards this, I wondered what had been the negative outcome of Mr Pace's visit to Penny Royal. He had been given a body formed of a tough and hard metallic glass: a layered thing which, according to Polity analysis, was as near to indestructible as something formed of conventional matter could be. Dropping out of the sky in a gravcar would be no problem for him – he would in fact be as difficult to kill as a battle drone like Amistad.

'State the purpose of your visit,' a voice demanded from the console.

I auged to Sepia. *'What's the best way to go about this?'*

She smiled, showing her sharp teeth. *'I've always found honesty is the best policy.'*

'I am here to see Mr Pace,' I replied.

The response was laughter. Obviously that 'state the purpose of your business' was just a way of opening communications, because the man speaking got straight down to the meat of the matter. 'The landing fee is five hundred New Carth shillings or equivalent in any other viable currency, including diamond slate. We also take Galaxy Bank transfers.'

'That's not a problem,' I replied. It wasn't: I still had plenty of portable wealth aboard and, according to my recent aug update, my service pension was nicely accruing interest.

'That's a C-class Polity destroyer you arrived in?'

'It is,' I replied, slightly puzzled and feeling the need to add, 'armed.'

'Does the mind have instructions in the event of you suffering some mishap?'

I got it then. The man thought I was one of Sepia's crowd, or like the shell people: that I had come here to alleviate my boredom. Having loaded much data on Mr Pace, I'd learned that Sepia was quite correct and that while in residence before he'd had many such visitors. They came because he was dangerous. They also came because he was very old – beyond the ennui barrier – and might have some insight to their condition. It struck me that visiting him bore some similarity to Perseus visiting the three witches: you might get the information you were after but would quite likely end up dead. And like a gambler throwing away his last cent on the longest odds possible, that was why they did it. Generally, if they managed to get to see him at all they never reappeared again. 'It has instructions,' I replied, not wanting to take the conversation any further.

'If you are visiting Mr Pace,' the man continued, 'we are prepared to waive the landing fee on the basis of us being designated the auctioneer of your vessel.'

I wondered how the hell that worked in the Graveyard. The space port I knew to be independent although it sat on Mr Pace's claimed property. I assumed that whoever owned it must have business links into the Polity.

'That won't be necessary – just send me precise landing coordinates.'

'If you're utterly sure,' he said. 'We can give cash and credit advances on all our facilities here and in Adamant Town on the same basis.'

I was getting tired of this. 'Alternatively I can land elsewhere since I don't see any barrier to my doing so.'

'The terrain is mountainous and you may experience—'

'This is the landing craft of a Polity destroyer,' I pointed out.

After a short pause he said, 'Sending coordinates,' and cut com.

As the coordinates arrived I loaded them to my aug, assumed manual control and took us down.

'Did you know that "visiting Mr Pace" has become synonymous in some parts of the Polity with self-euthanasia?' said Sepia.

'No, but I'm not surprised.' I shook my head. 'If your . . . erstwhile kind wanted some advice on how to just keep on living they'd do better visiting those Old Captains on Spatterjay.'

'Many do that too,' she replied. 'The opportunities for dying on that world are boundless.'

I didn't really have any answer for that.

The space port was a platform a mile square raised halfway up four half-mile-high corner towers. There were buildings along one edge and even more packed in on the floor below. The platform was scattered with ranks of shuttles or U-space-capable craft small enough to fit down here. The whole thing sat in a valley with a river running through and actually passing under the port. Further down the valley was the sprawl of a town, the houses constructed of atomic sheared blocks of the local stone evidently taken from a quarry cut into one of the slopes above. Various roads wormed away from this settlement, doubtless leading to others scattered over this continent and maybe all the way around the world. I didn't know. Though I'd loaded plenty of data about Mr Pace I hadn't thought to get detail on the planet he occupied.

'So what do they do here?' I asked as I brought the shuttle in between two of the port towers.

'Do?' Sepia echoed.

'This is the Graveyard and not some AI-cozened world in the Polity,' I explained. 'And I note there are a lot of ships here, not necessarily all with crew just coming to "visit Mr Pace". How do they earn their living here?'

'Oh, rare earths and gemstones, some strange biologicals from native slime moulds. And, believe it or not, tea.'

'Must be an adapted variety.'

'It is. They have valleys of tea oaks growing here. The trees were planted here before the war and survived it, though most of the original residents didn't.'

'I'm surprised,' I said as I brought the shuttle in to land. 'There must be a lot of places to hide in these mountains and anything that got all the people surely wouldn't have left much else.'

'Bio-weapon,' she explained.

'It's not named,' Riss interjected, 'just called number twelve.'

'You know this world?'

'I know of it. The weapon, number twelve, was a potent nerve agent.'

'Everyone?'

'Every single human being.'

'Inactive now?'

'Mostly,' Riss replied, in a way that wasn't exactly reassuring.

The shuttle settled on its belly, the remora clamp engaging because local information had it that this valley could get very stormy. Checking the package on local conditions in my aug, I found that we wouldn't need breathers or temperature-controlled suits if we went outside, but we would need insulated clothing and, it went without saying, waterproofs.

'Well,' I said, 'let's go.'

I didn't bother looking for anything in the shuttle's stores since the enviro-suit I was wearing would be more than adequate. Sepia was similarly clad so needed no extra clothing either. She did, however, holster a small pulse-gun at her hip and take her laser carbine. I just picked up one other item: the spine. Perhaps it would have been better had I left it aboard the *Lance*, but I felt I needed it with me and, as I was beginning to understand, it might be a lot more effective as a weapon than the carbine my catadapt companion carried.

We trooped out of the airlock onto pitted rain-swept plasticrete. As we tramped, and slithered, towards the nearby port buildings I noted in the puddles things that looked like jellyfish. When we reached the building, from one corner of which a drainpipe was belching water, I spotted molluscs like penny oysters stuck to the lower stonework, and was reminded of Masada.

'Any dangerous wildlife here?' I asked as I pushed open the door.

'Nothing we need worry about,' Sepia replied. 'We'll hire a clamberer in the port city below and that will take us straight to his castle – nothing should be able to get to us.'

The inside of the building was bare, with just a row of elevator doors across the back wall. I wondered where I was supposed to pay my landing fee.

'So what exactly happened last time you came here?' I asked.

'He wasn't here but I went out to his castle anyway.' She grimaced. 'I obviously wasn't as far gone as I thought because, when I finally got a look at the bone pile at the foot of his mountain I decided I didn't want to hang around.'

'His previous visitors?' I asked.

'Yes, his previous visitors.'

10

Sfolk

As he slid down towards the strange ship Sfolk saw Penny Royal come apart, taking on the form of a swarm of knives, which then shot down towards the vessel and disappeared. He arrived shortly afterwards – the huge ship looming around him like some vast city – boarded through a protruding open weave tube, alarmingly without an airlock, and began exploring. The AI wasn't confining him, seemed careless of him. It was time therefore to find a weapon, or some other technology to give himself an advantage. Even though he suspected he was powerless against the black AI, he had no intention of giving up.

He saw at once that this was definitely no human ship because the interior was made for something larger, but it hadn't been made for prador either because the tube he was traversing could accommodate no more than a prador of his size. Its strange weave also caught at his feet as he walked and he recognized none of the technology he could see, not a thing. It also occurred to him that he was walking as if in gravity, yet could not feel its pull. It was true that prador could survive in vacuum and so were less nervous of it than humans; however, Sfolk found it unnerving the way the open weave of the tubes and some areas of the hull enabled you to look straight out into open space. He was still baffled by his ability to breathe. Pausing where one wall of the tube actually formed the hull, if it could even be so described, Sfolk pushed a claw out through one of the gaps in the weave. Beyond that gap he could feel vacuum sucking at his claw joints and see vapour exiting them, yet in the gap he had detected no kind of force-field he knew. He guessed at some kind of meta-material effect integral to the way the strange materials of the ship had been woven together, but could not get beyond that.

Moving on, he came to a series of side tunnels and hesitated in exploring, but just then the lights came on. Where the macramé of the ship intersected in intricate flower-like patterns the threads began glowing, as if at an electrical short, that glow increasing until it became an intense blue-white glare. Penny Royal must be into the workings of the thing and powering it up, and this in turn gave Sfolk more confidence. He entered one of the side tunnels, finding it a little cramped but navigable, and went through it into a bulbous chamber.

A sanctum? Sfolk wondered. *A cabin?*

The chamber was spherical, devices like the nests of social insects attached all round, and in the lower hollow a strange thing like a lopsided basket holding a disc of green crystal a couple of feet across, spiky silver fingers touching it like the heads of data recorders or players, and which Sfolk suspected they actually were. Now floating, he propelled himself out into the chamber, caught a leg against one edge and pulled himself down to a macramé tree holding all sorts of glittery devices at the tips of its branches. He thought that some of these might be useful, but having no idea what their function might be left them alone. After a further inspection of his surroundings he departed the chamber and moved on.

The next two chambers were much the same, but in the last of them he picked an object because it might be a weapon. It was a tube of tightly woven threads with what looked like a handle on the side and inset gridded spheres that were surely a method

267

of adjustment. He moved on, holding the device in one of his under-slung manipulators, keeping his claws free. He would investigate it later.

As he continued exploring, he began to get some intimation of the internal layout of the ship. Towards the point of the leaf-like projection he found an object at the start of a long row of the same that was definitely a weapon, but was rather too large for him to cart around. It sat in its own little niche: a hard sphere ten feet across, as neatly inserted as an eyeball in a socket, extending what looked like one large cannon out into vacuum, a cluster of square-sectioned barrels alongside it.

After travelling for a further hour he realized he must have passed the point of the leaf and was now heading back into the main body of the ship. Here he found more cabins and one large chamber that seemed a recreation room for the weavers because it was packed floor to ceiling with all sorts of strange woven objects. Here he picked up a device with a large handle at one end – obviously made for something similar to a human hand but much larger – with one of those ball controls and what was obviously a trigger, though no protruding barrel, just a small polished disc. He held it in one under-hand and pointed it ahead before pulling the trigger. It just clicked and did nothing. He played with the ball control and pulled the trigger again. This time a yellow thread appeared, extending three feet from the polished disc. He waved this at a nearby sculpture and didn't even feel a tug as one large woven mass parted company with the rest. Further investigation revealed that the ball control could extend this line no further than the three feet, though it could increase its thickness to an inch.

It was some kind of atomic shear, then, just a tool, but one that could be usefully employed. Sfolk was delighted and now took out the other thing he had surmised might be a weapon, pointed it and tried the ball controls on that. However, no matter what he did, it just flashed a blue light at him from underneath the ball controls. Delight faded to disappointment, but he kept the thing. He knew that it wasn't necessarily broken. It could be some stricture that prevented it being fired inside the ship, it could be personalized – only capable of being fired by its owner – or it could require mental control. The possibility that it required power or fuel he dismissed, sure that all the devices here must be induction-charged in this basket of a ship, and that was why the shear was working.

Now impatient to move on, Sfolk began to travel much faster, heading towards where the leaf attached to the main body of the ship. At one point he found a long straight tunnel spearing in that direction and accelerated to a run which he maintained for a good hour. Eventually he reached a junction and from there found himself in a wide tube on one of a series of walkways that ribboned around a central bar, ten feet thick, of some highly polished material that threw back his grotesquely distorted reflection. Beyond this he passed further chambers containing technology as recognizable as that weapon, if only because the objects here possessed some bulk and were connected by black hexagonal-section pipes that might be power supplies or data-feeds. He also spotted objects that looked like the consoles humans used, a wall of golden bricks scattered with deep recesses that could have been prador pit controls, and a great stack of glassy octahedrons that could have been a prador screen array.

Some while afterwards, for he estimated he had travelled many miles, he finally entered the very centre of the snowflake, and was glad to see that it did seem like some control centre or inner sanctum.

Lying at the centre of this huge space, at the centre of the entire ship in fact, rested a massive object. The thing was pyramidal, with sloping woven sides sporting those inset octahedrons and consisting of woven mechanisms like models of some animal's intestines. It boasted bristling spines, an internal green disc and other items that bent out of reality into silvered tubes stabbing to infinity. This had to be the drive of the ship, or its control system, for arrayed all around it, squatting in cup-shaped baskets extended out on arms, with upright discs before them like either screens or control panels, was the crew.

Sfolk walked into this area, then with a shove of his feet launched himself from the floor. He sailed up and caught hold of one of those cuplike baskets and gazed at its occupant. The bones of the skeleton were black and grey and bore a faintly iridescent hue. One big arm, oddly jointed and divided towards the end, terminated in black talons inserted into the white material of the disc screen. Sfolk poked at the screen with one claw and found it soft; unpleasantly fleshy. Turning back to the skeleton to study it more closely, he saw sections of mummified skin, the remains of internal organs shrivelled to threads and hard nodules, but also implant technology laced through, silver weaving over bones and glinting jewelled beads. Of course the majority of this technology lay around and penetrated into the big domed skull, with its arc of eye sockets, and its protruding bird-like bill.

'Gabbleducks,' said Sfolk, using his speech synthesizer to say the human word describing those strange animals that inhabited the world of Masada.

'The Atheter,' Penny Royal replied.

Still holding his position, Sfolk used his palp eyes to check his surroundings again, but could see no sign of the black AI. He then paused, remembering all he had been taught about the Atheter, and rediscovered his capacity for awe when he thought about the device he now clutched close to his underside. How much prador technology would still be working after being abandoned for two million years?

'Cowards,' tried Sfolk.

In return he saw the gabbleducks all sitting here alive, occasionally twitching, and occasionally turning a head. He was aware of the passage of time in this image, and felt the internal twist of U-space constantly as he saw some heads bowing, a claw dropping, then the gradual onset of decay. No battle, then, no struggle for survival; they'd just sat here and died. Of course the images from Penny Royal could not have been real, because how could the AI have recorded an event that occurred two million years ago?

'I know about these,' said Sfolk. 'We are taught about the old races and know more about them than you Polity AIs suppose.'

He then felt a surge of objection that had him clutching tighter to the atomic shear. Penny Royal did not consider itself a Polity AI. Sfolk let that go even though to his mind it was the same as him saying he wasn't a prador. He was smart enough to know that you didn't get into aggressive arguments with something that could rip apart a space station without even trying.

'How did this ship avoid being obliterated by their mechanism?' He paused, not sure what this AI knew about the Atheter, then continued, 'They made a machine to annihilate their entire technology.'

'Yes,' replied Penny Royal acidly, 'I encountered it.'

Sfolk chose that moment to tip back his palp eyes and look up. The black AI was floating above him beside another of the cup-shaped baskets. Its form was that of a black sea urchin again, but it had also extended silver tentacles and plugged them into the soft matter of a screen up there.

'So how did this ship survive?' Sfolk repeated.

The reply was the twist of U-space deep inside himself, and some sense of annoyed impatience. He understood the first to be a clue and the second to be: use your brain. He thought about what it meant for the ship to be here. The Atheter aboard must have dropped it into U-space without some destination set, perhaps deliberately or perhaps because of some sort of fault. So while it was in U-space the mechanism had been unable to find it. Eventually the ship had washed up here – recently when thinking in terms of two million years. It could have been too inert to have been detected, or it could be that the mechanism had simply not got round to dealing with it before something more urgent summoned it to Masada, where, according to recent data out of the Polity, it was destroyed.

'What do you want of me?' Sfolk asked.

Penny Royal now detached from that disc screen and drifted across the chamber, finally coming to rest against another of those baskets. This one was much larger, the arm connecting it to the central machine much bigger too, and a series of disc screens was suspended before the basket. After a moment Sfolk propelled himself after the AI, finally catching hold of this larger basket and drawing to a halt. The skeleton here was huge, the bones thick and heavy and riddled with implant technology. Its arms did not terminate in claws but in numerous tubes penetrating the screens before it.

'The captain?' Sfolk asked.

A high-pitched whining ensued and the skeleton began to vibrate, then to crack and shed flakes. Both the skeleton and its implant tech shattered into a million pieces and with a thunderous crack collapsed into a central mass as if a singularity had been generated inside it. This spinning ball of flaked bone and pieces of bright metal and crystal then just shot away, arcing down towards the floor, spreading into a loose cloud and then settling.

'Here,' said Penny Royal.

The basket was big enough for Sfolk and, if he climbed into it, he could reach those screens. The prospect horrified him because he was sure the big gabbleduck had been more like a ship mind than any father-captain. He feared that Penny Royal might want a mind for this ship and Sfolk was the only candidate around. He immediately tipped back, extending his under-slung arm and activating the atomic shear, sure that if he didn't act now he would never get another chance. Some force snapped the shear from his grasp and sent it tumbling, then the same force took hold of him, hauled him up and slammed him down in the basket. He tried to throw himself clear, but instead watched in bewilderment as his claws extended and penetrated two of the soft screens.

'You know where to go,' said the AI, now drifting away again.

Sfolk only half heard that, for he was paralysed by horror at the feeling of something penetrating his claws and crawling up his limbs underneath his shell, like worms.

Amistad

The one thing about being the warden of a world like Masada was that it gave you time to think, and Amistad had been doing a lot of thinking. As he drifted above a misty cloud layer below aubergine skies he continued to try and work his way to the heart of the matter but, as ever, he was without critical data. Penny Royal was certainly making restitution for past wrongs, but in the process working towards something else. The hijacking of the *Azure Whale* with its three runcibles aboard was an obvious clue, but there were other more subtle indicators. Take Isobel Satomi. In her the black AI had created a dangerous creature that had built up a nasty coring and thralling operation, and it had then destroyed both Satomi and her operation. However, the upshot of that was that the Weaver had been provided with another biomech war machine which in its turn had repaired the older and larger Technician. Had this been an altruistic act on Penny Royal's part towards the Weaver? Amistad thought not.

Despite talk of a restoration of balance, Amistad was sure there had been some sort of exchange – that this had been in essence a simple commercial deal. Penny Royal had supplied the Weaver with the war machine and the Weaver was to give something in return. There had been much discussion of this among Polity AIs. Some of them believed the Weaver had supplied Penny Royal with that new version of the hardfield, while others named a thousand other possibilities related to the AI's capabilities. Amistad felt that the curved hardfield, with its anchoring in U-space, was entirely Penny Royal's creation. He also felt that the delivery of the war machine was not a deal being completed, but just a down payment. And now it seemed he might be right, because the Weaver was on the move.

Amistad dropped down through the cloud, grav-planing, moisture beading on his nano-chain chromium armour and running away in rivulets. He stabilized and gazed down at the border fence lying between the patchwork of squirm ponds where the big cargo shuttle had landed and the outer wilderness. Along the fence stood automated guard towers like giant flat-topped mushrooms made of a tough dull grey composite. Ranged radially on the upper faces of these a variety of weapons could be brought to bear – the cap tilting and turning to aim them. There were high-powered ion stunners that could drive away most of the life forms here, up to and including the wild gabbleducks.

There were lasers and projectile weapons for dealing with any that became stubbornly persistent – usually the siluroynes – and then there were the particle cannons which were fortunately rarely required. In a sane world a shot from a particle cannon should be enough to vaporize any being, but here they were just a deterrent to hooders.

Amistad scanned the wilderness for anything nasty, spotting at extreme distance a heroyne striding through the flute grasses, apparently unaware of the siluroyne stalking it. But they were a long way off and heading away, so Amistad mentally connected to the towers along this section of fence and deactivated them all. It wouldn't do for them to mistake the gabbleduck heading here for the wild variety. He then swung round and gazed across at the cargo shuttle.

There was always someone not prepared to take a hint. There was always someone for whom the lure of wealth would overcome any fear of Polity AIs. That someone, in this case, was unsurprisingly a hooper spaceship captain. Right now he was sitting out on one of his shuttle's landing feet, a rosewood pipe jutting from his mouth, a hood up over his head, waiting for his passenger.

The legal status of the single sentient Atheter on this world, and the world itself, had been problematic, especially when the case was being argued by a two-million-year-old Atheter AI. It had been a theocratic out-Polity world, after a bloody revolution it had been subsumed by the Polity but placed under lengthy quarantine, with the strange arrival of the Weaver it had become a protectorate world, with the advent of what was effectively a large sabre for the Weaver to rattle it had become a Polity 'associate' world – a designation never used before. The Weaver, exploring the new freedoms granted by 'associate status', had discovered that he had just about the same rights as a Polity citizen. Nobody had really minded about this, until it became evident that he wanted to use the runcible network. Fortunately, because of this world's previous quarantine, the only runcible in the system was positioned up on the Braemar moon, Flint. Polity AIs had agreed that the Weaver could use the network, then neglected to supply him with a way of getting to Flint. But the Weaver had established his own communications network, and now this shuttle had arrived. Amistad pondered the matter for a moment longer, then grav-planed over to the shuttle and landed heavily, right down beside the hooper. Perhaps there might still be time to scare him off?

The hooper hardly twitched. He puffed on his pipe a bit more, his face hidden behind a cloud of tobacco smoke, then waved the smoke away, before pulling his hood back to expose his bald-as-an-acorn head. He studied Amistad, his expression mildly curious, and Amistad studied him back. The man was big, heavily built, his skin blue with ring-shaped scars, but the fact that he was not wearing an enviro-suit, as Amistad had first supposed, and was showing no signs of getting out of breath, told Amistad that scaring him off was no longer an option. He was an Old Captain, he didn't really need the air, or at least wouldn't need it for some while, didn't really need much of anything to stay alive, and didn't really have much to fear from anything that might try to kill him.

'So you're the big-shot drone warden thingy here,' said the hooper, stabbing his pipe stem towards the drone.

'Yes, I'm Amistad.'

'You've come to try and persuade me to leave?'

Coercion wouldn't work, but maybe something else would.

'How much are you being paid?' Amistad asked.

'Enough,' said the Old Captain, which was the expected answer really.

'Whatever it is, the Polity can pay you more not to be here,' Amistad tried.

The man shook his head and tut-tutted. 'I can't be goin' and lettin' down a new and potentially important customer. How would that look?'

'One ton of diamond slate,' Amistad suggested.

The captain just stared at Amistad for a long while then reached into a pouch at his belt. Out of this he took a folded sheet of paper, opened it and carefully studied it. It was one of Spatterjay's famous paper contracts. They were even more un-breakable than a palm-and-DNA-scaled contract under runcible AI oversight, but Amistad was pleased to have managed to get the man to study the small print. After a moment he folded it closed again and shook his head, carefully returning it to his pouch.

Amistad sighed and then settled down, his belly plates against the mud. 'Okay, I give up. What are you being paid?'

The erstwhile war drone and warden of this world, then what could only be described as an adviser, knew he hadn't tried very hard, but he wasn't sure he wanted to. It struck him as petty the way the Weaver was being blocked, and Amistad was now frankly bored with the politics. He was coming to the conclusion that when Riss had invited him along with her and Spear he had made the wrong decision in staying. Responsibility was, he had de-cided, swiftly becoming a burden he no longer wanted to bear.

'Oh, just the usual,' the captain replied.

'And what's that?'

'A few hundred New Carth shillings.'

Cheap, then. The Weaver had quickly established itself a Galaxy Bank account and under the terms of various agreements was effectively charging the Polity, the human population and the dracomen, ground rent for the areas they occupied.

'And of course,' the captain added, 'having an ally with "associate status" who has a big-fuck AI that can tangle Polity AIs in knots might come in quite handy.'

Amistad got it now. Spatterjay, this man's home world, was independent but still fell under protectorate status. It might be that the rulers there wanted to move on to associate status and lose the world its warden and other Polity watchers.

'I see,' said Amistad.

Just at that moment there came the crump of an explosion and a flash. Amistad spun round and stood up higher to peer back towards the fence. A large hole had appeared in it, the narrow ceramal palings severed away, glowing hot where they had been cut. The drone sighed. This was a perfect example of how bored he had been getting here, since he was neglecting things like, for example, lowering a section of the fence to let the Weaver through.

The big gabbleduck was squatting on the other side of the hole. It now put away in a little holster on its harness the object it had used to cut the hole, then went down on all fours and ambled through. As it walked over, the captain stood up, took a remote control from his pocket and pointed it back at his ship. With a thump, a ramp door opened in the side of the shuttle and lowered itself to the boggy ground. The Weaver, meanwhile, had reached Amistad, who noted that it carried a large bag strapped to its side. A packed lunch? Its travel bag? It settled back on its behind again.

'The build has to be completed,' it said.

'What build?' Amistad asked.

'Then I get final payment, and no more need for this.' He waved one big black claw at the ship then, with a sigh, went down on all fours and headed for the ramp.

So what next? Amistad could see himself sitting on his viewing platform or cruising through the skies of this world. He would occasionally get roped into the negotiations between the Atheter AI and the human ambassador here, but the other negotiations between that AI and Earth Central it learned very little about until some new piece of legislation was being enacted. Perhaps there might be some action if those members of Tidy Squad due to be deported tried something, but it would be brief and efficiently quashed.

'Can I come?' Amistad asked.

The Weaver paused on the ramp and looked round. It studied Amistad for a long moment, then shrugged and beckoned with one claw. Amistad was already sending his resignation by the time he reached the foot of the ramp.

Spear

The space port official I had spoken to earlier was waiting in a second reception area at the foot of the elevator. He was a brusque little man who seemed to have been formed from soft lumps of pale dough, clad in a waterproof slick-suit and wide-brimmed rain hat. He again tried to obtain proprietary bidding rights on my ship or to get me to mortgage it against a cash hand-out, but when I showed no interest he tried something else.

'Exotic life forms have to be fully scanned and approved,' he said. 'There's also an import tax – payable in advance of the inspection.'

'What?'

He gestured at Riss and I wondered if he'd been born on this world and never left it. Riss, who until then had been content enough just to coil up on the floor and wait, rattled her ovipositor against the tiles and rose up to peer over the counter at the man.

'Exotic I may be,' she said, 'but life form I am not.'

'I'll need some sort of proof.'

'No you won't,' Riss replied. 'But you may be needing an autodoc soon.'

The man stared at her with his mouth hanging open, then abruptly turned a touch screen round to face me. The landing fee was there, the text red, along with a number of icons to select. I touched the Galaxy Bank – the icon itself reading my DNA through the screen, then a shiver passed through me as a scanner made a secondary check on my identity. After a moment the text turned to green and folded away.

'That's it, then,' conceded the man grumpily.

'We want to rent a clamberer,' I said.

'Base level,' he snapped, then rounded his desk and stomped over to the elevators. I presumed that meant he didn't get any backhanders from those who rented out the clamberers.

'Come on,' said Sepia, catching hold of my shoulder. 'I know where to go.'

We left the reception area to enter a street of bland apartments with bubble windows and small parking bays outside for field-effect scooters. Sepia led us down this to another bank of elevators. This took us down another level, where we had to walk through a shopping centre scattered with bars and restaurants from which staff eyed us hopefully.

'They make sure you can't just go straight down, rent a clamberer and leave,' Sepia observed. 'The space port owner wants visitors to spend as much money as possible here.'

On every one of eight levels we had to walk through some shopping area or other. Finally reaching the base of the structure, I saw a sign outside one establishment advertising clamberers to rent.

'Here?' I suggested.

Sepia shook her head. 'Outside they're half the price and better maintained.'

Thick doors of cut foam opened into an area where enviro-suits could be rented, then chain-glass doors led onto a crushed and bonded stone walkway, then some steps down to the flag-stoned street of the main valley town. Terraces of four-storey houses ran down either side of the wide street, small gardens to the fore often occupied by log piles and trees that looked vaguely like ginkgos. Ancient hydrocars were parked out front. Some of these houses had bubble windows while others had what looked like leadlight panes. The steep roofs were midnight black with high-conversion solar tiles, and smoking chimneys even pro-truded. It was still raining, gutters spewing water to run down channels in the street and into wide-gridded drains. Not many people were about, which was understandable.

We took a number of turnings, passed shopfronts, a hydro-gen charging station, some greenhouses. Crossed a bridge over a deep fast-flowing river, in which grew plants that clung to the stony bottom with claw-like roots and floated leaves, or fruit, like the hulls of sailing yachts, around them swam fishes that looked like salmon, but for the horns on their heads. Sepia finally brought us to the clamberer yard and pushed into a bubble-metal hut, while I paused to take my first look at a clamberer. This was an enjoyably novel experience, rare for me because it seemed none of the dead residing in the spine strapped to my back had encountered these either.

There were ten of them in the yard, each on four long limbs terminating in six-fingered gripping hands, and hunkered down as if trying to avoid the worst of the rain. They consisted of a bulbous chain-glass cabin with seating inside for four, and a sensory head protruding low down and to the fore on a jointed neck. The head looked much like that of an ant, a soldier ant judging by the size of the pincers, though I wondered about the purpose of the carbide chainsaw blades running along their inner faces.

'Seems a bit silly,' said Riss, black eye open as she doubtless inspected all the inner workings of the machines before us.

'I'm always prepared to bow to local custom,' I said.

'Maybe don't give anyone a ride this time,' she suggested.

It took me a moment to figure out what she meant, then I felt a chuckle rising up inside me. Yes, I did have a tendency to offer lifts. On Masada it had been a gabbleduck, and by Penny Royal's planetoid it had been Riss herself.

'We take that one,' said Sepia.

I turned. She was out again, accompanied by an amphidapt man who was smiling widely to expose tooth ridges and the white inner flesh of his mouth. He was obviously perfectly adapted for this environment because he was completely naked. He looked like a toad stood upright and given bat-wing ears.

'How much?' I asked.

'I've dealt with it,' she replied, holding up a key stick. She turned back to the amphidapt, 'I'll bring it back in one piece.'

He was now staring at Riss, and licking a serrated tongue over his lips. I supposed she might bear some resemblance to whatever food his form favoured – usually something squirmy, and raw, if other amphidapts were anything to go by. After a moment he got control of himself and withdrew his tongue, then reached up and snapped open and closed a webbed hand. 'Just remember it's on a ten-day auto return.'

'I know – I've rented from you before.'

He nodded. 'And you brought it back okay. Just this time, he's here . . .'

Sepia grimaced and gestured us to the clamberer, walked over and pulled up a wing door, then stepped inside. Riss shot inside after her, while I unhooked the carry strap of the spine. Then I followed, waving an acknowledgement at the amphidapt.

'Ten-day auto return?' I queried, once seated inside.

'Plenty of those who take clamberers out on a visit to Mr Pace never return. Strap in,' she added, having done so herself, as she inserted the key stick.

As I secured myself, something began to wind up to speed below the floor – probably a big flywheel driven by an electric motor. She took hold of a standard directional joystick and pulled it up, whereupon the clamberer lurched to its feet, raised its head and looked around as if blearily waking. In a moment it was in motion, stepping out through the yard gate then off down the flagstoned street.

'So what are the pincers for?' I asked.

'Tree-felling,' she replied.

I was glad the reason for them was so prosaic.

The clamberer took us out of the town and then down the valley road with a gait that reminded me of being on the back of an elephant. Only after thinking this did I remember I had never actually ridden an elephant, and that I was re-experiencing someone else's memory. The road ran down beside the river, then swept away to the right, where that terminated in a wide lake. Instead of following the road, Sepia directed our strange vehicle across the river, then along a rough almost non-existent track leading up the adjacent mountain. I noticed hardly any change at all in the vehicle's gait. Peering down through the curved glass of the cabin, I could see it smoothly gripping outcroppings where required, walking flat or adjusting the bend of its legs to give us a smooth ride. It was all very novel and quite enjoyable, but I couldn't see the point of it.

'Why the hell couldn't we have rented a gravcar?' I asked.

'Mr Pace doesn't allow them near his castle,' she supplied. 'In fact he has a couple of missile turrets there to act as a deterrent.'

'Why?'

'Who knows?' she shrugged.

'Well he does have reason to dislike aircars,' Riss muttered.

There was that.

Over the brow of the mountain, we clambered down past terraced fields packed with trees I presumed were tea oaks. Amidst them I could see robot pickers like metal swans running on caterpillar treads, their beaks snipping and vacuuming the tea shoots into their cavernous bellies. We crossed a small stream then mounted another slope and were soon striding across the flat top of a mountain, which I felt would have been a better location for the space port. After this we went down again then entered another valley which reminded one of my mental passengers of Glen Coe. It was getting darker now since we had arrived towards the end of the thirty-hour day, and I could see lights ahead. A further twenty minutes of travel brought us below Mr Pace's castle, where Sepia took us onto a road leading up. A few minutes later we crossed a stone bridge and entered a wide courtyard through a stone arch, where the clamberer squatted and its flywheel wound down.

'Okay.' Sepia pointed across the courtyard to an arched and studded wooden door. 'Last time I was here, and before I saw the bone pile, I hammered on that. Someone answered and told me that Mr Pace wasn't around and I could sod off.'

We clambered out of the clamberer and headed over, Sepia clutching her carbine close to her stomach and Riss now up off the ground, sliding through the air like an ophidian missile. Reaching the door, I banged on it with the base of the spine. Waited for a little while and was about to hammer again when the door swung open.

'Follow me,' said something.

I didn't realize what had spoken until I looked down and saw a small cylindrical robot on the floor. It turned on rotary flapper feet and took off down the corridor within. We followed, having to slow down as it clumsily negotiated a spiral stair. It then took us through further corridors with a distinctly medieval air, though the sconce torches emitted a gas flame of some kind, the pictures were memory paint, steadily changing scenes as we passed, and the one suit of armour in an alcove was a wartime exoskeleton. Big wooden double doors then opened to admit us into a room that wouldn't have been out of place in a Bram Stoker novel, but for its warmth and the fire burning in a huge grate occupying one wall, another room beyond visible through the flames. Meanwhile, the robot secured itself beside others of its kind in a stand like a shoe rack.

'Come in,' said Mr Pace.

He was standing with his foot up on the hearth, forearm resting against the mantel, gazing into the fire. I wondered why he had a fire burning here. Surely a man with a body made of metallic glass didn't feel the cold? I moved on into the room, Sepia at my shoulder, still tightly clutching that carbine. By the grim look to her face I reckoned she had lost any suicidal impulses and, in that moment, I suddenly had qualms. Until now the things I had been doing hadn't endangered anyone quite so vulnerable as Sepia. Yes, Flute had been in danger but was now the mind of a Polity destroyer, while Riss was something dangerous and hard to kill. That had now changed. Riss slid through the air past us, then dropped neatly to coil herself on a large circular pedestal table. There were ornate and not particularly comfortable-looking sofas before the fire. I didn't want to sit down. I walked through onto a wide carpet off to one side of the fire and halted.

'I tried to get in contact with you from orbit,' I said.

'Yes.' He nodded.

'And incidentally we're not here to relieve our boredom.'

He pushed away from the mantelpiece and turned to face us. With his obsidian face and white pupils he looked a demon perfectly appropriate to this setting.

'Of course not,' he said, 'you're a pawn in some complicated game Penny Royal is playing, and your arrival here is just one more obscure move.'

'All I've come here for is to ask you the location of that extremadapt colony Penny Royal apparently destroyed.' I paused for a second, a little irritated by being called a pawn. 'A question you could have answered easily enough while we were in orbit.'

'It's easy enough to give,' he said, and I felt a channel application to my aug. I denied it for the moment and made preparations to receive something hostile. Mr Pace shrugged and continued, 'But you won't be going there, since your journey ends here.'

Here it comes, I thought.

'Of course I could have sent you those coordinates while you were in orbit, but why should I do that when I wanted you here? Or, more specifically I wanted *that* here.' He stabbed a finger at the spine. The channel application was still there, ready for me to accept.

'What did Penny Royal do to you?' I asked, backing up a little and shooting a glance at Riss.

'I can stop him, but I doubt I can kill him,' she sent.

He spread his arms and gestured inwardly to his body. 'Penny Royal gave me exactly what I wanted. I am invulnerable.'

'Really?'

'Really,' he affirmed. 'Certainly this body can be destroyed but every time it is – five times thus far – I find myself waking up again here in the mountains of this world. The location is different on each occasion. Even dropping myself into a sun did not end me. Some mechanism rebuilds me here every time.' He paused and took a step away from the fire. 'I've never been able to find it.'

'You want to die?' I asked.

'I want to die,' he agreed. 'The old reach that ennui barrier that brings many of them here. I envy them because it is a barrier they can pass through in time, and so I kill them. Penny Royal made me invulnerable but made that barrier impossible for me to pass.'

'And what has that got to do with us, and this?' I held up the spine.

'I thought you were intelligent.'

I got it then. The spine recorded Penny Royal's victims, living and dead. He was recorded in it, and from it he was perpetually renewed. He wanted the spine because if he could destroy it, then he could finally end his own life.

'I could just hand it over to you now and leave,' I said.

'No.' He shook his head. 'I will destroy the spine and thereafter endeavour to foul the plans of that fucking AI to the best of my abilities. Until I am destroyed. You are part of those plans, an integral part, so I will now kill you and your companions.' Then he moved, fast, and the world slowed down around me.

In his first step he hit a barrage of fire from Sepia's laser carbine, complemented a second later by shots from her pulse-gun. This brought him staggering to a halt and set his clothing on fire. Meanwhile Riss streaked in from one side, the table smashed to splinters by the violence of her launch.

'Down!' she shouted, flipping over and coming at Mr Pace ovipositor-first.

I hesitated, then turned, threw myself at Sepia and snared her with one arm, bringing us both down on the floor. Glancing round, I saw that Pace had caught hold of Riss.

'Really, stab me?' he said, then flung her away contemptuously.

I buried my head under my arms just as the explosive gel she'd deposited on his chest detonated. The force of the blast tried to peel me up off the floor and burning debris rained down all around. When I looked a moment later Mr Pace was gone, blown back through his fireplace and into the room beyond.

'Let's go.' I stood, hauling up Sepia, and we ran.

I didn't know how long it would take Pace to recover from such a blast. Would such a thing even stun him? We charged out the way we had come in. Glancing back, I saw Riss acting as our rearguard, but still there was no sign of Pace. Finally we tumbled out into the courtyard and pulled ourselves into the clamberer.

'Fucking silly idea,' said Sepia, as she jerked up the joystick before the flywheel had built up enough speed, the clamberer lurching slowly to its feet. She sent it towards the tunnel just as the studded door blew out behind us, Riss streaking from it like a shard of glassy debris. The flywheel accelerated and the clamberer did too. It took us out through the tunnel and we were a hundred yards along the road when another blast ensued. Looking back, I saw rubble tumbling to fill up the tunnel, then Riss hit the glass of the cabin and stuck there, her gaze back towards the castle, black eye open.

'Fucking silly idea,' Sepia repeated.

I felt something still nagging at me and realized the channel application from Pace was still there. Taking all the mental precautions I could, I cautiously opened it. Nothing large came through; no virus or worm or other informational attack. What did come through almost escaped my notice at first, then I saw it: a simple text message giving galactic coordinates.

'I got the coordinates,' I said.

She glanced at me. 'If they're the right ones.'

I shrugged and firmly closed the channel to Mr Pace.

'And right or wrong,' she added, 'that bastard will know where we're going next.'

Soon we were climbing a mountain slope, moving a damned sight faster than we had on the way here.

'*Fuck,*' Riss sent.

'*What is it?*'

She sent me an infrared image of the castle, a clamberer scrambling down from its battlements.

'*How much of that explosive gel do you have left?*'

'*Not a lot,*' Riss replied.

I considered the terrain ahead, then the interminable and convoluted journey up through the small city below the spaceport platform, and wondered whether we were about to go anywhere at all.

11

The Brockle

The Brockle felt itself to be a thoroughly pragmatic entity and after a period of contemplation realized a number of things. The extensive data in the package from the watch station gave no indication of Penny Royal's location: only the odd communication from Amistad to Thorvald Spear did that. Also, the scale and complexity of what Penny Royal was achieving, at a distance, had firmly brought home to the Brockle another fact: it needed to be stronger, both mentally and physically, if it was to counter the threat the black AI posed.

The Brockle had considered upgrading itself before but no circumstances it had encountered had ever driven it to take that step. As it dropped the *High Castle* into U-space it began assessing resources. Plenty of materials and energy were available, but intricate planning was required. Now, in human form, it trudged out of its cabin, noted that Blite and Greer were asleep in theirs, and headed through the corridors of the ship to the advanced high-tech autofactory all such ships now carried.

As it walked, it probed ahead, assessing the capabilities of the machines available, and soon saw that most of what it needed was there and that ways could be rigged to provide just about anything else it could think of. The machines ranged from matter printers that could deposit composites in just about any form, an atom at a time, to gravity and hardfield presses capable of forming super-dense baryonic materials. Using the processing of its own units, it began designing further units incorporating extended processing and bulked-up power supplies but also physical capabilities it had not possessed before: state-of-the-art U-tech sensors and a distributed weapons system. While with a small part of its mind it concentrated on the details of the physical upgrade, it returned the rest of its mind to the design of that extended processing.

Here was where things could get a little sticky, for steadily upgrading that ill-defined capacity humans called 'intelligence' without extreme care could flip an AI mentality over into a state where the material universe ceased to be of much concern. In that state all thought became self-referential; the more prosaic aspects of reality became less interesting than mental constructs – one of those prosaic things being plain survival. Minds sank into the contemplation of the infinite and the infinitesimal: time, space, U-space and the proliferating dimensions, or the sub-atomic and the very grains of existence. It was a kind of mental event horizon which, when passed, was impossible to return through. As the Brockle contemplated this it had an epiphany.

That's how Penny Royal does it!

Out of physical necessity the Brockle had, over the ages, formed itself into a being capable of distributing its physical and mental parts. This shoal design had been useful for penetrating and assessing organizations, gathering and sorting multiple perspectives and launching subtle cascading attacks. But now it realized another advantage to remaining distributed: by buffering its separate mental parts, in much the same way humans were buffered from AI to prevent burnout, it could increase its overall intelligence while preventing that fall through the mental event horizon. Synergy, of course: the parts creating a greater whole while retaining enough separation to prevent what might be described as collapse. In essence it would be like using field tech to keep a bunch of super-dense components separate; components that would otherwise clash together and collapse into a singularity.

Finally reaching the autofactory, the Brockle was already relaying instructions and schematics to the machines within and they were setting to work. The factory itself was formed in the shape of an ammonite, with materials' feeds at its centre, super-conducting buzz-bars running around the coil fed by an exterior fusion reactor. The machines inside started at the centre with those for the gross forming of matter, the processes becoming more intricate as they followed the coil out.

The Brockle now stood before the exit for final products – a distribution face like a snail's clypeus. A hole in the face was circled by a series of hardfield projectors for conveying the factory's products outside. The aperture limited the scale of what could be produced, but there weren't any large components this ship was likely to need that could not be assembled from smaller parts. If a large component, like the actual hull of the ship, needed replacement rather than repair, it likely meant the ship no longer existed. The aperture was no problem, because the new units it would soon be producing were only twice the size of its present ones. However, their manufacture was a hugely complicated process and, since this was an upgrade, the Brockle needed to insert itself within that process.

The Brockle fragmented into a shoal of silver worms and sped through into the autofactory. At this end the interior was packed with glittering insectile robotics, field projectors, matter printers and atomic shears, but movement was limited to mere start-up and test routines. As it moved through all this, following the coil to the centre, it found itself having to take increasing care not to run afoul of the processes taking place. Nearer the centre were liquid metals flowing through complex field containment, atom-thick layers of crystal invisible to the human eye stacking themselves endlessly. Finally it found printer heads blurring around a growing shape that seemed to be formed of smoke. Here, then, was the point of insertion.

At the point of manufacture when it was required, the Brockle sent one of its units into that shadowy shape. Printer heads inverted, presenting micro-tools, which steadily disassembled the unit and redistributed its parts inside the shadowy mass. Connection wavered then died. The forensic AI felt itself grow a little bit less intelligent. It re-established intermittently broadcasting faults and calling for diagnostic analysis, which the Brockle as a whole ignored. It felt quite strange about the situation – drawing a parallel between the unit's apparent distress and that of the many victims it had disassembled.

The shadowy shape, now having gained more substance, moved on, still surrounded by the blur of matter printers, gaining further bulk around dispersed glittering parts of the original unit. The Brockle dispatched another of its original units to track its path out, while preparing to insert yet another one into another growing shadow. New components were inserted: flexible laminar power supplies, hardfield nodes, blocks of multi-spectrum quantum cascade lasers, organo-metal processing substrate, baryonic wires, micro-torsion motors . . . a list that went on and on as the new unit solidified and began twitching into life. It was no longer silver like the original units, but brown like old oak – the base colour of the newer and tougher materials employed. It looked like a giant flatworm, its flat profile and segmentation necessary if a number of these were to be able to take on a human form.

The mental connections began firmly establishing as the thing approached the exit aperture and the Brockle suddenly understood on a visceral level what it was doing to itself. The new unit almost overran its mentality as it established its position within the whole, within the hierarchy of mind. It was like reaching out to take hold of an unruly child, only to discover that child was cyber-enhanced and comprised of razors. What had started out as simply a matter of reconnecting, quickly turned into a fight for dominance. It lasted a total of just under two seconds but, in AI terms, that was an age. The Brockle gained control, subsumed the unit and thereby became stronger – its mentality expanding. In that moment it saw errors and better ways of doing things and reprogrammed the factory, improving the next unit that went through.

When its second new unit was, after a brief struggle, incorporated, the Brockle again reprogrammed the factory, but this time so quickly the matter printers hadn't time to lay down more than a barely visible metallic fog. While the third one went through, and the Brockle's intelligence climbed, it made a radical addition to the process. In simplistic terms it was a kind of complex origami – a way of folding in more matter, more components, more abilities. Another unit, and of course, why hadn't it seen that before? It was possible to route self-referencing information structures out as a U-space communication to itself. This meant that some thought processes could take, literally, no time at all.

As the hours, then the days and then the weeks passed, the Brockle found the location of its *self* now outside the autofactory and groping for ultimate truths and pondering the underlying structure of the universe. Wouldn't it be possible to take that matter-folding and U-space processing a stage further? Surely these presupposed the possibility of infinite processing? Glimmers of some numinous and deep understanding felt within reach, down there, down at the roots of the universe. Just a little way . . .

And then the Brockle pulled back and fought to re-establish itself, knowing that it had veered dangerously close to that mental event horizon – the point of flip-over into AI navel-gazing. Any further along that route and it would end up as a slithering sphere of brown flatworms, contemplating eternity until eternity ran out. Firm focus was required, purpose sharply defined, reason for being, retained.

Penny Royal . . .

The Brockle enjoyed feelings of satisfaction, for a microsecond. It was now much much stronger, both mentally and physically, and felt ready to face down the black AI. However, it was time to pay a visit to this Mr Pace.

Trent

Room 101 was shuddering and groaning in a way it had not done before, because the thing causing the noise and vibration this time was more comprehensively destroying it . . . and rebuilding it. Trent gazed at the images on the screen, at the reconstruction, the appalling amounts of energy and materials being thrown around. The machine doing this reminded him of microscope images he'd seen of some spores, but it was behaving like a multifunction printer-bot – those extrusions from its surface spewing out matter and weaving it together in a complex mass, while other extrusions were sucking up the matter of the station as if it was molten toffee.

'What the hell do we do?' asked Cole.

'Get them all into survival suits, I guess,' Trent replied. It all seemed unreal, yet on a visceral level he knew when that thing reached them they would be treated no differently from the

other matter the station was made of, and all would die screaming as it sucked them in.

Reece, the children, he thought. He had provided them with
survival suits but had been unable to obtain anything tougher.
He needed to see them and ensure they were ready . . .

Cole stared at him. 'Even if we have enough, or can make
enough in time, what then? They can't survive here.'

'Maybe if we move into the new structure . . .'

'And run out of air, water, food.'

'Then maybe we need to get aboard one of the ships.' Trent
tried to fight the rising panic that was an unforeseen aspect of
his empathy. It had been growing inside him ever since this had
started, because he'd already thought through the things they
were now discussing, and all his options were closing down.

If he did manage to get the increasingly ungovernable shell
people into survival suits and into that new structure, they would
last only as long as their suits, because everything they had
depended upon here in the station would be gone. He might get
the shell people to that damaged dreadnought in the nearby final
construction bay – maybe they could seal it and it could keep
them alive. Then what? They would only be able to go as far as
the hardfield barrier and there was no guarantee that the thing
currently eating the station wouldn't snatch the ship and render
it down to be deposited as part of this new structure. Would
Sverl open the hardfield barrier to let them out? No, because the
moment he did, the Polity fleet would turn everything here into
a spreading cloud of hot gas and burning debris.

'I need to speak to Sverl,' he decided. Reece would have to
wait because there was one option which involved less risk for
Sverl, and for that Trent would need to be as persuasive as possible.

Sverl hadn't been answering his calls, but he knew the erstwhile prador was outside the hospital, clinging to superstructure and on some level watching that object, though it was not yet visible from here. He turned away from the screens and made for the airlock.

'I'm coming too,' said Cole.

Trent shrugged. *Whatever.*

They both stepped into the airlock then headed out into the corridors adjoining the hospital. What, Trent wondered, would happen to Florence? In fact, what would happen to all the AIs here that Sverl had returned to sanity? Trent had seen them moving out of the way of the destruction but they couldn't keep moving forever. And what about Sverl himself? Trent needed to know his plans – if he had any.

Beyond the corridors he reached a section of the station that had been just a gulf before – superstructure obliterated in some blast. Now bracing beams webbed the gap, and up on one of them squatted the silver shape of Sverl, completely alone now. Trent launched himself from the terminus of a corridor, using his wrist impeller to direct himself to the beam concerned. He landed on the beam, which was a yard-wide Z-form fashioned from bubble metal, and gecko-walked along one face to confront Sverl.

'I've been trying to speak to you,' he said over suit radio.

'And I have too,' Cole added.

'What are you going to do?' Trent asked.

Squatting on the beam like some strange technological tick, Sverl faced towards the end of the station steadily being destroyed and remade. After a moment he snipped his claws at vacuum – that almost seeming a gesture of defiance against that distant thing – then turned towards them.

'It isn't Penny Royal technology,' he told them over their radios.

'What?' Trent asked.

'It should have been obvious to me the moment it started remaking the station,' Sverl explained. 'It is weaving it into a very strange meta-material object.'

'So?'

'It is *weaving*.'

'I still don't see the point –'

'This is Atheter technology, don't you see?' Sverl paused, vigorously waving a claw in his excitement. 'This is how Penny Royal was paid! This is what it got in exchange for what Isobel Satomi became.'

Trent unconsciously reached up to touch his earring, only his fingers rapped against his suit helmet.

'It doesn't matter where it comes from,' said Cole. 'When it reaches us we're dead.'

'It did not destroy the runcible,' Sverl noted.

'But it has wiped out three AIs that didn't get out of the way quickly enough,' said Trent.

A dismissive wave of a claw. 'We are here for a purpose.'

'Are you sure about that, Sverl? Or could it be that we're just lost wax?'

'Lost wax? I'm not familiar with that.'

'Search that massive mind of yours.'

After a moment Sverl said, 'I see: a component is made of wax, the mould formed round it and then the wax melted out before the liquid metal is poured in. You have some interestingly antique knowledge in your mind, Trent Sobel.'

'But you get my meaning.'

'You're implying that we're disposable – that our purpose was to bring about the current process and that whether we survive it or not is irrelevant.' Sverl dipped as if trying to nod like a human. 'I cannot believe that.'

'Well maybe you're right about you, and maybe you can survive by moving yourself into the new structure.' He paused, stabbed a finger at his chest then at Cole. 'We could survive if we went with you, as could those of the shell people we could provide with space suits. But that leaves over a thousand of them whose life-span would be that of their survival suits – four days maximum.' He paused again, sensing somehow that Sverl was waiting for something, continued, 'And no, if we board a ship we won't be able to get clear of the reach of that thing while you have your hardfield up, and I know you won't be dropping that.'

'What can I do?' asked Sverl.

'You already know,' said Trent.

'You want me to open the runcible to the Polity network.'

'It doesn't have to be the whole network – it can be limited to one gateway. You know that.'

'It doesn't matter. The Polity will respond, fast. Even if the AIs don't have the time to send an assault force they will have time to send a CTD or two.'

Time now to play his ace, Trent felt. 'But that's not true of one runcible gate.'

Sverl, who until then had been fidgeting as if very uncomfortable with this whole exchange, now froze. 'Explain.'

'There's one runcible gate where a Polity assault force could not be quickly deployed. There's one planetary system where major Polity weaponry has been outlawed.'

After a long silence Sverl said, 'Masada, of course.'

'What's this?' asked Cole.

'The Atheter, the Weaver,' Trent explained. 'It's been struggling for independence from the Polity and since regaining weaponry of its own has been in a position to negotiate . . . well, demand that Polity forces withdraw from its system.'

'But have they?'

299

'They were moving out when I escaped with Blite and his crew, and everything should be out of the system by now. On the one hand they don't want to piss off the Weaver, but on the other they know they can move assets in pretty quickly if there's a problem.'

'It seems another circle closes,' said Sverl speculatively, then, 'Get the shell people to the runcible. I will open it to Masada so they can go through.' He tapped a claw against the beam. 'And it seems that at last you will have saved them.' Before Trent could make any response to that, Sverl had leapt from the beam, and sped away under the impetus from some unseen drive.

'Come on,' said Trent, heading back towards the hospital. 'We've got an evacuation to organize.'

Sverl

As he watched Trent go, Sverl contemplated what to do next, meanwhile taking a peek through remaining sensors at the Polity fleet out there. The ships were just hanging in vacuum and didn't seem to be probing for weaknesses, which was worrying. It was almost as if they were waiting for something. He allowed a mental sigh then withdrew his attention from them, focusing instead on his children.

'Bsorol, Bsectil, all of you,' said Sverl to his children, 'abandon your work there and come forward. Bring all your tools and weapons – everything you can. Go here.' Sverl sent them the coordinates of a small hauler in the final construction bay adjacent to the hospital. The ship had plenty of hold space and, just a minute before, Sverl had dispatched robots to fuel it and run maintenance checks. Sverl estimated he had four hours to get the vessel ready. He would have liked to have used the big dreadnought in that bay, but it would have taken longer to get ready and he suspected it was too large to get past the Atheter device currently eating Room 101.

'Why?' asked Bsorol.

'Because I say so,' Sverl replied.

'If we don't get this drive fixed we're stuck here,' Bsorol argued.

Sverl allowed himself another mental sigh. Time was he could just deliver his orders and they were obeyed. Here then was the penalty for allowing his children to think for themselves.

'Because, Bsorol, I don't think that device is going to stop when it reaches the drive. I think all your repairs will be for nothing,' Sverl explained. 'I also think it highly unlikely that whatever Penny Royal is creating here is going to be left sitting under a hardfield waiting for the Polity to find a way to destroy it.'

'Perhaps we should go with the shell people,' interjected Bsectil.

Sverl wanted to ridicule that idea, but then had second thoughts. Perhaps that was what they were supposed to do? Having started the process here, were they the 'lost wax' Trent Sobel described, and was the runcible the hole they were supposed to escape through? No, he did not want to believe that. He was staying and that was all. Except . . .

'I am remaining here. You may, if you wish, depart through the runcible with them,' he said. 'Perhaps the Weaver can find a use for you.'

He waited for their immediate response of protestations of loyalty to him. He waited for them to tell him they would remain here, and he waited . . .

'It's a thought,' said Bsorol.

'The Weaver has his weapons but he doesn't have troops or

much in the way of an able workforce,' said Bsectil. 'I bet he's recruiting.'

'He might question our loyalty,' said Bsorol.

'True,' Bsectil agreed, 'except this isn't about loyalty, but wages.'

Sverl felt as if his innards were coming to the boil, even though he didn't have any. Instead he took a look through cams in the engine section and saw his two first-children, and his second-children, rapidly collecting up their tools. Suddenly he realized they had been playing with him. His next prador instinct was to find some way to punish them, but then he decided he was better than that.

'I leave the choice entirely to you,' he said calmly, before turning his attention elsewhere.

The hauler was small enough and, once fuelled and some of its thrusters replaced, would be fast and sufficiently manoeuvrable to get past the Atheter device and go deep into the structure it was building. What he needed to find out now was whether it would be allowed past. His attention fell upon a heavy construction robot not much smaller than the hauler. The thing was fully functional – a great slablike object with rocket motors, power supplies and grav-engines at either end and arms sprouting all around its rim. Like many others of its kind, it had already been used in clearing up some of the mess in the station and in rebuilding an area close to its location, currently being annihilated by the Atheter device. Sverl gave it its instructions, and set it in motion.

Like a great flattened spider, the robot hauled itself along some beams then waited until the device had collected up its latest batch of materials and headed off for the rim of the growing hemisphere. The robot propelled itself out, fired up a rocket drive that sent it across a gap strewn with floating debris and inside the hemisphere. Now, peering through cams on the thing, Sverl was able to run deep scans and study the massive bracing cross-struts more closely. He saw that they were a basketwork of concentrically laminated composite threads, hollow at the core. They possessed some elasticity but were designed to dampen and then resist massive stresses. Though they looked flimsy they were much stronger than the original composite beams of the station – atomic forces working in concert, piezoelectrics generating electrostatic binding and micro-hardfield reinforcing. Elegant, beautiful.

The robot reached the furthest inner face of the hemisphere, settled on a bed of woven composites and put down gecko feet. Sverl now watched the Atheter device finish its run around the rim of the hemisphere then return to the station itself to tear up more materials. It was getting closer to the hospital and the barracks, and, clad in survival suits, the shell people were coming out. Sverl, however, kept his attention focused on the device as it headed out to weave another section of hemisphere and then returned. At length it seemed that the thing was ignoring the stray robot, which meant it might be safe for him to follow it into the hemisphere. Next he returned his attention to the hospital.

People were streaming down the nearby corridors and launching themselves through the new beam-work, directly visible to Sverl now. They looked like a human swarm being disturbed from a nest. Cole was leading the way to the runcible while Trent was in the barracks ensuring that everyone left. A peek inside showed he was having trouble with just three individuals – a surprisingly small number considering the nature of these humans.

'You're leaving now,' he told the group he had been arguing with. 'If you don't, you die.'

'That is our choice,' said one individual. 'I want to stay here and see what happens – I'm prepared to take the risk.'

'I'm betting Sverl and his children are staying,' said another.

'You've done enough, Sobel,' said a third. 'We're adults and we make our own choices.'

They were gathered by the airlock. The surgical robot that had named itself Florence loomed in the background and behind it Taiken's wife and her two children. Florence had acquired gecko-stick caterpillar treads and was much faster than before, which she now displayed. The argumentative three only had time to turn as she rushed them, then three shots from an ion stunner dropped them jerking to the floor.

'You can carry them?' Trent asked.

The robot was already unfolding a large sack made from bonded-together body bags. 'I can.' While it opened up the bag, Sobel went to each of the prostrate forms and sealed up the survival suits of two, then laboriously pulled a suit onto the one who hadn't been wearing one.

'When does it end?' Sverl asked him through his suit radio. 'Responsibility is difficult to put down when it is taken up.'

'It ends once they're through the runcible.' Trent finished sealing the suit of the last of them and stepped back. Florence now moved forwards and loaded all three into the big bag, hoisted that up easily and headed for the airlock.

'Hence your eagerness to ensure they all go through the runcible?'

'Yeah, hence that,' Trent replied, now heading back to Taiken's wife.

Next, watching from outside the hospital, Sverl tracked the robot, driven by a compressed-air impeller, following the stream of shell people heading for the runcible, Trent not far behind with the woman and two children. It was likely that Florence would be going through the runcible. The robot was run by a submind of the hospital AI, which had been destroyed long ago so now there were no minds in that structure to save. However, scattered throughout the station were all its other AIs, and they needed to move.

Sverl sent data to all the AIs aboard. The results so far showed that if they made the trip across they wouldn't be harmed, but if they stayed in the station they certainly would be. He did not offer them the choice about moving because they were completely under his control, and he had fewer qualms about the sanctity of the free will of others than Trent Sobel. The first of them was making its way across as the Atheter device reached one of the deactivated runcibles. This might be interesting, Sverl felt, because the runcible, even though inactive, wasn't composed of merely normal matter.

Straight away he saw that the device's approach had changed, for it dismantled the runcible rather than suck it all straight down. When it hit a component made of baryonic matter it paused, opened a gap in its surface, and took the thing in whole. Its projections then withdrew, the whole thing collapsing down to a sphere again. Then it pulsed, expanding massively as if muffling a contained explosion.

Indigestion? Sverl wondered.

After a pause, it regrew its extrusions and carried on as before, stripping away all the runcible's structure until nothing was left but the singularity case. This, apparently, was too much for it because it snared the thing at the end of one extrusion, and then with a slow heave sent it on its way into the hemisphere. Immediately tracking its course, Sverl saw that the case would land in a hollow made in the base of one of the support struts – one obviously made to receive it. He now turned his attention away from it, and to the functional runcible lying beyond what had been his abode for a while.

All the shell people were in position, gathered on a platform at the end of the destroyer assembly tube extending past the runcible.

'Trent,' Sverl said, 'send them towards the meniscus.'

'Sure thing,' Trent replied.

'Make the connection,' Sverl instructed the runcible AI.

The meniscus rippled as if a stone had been dropped into its centre point. The area on the other side remained visible, but also receded to impossible distance. Sverl felt the power draw and, touching the runcible AI's mind, read the mathematical description of a tube which possessed no length, connecting over a vast distance. The connection was accepted, firmed and established, and thousands of other options opened. Still under Sverl's instruction, the AI blocked all those options, which wasn't an easy task because the runcible they had connected to could be used for rerouting.

A moment later the first of the shell people arrived at the meniscus and dropped through it, ceasing to exist here and doubtless stumbling out of the smaller runcible on the moon of Flint in the Masadan system. Everything would have been corrected for at the other end. The energy they were carrying because of the different relative motions of the two runcibles would be dumped into runcible buffers. The energy they had acquired throughout the transit which, unless buffered, would have resulted in them exiting the runcible at close to the speed of light, was drawn off too, but bounced in a retransmission loop, never actually leaving U-space and so never actually existing. One after another they went, the surgical robot Florence carrying her load through too, shortly followed by Taiken's wife and children. By the time they were all gone the Atheter device was tearing apart the hospital in which they had returned to consciousness.

Sverl felt relieved of at least some pressure when that last shell person blinked out of existence. He eyed the platform they had departed and saw one figure still standing there. Trent.

'You have one minute,' said Sverl. 'Make up your mind.'

He stood with his head bowed for a moment, then finally sighed, 'Okay,' and launched himself towards the runcible.

'Goodbye, Trent,' said Sverl.

'Bye,' Trent replied, and disappeared through the meniscus.

Sverl hesitated as he saw another shape shooting towards the meniscus, watched it pass through, slightly puzzled by Mr Grey's decision to go, then instructed the runcible AI, 'Close it.'

'I can't until transmission completes,' the AI replied.

Sverl had delayed just a moment too long, because the runcible buffers were registering a load. Something was coming through from the other end.

Trent

Watching the last of the shell people fall through the runcible Trent had felt relieved. He felt he had discharged his responsibility and his conscience had no more call on him. On the other side of that meniscus the shell people would have to find their own way because the responsible thing to do with people was to allow them to make their own decisions, for good or ill.

When Reece and her children had gone he had intended to follow immediately, but then realized something else was happening inside him. Things were loosening, snapping away, folding out of existence. The feeling was an odd one, but in a strange way he recognized it. He suddenly understood he didn't have to care.

It was this feeling that momentarily held him on the platform, but then the knowledge that he could *choose* to care impelled him towards the runcible. As he said his goodbyes and fell through the meniscus, he felt some concern that this was a decision he could not change, but almost at the point of transition he knew it was the right one.

From the perspective of the traveller the transition is supposed to be instantaneous. Quince, the collective term for runcible travellers, are supposed to scream for that instant, but Trent found himself floating in greyness. Perhaps his transition had been instantaneous and what ensued was just a mental artefact – something set to 'play' at this moment.

'Are you an evil man?' a hissing voice queried in his mind.

As he tumbled in grey void, Trent thought of people he would like to kill – the few who had escaped him over the years. He visualized killing them in the most gruesome ways possible and he didn't flinch at the prospect. He knew, with utter certainty, that the imposed empathy was gone now and that he could kill again. However, he also knew that from now on he would avoid killing, unless it was absolutely necessary. What had changed, he understood, was that in the past necessity had not even come into the equation.

'No, I'm not,' he replied, suddenly uncomfortable with the knowledge that before Penny Royal had touched him he would have answered that question exactly the same.

'Because you could feel the pain of others and your conscience castigated you . . .'

'Yes. But no longer, it seems.'

'And now?' said a remnant of darkness residing in his skull.

'I choose to be good,' Trent explained.

The remnant whipped away, like a scrap of black silk caught in a breeze, and as it went it emitted a sound that might have been laughter, or crying. Trent looked around as if he might see the thing, but all he could see was grey, extending to infinity, and also seeming to have no depth at all. He wanted to scream, but found it locked in his throat. Unbearable tension stretched him then, and snapped him through and out into the reality of the runcible chamber on the moon of Flint in the Masadan system. As he stepped out on the black glass dais he felt a large shape looming to his right, but as he turned towards it the thing disappeared through the meniscus.

The chamber was in chaos, with thousands of erstwhile shell people milling about and a small staff of runcible technicians clad in blue overalls trying to impose some order. Those nearby were all gazing towards the runcible, expressions surprised or baffled, and he knew they had been watching the large thing that had just gone through past him. Stepping out further, he gazed beyond those nearby and saw some wearing a different uniform: the cream and yellow of runcible security – ECS. Perhaps he had made the wrong decision coming here? No, though the runcible on Flint was run by the Polity, that political entity had no power of arrest in the Masadan system. As he understood it, the cops here now had to ask permission of the Weaver.

'Come on,' said a familiar voice over suit com, and then a hard skeletal hand came down on his shoulder. He turned to find Mr Grey standing there.

'Why?' he asked.

'Why what?'

'Why did Penny Royal give me empathy, and then take it away again?'

'Sanity? You want sanity?'

'Just an explanation.'

Grey looked as if he was grinning insanely. But then, as he was a strangely painted ceramal skeleton, he always looked like that.

'Explanations,' he said, reaching up with one hand and click-ing his fingers together like a ratchet. 'Clickety click,' he added, which was a new one.

'Yes, explanations.'

'You are Penny Royal in microcosm,' said Grey, his voice now taking on a more sombre tone. 'The elements of choice and environment that turned you into a killer were the same in essence. The killer in you was taken away and the rest allowed to re-establish itself, just as it was with Penny Royal. Your empathy wasn't an addition, just unused and raw when you used it again.'

'You're talking about Penny Royal's eighth state of con-sciousness – its evil.'

'If you like.'

'I was an experiment – a test.'

'To see,' said Grey, 'if you would still be you. Are you?'

They moved through the milling crowd. Trent opened his visor then collapsed his suit helmet down into its neck ring. The air here was cool on his face, smelled of unwashed people and iron. He saw two of the ECS people watching him, but that was all they were doing, probably because of the company he kept. Next he scanned the crowd for Reece and the two boys.

'I'm me as much as anyone is the same person after the pas-sage of time,' he replied.

'That's good,' said Grey.

'So I am Penny Royal in microcosm, and a test.' Trent pon-dered that for a moment. 'So are you saying that Penny Royal intends to reincorporate its eighth state of consciousness?'

'I am.'

'Perhaps I made the right decision in coming here, then, because we can be damned sure Penny Royal hasn't finished with Sverl or Room 101.' He paused for a second to study the skeletal Golem, but of course there was nothing to read. 'Is that why you're here? Survival instinct kicking in?'

'I don't have one,' said Grey. 'And you weren't the only microcosm or test . . .'

'You too?' Trent asked.

'Yes.'

Trent understood. Penny Royal's Golem had been killers; Mr Grey had been a killer.

'So what now?'

Mr Grey gave an eloquent shrug. Trent moved off through the crowd, checking the faces of all those around him, but he was found when a small hand closed on his own.

'Robert?'

The boy tugged at his hand and led him over to where Reece and Ieran were waiting.

'Where do you go now, Reece?' he asked.

She gazed at him, obviously annoyed. 'Where do you think?'

'The Polity?'

She reached out and grabbed hold of the neck ring of his space suit. 'Stop being a bloody fool.'

'Let's go to Masada,' said a voice nearby.

They all turned to look at Mr Grey, grinning again. Trent was trying to decide whether or not he liked the idea of the Golem tagging along like this. Then he considered the idea of heading to that new world. Why not? He wouldn't be arrested on Masada and it might be an interesting place to be as the Weaver asserted his power and drew his world further away from the Polity.

'Will they let me leave?' Trent nodded towards the ECS officers.

'They've no choice,' said Grey. 'There's a ship here run by an old captain out of Spatterjay ready to take anyone there who wants to go. The Weaver has ordered that no one is to be inter-fered with; no one arrested.'

Trent glanced a query at Reece. She gave him a warning look then scanned their surroundings. 'So how do we get to this ship?'

Trent reached up and fingered his earring. He should be able to find a way to access his Galaxy Bank, then maybe rent or buy some property and thereafter there would be no need to rush to any decisions. Perhaps together they could go take a look at what Isobel Satomi had become. Time for a holiday, and a bit of sight-seeing, then he could think about what to do next and just how evil or otherwise he wanted to be. Gazing at Reece as she moved off towards what looked like an exit, he thought, *Not so much.*

12

Spear

The other clamberer was catching up with us but I wasn't surprised. Mr Pace was the top dog here so his owning a souped-up version of this vehicle was almost inevitable. I was just thankful for his apparent aversion to gravcars, else he would have been on top of us by now.

'The cliff,' said Riss, her voice issuing from the console. 'Go up the cliff.'

I glanced at her, then to where she was looking. On our way here we'd come down a long slope to reach this valley from a plateau above, the one that I had thought would have been a better location for the space port. Sepia turned our clamberer in that direction. Having an idea of what Riss intended, I decided to also take out some insurance. The shuttle's computer system was as open to me as that of the *Lance*, but I wasn't that confident of getting things right at a distance. Now routing all our coms through the clamberer's console and making a link to the *Lance*, I said, 'Flute, can you see us?'

'Watching you even now,' Flute replied. 'You seem to have a problem.'

'I want you to take control of the shuttle and bring it over here – bring it down on the plateau above.'

'Launching now,' Flute replied.

We reached the base of the cliff, where the clamberer hesitated as if silently wondering if we were sure. It found a grip with one of its limbs, reached up with the other, then began hauling us up the cliff face. In a moment we were pressed back in our seats, the clamberer tearing out a chunk of rotten stone as it scrabbled to get a grip with its lower limbs.

'He'll know what you've got now,' I said.

'And?' Riss enquired.

'If you leave something on the rock face for him he'll probably go round it.'

'Yes, I thought of that.' After a pause, during which I suspected Riss was considering other possibilities because she *hadn't* thought of that, she said, 'I'll put a charge on the leg of his vehicle.'

'All the legs would be better,' I suggested.

'Not enough for that,' she replied.

The clamberer began steadily making its way up the cliff face, scaring from a nearby crevice a thing looking like a bat fashioned out of glass. I looked round to see Pace's clamberer quickly drawing in below us and watched as it pursued us up the cliff with greater agility than our vehicle. We were about halfway up when Riss unpeeled from the glass.

'Wish me luck,' she said as she departed.

I tried to track her but soon she disappeared as her chameleonware engaged. When we were three-quarters of the way up, with Pace's clamberer just ten feet behind us, Riss returned, landing against the glass with a thwack. I looked back in time to see the explosion, halfway up the right forelimb of Pace's vehicle. With a crump the limb parted, the glare of the explosion leaving afterimages in my eyes. Our clamberer lurched in the blast and hung on, while the one below peeled away from the cliff face.

'We got him?' Sepia asked, concentrating on her controls.

'Sort of,' I replied.

I watched as his clamberer swung back into the cliff and continued to climb, slower now because it had lost a limb. As we came over the cliff top I could see the glare of atmosphere rockets haloing our approaching shuttle. But I knew it would not be quick enough.

'Put us down, now,' I said.

She peered at me. 'We'll probably be safer inside . . .'

'But then I wouldn't be able to use this vehicle to stop him,' I replied.

She held my eye for a second longer then settled the clamberer down. Meanwhile, I was in the vehicle's computer system, searching for a way to control it remotely. There were safety blocks I couldn't get past just using my aug, but almost without thinking I accessed the spine and the memories of Penny Royal's victims, many of whom knew ways to subvert systems like this. As we spilled out into a cold drizzle, stone slippery underfoot, I mentally seized control of the vehicle and had it standing and turning just as Pace's vehicle reached the cliff top. Sepia turned and opened fire with her carbine, the shots leaving glowing holes in Pace's clamberer without really slowing it.

'Run!' I shouted, seeing that the shuttle was coming down a few hundred yards away. Sepia glanced at me, picked up through our connection on what I was doing, then turned and sprinted, moving cat-fast, of course. As I followed, a portion of my focus remained in our clamberer. I sent it forwards to slam into Pace's vehicle, subverted its usual safety routines and had it grab the other clamberer's forelimbs and struggle to push it back towards the cliff edge. Poised there for a moment, they looked like grappling robotic wrestlers. Ahead, atmosphere rockets slowing it, the shuttle came down. Even as it settled, Sepia opened the door and darted inside. Meanwhile, Pace had opened the door of his vehicle and thrown himself out. Behind him both clamberers toppled over the edge of the cliff, but he hit the ground running.

I followed Sepia inside, ran through into the control cabin as we launched. Glancing at the screen, I could see we weren't going up quickly enough. Snapping out of the system of the clamberer, which had yet to fall all the way to the bottom of the cliff, I slid next into the system of the shuttle, making instinctive calculations and firing up one steering thruster. The shuttle lurched round, sending us both staggering inside and a second later I fired up one of the atmosphere rockets. The shuttle slewed and dipped, its nose grinding against stone, but subliminally, through an exterior cam, I saw Pace blown backwards across the plateau in the drive flame.

'We're good,' I said, as we rose and I finally got to a seat.

A fraction of a second later I saw five bright stars streaking towards us through the night and felt the bottom fall out of my world. I had some very effective abilities, I could think fast and react fast, but what the hell could I do about missiles launched from Mr Pace's castle? I might be able to evade one or two, but not all five. The night then lit up in a series of detonations and I glimpsed one missile spiralling down out of control to blow a crater in the side of a nearby mountain.

'You could have done that earlier,' said Riss, shimmering into existence on the console, peering out at the rising cloud of burning debris.

'Certainly,' Flute replied from the console, 'but I didn't want to interfere in case there was some purpose to all this running around.'

As I clipped across my strap I felt stupid. In the heat of the moment I'd completely forgotten that I had an armed Polity destroyer sitting in orbit, and that just with a thought I could have had it obliterate Mr Pace. But through the sheer relief I felt as I slumped back in my seat I also felt puzzled. Surely Mr Pace had known that too?

Sverl

'Drop everything but your weapons!' Sverl ordered. 'Get to the runcible now!'

But, even as he delivered those orders to his children, Sverl knew he might already be too late. Hadn't it been naive to think that the Polity AIs had obeyed their own laws and removed their military from the Masadan system? Wasn't it naive to think that they might not have a CTD or two to sling through at him? No, Penny Royal could never be described as naive. It felt inevitable that Sverl must open this runcible to Masada, while he felt sure that the black AI would never open what it was building here to such an obvious possibility of destruction.

Black spiky objects sketched a line down the meniscus before a large shape came through and began flailing about in zero gravity. The great bulky creature was almost comedic . . . Almost. Sverl gaped at the gabbleduck, at this resurrected Atheter called the Weaver, then suddenly realized that it had stepped through from the pressurized base on Flint straight into vacuum and might be dying. However, as he was about to change his orders to Bsorol and the rest, the beast abruptly stabilized, folded up its back legs and sat there, pyramidal in vacuum as if some invisible surface had materialized beneath it. A brief scan brought back some very odd results, but there was a bubble of air around it, under pressure, though the method of containment was beyond baffling. The surface of the bubble was constantly writhing . . . in fact it was *weaving* itself together.

Sverl felt his panic subside. So this was what Penny Royal had intended . . . His calm lasted for just a second until the other shape came through. Had the black AI intended this too? It was a gleaming scorpion, immediately stable in zero gravity and revolving slowly to take in its surroundings. This was marginally better than a CTD but could be worse than an assault force. The scorpion was Amistad, a war drone of the old school, upgraded to the status of planetary AI certainly, but doubtless still retaining his old weapons. He was densely packed with technology, possessing the kind of power supply that could run a small attack ship, deploy particle beams, cross spectrum lasers; he probably had a high-spec railgun and a wide selection of missiles and mines . . . things could be about to get very nasty, very fast.

'Runcible link to the Masadan moon Flint is now closed,' said the runcible AI.

'Very good,' Sverl replied.

'Hello, Amistad,' he sent.

'Sverl,' Amistad replied. 'Don't get twitchy on any triggers – I'm just here as a tourist.' The drone now drew to a halt facing what had been the nose of the station. 'Interesting view.'

There were now gaps through the body of the station, and the light of the hypergiant glaring in was reflected in shades of gold from the seemingly organic inner structure of the hemisphere. Even as Amistad watched, the facing side of the final construction bay adjacent to the hospital began to disappear, letting in more of the glare. Sverl, the whole station effectively transparent to him as he gazed through surviving station cams, saw that the device had returned from weaving around the edge of the hemisphere to rip up and digest more materials. Checking the progress of the work it had done, he could see that the hemisphere was more than half done, and the device would soon be on the way back to complete a sphere.

'And what will your Polity masters think of that – the ones who sent the fleet that has been attempting to destroy this station?' he asked.

Amistad waved a dismissive claw. 'I would dispute that I have any "masters" since I submitted my resignation before I stepped through this runcible.' He paused for a second, then added, 'Anyway, seems to me that fleet might be redundant now. My "masters" didn't want you getting your claws on wartime weapons production. Yet that seems to be rapidly disappearing.'

Amistad now turned and tipped up, his front end pointing directly to where Sverl squatted on a beam. Just then Bsorol, Bsectil and Sverl's remaining second-children rounded the runcible, spread out through the space beyond, forming themselves in a loose sphere around the scorpion drone and the Weaver. Sverl was impressed by their discipline. They had intelligently assessed the threat and moved to contain it but without being ordered to, had not fired a shot.

'Remember what I said about triggers,' Amistad reminded them and, perhaps just to drive the point home, the space all around him and out to Sverl's children briefly filled with the flicker of targeting lasers. In response, a few Gatling cannons began spinning and targeting lasers flickered again, this time from the prador.

Sverl remained undecided. If he kept his children there, despite their apparent adulthood, the chances of a slip-up would keep rising, but if he withdrew them that might just be what Amistad was waiting for. No, in the end he decided to trust in Penny Royal's plans, uncomfortably reminded, as he so decided, of Spear's comment about him having found something to believe in.

'Bsorol, Bsectil, withdraw and carry on as before,' he instructed. 'Move your stuff to the hauler.'

Throughout all this the Weaver remained squatting in vacuum, turning its head occasionally to gaze either at Amistad or out at one of the prador. It was as if the creature considered itself a spectator and not a vulnerable organic life form sitting right in the middle of enough hair-trigger armament to flatten a major city. Sverl also sensed from it, he wasn't sure how, a degree of suppressed amusement, as if at any moment it might bellow with laughter. But then, as the prador began to break up their formation and move off, it too, moved.

It began drifting away from the runcible and turned to face towards the device it had been instrumental in creating. The device began jerking like some beast being stabbed. Then all at once the device just stopped.

Sverl transferred his attention back to the Weaver, who was heading, like some insane alien Buddha, for one of the gaps broken through the body of the station. It had raised an arm and held some intricate but flimsy artefact in one of its heavy claws. Sverl had no doubt that it had just shut down the Atheter device, but what now? He decided he wanted to take a closer look – see with his own eyes. He ran along the beam, launched himself, fired up his internal grav-engine and planed after the Weaver. As expected, Amistad was soon travelling beside him.

'Can you do anything about that fleet?' Sverl asked.

'I'm talking to Garrotte right now,' Amistad replied. 'He's not happy about me being here and seems to think he can give me orders. I guess that's what happens when you stick an attack ship mind into a dreadnought. Napoleon complex.'

They came in behind the Weaver as he floated through one of the gaps, in the bright glare almost lost even to Sverl's sensors. Checking, Sverl found that it wasn't just the light from the hypergiant he was having to deal with but also radiation in some odd bands across the EM spectrum from the station structure: infrared and microwave, gamma radiation and for some reason a singular high spike in the ultra-violet. Some sort of tenderizing process the device used on the matter it was shortly to ingest, Sverl supposed.

'So why do you think he's here?' Amistad asked.

'I'm not sure,' Sverl hedged.

'Yes you are,' Amistad replied. 'This is Penny Royal's payment for providing a bio-mech war machine. But the Weaver's presence here perhaps tells us something else.'

'Like what?'

'Do you think that Atheter device required any form of *actual* intervention from the Weaver?'

'No,' Sverl replied. Atheter technology looked as if it might be more advanced than that of the Polity. It didn't seem likely the Weaver's presence was required, unless it was for some obscure cultural reason.

'The deal's not done,' said Amistad.

'Ah . . .'

Now that would explain things. The object steadily being constructed here might be part of an ongoing transaction. Perhaps the Weaver was here to see the deal through to completion. He had probably left out something essential, or was retaining control until Penny Royal made the final payment.

'I wonder what that final payment might be,' Sverl said.

'Me too,' said Amistad, distracted.

'Do you think Penny Royal will be coming back here to make it?' Sverl asked, sure that the answer was yes. 'And to collect the final product?'

'One might suppose so,' Amistad replied. 'But whether there will be a final product here to collect is open to debate.'

'What?'

'I just got warned by Garrotte that I have one solstan day to leave this place,' Amistad replied. 'And now he's sending me an image feed.'

Even as Amistad spoke, Sverl's sensors were warning him of further U-space signatures: more ships arriving. Amistad wanted to widen their com channel and Sverl was instantly suspicious, because this could be a method of attack. But he dismissed those suspicions. Amistad had weapons to deploy, so he didn't need to use informational warfare. He opened up the channel.

Ships slid into the real far-out past the hypergiant sun. Sverl recognized the long lethal-looking things at once as those of the King's Guard returning. For just a brief second he hoped these might be a problem for the Polity fleet, but then knew that wasn't so. Garrotte would not have given that warning and sent this feed to back it up. It seemed the Kingdom and the Polity were now allied in some sort of response to what was happening here. Sverl counted twenty King's Guard ships, but there was another ship as well. This he recognized too: a great bulky mass like a titanic clam with big old nuclear drive engines to the rear and massive grabs spread to the fore. He had seen such vessels in Kingdom shipyards during the war. They were tugs made for shifting great masses like enormous damaged ships coming in for repair, a bit antediluvian now but still good for their job.

'This doesn't look good,' commented Amistad.

'Quite,' Sverl agreed.

The Brockle

The moment the *High Castle* surfaced from U-space, the Brockle began delving into all available data channels and quickly learned some interesting facts. It had missed Thorvald Spear by a matter of days. The man had come here to visit Mr Pace and had only narrowly managed to escape with his life. Whether this was due to Mr Pace's tendency to kill his visitors or because

Spear had done something to further upset the man, the Brockle had no idea. It was, therefore, time to investigate.

Focusing sensors on the planet below, the Brockle studied the man's castle. There was damage to the entryway, and some positively antique robots were repairing it, while on the roof a shuttle was being fuelled and loaded with crates. The Brockle withdrew its attention momentarily to focus on a ship in orbit: a large egg-shaped craft with three U-nacelles extending from its equator. A brief probe revealed that the thing was going through test routines. From what it had learned upon its arrival here it knew this spaceship belonged to Pace. He was preparing to go on a journey. The Brockle returned its attention to the planet below.

Auto-handler drays were driving up a ramp in the side of the shuttle and depositing the plasmel crates inside. And Mr Pace was there, watching, his arms folded. The Brockle used passive sensing on him at first, but got no readings off him at all. He was like a mobile stone. Active sensors revealed a body with a strange molecular structure. Pace was tough, but pliable – the material of his body a nano-layered composite of metallic glass that was tougher than the advanced armour on those pieces of the *Black Rose* still sitting in the science section aboard the *High Castle*. There were AI crystals in there too, distributed so his brain wasn't located only in his skull. Strange forms of carbon abounded, including diamond films. Graphene and molybdenite processing nodes were scattered throughout, while his nerve impulses were transmitted by nano-lasers. This was all very interesting but didn't get the Brockle any closer to what it wanted to know.

Suddenly Mr Pace turned and looked up, straight towards the location of the *High Castle*. Unclear as to why, the Brockle felt a stab of fear.

Mr Pace was a complicated and interesting creature and it

wasn't beyond the bounds of possibility that he had a way of sensing if he was being scanned. Also, the *High Castle* was a big ship which would be clearly visible from down there, if not from the sensors of Pace's nearby ship. The Brockle shrugged off its fear, assuming it stemmed from some remnant of its former human self, and now began to pull itself back together to regain its human form.

The process was much quicker, but the result wasn't pleasing. The Brockle was reminded of the time aboard Par Avion when it had been necessary to form some of its units into a piece of hover luggage. Despite maximum compression of its units, the resultant human form stood seven and a half feet tall and possessed an extreme girth. But did it matter? Humans, as they had spread out in the galaxy, had taken on all sorts of strange forms when adapting to environments, and many changed themselves radically for aesthetic purposes. There were inhabitants of low-gravity worlds who stood taller, squat troll-like humans on heavy-gravity worlds who were shorter and wider. Some had adopted wings, others had made themselves indistinguishable from terran cetaceans. It was all of no consequence for now the Brockle's purpose wasn't subterfuge: it no longer needed to blend in and avoid being noticed.

Coming into the corridor, it saw Blite and Greer ahead of it. Seeing it, they registered shock, then terror. With its intelligence levels higher now, it knew there was little more to learn from them. Briefly it considered erasing them both, but decided against that. They were weak human beings who in no way could hinder the Brockle's plans. Also, their potential value as hostages should not be discounted.

'Come with me,' the Brockle commanded and trudged towards the door from the lounge, the floor bowing slightly underneath its feet.

The two stood up, looking confused and worried. Only as they did so did the Brockle wonder why it had ordered them to come with it. Was it still so insecure that it dared not leave them alone aboard this ship? Was this another remnant of its past impinging? This was ridiculous really because it could keep watch on them even from down on the surface and easily enough foil any plots from there. Analysing its own thought processes, it could find no answer; however, it did find an answer to why it did not immediately change the order and tell them to stay: dumb pride.

'What do you want?' Blite managed. Greer glanced at him in panic as if he might be provoking a hooder.

'What do I want?' the Brockle repeated, its massively expanded intelligence for a moment providing far too many answers, and very little in way of choosing between them. 'I want to save the Polity from its own folly by destroying Penny Royal.' It paused for a moment then added, 'And because of what I've done to get this far, my reward would be death, though I will choose exile.'

'Feeling underappreciated?' Blite asked.

Greer was now backing away from him. Obviously Blite had had enough and was intent on getting himself killed.

'No, I perfectly understand the consequences of my actions.'

'But it must be hard when you're being so *altruistic*.'

'Blite,' said Greer, 'please.'

He glanced at her, then shoved his hands into his pockets and dipped his head in acquiescence. The Brockle watched him for a moment longer then turned to head off through the corridors of the ship, and the two of them trailed along behind. The route took it past the open door into the science section, through which Blite and Greer looked and then wished they hadn't. The

325

Brockle made a note to itself to clear up the mess in there, and also to examine further those remains of the *Black Rose*.

Finally, they reached the *High Castle*'s shuttle. The shuttle was state-of-the-art: a packed brick of technology a hundred feet long, a combined chemical and fusion drive, grav-engines, its own hardfields and enough power, strengthening and negating internal grav to enable it to land on a giant world while keeping human passengers alive. The doorway opened into a long compartment that could be used either for passengers or cargo – chairs folded down into the floor. The Brockle ducked into the cockpit, having to deform its shape to get through. It fired up the shuttle's systems and before it took the shuttle out, checked to see if its passengers were strapped in, then experienced a moment of complete confusion as to why it had bothered.

Thrown by a maglev sling, the shuttle shot out into vacuum. Then, as it hit atmosphere, the fusion torch winked out and grav-engines took over. The Brockle dropped the craft hard through a rain storm, which seemed to be the standard weather here, and fell like a brick towards the valley in front of the castle. A mile above the valley it decelerated on grav and the burst from a chemical rocket, folded down pneumatic feet and landed just about as hard as it could, and still no disturbance was felt inside.

The Brockle turned and headed out of the cockpit as the vessel settled. It eyed its passengers then gestured peremptorily before heading for the door, opening that on to the rainy night and walking down a ramp that bowed under its weight. The two followed obediently but then, upon reaching the bottom of the ramp, they broke away and ran off into the darkness as fast as they could. The Brockle watched them speeding away and considered bringing them back, which it could do as easily as thinking. But, it now questioned their utility as hostages. Perhaps its hidden reason for bringing them down here had been precisely for this – to find a way of releasing them. It shrugged and heaved its gargantuan form on into the darkness.

Sverl

Sverl and Amistad now found themselves beyond the chewed-off end of Room 101, floating in vacuum out from a wall of wreckage thirty miles wide and fifteen deep. The Atheter device was just hovering out from the remains of the last structure it had been digesting, the Weaver slowly drawing closer to it. Beyond them the hemisphere loomed – a great disc filled with golden bones. As the Weaver drew within a few miles of the device, the thing started revolving in place, then slowly began to shift to one side. Sverl scanned it with everything he had available. The density of the thing was much higher than it had been before, complex networks like veins and capillaries flowed with molten materials, all routed to those protrusions from its surface.

'Looks like the head of a sundew,' Amistad commented.

Sverl checked the reference, found images in his extensive files of the terran insectivorous plant, and had to agree.

'I thought big printer-bot when I first saw it working,' Amistad continued, 'but those sticky-out things bear more of a resemblance to spinnerets.'

Sverl now had to do some further checking, wondering if Polity drones always referenced obscure stuff about terran biology and culture, for that had been the drone Arrowsmith's habit too. He then briefly lost himself in a fascination with terran spiders. Yes, the similarity to how spiders made their webs was there. Belatedly, Sverl felt a moment of worry when he considered other possible similarities concerning insect traps and dry little corpses sucked of fluid.

Still revolving, the device halted at a point which, after just a brief check, Sverl found lay on a line running from the centre of the hemisphere and through the middle of the station. It then moved back in towards the station and started carving again, rotating around that axis as it did so, drilling into the structure.

'What now?' he wondered, then fired up his grav drive to take himself after Amistad, who obviously wanted a closer view.

Within a few minutes they came in behind the Weaver, who was following the device through the hole it had already carved half a mile into the station. The thing was working differently now because its reach was limited to its diameter. All around, beams, pipes, factory units, transport systems – everything packed into the station – had been neatly sheered through, the cut faces often mirror bright. Sverl even saw half a fusion reactor, utterly dead inside now after safely shutting down. Was this alteration a tweak? Had the device not been running properly before?

'We're in the hauler,' Bsorol informed him.

'Very well,' Sverl replied, quickly checking the status of the repairs to that ship. 'When it can fly, take it out of the station and into the hemisphere. Dock near the rim for now – we don't want to sit ourselves in a possible trap.' It was the stuff about spiders that had instigated that last comment.

'Anything else?' Bsorol enquired.

Sverl had been modelling possible future scenarios for some time to try and figure out what preparations he could make. To the complex computer models he had added all sorts of possibilities concerning what might be happening here. However, in all honesty, he had no idea what Penny Royal was up to. Nor, taking another brief look out beyond the station, what the combined Polity and Kingdom response to it would be.

'Have you got any suggestions?' he asked.

'Can't think of anything,' Bsorol replied.

'Me neither.'

The device continued cutting straight through the station. Soon it was slicing through the gridwork of new beams before the working runcible. If it continued along this course, it would carve into the frame of the runcible because the thing was offset from the centre line of the station.

'What do I do?' the runcible AI asked, some urgency in its enquiry.

'Let's just wait a moment,' Sverl replied.

The device halted before reaching the runcible, drifted to one side, then forwards again, and began carving round the runcible frame through all the support structures, but now leaving behind a band of woven matter. Studying closer, Sverl saw that the support beams, power supplies, optic feeds and other equipment had been connected to the inner face of that band.

'Report,' Sverl instructed.

'Brief errors, immediately corrected,' the AI supplied, also sending a data package. Sverl examined the thing. While carving out the runcible from the body of the station the device was immediately connecting it up again. The point where it was cutting had been carefully chosen. Any closer in and it would have wrecked some critical support mechanisms. But then Sverl wondered if that would have mattered – the thing could probably have replaced them.

'So the runcible is being kept,' observed Amistad.

'A U-jump missile in here would destroy even Atheter tech,' Sverl replied.

Over the ensuing hours, the device carved the runcible clean away from the body of the station, leaving it sitting in that woven ring, held in place by strands spiking out from it to various beams. Once this was done, the device set itself back along its previous course, except it started on the other side of the runcible. As it continued, it grew larger and larger, now five miles across. It had grown by another mile by the time it carved through the back of the final construction bay and was a further two miles wide when it reached an inactive runcible and absorbed most of that.

'Like an owl pellet,' Amistad observed.

The drone was referring to the singularity canister the device had left behind, anchored by woven bands to a beam.

Three-quarters of the way down the length of the station and the device had grown to ten miles across, with Sverl and Amistad progressing behind it. The station's profile was vaguely rectangular and measured thirty miles by fifteen, meaning it had been effectively gutted.

'Doesn't leave much in the way of debris,' Amistad commented.

Sverl turned his attention to a wall that lay five miles away, he saw severed pipes and powder feeds. Many of these should have been leaking materials, so the device's reach must be a little more than its diameter. It must have been sucking dry the reservoirs those pipes and feeds led to, either that or blocking them deep inside. As he considered this and wondered what else he might be missing, a subprogram he had set running in an external sensor array alerted him. The ships out there were on the move again.

The big tug was now heading towards them, while the other ships were forming up all around it. Did they intend to try relocating the surrounding hardfield and thus the station itself? What would be the purpose of that?

'Father,' said Bsorol, interrupting his thoughts and opening a cam feed.

The viewpoint was from the edge of the hemisphere. It showed a swarm of objects crossing from the ragged end of the station there. Close focus revealed hastily rigged forms of transport: impellers strapped on, robots gutted to take new loads and straight escape ejections. The AIs were heading across.

'I instructed them to leave,' Sverl said.

'Yes,' Bsorol replied, 'but see what's happening now.'

The image feed sped up, showing the AIs spreading out in the hemisphere and anchoring themselves. About half of them had gathered in an area in the apex of the hemisphere, while all the others had spread out in a suspiciously even pattern. The cam view now focused on one of these. This AI was sitting in the stripped-out back of a scorpion-format robot, which was gripping the base of one of those cross-strut 'bird bones'. While Sverl watched, a rod like the shoot of a plant oozed up from the underlying mesh, spread threads all over the robot and, coming apart, it and the AI began sinking into the base of that strut. Sverl immediately checked his comlinks to all the station AIs. They were still open and the responses from the AIs showed a strange lack of concern.

'Positioning,' they replied, 'have reached insertion point.'

Delving deeper, Sverl soon found that apparently *he* had given instructions about where they should place themselves in the hemisphere, and about how to integrate. Of course those instructions must have issued from the physical and mental centres of these entities, from the black diamonds in them. How to respond? The answer was the same one as before: do nothing, hope for the best.

'And now it's approaching the drive,' commented Amistad.

'Whatever Penny Royal is building . . . or rather having built here, I'm sure needs to be moved,' Sverl asserted.

'Well, if you suppose it needs to be moved, then you must have some idea of what it's for,' said Amistad. 'So what is it for?'

Room 101 was being converted into a huge spherical object, a thing woven by (and packed with) Atheter technology. Was it a ship of some kind, or just another immobile space station? Why did it need the huge strength it obviously possessed when, as far as Sverl could see, it had nothing that looked like offensive weapons? Why had the AIs been evenly distributed around inside that hemisphere and linked in to the underlying system? Why were half the AIs gathered in that one spot? The answer to this last was obvious: they were ready to distribute themselves just like their brethren when the sphere was finished. Yet Sverl was no nearer to knowing why.

'I've no idea,' he replied. 'I just feel that whatever Penny Royal intends has got nothing to do with this system . . . it's . . . too remote.'

'In the Polity then, or in the Kingdom?'

Perhaps this entire thing was some kind of weapon. Penny Royal hadn't been the nicest of entities in the past and on Masada it had regained its nasty aspect in the form of its eighth state of consciousness. Could it be that all the good deeds were just a cover and Penny Royal was returning to what it did so well: fucking people up? Just on a grander scale than ever?

Looking out, he saw the Polity ships had accelerated and, as they approached the hardfield, their formation was spreading. Still he had no idea what this was all about.

The device now reached the rear of the compartments containing the U-space drive of the station, and it did not slow at all. It chewed its way through and, slightly offset from the drive itself, sliced down along it just as if it was any other part of the station. As it did this, iridescent surfaces cut across vacuum behind the device, then something exploded. The blast, brighter even than the penetrating sunlight, was followed by an expanding sphere of luminous fire. Sverl registered the temperature of his skeletal ceramal body rising rapidly, and cautionary reports began scrolling in his mind.

We're too close, he thought. But the Weaver was closer still.

The sphere of fire continued to expand, and washed around the bubble enclosing that floating gabbleduck. It then began to break into streamers and slow. Next, all at once, it started retreating, back towards the Atheter device and disappearing into its protrusions as if they were vacuum hoses sucking up smoke. And the device moved relentlessly on.

'What were you saying about this thing needing to be moved?' Amistad enquired.

Sverl groped around for a clever reply, but settled for, 'Screw you.' He would have done better but his concentration was now focused on that big tug out there, closing in on the hardfield and now decelerating to reduce the impact.

'You're seeing this?' he asked.

'Certainly,' Amistad replied. 'I penetrated your systems about twelve milliseconds after I arrived here.'

Big-head, thought Sverl.

The other ships were now spreading out around the sphere, weapons definitely to bear. Why? Then Sverl understood. He could respond to this tug by briefly shutting down the hardfield and repositioning it further out, thus chopping the tug in half. The ships were just waiting for that brief shutdown. Was that the purpose? To try and elicit that kind of response from him?

The tug now impacted and Sverl felt a shudder deep in the core of his being. What would happen? Would the field shift, would the station or, rather, what remained of the station, drift over to one side and impact against its inner curve? He ran some analysis, having to delve into some of the exotic math related to how the whole thing worked. No, if it was even possible to move the hardfield, the object inside would move with it. The reason for this related to the entire mass being fixed to the energy sinks into U-space: stasis forces were at work here that operated on the large scale but not the minor scale, which was why they could actually move within the field. In its way the effect was comparable to weak atomic binding forces.

Sverl focused exterior sensors on the relative positions of a series of astronomical objects in the system and began collecting data and measuring. Meanwhile the tug's nuclear engines were firing up. As he waited for results, he wondered why the hell they had chosen such an antediluvian vessel for this chore, whatever it was.

There.

The hardfield, and thus the station, was now on the move.

'I'm puzzled by the purpose of this,' he said.

'Are you really?' Amistad asked.

'I wouldn't have said so if I wasn't,' Sverl replied.

'Well,' explained Amistad, 'when someone is giving you a shove, it's worth glancing in the direction of that shove to divine its purpose.'

Sverl immediately focused exterior sensors in the aforesaid direction.

He looked straight into the face of the hypergiant sun.

'Oh,' he managed.

13

Sfolk

His claws trapped in the soft screens by Penny Royal, Sfolk struggled in the basket that had contained the original captain of the ancient Atheter starship, the squirming of something from those screens continuing up under the carapace of his claw limbs. It wasn't painful but then, as Sfolk understood it, a lime worm infection wasn't painful until just before the point when the things started eating major organs. His legs scrabbling for purchase in the basket, he tried to heave his limbs from the screens, but the screen material just stretched a little way towards him then snapped him back when he stopped pulling.

In a moment the sensation reached where his limbs joined to his main carapace, whereupon he could feel it deep inside him but much duller, since there were few afferent nerves there. His vision through his palp eyes fizzed for a moment, showing him deep vacuum and distant stars, while the vision in his main eyes overlaid that with a mathematical display. Diamond-pattern gridlines scrolled across, shapes that might have been glyphs appeared, some of them changing incrementally, curves and geometric patterns sprang from this, then, with an internal snap, his vision returned to normal. The starship was making some kind of connection to him. He felt something twist in his visual centre and elsewhere, and the legs on one side of his body collapsed. He folded the rest of his legs to bring his other side down and settled in the basket – it being obvious now he wasn't going anywhere.

Next that other vision came back, but this time swapped around, and the grid formed in a familiar hexagonal pattern. He tried to move his palp eyes, but instead found the graphical displays shifting in response and those glyphs, which he just knew to be numbers, were changing too. He wasn't stupid. He had an aug and recognized that he was undergoing a similar connection routine. Concentrating, he found himself able to shift individual lines, alter geometric shapes, reweave the whole display. Another snap ensued, and suddenly the numbers were prador number glyphs and other instructional glyphs were appearing. The mathematical display divided and divided again. In each section were clear prador glyphs overlaying everything else. One said manoeuvring/relocation, another was a general-purpose word combining armour and energy shields, yet another kept changing, as if whatever program was now running was having difficulty finding an adequate prador explanation. The last, however, was clear, unchanging and very, very attractive. It said 'weapons'.

Feeling a prompt inside him like the beating of a heart, he resisted the immediate instinctive urge to select weapons and instead chose manoeuvring/relocation. This display expanded to fill the vision of his palp eyes. All at once he recognized everything there: the 'small shift' drive based on something similar to a combination of Mach-effect and grav-engines with finesse of control to move the ship incrementally and the power to sling it about in realspace at speeds up to a quarter of the speed of light; the fusion/ionic drive that kicked in at that point to take it all the way up to just below the speed of light; and last of all the U-space drive. This last he found himself able to understand on a basic level, until he found the links through to the weapons system, to astrogation maps that filled his mind in three dimensions, and to the terrifying optional manoeuvres – one of which involved U-jumping into the heart of a star, then out again. As he tried to access all this, his ganglion began to ache and reality took a sidestep and tried to escape him, and he was back in the simple stuff. Later, perhaps.

Sfolk tried simple manoeuvring, weaving the pattern to spin the ship around slowly. He at once felt the movement and saw the star fields displayed in his main vision shifting round. What would happen if he tried something more violent? Would he end up pulped in this basket? No, he realized, because the damping field would kick in. Care should be used, of course, because that field would halt all the processes of his body and slow down the boosted processing of his mind. Sfolk halted the ship, dismayed, aware that he was thinking about stuff he simply hadn't known a moment ago. However, he had experienced something similar before with his aug, and his dismay waned.

Next he tried to focus with his main eyes because, perfectly knowing his position in this system, he *knew* he was facing the Junkyard. Nothing happened for a moment, then new options dropped into his mind. He chose the easiest of them and found himself gazing on one of the wrecked hulks as if it was just a few hundred feet away, every detail clearer than he had known before. He focused again, in a different way, and could see even more detail while still able to see the hulk as a whole. How far could this take him? He pushed further, microscopic detail open, another option opening to give him an analysis of the hull metal, its structure, composition, weaknesses and strengths. At this point the pain returned and he understood that, though he hadn't reached the limits of this system, he had reached the present limits of his own mind. He retreated, tried other options. While simultaneously moving the Atheter starship towards that hulk, he steadily widened his vista. Pain returned and he accepted that he did not have the capacity for three-hundred-and-sixty-degree vision.

Not yet.

Acceleration pushed him back, and then the basket reoriented so he was being pushed down on his belly plates. He increased acceleration, and felt an impact just before the air seemed to harden around him. His mind slowed, he felt as if he was dying, everything inside him paused for a second. A moment later he was exiting from the other side of a spreading cloud of wreckage. Minimal damage, repairing, something informed him. He realized he had just rammed that hulk and obliterated it. Suppressed dismay began to transform into creeping delight and, while still mentally hanging onto the manoeuvring controls, he decided to take a look at weapons.

What toys . . .

The prador mind, he found, was better at grasping this, but only marginally so. However, though numerous toys were detailed, many of them were offline, or warned of fatal energy drains. There were beam weapons described not so much by the coherent energies they could unleash, but by what they were capable of destroying. These energy weapons also opened into a cornucopia of hostile computer life that could be transmitted, but that was far too complicated for translation and remained stubbornly in a form beyond Sfolk's grasp. There were shearfields that could be extended beyond the ship like hardfields, and which could be shaped to chop up items in any way desired. Weapons for deploying gravity pulses, waves, the kind of collapsed space generated by a singularity, but, looking further at those options, Sfolk found linkages to the U-space drive and further complexity that lay beyond him. All of these, apparently, could cause fatal power drains – fatal being defined as energy usage that would kill the ship's ability to move.

Sfolk paused for a moment, remembering his earlier thoughts about the atomic shear he had picked up – thoughts that had arisen in a mind that seemed a bit dull to him now. That anything was working at all should be a matter for awe. This ship, which he had just crashed through a hulk to receive only minor damage, was two million years old. Sfolk continued to ponder that, almost out of respect for the vessel around him, then, with the glee of a second-child provided with his first Gatling cannon, focused his attention on the coil guns.

The Brockle

The Brockle tramped on through rainy night, the soggy ground squelching under its huge weight until it reached the road leading up to the castle. Mentally probing ahead, it delved into the antiquated computer system of that building, along with its robots and cams, and kept an eye on Mr Pace.

After watching cargo being transferred to his shuttle for a while longer, Mr Pace smiled bleakly and returned inside, making his way down through various castle passageways then up a spiral stair and out atop a castellated tower.

Reaching the archway into the castle and seeing it still partially blocked with fallen rubble, the Brockle paused for a moment, then, with a clap of its hands and a whoomph like a grenade going off, divided into a hundred oaken segmented units. It swarmed up a slope of rubble and through the narrow gap at the top, past a primitive printer-bot exuding high-bond cement to stick blocks of stone back in place in the fallen ceiling, then down the other side, slamming back together at the foot of the slope in gargantuan human form again. It stomped on across a courtyard, smashed open a studded door with a nonchalant flip of its hand, and made its way into the musty torchlit ways of this edifice.

While in the computer system of the castle *and* watching Mr Pace, it was also aware that it was being watched in turn. Mr Pace knew it was here, yet his reaction was puzzling. He had not tried to launch his shuttle to get away – which of course the Brockle would have stopped. Perhaps he knew the futility of trying to escape. As it was, it seemed he had chosen a place to wait.

Within a few minutes the Brockle was climbing the same spiral stair as Mr Pace, then stepping out onto the wet stone at the top of the tower. The rain had stopped now and overhead the cloud was breaking, while the sun was lighting up the sky behind the mountains. The Brockle eyed Mr Pace as he turned from the battlements – a vaguely amused expression on his adamantine face.

'So what are you?' he enquired.

'I am the Brockle.'

'Ah, yes, I know about you,' Pace replied. 'I always wondered, if I was ever captured by the Polity, if you would be able to break the link. Perhaps now it has been ordained that I find out.' He paused thoughtfully for a moment. 'Or it might even be that you're a random element and none of this has been planned.' He shrugged.

'Where is Penny Royal?' the Brockle asked, taking a step forwards. It then paused as something crunched underfoot, and looked down at the crushed mess of some mollusc. Scanning about the top of the tower, it now saw that the stone was covered with things like terran snails, only with the shells sideways extended so they looked almost like little scrolls. Why hadn't it noticed these before?

'What is your interest?'

'I intend to destroy that AI.'

'Then our interests are similar . . . in a curious manner.'

Now much closer to the man, the Brockle scanned him on deeper levels. Though his mind was distributed, it should be possible to read him. However, it was nearly impossible because to make the connections would require punching through his outer layers of metallic glass.

'Where is Penny Royal?' the Brockle repeated, then looked down.

One of the snail things had just crawled onto the ersatz toe of its boot. It kicked the thing away and returned its attention to Pace, just as a channel opened from him. As the Brockle received coordinates it tried to gain access to him through the channel. The man struggled mentally, but severed the link by powering down the transceivers in his body. He staggered back and rested one hand against the battlements.

'Now, now.' He held up his other hand and waved one finger. 'You have what you came here for. That's the last known location of Penny Royal. Spear and his companions are heading there even now, and I must pursue if I'm to get what I want from that man.'

'So what do you want from him?'

'A way to kill and a way to die.'

This obscure statement rather confirmed what the Brockle had felt as it approached this castle: Mr Pace was a repository of information about the black AI and should not be . . . neglected. It took another pace forwards, crushing another mollusc underfoot, looked down again then around at the rest of them and felt unreasonably annoyed. What was the point of the damned things?

'Perhaps we can join forces,' Mr Pace added.

'In what manner?'

'We both want similar things . . .'

The Brockle weighed up what use Mr Pace might be, and

decided his information was primary, but his physical presence unnecessary. Also, Mr Pace was at the top of a long list of people the Brockle had expected, at one time or another, to pay a visit to it while it had been aboard the *Tyburn*. He was one of the criminal overlords who ran the Graveyard; a man guilty of many murders and other atrocities. Taking him apart was perfectly justifiable for the Brockle's own ends and to the AIs of the Polity.

'Data is what I want now.'

The Brockle fell forwards and separated with a thunderclap, shoaled towards Mr Pace and engulfed him. He didn't struggle, which was somehow as irritating as these molluscs squirming underfoot. The Brockle blunted chain-diamond saws against his skin, tried peeling away layers with nano-shears but recognized that would take forever, then tried to punch through with the hardest micro-drills at its disposal. It became aware then of a strange sound it took a moment to analyse.

Then it realized Pace was laughing.

Irritation turned to anger. The Brockle concentrated on suppressing that while minutely examining the outer Mr Pace. He was tough, but his outer layers also reacted like projectile armour: hardening at points of impact and distributing load. Micro-fractures were the answer. Mr Pace needed to be subject to a massive shock and, no explosives being immediately available, the Brockle hoisted him up and over the battlements. Some kind of change then ensued: Pace grew rigid and a sort of power surge began to build inside him. The Brockle dropped him, then followed him down. Pace tumbled through the air, a grin fixed rigidly on his features, struck the hard stone below the battlements with a sound like a dropped bell, and shattered. The Brockle swarmed over the pieces, which were steaming in the damp, then fell on them quickly, groping for connections and data to download. Even as it made connections, the data, in quantum storage, began losing coherence as the power earthed out of those pieces.

Connection . . .

The Brockle found something it had never encountered before in all its victims, all those people and machines who had committed every atrocity imaginable. It found true immutable insanity, then the sound of laughter, steadily receding. Desperately, it snatched at diminishing data, incoherent chunks falling into its mind. Then it was gone; Mr Pace was gone. Swirling up, the Brockle raged. Individual units snatched up pieces of the man and scattered them, tore at the underlying stone as if in pursuit of the earthed out data and left glowing scars. Then it slammed back into human form and found itself stamping on remaining pieces, shattering them to black glassy sand. After a while there were no more in immediate reach and it turned to the tower, punching a hand through the nearest door and ripping it off its hinges.

As the Brockle climbed the spiral stair it felt the madness receding. It had got what it had come here for, and more, but not all of Mr Pace. The man had used the Brockle as a method of suicide and, at the last, had deliberately made alterations inside himself so he would shatter. He had done this either to keep something from the Brockle or perhaps, for no reason at all. There was nothing more to be gained here. It was time to go after Penny Royal.

Still, the Brockle climbed to the top of the tower, walked out on the wet stone and stamped on every one of those molluscs it could find. This wasn't rational, it knew.

Didn't care.

Sfolk

The six coil guns, spaced equidistantly around the perimeter of the ship, protruded from each 'leaf' of the starship's body. They could still be used, though their supply of missiles had been depleted . . . two million years ago. They could fire objects on a sliding scale of speeds, where the old prador guns had two speeds: fast for inert slug, slow for self-drive anti-matter or fission missiles whose internals fast acceleration might wreck. Muzzle fields could also set them spinning or tumbling, just like bullets from some hand weapons, though Sfolk could not see the purpose of that in ship-to-ship conflict. Some of the missiles, in fact, just one of those remaining, contained a very odd design of Mach-effect engine which it took him a little while to understand. When he did, he clattered his mandibles in amusement. The gabbleducks could shoot round corners.

Now swinging the starship round and back towards the Junkyard, Sfolk called up targeting graphics, but then had to stop all of them loading to his mind because inset tactical displays were coming on he was failing to grasp. But again, maybe he would understand them later. For old times' sake, though he hadn't actually taken part in the prador human war, he selected a defunct Polity attack ship, an old-style vessel like a length of sawn-off rectangular bar-stock with two protruding U-space nacelles, both of which had been stripped out by extremadapt salvagers. Part of the hull was missing near the nose, the interior hollowed out, where they had stripped out the weapons system too.

Sfolk focused close on it and, the moment he did, objects inside the hull were outlined and projected outwards. Target assessments were made, the remaining internal system was plotted out and a conclusion drawn: invalid target. He checked through his system looking for something he was sure would be there and, sure enough, he found it: override. One of the coil guns immediately went live, loaded a missile and fired. The thing that exited the gun was two yards long and surprisingly thin. The muzzle fields set it tumbling on its course, without orders from Sfolk – automatics taking care of that. A microsecond later it struck the old derelict and punched through it in a flash of light. The impact was so hard that metal turned instantly to sun-hot vapour causing an explosion akin to that of a tactical nuke. Sfolk had time to register that it had struck at the point where such ships usually contained their AI before the ship separated on the blast, completely sliced in half.

The two halves tumbled away from each other, glowing at their severed ends. Old Polity attack ship it might have been but it still possessed seriously tough armour. Had it degraded over time, or had the salvagers stripped away inner s-con and impact-absorbing layers? A missile hit like that should not have cut the thing in half. Certainly the impact would have been severe but such missiles usually turned to plasma at that point. Focusing beyond the wreckage Sfolk finally found the missile – a blurred wheel continuing on into deep space. It should not have survived but that it had now explained the strange muzzle-field effects that could be imparted. Sfolk next tried to find out more about the missiles themselves and as the system struggled to offer up translations he finally realized the things were fashioned of a form of matter that was just untranslatable, which probably meant it hadn't been either discovered or thought of by the prador.

What next?

'Recharging.'

'What?' Sfolk clattered.

That seemed like a communication from Penny Royal, yet he felt sure the AI had left the ship. He found himself laying in a course to the nearby sun for, of course, recharging. On one level he felt he should feel resentment about being so commanded and being unable to disobey, but it seemed a stray querulous objection that faded even as he considered it. His awareness remained complete, but his motivations had changed. This was an order he was glad to obey – obedience to it was an integral part of his being.

The starship accelerated smoothly, passing between the two halves of the Polity attack ship then swinging round and centring on the red giant – the thing now filling most of the view, its light penetrating the basketwork structure of the ship. As he headed towards this, Sfolk began to grasp the purpose of that remaining mathematical display struggling to interpret itself, now settling on the quite odd combination of energy and a series of universal constants, which kept flickering, as if they were not constant. Stripping away layers he did not understand, Sfolk finally revealed a simple input, output and store display. Output exceeded input by a large margin and the store seemed to be approaching some red line. The moment it hit that, the drive shut down. However, checking navigation, he found that 'position' had been released and that his initial acceleration was taking him towards the sun. A moment later he understood the implication of that 'position'. The drive system he was currently using could ramp up at high speed but, apparently, it could also stop him dead when switched off. The system had chosen the option not to do so, because the ship needed power.

Over the ensuing hours Sfolk concentrated on learning more of the system, steadily finding that things he had not understood when first taking this position were now becoming clear to him. He even began to make some inroads into that connection between the U-space drive and the weapons system, and started to discover a cornucopia of weapons, and methods of attack. He also began finding numerous methods of defence, many to protect this ship from things he was sure existed neither in Kingdom or Polity arsenals. He now also had more time to think about what this all meant.

The Atheter had been penetrated by the civilization-killing Jain technology. This had led to centuries of civil war and finally to their insane choice to reduce themselves to animals. It was a solution of sorts, for, no longer having a civilization, there was nothing for the Jain tech to key into and subsequently destroy, but it wasn't one the prador would have chosen, nor the humans, as far as Sfolk understood them.

So, centuries of war and the kind of technical development that was driven by war. It struck Sfolk that they had weaponized just about every aspect of their technology. Like the Polity, they had started a line of development into U-tech and now Sfolk was seeing the results of that. The prador in him was highly excited but something else in him was growing steadily stronger.

The prador would give the Kingdom to one who brought this ship to them, he thought.

A moment later, he realized he had been thinking of the prador as something separate from him, as though he was on the outside, a spectator.

Energy input from the sun ahead remained steady while the store nudged that red line then slid past it. Again the drive fired up – the ship centred on the vast orange-red sphere lying ahead. Sfolk tried to take control, sure that an offset course would be better, but the controls didn't respond. After a moment he got a message whose rough translation was: energy situation critical, automatic charging – emergency override only. Sfolk relaxed in the embrace of the superior technology of the Atheter. He watched the store bar extend beyond the red line then close in on its end. The input bar had also increased while the output remained steady. Was that enough? No, because once the store bar reached its end the display changed to show three more bars that were all but empty. It took him a moment to interpret the surrounding translations and, when he did, awe tightened his guts. The bars were the same as before but the scale had increased by an order of magnitude, and the energy levels for input, output and store were mere red slivers at one end. Running some rough calculations, he realized that this vessel could handle levels of energy a hundred times those in a prador dreadnought . . . and that was supposing the scale did not go up another order of magnitude later.

The sun grew brighter and bigger. Without magnification it now filled the view ahead. Checking the distance, Sfolk saw that the starship had reached a point where a prador vessel would have needed to start shedding heat, but the system for doing that in this vessel was still offline. He felt a little worried about this and looked throughout the system for temperature anomalies. There was none. The heat was being converted straight into 'stored energy'. He next began checking the nature of that storage but found himself looking at U-space math that set his ganglion aching again. However, he understood enough to realize that the 'store' seemed to be some kind of blister in the U-continuum; some kind of potential difference between realities: a *twist* that was steadily winding tighter.

To the right now Sfolk watched a mass ejection, cutting up through the helium fusion of the outer layers of the sun. It was the kind of thing that would have fried a prador dreadnought, yet here he was sliding past it in a ship made out of basketwork. He clattered prador laughter, a slightly hysterical bubbling underlining it. Soon the shape of the giant sun was no longer visible because the ship was in the edge of the fire. Input had increased to a third of the way along the new bar. The store was up to a quarter. Sfolk really felt it was time for the ship to slow down and, thankfully, that is exactly what it began to do.

Still no heat anomalies . . .

Cam input was filtered to down below one per cent, but still what he was seeing seemed painfully bright. Outside, sylphs of fire raged and twisted, glutinous as something organic. Spirals twisted into existence then disappeared in a flash to leave oily smokes of darker matter. He checked readings, then rechecked them. There was no doubt now: he was sitting in the middle of a helium fusion fire. He should be a cinder, and a short-lived one too. What would the prador think of this? What would the humans or their AIs think?

Sfolk was sitting inside a two-million-year-old Atheter starship, bathing in the surface of a sun.

Blite

As the shuttle lifted and disappeared into cloud, Blite dropped the visor then the concertinaed helmet of his space suit and breathed an easy breath. They were safe. The Brockle was gone. He glanced across at Greer but her visor was still closed and she was still doubtless using its light-enhancing and magnifying facility while she gazed down at the castle. Then, after another moment, she lowered her visor.

'That's it, then,' she said.

'Yes, that's it,' he agreed, but then something errant and out of his control inside him added, 'Maybe.'

'Did really well, didn't we?'

'We're wealthy,' said Blite.

'We have no ship. Brond is dead and we've lost Ikbal and Martina.'

Blite nodded. During its frequent interrogations of them, the Brockle had revealed that it knew more about Ikbal and Martina than it could possibly have learned second-hand. Then, when the time was right during those interrogations, it revealed how it had killed them . . . and yet not killed them. It had destructively recorded them.

'They're finished,' she added. 'That thing goes up against Penny Royal and there won't be anything left.'

To her mind, Brond was gone, irretrievable, but the Brockle had recorded Ikbal and Martina, and if it were to release their recordings, their resurrection was possible. She obviously wasn't thinking clearly and had forgotten what the wealth he had mentioned was based on.

He turned to look back into the cave behind them. Something caught his attention, but he couldn't process it yet.

They had chosen the cave as a refuge, as a place to hide, but Blite was realistic enough to know that if the Brockle hadn't wanted to let them go, they would not have escaped. He looked up at the cave roof, at its walls and then down at the floor. The packed earth below and the red Mandelbrot lichens on the walls went some way to conceal it, but he could make out the odd striations on the wall and he could see that the cave was perfectly circular. Something about it niggled at his memory.

'So what the fuck do we do now?' Greer asked.

'I'm thinking,' said Blite and walked over to the wall, pulling off his gauntlet. He ran a finger over the stone. It was glassy and he guessed that if he tried to scratch it with something he'd make no mark at all. It was heat-compressed and toughened stone and now he remembered where he had seen it before. He had studied images like this – what spacefaring adventurer in the

Graveyard hadn't? This looked like the kind of tunnel bored through Penny Royal's planetoid.

'Still thinking?' Greer asked.

Blite nodded, walked deeper into the cave and stooped to pick up one of the items lying on the floor. It was the discarded tooth of a rock-boring machine, but not the kind that had made *this* cave. He raised his visor and increased light amplification. The back of the cave was a flat wall, filled in with foamed stone. A borer had been used to cut through that and a yard-wide hole stretched back and back into blackness.

'What is it?' Greer asked.

'I don't fucking know,' he snapped.

But was starting to get some idea. Mr Pace had been changed by Penny Royal. This cave looked like those produced by Penny Royal and then filled in. It struck him that the rock-borer that had been used here might well have been Mr Pace's and that he had been trying to find something. What, Blite had no idea. He turned away from the rear of the cave and walked back out to the entrance.

'Maybe we can find some transport there.' He pointed towards the castle. 'Then we get to the nearest space port.'

'Then where?'

'You can go wherever you like,' Blite replied, stepping out.

'What about you?' Greer asked, following.

'Those memplants we delivered and were rewarded for were recordings of Penny Royal's victims,' he said. 'Did the AI destructively record them when it killed them, like the Brockle did with Ikbal and Martina? I don't think so.' He turned towards her. 'Do you remember what was said when we handed them over?'

Greer frowned, shook her head.

'Almost twice the total of known deaths, including ones

beyond those directly attributable to the AI, many killed as secondary results of its actions. That means people killed when the AI wasn't even there.'

'So . . .' Greer looked confused, then a light ignited in her brain. 'You think it was recording some people all the time?'

'I think it's worth checking.'

'Penny Royal has recordings of Ikbal, Martina and Brond?'

Blite shrugged, concentrated on his footing down the slope.

'So what are you going to do?' Greer asked.

'We were forced to transport Penny Royal at the beginning. Then we stayed with the AI out of curiosity. Now I feel chewed up and spat out. But I have to get back into the game because I feel responsible for my crew.'

'You're going after the AI again?'

'I'll buy a ship, track it down – see if I can retrieve our friends. What you do is up to you.'

He expected her to say, quite forcefully, that she was going her own way or that she would accompany him, but she was silent. He glanced at her, saw she was thinking.

As they trudged back along the valley the sun broke over the mountains. Its light was a strange organic pink, while the cloud immediately around it looked like diced liver. Rain was spitting down, forming into droplets on their suits like a spray of blood, then quickly dropping away from the frictionless material. The ground underfoot was boggy and thick with sphagnum moss and purple clover and oozed yellow water at each step. Scattered here and there were plants Blite recognized as no Earth import: flat rhubarb-like leaves of dull white veined with vermilion, supported on thick almost muscular stems, and slowly propelled along the ground by rhizomes like creeping hands.

By the time they reached the plasticrete road to the castle, the gap in the cloud had closed again, all above a rumbled ceiling the colour of baked clay bricks. As they drew closer, Blite eyed the pile of rubble in the main entrance, crawling with robots, and turned to the left, heading towards that castellated tower – the one with a door that the Brockle had kicked in.

'I'll go with you,' said Greer just as they rounded a corner to come back in sight of that door, adding, 'What the fuck?'

Something was happening at the base of the tower. Over to one side it seemed the ground had burst open to let something out. This massive form was now hunched over where Mr Pace had fallen to the stone. Blite recognized it. The dull grey object was five feet wide at its thickest point and looked like a giant dust mite. It was in fact the kind of drone seen during the war whose speciality was usually informational warfare. It was the kind of thing that didn't actually go in at the front line but remained behind it, fucking up the enemy's coms. However, this one had been altered at its front end. Above the splayed insect legs with which it clung to the stone, its long head, which usually sported a hundred different ways of tapping into computer systems and even organic minds, had been replaced with something else. This object protruded like the guts of a piano. Its intricate component parts were constantly in motion, while the robot was steadily swinging it back and forth over the ground as if combing for something. Blite began to walk towards it.

'Are you sure this is a good idea?' asked Greer.

Blite hesitated momentarily. Certainly these drones were the kind that remained behind the lines, but they had never been without their defences. That thing squatting ahead could probably kill him without even pausing in whatever it was doing. Nevertheless, Blite kept walking. As he drew closer, he soon heard the hissing and chittering of matter printers and saw that there was some object being fashioned below that slowly traversing head. Closer still and he made out a black human spine and partially formed skull supported off the ground by threads of glass. Scanning round, he could see none of Mr Pace's remains. Perhaps the thing had gobbled them up for reprocessing – that perhaps being easier than using new materials. Mentally reviewing what he knew about Pace, he realized this must be the solution to the question mark about him. He had supposedly been indestructible, but nothing is indestructible. Something rebuilt him every time he was destroyed, and here it was.

Next he walked over to where the big drone had burst from the ground, and saw a round tunnel, just like the one they had been hiding in, spearing down into the depths. The tunnel did not look freshly bored so perhaps there were many of them riddling these mountains and leading to this creature's abode. Perhaps it only filled them in when they had been discovered – like the one where he and Greer had hidden themselves.

'Come on,' he said, gesturing to the wrecked door.

Greer nodded and moved towards it ahead of him, saying, 'Maybe we should get a move on. I don't want to be around when he . . . wakes.'

She had obviously understood too.

Rather than climb the spiral stair, they traversed a corridor running round the base of the tower, then kept going through doors and along passageways. They soon found themselves lost inside the building, checking rooms, glancing out of windows to try and locate themselves, searching for some form of transport. Blite tried an antique-looking console but, though it came on, he could not access it.

'We should have just walked away,' said Greer.

'In what direction?' Blite snapped, though he was rapidly coming to the same conclusion.

The castle was spartan inside, but what home comforts did a man seemingly made of obsidian need? They found what looked like guest rooms, but old and dusty and scuttling with grey cap-top beetles and yellow spiders. It was almost with a feeling of inevitability they paused to gaze upon a human skeleton lying on the floor of one room, a pulse-gun lying a few inches away from an outstretched hand. Blite picked the weapon up, checked the charge and found it full, gratefully shoved it in his belt but knew it would be no use against a resurrected Mr Pace. Then, while they were trying to get a higher view of their position, just so they could find a way out again, they walked out onto a roof port and a shuttle, its hold door open down as a ramp, crates stacked inside, a couple of auto-handler drays parked nearby.

Blite eyed the vessel with interest, but then grimaced. Its security would probably be impossible to penetrate and, even if not, where would they go with it? They might get off-world and even enter the spaceship it belonged to, but then their chances of taking control of that would be even more remote. He scanned around and, over on the far side of this roof port, saw a gap in some railings and what looked like the edge of a stair leading down. That was over towards the edge of the castle so at least it looked as if they had found their way out. Before he even started towards this, Greer was ahead of him – having herself assessed their chances of taking the shuttle.

He followed quickly, catching up with her as she paused at the top of the stair. Glancing down, he saw that this was indeed a way out. Unfortunately a figure was climbing the stair – the figure of a naked man seemingly fashioned out of black glass.

14

Sverl

'And now that is the only way out,' said Amistad, gesturing with one claw.

Sverl stared at the drone, then where it had gestured towards the centre of the vast sphere they occupied. He could see nothing but the jungle of bracing struts but he knew Amistad was referring to the remaining workable runcible the Atheter device had fixed in place there.

One hour . . .

The big tug out there was working diligently, accelerating them towards the hypergiant. Though they were completely enclosed by the Atheter sphere and he couldn't directly see that vessel now, its steady pull would, in one hour, take them past the point where hardfield drag in U-space could resist the gravity of the sun. Thereafter, if the tug continued, they would end up in fusion flame within ten hours. What then? Running calculations, Sverl wondered if there was a level of energy the hardfield could not divert into U-space. It would seem so, else why were the Polity and Kingdom forces out there conducting this operation? Or was it that they thought dumping the entirely modified Room 101 into the sun was the best they could do to counter the threat it posed? Getting out of a hypergiant's gravity well would be no easy task, especially as they were now lacking engines.

Or was it the case that, despite the resistance of the hardfield, they would still end up boiling inside here? EMR was getting through the hardfield out there and the sphere was not completely opaque to it. It was now much brighter in here and the temperature had already risen a few degrees – the intense sunlight penetrating through the microscopic holes in the surrounding structure. No, even as he considered this, Sverl studied the system controlling the hardfield and saw that there was a way to alter its opacity, and that the Weaver, who now controlled it, could make it completely block the EMR. However, his latest inspection of the system resulted in him understanding other aspects of its function too: the twist it fed in U-space was the key and, if that key was turned too far, they were doomed.

'So should we leave?' Amistad asked.

'Should have left a while ago,' grumbled Bsorol from where he was clinging to one of the nearby struts.

'You don't *mean* that,' said Bsectil, from lower down the same strut.

'Maybe, maybe not,' Bsorol replied cryptically.

'What do tricones taste of?' interjected one of the scattering of second-children, obviously wanting to join in but not quite understanding how to.

Sverl scuttled round and looked directly at them, clattering his mandibles together in irritation, then further annoyed because he hadn't thought to transmit the sound, non-existent in vacuum, of that. When no further comments were forthcoming he inspected his other surroundings. He and Amistad were standing on the hull of the hauler – abandoned by his children, who apparently wanted a better view of proceedings. The hauler rested against the woven matter of the inner surface of the now-completed sphere. There were no holes in that surface large enough to admit anything bigger than a molecule.

'Strange relationship you have with your children,' commented Amistad, 'for a prador.'

NEAL ASHER

'But an interesting one,' suggested Sverl.

'Uhuh . . . so, *do* you think we should leave?'

'We don't have to decide yet,' Sverl replied vaguely.

He would wait until the very last moment – the point when they reached imminent destruction – and then he and his children would go through the runcible. What kind of reception they might receive on the other end might prove interesting. However, there was the gabbleduck to consider.

Sverl gazed through some of the remote probes he had dispatched throughout the interior of the sphere. The Weaver was now using up the device that had built this sphere. Still hanging Buddha-like in vacuum, the creature was watching the whirling sphere – now just a couple of yards across. The thing had eaten the last of the original station some hours before and had then steadily shed matter as it finally wove the two hemispheres together into one complete sphere. Recently it had built a stalk extending from an inner surface and was now moving in a steadily widening spiral as it built a platform on that, while itself steadily shrinking.

So, what did the Weaver intend?

He must surely be aware of their situation, but seemed to be paying it little attention. Would he decide, over the next ten hours, to abandon this place? If the Weaver did leave, Sverl decided that he would follow.

As the last hour slunk away, the device completed the platform and had by then reduced itself to a translucent object just a foot across. The Weaver held out one claw and, after its last pass, the thing rose and headed towards the Atheter, steadily shrinking as it did so. Scan readings showed that its mass was now negligible. At the last moment, as it finally reached the Weaver's claw, it collapsed into something the size of a marble. The Weaver pinched it between two talons then inserted it into a small container hanging from his tool harness. That was it then: a thing that could tear apart and remould a giant space station now reduced to an object smaller than a human eyeball.

'You were watching?' Sverl asked.

'Of course,' Amistad replied, 'and probably thinking the same thing as you: a creature capable of creating and manipulating technologies like that might not be too worried about anything Polity and Kingdom ships could do.'

Sverl hadn't been thinking that, but he was now. In reality the Polity AIs had been quite correct to try and limit and contain the Weaver. The creature was, after all, the product of a highly advanced civilisation that had been fighting internecine wars, involving Jain technology, for millennia.

The Weaver drifted forwards and settled down on the platform. He made a few seemingly negligent gestures with his claws and in response globular shapes oozed from the substance of the platform and began to sprout and rise like fungi – stretching up into stalks topped by wide flat plates. Waving one claw again caused one of these stalks to bow towards him, presenting a flat plate. The Weaver inserted a claw into that plate and manipulated something. All around, the massive structure heaved and tightened and filled with electrical discharges like St Elmo's fire. The Weaver watched all this for a long moment, then swung his head round to gaze directly at the probe through which Sverl was watching. Then he gave a gabbleduck grin and suddenly Sverl found his access to exterior probes no longer blocked.

Over the last few hours there had been some changes outside. Ships were now on the move around the sphere. Sverl was at first puzzled by this until he saw some of them shedding heat with thermal lasers and plasma or gas ejections. They were circling now to take turns in the shadow of the sphere to shed this heat. Meanwhile, the vastness of the hypergiant was more evident

359

than ever – filling the view in one direction – while the stars were no longer visible and all seemed bathed in liquid light.

'The opacity of the field is dropping,' Amistad observed.

It was already brighter inside the sphere and Sverl's probes outside began filtering EMR to prevent their internals being fried. They would, he calculated, last just an hour more at this level because, unlike the ships out there, they were unable to dump heat. He then recalculated, because the hardfield's opacity was still declining, and now basing his calculations on that rate, realized his probes had minutes only. Meanwhile, internally, he was picking up on massive surges and transferences of energy.

Soon, exterior probes began blinking out, yet, even as they did so a new channel was offered up in their place. Sverl was wary of accepting because, as ever, the kind of bandwidth for video offered plenty of space for a nasty informational weapon. But this channel could only have been opened by the Weaver and, just as with Amistad, that creature would not need to use computer attack if it wanted to be rid of Sverl. He opened it and found vast options for exterior sensing available to him. This was like keying into a massive pin-cam system, spread out over the entire outer surface of the sphere. As he explored this he noted further changes. The Kingdom and Polity ships were withdrawing. It seemed they were now struggling with the temperature and decided they had escorted the prador tug far enough. Sverl watched them intently, trying different views all the way around the sphere.

Now, he thought, *do it now*.

But nothing was happening.

'They're withdrawing,' he said to Amistad. 'That tug needs to be dealt with.'

'Then tell the Weaver,' Amistad replied.

Sverl searched for a way to contact that distant gabbleduck, then decided just to use the link he had to the exterior cams.

'Surely time to reposition the hardfield and deal with that tug?' he suggested.

Strange glyphs of some form of text appeared in his visual field, an odd smell impinged on his consciousness and he understood in a moment: pheromone communication. Next came something completely nonsensical, followed by a single view of just to the side of where the tug's claw arms rested against the hardfield. Areas all across the claws glowed and Sverl understood this was the Weaver's way of highlighting something. He focused in on one of them, and there saw a slight bulge in the metal.

'What is that?' he asked.

Strange noises and smells ensued, then words: 'Total yield: four gigatons . . . or thereabouts.'

Sverl no longer possessed an organic body but he felt the phantom sensation of his guts knotting up and the urge to pull in his limbs under his non-existent carapace to protect them. It was such a simple trap. If they had shut down the field and extended it to chop through the tug it would have resulted in its front end being inside the field. And it was at the front it had concealed a large collection of CTDs, which would have then detonated.

'Phew,' said Bsorol. 'That could have been nasty.'

Hearing Bsorol's voice, Sverl ran checks and saw that his children had linked into the sphere's system – its computing – shortly after him. He had not given them permission to do so, but now they had moved beyond the father-captain and pheromone-enslaved children relationship. He would have to accept it.

They carried on towards the sun. Sverl registered the EMR levels continuing to rise, while some areas of the metallic interior were beginning to emit in the low infrared. After a further four hours, Sverl's children went back inside the hauler, either to cool off their armour or out of boredom. Sverl and Amistad, being creatures of metals, meta-materials and pure mind, could last longer. Surprisingly, whatever form of cam hardware the sphere used continued to survive even while it gave a view of the tug as its engines went out then pieces began to drop away from it. The thing did not possess exotic metal armour like a prador warship so could not survive for much longer. Sverl watched the thing begin to sag, twisted by tidal forces in the hypergiant below. It parted company with the hardfield, and shortly afterwards some of its materials began to burn, leaving coloured streaks in the furnace. Then, with an almost physical thump, the EMR began to drop and he registered a weird and dispersed U-space signature. Light levels quickly fell as the hardfield grew opaque, and it was now feeding energy back into that underlying U-space twist. Sverl understood: the Weaver was charging up the sphere – filling the underlying U-space reservoir to its limit. However, this could not go on for much longer, for they were now bathed in a glut of fusion fire.

'I would say,' said Amistad, 'in the next two or three minutes.'

'What?'

The tug was now an unrecognizable burning mass. Then, just a minute later, an external flash briefly overloaded even this magical Atheter technology. Of course, the CTD canisters had given way. Sverl felt a surge that sent even him staggering as the sphere rode on a wave of fire across the face of the vast sun. Then came the wrench, and Sverl briefly registered a hundred gravities of acceleration before surrounding vacuum filled with an amber field effect, imposing an immobility that reached to the core of his being. The sphere was now rising out of the fire, a mass ejection from the sun reaching up beside it as if, like a titanic fire elemental, it wanted to drag it back down. And next the U-space twist relaxed just a little, flinging out a surge of energy. This energy was directed at a U-space drive that Sverl could not pinpoint – his scanners registered it all around him. The sphere folded into that continuum, the sun inverting impossibly and falling away.

And they were *travelling*.

The Brockle

Back aboard the *High Castle*, the Brockle fought to subdue info-tive madness as it examined the extra data it had extracted from Mr Pace. Surely it should now head off after Thorvald Spear to the last known location of Penny Royal? No, because already the data from Pace was etching out a larger scenario. Despite his madness, his ennui and his attraction to his own death, the man had still managed to function, powered by his hatred of Penny Royal. He had split himself mentally to survive, much as the black AI itself had and, via the sprawl of his Graveyard criminal operation, succeeded in gleaning every available scrap of information about the AI.

The spine . . .

Yes, that object was apparently a weakness Penny Royal had deliberately introduced, a way the AI could be killed. This was what Mr Pace had been after – still was, in fact, because it now seemed his destruction had not actually resulted in his death. But didn't he understand the consent utterly integral to both the creation of that object and its use? A larger game was afoot.

The Brockle needed data, and it needed greater capacity, so it instructed the autofactory to begin producing more units, then probed towards Mr Pace's ship here in orbit over his home world. The data it had extracted from him had revealed much about his information network, which extended into both the Polity and the Kingdom. Within his ship he had U-space transceivers and a complex computer system for sorting the masses of information he received there, all overseen by a distinctly odd ship mind. Tentatively probing the thing, the Brockle discovered it to be a prador mind but not of the usual sort. It was alive, after a fashion, in a state somewhere between hypersleep and consciousness. It was, the Brockle divined, the mind of a prador female. Its thought processes did not include anything beyond the language of mathematics, though there was a conventional language centre there, sitting offline for some reason. Pace delivered his instructions to it via a simple holographic touch display. It was, of course, completely vulnerable, and the Brockle was about to take control of it before he was interrupted.

'Hey ho,' said a voice. 'I see you got there.'

It was an uplink from the planet below. The Brockle peered through sensors and saw Mr Pace climbing steps up the side of his castle.

Already?

The Brockle focused more sensors but, beyond discovering a recently used tunnel, could find no trace of whatever had rebuilt or built anew this Mr Pace. Further probing revealed a network of tunnels spread out through the planet's crust. It ceased scanning these after it had detected four thousand miles of them.

'Got where?' the Brockle replied, stamping on a surge of rage and meanwhile beginning to integrate a new physical unit issuing from the autofactory.

'Ultimately you will learn where Penny Royal will be, but by then it may be too late.'

'You are not sane,' the Brockle observed.

'And you are?' Pace shot back. 'Perhaps you should check the main Wasteland feed.'

Now ignoring the female prador mind, the Brockle instantly located that feed in the system of Mr Pace's ship. It hesitated to cut into the data flow, suspecting some kind of trap, for Mr Pace had already proven more capable than it had supposed. But then it cut in anyway. The feed was from an old prador satellite that had been set, over fifty years ago, to watch Room 101 factory station. The first telemetry was a shock and left the Brockle momentarily baffled. It then dug in and began parallel processing every thread of the feed, previously recorded data, absorbing everything there whole into its mind. And it was dumbfounded.

Since the Brockle's last view of Room 101, the station had been turned into a massive sphere. Apparently the Weaver and Amistad were aboard, and apparently the sphere was Atheter technology. A brief alliance had been forged between the Polity and the prador to deal with the potential threat this sphere represented. A massive tug had been brought in to dump the thing into the nearby hypergiant sun. This effort had failed when the sphere, without any evident U-space drive, submerged itself in underspace just as it was falling into the star.

'Pretty, isn't it?' said Mr Pace. 'You see, that's where Penny Royal is going and of course we know where *that* object is going.'

'Some clarity would be good.' The Brockle meanwhile gazed at the Polity fleet, complemented by twenty King's Guard ships, scattered around the hypergiant. What were they doing? Procrastinating?

'Consider the data being collected at the Well Head,' said Mr Pace, as he stepped out onto the roof of his castle.

The Brockle located this data in Mr Pace's systems and, just microseconds later, everything slammed together in a coherent whole. It knew the purpose of that giant sphere with its ridiculously powerful hardfield. It knew what Penny Royal intended and recognized the temporal debt the black AI intended to pay back. It also knew why those Polity and prador vessels weren't on the move. Doubtless the U-space signature had been easy to read and, having divined the destination of the sphere, the AIs had, just like the Brockle, worked out the rest. They had decided to stand down and let Penny Royal finish what it was doing because of the dangers inherent in that temporal debt *not* being paid.

'I cannot allow this,' it said.

Mr Pace had other immediate concerns down on the planet, specifically Blite and Greer. But the man was no longer important, nor was where he was going. The Polity fleet and, if possible, the prador, must continue with their mission and destroy that sphere. Yes, the temporal problem might tear open a massive rift in space-time. But surely that was preferable to allowing the black AI to open the door for itself to super-dense infinite processing, and eternity?

With a thought, the Brockle threw the *High Castle* into U-space, its destination chosen. No, it would not be pursuing Thorvald Spear as Mr Pace doubtless intended to do. Spear was a sideshow, a subplot, because the real event was here. Mr Pace had understood a lot, but nowhere near enough. He thought it would be possible to get to Penny Royal before that AI effectively made itself invulnerable. What he had missed and what the Brockle now understood was that the aspects of Penny Royal people now saw were no more the whole AI than one of the Brockle's own units was all of itself. What Mr Pace had also missed was that Penny Royal's greatest moment of vulnerability was when it gathered all of itself together inside that sphere and prior to the time when it dropped that sphere into the Layden's Sink black hole.

Spear

We exited U-space with a thump and a shudder and, as I opened my eyes, it felt as if the *Lance* was revolving axially. Since nothing was being thrown about in the cabin, I knew the sensation was due to my primitive brain interpreting something it hadn't been evolved to deal with. I think it just slotted it into the memory bank labelled 'too much to drink'. Turning my head, I gazed at the tangle of long gold-blonde hair, the long ears, long neck and distinctly female back beside me. It seemed Sepia had been unaffected by our exit into the real, because she was still snoring gently. I swung my legs over the side of the bed, stood and walked to the room's shower cabinet; only when I was in there did I start asking questions.

'*That didn't feel right,*' I auged.

'*You were given coordinates,*' Flute replied, '*but no detail.*' A system map arrived in my aug and I studied it closely as I washed myself: red giant sun, scattering of planetoids, what looked like technological debris smeared part of the way round the sun on its way to forming a ring, and then the orbital part- ner, which was strange. The singularities spinning about each other, and spinning individually, were too evenly matched. Their spin and mass were the same – far too close to be anything but artificial. We'd arrived at an artefact probably created by one of the old dead races. I shivered despite the warm water.

'We've arrived?' asked Sepia.

I again felt the tightness and organic thrill of seeing her naked and wanted to just get back into bed with her. But there were things to do, matters to investigate and, anyway, we'd been making pigs of ourselves for some time now. Precisely this kind of distraction was why I'd set my internal nanosuites to suppress my libido. Intellectually I knew that for best efficiency I should do so again. However, on a visceral level I just didn't want to. As I dried myself, I shot her the data Flute had sent me, then tried to ignore her nakedness as she flopped back on the bed, one arm above her head, legs open and one knee up, her other hand down stroking her inner thigh.

After drying, I grabbed up clothing and pulled it on, auging through to get a better view of that debris field. Ships, many ships from throughout the ages of space travel – both human and prador. What was this place? I replayed the scene Amistad had allowed me to view but was none the wiser. Had there been some battle here? No, because if that had been so the ships would have all been from one age.

'What the hell is this?' I asked out loud.

'It's a maelstrom,' Flute informed me via the intercom. 'Or a tide pool.'

'What's that?'

'That strange U-space effect we had when we surfaced is part of it,' the second-child mind explained. 'The spinning singularities have an effect similar to a U-space mine or missile: they drag things out of U-space.'

'I don't think your analogies are very good, prador-child,' interrupted Riss via the same intercom.

'Well what would you use, smart-arse?'

'The underlying area of U-space is like the sides of a pitcher plant,' said Riss. 'Anything drifting into the vicinity slides down and arrives at the Lagrange here.'

'Well, as analogies go, that wasn't much better,' said Flute, then to me, 'You know those debris fields of plastic that they had building up in the oceans of Earth? Well it's a bit like that.'

'How about,' I suggested, 'you just tell me what happens here.'

'Okay,' said Flute. 'The effect created by those singularities, in conjunction with the sun, draws debris here in U-space and ejects it into the real here. Since most "real" debris in U-space are ships with screwed drives or parts of the same, that's what we've got.'

'So in a way like some of the mechanisms used to clear up the orbital mess around Earth before the First Diaspora,' I said.

Neither Riss nor Flute replied to that as they doubtless absorbed the implications of the word 'mechanisms'. I continued, 'So who did Penny Royal "slaughter" here?'

'There have been rumours,' said Riss.

'Rumours?'

It was Sepia who replied by sending me a data package. I opened it at once. It seemed to be a collection of rumour and hearsay, but it did all pertain to a system that looked like this and had a debris field like this too. Details were vague but I got the gist: a colony of human salvagers who stuck the survivors they found into an arena to fight to the death for their entertainment. It was the kind of piratical stuff often dismissed as just stories . . . but then the pirate Jay Hoop and his renegades had seemed just as unlikely, and had been all too real.

'There is another debris field,' Flute added, now giving me another view.

By now I was dressed while Sepia had moved to sitting on the side of the bed and looking disappointed. Finally she stood up and walked to the shower with an exaggerated sway to her hips. I sighed. What was it about sex that seemingly regressed people to just a few decades old? Perhaps I had made a mistake getting this involved? No, I dismissed the idea. Taking our relationship on to pleasant recreation didn't presuppose all the problems of adolescent human mating. I was over a century old, in real terms, and she was much older. She was only playing a part to relieve her boredom. I concentrated on the view Flute had sent me rather than on Sepia soaping herself in the shower.

The new debris field was sparse and expanding, but plotting the tracks of each of the pieces back soon demonstrated that they all came from a centre point that had come apart a few months ago. Speed and direction of travel showed that whatever had come apart had not done so explosively. This looked more like the debris pattern created by a spinning object with extra impetus given in some cases by explosive decompression –

'Organo-matrix space station hit by some kind of nano-deconstructor weapon.' Of course, Riss's martial mind had got there before me. 'The inhabitants were extremadapts,' she added.

'How do you know?'

'Flute,' said Riss.

Obviously some coordinates had been relayed because now I got images focused in on one point in space. I gazed upon a drifting spaceship – a system-class hauler – then, through a cockpit screen, at the merman who controlled it. He was sprawled and bloody – looking as if he'd been hit by explosive shells.

'So,' said Sepia, stepping out of the shower and drying herself. 'An extremadapt colony of salvagers with some nasty habits destroyed by Penny Royal. What's that all about? And does it get you any closer to finding the AI?'

'You're scanning, Flute?' I asked.

'Something on one of the planetoids,' Flute replied. 'Anomalous – strange readings.'

Well, if I was looking for Penny Royal, then those were exactly the kind of readings I expected to find. 'Take us there.'

'You're considering using your nascuff,' said Sepia as she now dressed.

Now that she mentioned it, I was. I peered down at the narrow bracelet about my wrist. The idea had been floating about in my consciousness from the moment our U-space transition woke me. Adjust my nanosuite and all the complications of sex would be gone. Sepia would just become a pleasant companion and I would no longer be subject to base-level drives and could concentrate on more important matters.

'I wish you wouldn't,' she continued. 'Limit your experience of life and the ennui hits earlier.' She looked up as she pulled on her knickers. 'In your case I guess it will hit shortly after you've concluded your business with Penny Royal . . . supposing you're still alive then.'

'I'm only just over a hundred years old, you know,' I observed.

She shrugged. 'A number of centuries back you'd have been grateful for the hard-on at that age.'

'So crude,' I said, grinning, and headed for the door.

As I entered the bridge the screen-fabric lining came on, the red giant sun centred and frames picking out the scenes I had just viewed through my aug. Riss was coiled on the horseshoe console as usual. I took my seat, eyed the vector digits changing along the base of the fabric then turned my attention to the frame showing the dead extremadapt. With a thought I expanded the frame to get a better look. The merman was only just in one piece and I noted big slices across parts of his body.

'So what do you reckon happened to him?' I asked.

Riss swung her head towards me, black eye open. 'That I've been trying to figure out.' She turned back towards the screen and gridlines appeared over the remains. She then lifted them out of the cockpit onto a second blank white frame. Some severed

371

pieces of tentacle then followed, orbited the corpse for a moment then shot back and attached, while all the other wounds closed up. Something then exploded inside the man's body, hurling out shrapnel to remake the wounds and sever off pieces of tentacle, blowing open the body so it was once again as I'd first seen it.

'Explosive shell, then,' I said.

'Yes, I thought so,' said Riss. 'But there are anomalies.'

The image contracted – the merman returned to a semblance of life. The wounds began appearing again, matching up with lines scribed out from a centre point in his body. Those lines thickened at their base point, sliced off tentacles, formed into an object like the head of a medieval morning star, then the whole thing shifted out of the body, tearing the final massive wounds that had opened the man's body. I stared at that thing, hovering just out from the corpse, not wanting to admit what I was seeing.

'Then,' said Riss.

The star folded itself up, then passed through a surface that had just appeared, leaving a vaguely octagonal hole. Riss banished the blank frame and brought an area of the hauler's screen into view. The hole was there, blocked from the inside with a mass of solid white foam from an emergency auto-patch. I stared at that for a long moment. The screen was almost certainly chain-glass, which meant it should either be whole, or dust. The only way a hole could be made through such glass was by the intricate manipulation of the chain molecules.

'Penny Royal,' I said.

'If so,' said Riss, 'then in a smaller form.'

'Or part of Penny Royal,' said Sepia, entering the bridge.

'And there was I thinking it had joined the side of light,' I commented.

Sepia sprawled in the acceleration chair she favoured. 'Well, if these extremadapts were playing nasty games with any crew they took from those ships, they probably deserved what they got.'

I nodded. Sure, if they had been murdering people here, then under Polity law they would be under death sentence, but I couldn't help feeling that the 'slaughter' Penny Royal had committed here was not due to any sense of justice in the AI. Perhaps it was trying to do good, but still enjoyed returning to old nasty habits; exotic murder fitting like an old worn glove.

'Okay, let's take a look at this planetoid.'

A new frame appeared on the screen, along with scrolling stats frames in a console display along the bottom. I ignored that, loading those stats straight from the system into my aug. It was a planetoid similar in size to Ganymede. But there the resemblance ended: it was ruggedly mountainous with needle peaks punching up like fairy towers through methane clouds. There were methane lakes down on the surface, a metallic gleam in many rocky surfaces. I checked its density and saw that it was high. The thing's consistency was more like that of a metallic asteroid than a little world like Ganymede. Remembering what Sepia had said about people of centuries ago I wondered how one such would react to this: a world heavily laden with metals that had once been precious: gold, platinum and iridium.

'And the anomaly you were talking about, Flute?' I said.

Another frame overlaid the planetoid and in that appeared a baffling shape like a twisted-up fragment of glowing silk. Data then arrived in my aug. This shape was the best visual illustration he could do, because the anomaly was a combination of U-space and exotic matter. It was on the other side of the planetoid, which wouldn't have mattered if the thing hadn't been formed of such dense metal.

'Maybe a probe?' suggested Sepia.

I grimaced.

'We can get there just as quickly with this ship,' she agreed, reading me on a level that seemed one stratum down from our open aug connection.

Over the next hour we pursued the planetoid and swung round it to get a view of the other side. When we finally got a good look at it on the screen fabric, I felt my stomach tighten and something cold crawl up my back. I was suddenly aware, via my connection to the spine, of the odd feeling of standing in some vast arena, and the presence of a crowd that had abruptly lapsed into expectant silence. Sitting in the middle of a crater, whose metallic edges cut up into the meagre air of that place like blades, was an object that seemed to be some strange plant, exotic yet familiar. Surrounded by a scattering of spherical devices, much like those independent hardfield generators Sverl had been making, was a tree of entwined silver tentacles topped by a lethal spiky mass as of a giant black sea urchin.

Penny Royal.

'I don't know why,' said Sepia, 'but I wasn't expecting that.'

The crowd in my mind sighed with a mixture of many conflicting emotions.

'Sit us geostat, Flute – I'm taking the shuttle down.'

'Easy target,' Riss mentioned, by the by.

'I think we've moved beyond that, don't you?'

'Just saying . . . '

'And a target that would end up wrapped in an impenetrable hardfield the moment we started slinging railgun slugs at it.'

'True enough.'

I focused on Sepia. 'You'll be safer here.'

'Always the comedian,' she replied.

I'd expected nothing else.

'Come on then.'

She watched me as I walked over to the wall, detached the spine from its clamps and shouldered it, then she turned to head for the shuttle bay ahead of me.

In the annex leading to the shuttle bay we shed our clothing, pulled on undersuits, then donned favoured space suits. We didn't talk much, but maintained a constant low-level *touch* through our aug connection. When I opened the door into the shuttle bay Riss went through ahead and soon all three of us were ensconced inside that vehicle. The bay quickly emptied of air as the shuttle turned towards the space doors, which then opened on the glare of the red giant out there. Almost as if this had instigated Flute taking a look, the ship mind said, 'There's something odd on the sun.'

'What?' Sepia and I both asked simultaneously.

Flute opened a connection to the array he was using, first showing the sun at a distance then focusing in close, then closer until we were lost in the surface of fire. A swirl appeared, accompanying U-space data scrolled down in a sidebar. Towards the centre of the swirl lay something dark. The colours changed as different filters were used and different EMRs were tried, stripping away layers to reveal a strange, even formation – a pattern that should not be able to exist down there in that furnace.

'What are we seeing here?' I asked, even as we slid out between the space doors.

'An energy sink,' Flute replied. 'The object appears to be soaking up thermal energy almost as if there is a hole there through to U-space.'

'A runcible gate?' I asked.

'No – it's not working like that.'

'Another question to ask Penny Royal, then,' interjected Sepia.

'Keep an eye on it,' I instructed as I turned us on steering thrusters and kicked in the fusion drive.

The planetoid swung into the main screen and, after a brief period of acceleration, I knocked off the drive. We drifted down, the meagre gravity taking hold of us and drawing us in. I considered swinging round the thing once, then decided against it, switching over to grav-engines, turning us again and tapping fusion for a second to bring our speed down. A few more adjustments with steering thrusters and I had us on a nice vector that would direct us low over Penny Royal's location. I could then bring us down in one of the few clear areas I could see – an area that glinted with a strange metallic iridescence. Brief analysis revealed it to be a basin almost entirely consisting of a grit of bismuth crystals. I wondered then if this entire planetoid was as unnatural as the two spinning singularities nearby. The heavy concentrations of certain elements seemed to indicate so.

'Have you handled this shuttle much?' Sepia enquired.

'Once before,' I replied casually.

'Yet you've used none of the automatics . . .'

I dipped my head in agreement. I'd never been a shuttle ace and had always used automatics whenever they had been available. However, the clamouring crowd in the spine contained many seat-of-the-pants pilots and it seemed the sum of their experience had filtered through. I hated the idea of using automatics – sacrifice the pleasure of flying something yourself? This had never been a concern of mine before.

As we dropped lower I could see that this was certainly a place where you wouldn't want to land carelessly. The mountains were like the jags and shards resulting from a major space station being blown open. Some of them stood like scythe or sword blades. Baroque sculptures of the kind found when streamers of molten metal solidify in vacuum abounded. Everything down there looked sharp. A perfect setting for Penny Royal.

When it was in sight, I focused on a close-up of Penny Royal. I felt the sharp intake of breath in a thousand non-existent throats, overpowering terror and in some cases a weird perverted eagerness. Struggling for a moment, I managed to damp my connection to the spine just enough so that I remained functional, but I couldn't completely cut it out now. Glancing across at Sepia, I saw that she looked a bit sick and felt the sluggish effect of feedback dampers at her end of our connection. She was taking precautions.

As we passed over the crater I spun the shuttle on steering thrusters and allowed it a couple of stabs of its main drive to bring us to halt relative to the surface below. I then used grav to bring us down, settling with an audible crunch which only made the silence in the craft louder.

'Right.' I stood up, picked up the spine, closed up my helmet and my visor.

Sepia stood as well and, even though our connection was sluggish, I could sense her reluctance. We headed for the airlock, and this time Riss trailed behind rather than shot ahead. Something about this situation didn't feel right, didn't feel complete. I went through first, clambering down the ladder onto ground scattered with iridescent metallic crystals. Riss shot out ahead of Sepia and rose high in the thin atmosphere to peer towards the crater while Sepia climbed down the ladder.

As Sepia and I reached the rim we carefully negotiated our way between the monolithic jags of metal, feeling like ants in a scrap shredder. Penny Royal came into sight just as we reached an incline of white chalky rock and drifts of dust – probably some sort of metallic oxide.

I paused to gaze at the AI, time shuddering to a halt around me. My internal crowd seemed to be cheering and jeering like spectators at a Roman arena, at a hated or beloved gladiator stepping out onto the sand. Penny Royal was in constant motion, somewhat like a sea urchin, the spines not only shuffling but moving in and out, shimmering from spikes to flat blades, breaking into collections of blades and reforming. I studied it for a long while, checked distances and scale in my aug. There was no doubt: the AI was nearly four times larger than it had been on the other occasions I had seen it.

There was something else here too, related to my own personal glimpses of U-space and the collective knowledge of it in my mind. I was seeing three-dimensional shapes in their transition through the fourth dimension that is time. They were all I could see as a linear-evolved organic creature of the real but I knew, with a terrible certainty, they were just one facet of something with many more dimensions, and with far greater complexity, than that. I was the Flatlander seeing just the two-dimensional slice of a cube. Penny Royal was here, but it was elsewhere too. I sensed for the first time how vast it was.

I moved closer and at that moment six white ovoids that were scattered around the AI, each a yard across, rose from the ground and sped out. A moment later, a hardfield surrounded us, separating us from the shuttle. We were trapped.

'*You have come,*' the AI's voice whispered in my mind, '*to learn how to kill.*'

Blite

Blite walked over to the bulkhead and slammed a fist against it. He was getting very tired now of being a prisoner – both of circumstances and hostile creatures, like Penny Royal, the Brockle and this Mr Pace. When they'd seen him rise up the stairs they had frozen, and he had captured them fast and easily – by knocking them both out.

'What does he want with us?' Greer asked. 'What *can* he want with us?'

They had been unconscious while Pace loaded them onto his ship, but Blite felt them dropping into U-space just as Greer woke up to a vomiting fit. In fact, it had probably been the sensations of that drop that had helped her on her way.

'I don't know,' he replied.

The area they were in was spartan: just a room shaped like a comma with ceramal walls, floor and ceiling, the point of the comma where Greer had thrown up and a mass of plasmel crates occupying most of the rest of it. These were secured in a pallet frame. Blite walked over to them and flicked open the latches on the top one. Lifting the lid, he gazed in puzzlement at the contents, reached inside and pulled out a glass statuette. It was big, heavy and quite beautiful. After a moment, he realized it depicted a hooder, partially coiled and with front end raised as if ready to strike. Even as he held it he felt it growing warm in his grasp, lights flickering on in its translucent depths. When it began to move he quickly dropped it back in the crate. As the lights faded it returned to its original shape and froze again.

What the hell?

'Art collector?' wondered Greer, standing at his shoulder.

'Artist,' replied a voice.

They turned to find Mr Pace standing just a short distance away from them, a bulkhead door open behind him. Blite took a calming breath. This guy moved far too fast and silently for comfort.

'Why did you bring us here?' he asked.

'I knew there would be someone,' Pace said. 'Come with me.'

He turned and headed for the door. Blite glanced at Greer, who shrugged. What choice did they have? They stepped out into a corridor to see Pace disappearing out of sight. He was gone by the time they saw the dropshaft at the end of the corridor. Here Blite hesitated, then again shrugged and stepped in. If Pace wanted them dead, he hardly needed to tinker with a dropshaft gravity field to kill them.

They wafted up one floor, the irised gravity field holding them in place so they could step from the open shaft onto a circular area with doors all around. Mr Pace was waiting by one of these doors.

'Here,' he said, pushing the door open.

Blite walked warily past him into the space beyond, expecting another prison of some kind. He found himself in a strange cabin. It smelled like a greenhouse, while over to the right stood a weird-looking tree. In the centre was a seating pit with a central com-column, while off to the left was what looked like a bed . . . or a huge lily pad.

'I don't often have guests,' said Mr Pace. 'This is the only cabin available.'

Blite turned to peer at the man. He was, of course, quite expressionless, except for that slight, fixed smile. Well, if he was going to call them guests and not lock them in the hold, that was fine . . .

Pace pointed to the tree. The thing had big leaves that looked like those of a ginkgo, gnarled bluish boughs, and was scattered with fruits of all different shapes and colours. 'Sustenance is there. Toilet and bathing facilities are there.' He now pointed to what was effectively a hole in the floor with a thing poised above it like the giant looped-over bloom of a trumpet flower, though one rendered in shades of reptilian green. 'Keep this with you at all times.' The man now held out a short cylinder of black glass much like the kind he himself was fashioned from.

'I'll ask as politely as I can, again,' said Blite. 'What the hell do you want with us?'

Pace just stood there holding out the cylinder until Blite reluctantly took it. 'All you need to know,' he then said, 'is that the cargo has a buyer in the Polity who will pay well for all of it and who will never break it up.'

'What?' The man was baffling.

'I care about three things in existence,' said Mr Pace. 'My prime concern is my collection, which gave me solace while I made the pieces, at least. My last concern is about trying to exact some vengeance against Penny Royal.' He turned and headed towards the door.

Blite was about to call after him, but then decided it wasn't worth the risk.

'He didn't tell us all three,' said Greer.

'Uh?'

'He told us his prime concern and his last one, but not the one in the middle.'

Blite nodded, peered down at the glass cylinder, and felt he had an inkling of an idea what that third concern might be.

15

Crowther

Poised at the interface of Lunar Runcible Twelve, Isembard Crowther suppressed his frustration as he tuned down his implants. Being a haiman, he had discovered that one of the drawbacks of his extensive augmentations was that if he kept them running at maximum efficiency he experienced something quite unpleasant during runcible travel. Popular culture called it 'the scream' – the human response to the brief eternity spent between runcible gateways, and one never remembered by humans. As a haiman, he found that his implants recorded stuff during transition that fed back into his human mind shortly afterwards. If he didn't tune things down, he always felt, later, that his mind was somehow sitting outside his body and, during the ensuing minutes, pouring back into it like some proto-organic sludge.

He stepped through.

That brief eternity later he stepped out of another interface thousands of light years away aboard the Well Head space station, pondering his latest visit to Earth and what he had achieved. He had now all but finished his historical reconstruction of Panarchia – having moved beyond the war to the final colony. The people of that colony, right here on the line between the Graveyard and the Polity, had been a dubious crowd of pirates, criminals and Polity dropouts who, over eighty years, built up a small city that was mostly a lawless trading post. Panarchia had, by its position, been a good place from which to smuggle goods from the Polity to the Graveyard and vice versa. The smugglers had considered themselves quite smart, little knowing that they were under close surveillance, but allowed to carry on because the world was an ideal entry point to the Graveyard for Polity black ops. In recent years the city had been abandoned as Panarchia became increasingly saturated by the EMR output of the black hole Layden's Sink and its accretion disc, becoming subject to increasing seismic activity, and as its environment underwent radical changes. However, despite bringing much of the history up to date, it had been, Crowther felt, an ultimately fruitless visit to Earth. He was still no closer to resolving something that had been bugging him for some months now: Penny Royal.

Why had a rogue AI risked itself to penetrate prador lines only to anti-matter bomb eight thousand troops who had been doomed anyway?

The area spanned by the small runcible in the Well Head was an oblate chamber a hundred feet from end to end and seventy feet wide. It was zero gravity and, as usual, Crowther found himself drifting through air without any way to get himself to a solid surface. This was one of the security precautions, while others were dotted around the chamber walls. He eyed the various scanning heads and felt his body flush hot as it underwent active scan. He looked at the other devices in the station that could turn him into a hot cloud of component atoms in a moment and, as always, felt slightly thankful when a hardfield sprang into being beside him and gently propelled him towards the small exit tunnel. Such security, of course, was standard in a research station like this, since it was just the sort of place your average separatist terrorist, with a Luddite hatred for any kind of technological advancement, would like to blow to smithereens.

Landing gently on the lip of the tunnel to his quarters and feeling the pull of grav-plates, Crowther stepped on through. Re-engaging his augmentations, he felt Owl's request for contact and allowed it, in full. Station data immediately began loading and he discovered that another data pulse had been picked up from the Layden's Sink black hole while he had been away. Again it was mostly technical data.

'And interestingly,' said Owl, 'the data renders possibilities for U-space/hardfield interactions.'

'Interesting,' Crowther agreed.

Of course he was interested in the black hole data, but his secondary interest in history had been steadily supplanting it. There was a good reason for this because, in the end, the mystery of the source of data from the black hole did not lie in its technical content, but in events. A lot of it could have been coincidental but for that phrase he had encountered amidst the data: *Your greatest fear – the room stands open.* The black hole. The black AI. Room 101. Crowther was haunted by the feeling of a connection he did not yet understand . . .

'Did we get any of those odd phrases through this time?' he asked.

'Certainly,' Owl replied, and sent him the data.

In his room, as he shed his clothing to expose the data ports running down his spine and along his arms, Crowther puzzled over the phrase, 'Beware of scorpions,' then decided that one was probably going to be vague enough to share. It was also vague enough to have millions of interpretations and, like something from a Delphic oracle, would doubtless only reveal its true meaning after the fact.

He took a necessary decontamination shower to free himself of every external microbe while his inner systems dealt with anything else he might have picked up, then stepped through the clean lock into the short pipe leading to his interface sphere. Once inside the sphere and settled in his cradle seat, he relaxed and sent the connection order. All down his back he felt the bayonet data plugs inserting. Resting his arms down, he felt optics plugging into the interfaces there. His world expanded to include the sensory arrays of the station and much extra processing. He gazed out across the accretion disc and, back-filling recent history, saw that there had been a pause in in-fall debris caused when a recent detonation at the event horizon blew everything back. For five hours Layden's Sink had been utterly exposed, and would be exposed for a further two. He gazed upon darkness. It was boring, though of course everything it implied was not. Next he looked around for Owl and found the drone to the fore of the station, over where the hardfield projectors were housed.

'You're probing them?' Crowther queried.

'We may, with a little tinkering, be able to utilize this,' the drone replied.

Owl was referring to the recent data which, even as he settled himself in and inspected his surroundings, he had already been absorbing into his enhanced mind. He could see at once what the data implied, but wasn't exactly happy about the idea of trying to apply it. So, it would appear that a link could be made from the hardfields through to the runcible of the station. This would require taking the runcible off standby, but it would mean energy from any massive impact on the hardfields would be routed back through it into U-space. But what would happen to it there? Ensconced in his interface sphere, Crowther raised an arm trailing optics like wing feathers and scratched his head.

Just as it annoyed him when Owl started tinkering, it also annoyed him when the drone was ahead of him. He now routed the data to different levels and methods of processing, routing 'real-world' implications back to his over-conscious. It took him hours to get there: the energy would create an even and controlled disruption, a distortion almost as if the non-fabric of U-space was being put under tension. This implied that the reverse could apply; that the distortion could be tapped for energy.

Crowther suddenly shivered as he absorbed the implications. The process was practically infinite . . . no, no . . . once the distortion . . . once the *twist* passed beyond a certain point – call it three hundred and sixty degrees – the whole lot would fly back out, almost like a pressure valve breaking. Then what? The idea of such a feedback had further implications concerning the geometry of hardfields; this meant it wasn't two dimensional . . .

'Got it,' said Owl.

The drone had been very busy. The runcible was muttering and ticking, ripples running across the interface, while maintenance robots in the nose of the station had made alterations to one of the spare hardfield projectors – adding components from one of the contained manufactories aboard, while also extracting some others. The thing was powering up now and the circular scale of a hardfield appeared a hundred yards out from the station.

'You've got what?' Crowther asked. 'Looks like a standard hardfield to me.'

'Watch,' Owl instructed.

Something odd began happening with the hardfield. While these things were refractive, it was usually just in the same way as a simple sheet of glass. Now, however, as he watched, the hardfield began distorting the view across the accretion disc beyond it; it was lensing. Before Crowther could begin taking his own measurements Owl routed further data to him. The hardfield was now bowed – it bore the shape of some huge contact lens.

'Now let's test it for impact,' said Owl.

A second later a sensor probe of the kind they occasionally shot at the event horizon of Layden's Sink launched from the rear of the Well Head. It hurtled out into vacuum, transmitting telemetry as it swung into a curve bringing it back towards the station. Yes, this was it, this was precisely the kind of thing Crowther didn't like about Owl's tinkering. Sure, test out some theories, do a little experimentation, but really, try not to kill your companion observer in the process.

As the missile became a dot haloed by its single burn fuser, Crowther was all too aware of just how tough an object it was. The things were made in a gravity press much like some U-space drive components. Despite the armouring and defences the Well Head possessed, that missile, unless intercepted by a hardfield, would punch right through it like a bullet through a pineapple. And now, of course, the hardfield due to intercept it was one that had been *tinkered* with.

'Perhaps a backup field?' Crowther suggested.

'Not required,' said Owl dismissively.

A few seconds later the missile hit the convex field, and all its mass turned to plasma in an explosion that spread in an instant to a mile across. While measuring the effects of this, Crowther eyed the hardfield. The thing had turned completely opaque – a black dot like an eyeball at the centre of the explosion. Meanwhile, the projector wasn't buffering energy but emitting a U-signature.

It was working . . .

The next microsecond, the hardfield projector's temperature increased a thousand degrees. The microsecond after that a safety trip cut in and opened the ejection port leading to the opposite side of the station from the projector and, as the U-signature cut out, belated kinetic energy complemented the heat energy, and shot the molten and radiating projector out into vacuum.

'That could have gone better,' said Owl.

Feeling very pleased with himself now because, through his own calculations, he had divined the problem, Crowther said, 'The U-space tap needs to be integral to the projector. I know that should not be relevant, since there is nominally no distance in U-space, but at these energy levels you cannot neglect quantum tunnelling at the interface.'

'Oh. Right,' Owl replied.

Now feeling expansive, Crowther continued, 'You do of course understand what this implies? The hardfield curve can be extended and actually link up. No more scaling of fields, fully enclosing fields, weapons systems fed by the U-twist.' There he paused because, in reality, he hadn't thought about that last bit deeply enough. Again the implications: weapons systems drawing on the kind of power output you might find at a major runcible terminus, but certainly not aboard any Polity ship he knew. He was appalled.

After a pause he muttered, 'Fully enclosing hardfields . . . perhaps we should . . . look at this again.' Damn, he hoped this was again behind the curve. He'd heard nothing about such fields from EC but they were probably in development somewhere in the Polity. Better there than anywhere else. Like the Kingdom, for example.

Over the next few days, and with no recent data surges from Layden's Sink, they worked together on designing a hardfield projector. Still, Crowther knew that even if no such projectors had been developed in the Polity, since his transmission of the last data package, some serious AIs would be working on them. In fact, they would almost certainly come up with something before he and Owl did. Two weeks later, with plans put on hold as he studied new data again seeping from the black hole, Crowther peripherally picked up a U-space signature back towards the far rim of the accretion disc, out towards the Panarchia system. He supposed another Polity research vessel or private sightseer had arrived.

'Well, someone got there before us,' Owl commented.

'How so?' Crowther asked.

'Spherical hardfield.'

'*What?*'

Keeping the Hawking dish focused, Crowther redirected his other sensors away from the black hole and back towards that U-signature. Whatever had arrived was light minutes away so no realspace EMR had arrived yet, but the U-space signature was weird, disperse, and in that underlying continuum sat a massive distortion – a twist. Measuring this and deploying new esoteric math, Crowther realized why Owl had said that there must be a spherical hardfield out there. Minutes later, when the EMR reached the station, Crowther gazed in glorious Technicolor at their new arrival.

'Fucking hell,' said Owl.

'Indeed,' said Crowther, surprised to hear that from the normally precise and acerbic drone.

Out at the edge of the accretion disc, and now heading in under some kind of drive actually clawing at the fabric of space, came a spherical ship, enclosed by a truly immense – and spherical – hardfield. But then the hardfield had to be big, since it was enclosing a ship nearly fifty miles across.

Spear

I began to walk towards this larger form of the black AI as it now lowered itself to the grit in urchin form, spines shuffling, moving in and out, changing shape and *energetic*. Was it *really* programming that made me open my connection to the spine and, for the first time, experience its full impact, or my own choice? The crowd filled me and I felt Sepia's sudden panic and her severing of *our* connection. I paused and looked back at her. She was down on her knees with her gloved hands against her space helmet, clutching and shaking her lowered head. But the crowd overrode my reaction to that because I was both me and all of them, and now I was reaching out to Penny Royal for resolution.

And then I was in and though I numbered in the thousands I was still small in this new hellish vastness. A great cavern of black crystal surrounded me, its walls within touching distance or a thousand miles away, the cavern extending ahead to the eye of infinity. I could sense the eight states of consciousness – their interplay, alliances, the pure vicious evil of one of them – and saw in this whole a reflection in myself. I too had those within me who were vicious and who only had their one response to the world. I suppressed them. I was a synergetic combination of all, an alliance, and yet I was still me.

The scale and the complexity I found around me were awesome, yet I could also see that the relationship, through the spine, was comparable to the connection I had made with Riss, to Mr Grey, to any other robot or AI I cared to infiltrate. With the spine I was like a chain-glass decoder. I could press myself in here and everything would unravel. I understood then that as well as giving me reasons to kill it the AI had also provided me

390

with the means. Was this what it meant when it said, *You have come here to learn how to kill?*

'Not yet,' Penny Royal told me.

Through the all-encompassing vision of the AI I saw another ship arrive and recognized it. Belatedly Flute informed me, 'We've got a visitor.'

'I know,' I replied. 'Just keep watch – I'll let you know if you need to take any action.'

'Why is he here?' I asked Penny Royal.

'You know.'

Of course I did. Mr Pace was here for me, for the spine, for Penny Royal. He knew precisely what I was. He needed to take the spine away from me because he believed that with it he could kill Penny Royal and then he himself could finally die. As I watched the ship coming in fast, I realized there had to be more to it than that. I was the judgement the AI had created for itself. So where exactly did Mr Pace fit in? If I wanted to see Penny Royal dead all I needed to do was hand the spine over to him. All the AI's manipulations would then mean nothing; all its preparation of me. I knew the AI's crimes because I had experienced them thousands of times over. Did I want to see Penny Royal dead?

'All I need to do is give this to him,' I said.

'Then you have failed,' the AI replied, after a pause adding, 'to understand Mr Pace.'

Really?

I reached deep into the spine and, in another respect, out towards that ship. In the tangle of a thousand threads I found his. The totality of his life resided in his body while perpetually recorded to the spine. From there it was relayed through U-space to Pace's home world to update a third recording of the man residing in the extended mentality of what had once been a war drone. Damn me if I didn't recognize the signature of the mind of the thing, but I couldn't place it. I glanced at Riss, and only learned why I had done so when she said over suit com, 'When I was on Room 101. The first time.'

I got it then: the drone on Mr Pace's world was one of those who had escaped with Riss, whose memory of the whole episode I had experienced. Further reflections and shadows here, for this was a drone that had wanted purpose just as desperately as Riss. Penny Royal had given it such a purpose, of course, when Mr Pace had come begging. And now the drone perpetually recorded Mr Pace and resurrected him every time his body was destroyed, or otherwise burrowed aimlessly through the crust of that world. There seemed to me a lesson in this . . . a case of be careful what you wish for.

Now I focused fully on Mr Pace and, just as I had with many others residing in the spine, *experienced* him. It was a brief sojourn in a mind that was an abyss of despair, only stirred to action by the prospect of murder. I divined then why he had been aboard the extremadapt station. He had found something in a piece of green memory crystal: some hint to the location of an Atheter starship. There, he felt, would be the technology that could free him from his unique damnation. He knew there was something on his home world that resurrected him each time he destroyed himself and he was powerless to stop it. He had decided his best option was to obliterate the world – a task such a starship could easily achieve.

Had Penny Royal destroyed the extremadapt colony to drive him away? I could make no sense of it but, nevertheless, Mr Pace was coming in fast and now I did, if imperfectly, under-stand him. Sure, if I handed over the spine he would use it against Penny Royal. But first he would use it against me. He had to get to me, though, and there was this hardfield . . .

Even as I thought that, the hardfield went out and one of the projectors came in low over my head to land between me and the AI. The hardfield came on again, surrounding it, and leaving me outside. I turned away, some intimation now of what Penny Royal wanted here.

'Sepia . . .' I groped to re-establish our connection, but the attempt only raised a squall of error messages. I began trotting towards her, now using my suit com, 'Sepia, head for the shuttle. Fast.'

'What? Why?'

'Mr Pace just arrived and he's going to try and kill me.'

She turned round and set off in loping paces towards the shuttle.

'Too late,' said Riss direct to my aug.

Even as I heard her words, the railgun missiles hit.

The Brockle

The *High Castle* slid out of U-space and immediately concealed itself under chameleonware. The 'ware was good, but still would not be enough to conceal it completely from the Polity ships. They would know that something had arrived, they just would not know what or where. The Brockle surveyed the scene.

The twenty prador ships were in a loose formation separated from the Polity fleet by a hundred thousand miles. The latter had its two dreadnoughts, close together between the prador ships, and the seven attack ships, which were arranged in a ring formation oriented towards the hypergiant. Com activity was high and the Brockle, possessing the requisite codes, keyed into it. Both sides were preparing to leave, their brief alliance over, but some diplomacy was ongoing, in an attempt to create closer ties.

393

The lead Polity dreadnought was transmitting data on the Well Head, the Weaver and the war drone Amistad to the lead King's Guard ship, while in return the Polity was getting much data on Sverl and other renegade prador past and present. This was necessarily a slow and very careful process because, despite a hundred years having passed since the end of the war, the parties represented two civilizations that had come close to exterminating each other. They were also, the Brockle realized, checking each other's trustworthiness by comparing received data against what they already knew. It seemed a shame to break up the party.

Now turning its attention to the *High Castle*'s weapons systems, the Brockle made its selections and chose its targets. It fired two Polity U-jump missiles athwart the hypergiant. They would materialize in vacuum beyond the sun to await updated coordinates on their targets, at which point they could jump back in again. It next turned its attention to the two highly modified U-jump missiles and fired them off. These were bulky oblate objects with single-burn fusers attached, their U-signatures varying from the Polity norm and with deliberate inaccuracies introduced. Unlike the first two missiles, they were not capable of materializing actually inside a target. These the Brockle dispatched out towards the asteroid belt here, where they too would await updates on their targets. The Brockle then cut its chameleonware and under fusion accelerated in towards the massed ships.

Fleet communications immediately opened to the *High Castle* and this of course was because the ship had been expected. Its apparent mission had been an investigation of the situation with Room 101 after the fleet had dealt with the problem. It had also been tasked to intervene if the problem turned into one that couldn't be solved with the simple application of CTDs and particle beams.

'You're late,' said the Garrotte AI.

The Brockle opened up the bandwidth of communications just enough, puppeting through the *High Castle* AI which was not simply under its control, but had become just one unit in its extended being. Now, since it had realized that what had been seen of Penny Royal was not the whole of that entity, the Brockle had allowed itself to grow physically larger – the conglomeration of its units forming a sphere measuring twenty feet across – and mentally larger. Now it was *really* ready to deal with Penny Royal.

'The nature of our mission as it now stands required my disembarking my human crew,' the Brockle replied. 'We need prime manoeuvring capabilities for AI-on-AI conflict.' It had happened before when the Polity had needed to deal with renegade AIs – when ship AIs pushed systems beyond tolerances that might leave humans smeared about the interior.

'What mission?' Garrotte asked.

'Close U-space com and await delivery of physically transported data. Cut all com to our prador friends here,' the Brockle instructed. 'I am now, as per plan, taking command.'

'That bad?' enquired Garrotte.

Via its links to the two destroyers and seven attack ships the Brockle observed its orders being obeyed. All com shortly switched over to laser or microwave beam. Communication channels that had been open to the twenty King's Guard ships cut abruptly, but the Brockle quickly opened its own channel to the chief Guard ship because it would be needed later. Those ships began changing formation at once – suspicious of their Polity allies after the abrupt cut in com. The prador in charge tried to ask questions, but the Brockle put it on hold for the moment.

Garrotte had also issued other orders and, in response, the human crews aboard the two dreadnoughts were heading for aqueous-glass stasis tanks. In these they would sink into hyper-sleep, the two-state glass penetrating their bodies and then hardening to the consistency of diamond. In this condition they were no more vulnerable than the crystal of the AIs controlling their ships. The *High Castle* also possessed this facility, which was worrying, because Garrotte and the other AIs might wonder why it had not been used. Too late to call back the lie.

'U-com has been penetrated,' said the Brockle. 'It is possible that ships here have been penetrated too, and that includes those Guard ships.'

'Understood.'

'Physical data units will be dispatched shortly.' As it said this, the Brockle began breaking off clumps of units of itself of much the same mass as its original form aboard the *Tyburn*. These it quickly dispatched through the altered interior of the ship, down tubeways to a series of eleven sensor probes it had prepared on the journey here – the two spares in case of failures.

'But I'm still puzzled,' said Garrotte. 'Our last order from Earth Central was to stand down.'

Despite, or even because of, its much-expanded intelligence, the Brockle felt a surge of irritation at the other AI. Knowing the Garrotte's history, it said, 'You, of all AIs, should know the penalties for arrogance and underestimating an enemy.'

'Yes . . . but surely the greater enemy here is the possibility of tearing open space-time. We were told to stand down because of that. Penny Royal's transformation is secondary . . .'

'You were told to stand down because that is precisely what Earth Central wanted Penny Royal to hear.'

'Oh.'

'Yes, "oh". Do you fully understand what is happening here?'

'I think so,' Garrotte hedged.

'The limitations of AI are physical,' the Brockle lectured. 'The amount of energy available, barriers to the transmission of data through matter, and the processing of data in matter even when using quantum processes. And, of course: time. An AI can lodge itself in U-space and defeat some of the temporal problems, but to maintain itself in that state requires vast amounts of energy from a realspace source. And there are other limitations too.'

'Like the Jain AIs,' said Garrotte.

The Brockle hesitated for a microsecond, long enough to retrieve relevant data from the *High Castle* AI's memory. How had it missed that? Apparently the Jain AIs had taken their own route to transubstantiation and so embedded themselves in U-space. Except that it now seemed the energy sources that had maintained their state had died long ago, and they thought long slow and indifferent thoughts in that continuum; they had regressed, forgotten . . .

'Like the Jain AIs,' the Brockle agreed. 'But Penny Royal's route is different. If it can survive dropping itself into Layden's Sink, if it can pass the event horizon and establish itself intact in the compressed matter of a black hole, it can deploy the U-space feedback technology it possesses to order that matter. In such a state it would have taken itself beyond time and would have practically limitless energy at its disposal.'

'But it's not a case of *would*, but of already has.'

Yes, that was the whole point of the data being collected at the Well Head: the contention being, now that they knew the AI's destination, that it was Penny Royal sending that data – a version of the AI that had taken itself beyond both temporal and energy restrictions. The contention was also that if they tried to stop Penny Royal entering the black hole and actually suc-ceeded, this act would create a paradox that could rip open space-time across a hundred years and a thousand light years. The Polity might not survive that; the Kingdom might not survive it either.

The Brockle's units were now loaded to their probes, the first of these lining up for a slow-shot through one of the railguns. The Brockle targeted the *Garrotte* and fired the first probe.

'There you are wrong,' it said. 'Data from the Well Head is much more open to interpretation than that. There is no way of identifying the entity within that black hole as Penny Royal. In fact, there is more data to indicate that it is another AI that entered Layden's Sink.'

It was all complete fabrication, but the Brockle was in no doubt that Penny Royal had to be stopped at all costs. It then reconsidered. Perhaps it was true? Perhaps the full circle of destiny *was* closing? Perhaps the Brockle itself was the one to enter the black hole . . .

The probe shot across towards the big golden lozenge of the new dreadnought named *Micheletto's Garrotte II*. There a fast-retracting hardfield decelerated it a few miles out from the hull. The hardfield then went out and an access port opened. The probe next used its own chemical drive to take it towards that port. Meanwhile the other probes were launching and on their way towards the other ships.

'Really?' asked Garrotte.

'Really,' the Brockle confirmed. 'We have to stop Penny Royal entering Layden's Sink because that will actually cause the temporal rift. The black AI has been trying to convince us that we must let it go, but in reality is trying to cause catastrophic damage. Do you not see that this is exactly what Penny Royal has always been about?'

The probe was now inside the dreadnought and Garrotte was inserting a physical optic connection. Having learned from its takeover of *High Castle*, the Brockle was aware of how danger-ous this situation could become, and how easily it could fail at taking full control of this fleet. Elements of chaos now needed to be introduced.

'Why does Earth Central believe we have been penetrated?' Garrotte asked.

'Penny Royal is maintaining its distributed being in U-space,' lectured the Brockle. 'How likely do you think it is that you have not been penetrated?'

'I see.'

'The data in those probes will confirm when I release them,' said the Brockle. 'Stand by.' It put the com channel to Garrotte on hold. Now the prador.

Already it had studied the deal struck between the Kingdom and the Polity. Having learned that the renegade prador Sverl had effectively been turned into an AI, the king had not been happy at all. That Sverl was a renegade prador-turned-AI in control of a wartime Polity factory station made things some-what worse. But then events had moved on. Reviewing previous communications between the king of the prador and Earth Cen-tral, the Brockle was surprised at the intelligence the former demonstrated. As the situation had changed, with Room 101 being turned into a sphere, the king had grasped the situation at once and immediately made a shipyard tug available – had in fact suggested the solution. With the sphere dropping into U-space, its signature indicating its destination as Layden's Sink, and then being apprised of what was going on at the Well Head, the king had quickly grasped the implications of that too, and also agreed to stand down.

'I am sorry for the delay,' said the Brockle to the large armoured prador now appearing in internal visual spaces. 'We have a serious problem.'

'You are the *High Castle* AI?' said the prador.

'I am.'

'Polity orders were for you to take over control of the *Polity fleet* after Sverl had been dealt with, or in the event of matters . . . becoming more complex.'

Noting the emphasis, the Brockle replied, 'Matters have become considerably more complex. I have evidence that three attack ships here –' the Brockle selected three at random and sent their locations to the prador – 'are definitely now under the direct control of Penny Royal, while there are others that may be. You are aware, for example, that the AI of the *Garrotte* was once a captive of that AI? I have dispatched probes under the guise of direct physical data transport to all ships, but the probes contain subminds of a forensic AI called the Brockle, which will attempt to deal with the problem.'

Already energy readings from the prador ships were changing and their formation shifting yet again. The previous cut in communications had made them wary of their allies, but now they were fully orienting towards a fresh danger and readying their weapons.

'And why are you informing me of a problem that is now essentially a Polity one?' enquired the prador.

Garrotte was now urgently trying to get in contact. The Brockle opened communications again to deliver a warning: *'I don't like this at all,'* the erstwhile forensic AI said. *'That prador formation does not bode well.'* It simultaneously but separately said to the prador, 'I am informing you because, though I have ordered a shutdown of coms between the Polity fleet and you, the subverted ships may try to open com. This will be an attempt, using the computer worm Penny Royal used to take over those three ships, to seize control of your fleet. Be utterly aware that this worm is capable of being transmitted piecemeal at narrow bandwidth.'

'*I know it doesn't bode well – that's why I was trying to get in contact,*' said Garrotte.

'We do not have AIs aboard to be usurped,' the prador observed.

'But you do have first- and second-child ship minds that are equally as vulnerable,' the Brockle told the prador, while simultaneously telling Garrotte, '*Pull your attack ships in – flat wheel formation in response.*'

'*Understood,*' Garrotte acknowledged.

All the probes had now arrived and been taken aboard the Polity ships. All those ships were making physical connections to the probes in an attempt to download the data they contained, but of course there was no data there – just collections of units conglomerated into subminds that were more powerful than the Brockle's original self aboard the *Tyburn*, while the remainder of the forensic AI was now somewhat reduced, but still a writhing ball fifteen feet across.

'Then it is time for us to depart,' said the prador.

'Meaning I cannot call on your assistance?'

The subminds were studying the ships they were aboard, finding ways to shut down internal scanning and security around them and designing appropriate attacks. Perpetually updated on this, the Brockle itself noted that the problem with the attack ships was accessibility. They were so packed with hardware that there were hardly any spaces to worm through. However, the submind designated number six found the answer: the ship-mind ejection ports. To access such a port would require the sacrifice of one unit each – converting a large portion of its meta-material mass into a catalytic thermic lance. All the Brockle's subminds in the attack ships began preparing themselves for this.

'This is getting a little fraught,' said the prador, obviously acknowledging the change of formation in the Polity fleet. 'If the assistance you require entails firing on Polity ships, I think not. The king is all for mutual cooperation when it suits both our interests, but actions that could be misinterpreted and lead to war, are not in our interests. This is something you will have to deal with alone.'

The main problem with the dreadnoughts was the distance of the subminds from the ship AIs. The Brockle was amused to see that the solution to that was again the ship-mind ejection tube. It seemed their concern for their own survival was the weakness to be exploited in both cases. The subminds were ready, and it was therefore time to set the whole plan in motion.

'I'm afraid the indications are that Penny Royal has also penetrated the prador fleet,' it told Garrotte, while to the prador it said: 'Then I bid you goodbye,' briefly amused by its own underlying meaning there as it sent its instructions to the U-space missiles.

The massive extended teardrop of the King's Guard lead ship, gleaming gold and the peak of prador weapon technology, bucked, briefly expanded at its waist, and simply blew apart in an explosion that glowed borealis green in the pink-champagne light of the hypergiant. The Brockle thought this beautiful as, still hurtling in towards the two ship formations, it initiated the internal structural force-fields that were a requisite for a firing of the *High Castle*'s gravity-wave weapon. Meanwhile, what appeared to be a prador kamikaze materialized just a few hundred miles out from the Polity fleet and fired up a fuser drive, its speed ramping up under thousand-gravity acceleration.

The Polity formation broke, ships slamming immediately into similarly massive accelerations as they scattered. They could take out the kamikaze, but guessed the thing was a planet-breaker loaded with CTDs that would detonate once their anti-matter vessels were ruptured. Shooting the thing was about as smart as shooting at a grenade sitting on a shelf across a room.

The second apparent kamikaze appeared from sunward, changing the ship scatter pattern, while the second Polity U-jump missile blew the tail from a second King's Guard ship and sent it tumbling. The first kamikaze detonated, its explosion surprisingly weak. And now the ships were responding to attack. Particle beams lanced out from the prador ships and splashed on sudden scalings of hardfields. Swarms of railgun missiles filled intervening space.

Antiquated, thought the Brockle, as it fired its gravity weapon. 'Take them out!' it then ordered the Polity fleet.

The gravity wave hit: a space-time ripple passing through two prador ships and wrenching them into twisted wrecks. One of them blew open lengthways on a disc-shaped explosion. The *High Castle*'s gravity wave firing appeared ill-aimed and ill-timed, because it continued, somewhat weakened, straight into the Polity fleet. It wasn't enough to kill ships, but it did cause damage and disruption. However, one attack ship disappeared in a bright flash, its substance fading like shadows – one of the hardened CTD cases that should have protected it from the gravity wave must have possessed a fault. The Brockle felt the pain of its submind there expiring. Meanwhile its other subminds were now out of their probes and heading for those ship-mind ejection tubes.

Firing now from the Polity ships as white lasers stabbed out to incinerate railgun missiles, then switched to particle beams as it became apparent that some of those missiles were prador exotic metal. But still, it was no contest. Two of the attack ships began peeling off splinter missiles, which then blinked out of existence. Three prador ships, one after the other, bucked, briefly expanded, then exploded like petrol-filled balloons. The rest of their formation began pulling away and, as another two ships were simply annihilated, the Brockle felt two attack ships fall under its control.

'We can let them go,' said Garrotte, calm, forgiving, and utterly unaware as yet of the submind now cutting through the locks on its escape hatch.

The Brockle contemplated the remaining eleven prador ships. They had their hardfields up and were withdrawing just as fast as they could. They were just seconds from U-jumping away, their drive fields actually managing to overcome local disruption, but they were totally vulnerable to U-jump missiles and could be destroyed in a moment. What to do? Did allowing them to go undermine the Brockle's story about them having been taken over by Penny Royal? Would it be best for them just to disappear and thus delay news of what had happened here getting out?

As the remaining four attack ships fell under its control, the forensic AI realized it did not matter. Whether AIs that were under its control knew it had lied was irrelevant and, as for the news getting out, the Brockle knew that the prador ships would have been constantly relaying data to the Kingdom.

'Yes, let them go,' it agreed.

'What the –' began Garrotte, then a submind unit silenced it by severing optics, while the other wrapped around it and injected nano-fibres. A moment later the other dreadnought fell.

Done.

In virtuality the Brockle sensed eight AI ship minds like tumours in the loose spread of its being. As it steadily took them apart, completely supplanted them, absorbed them, they became part of its being. It wasn't murder because, in a sense, they still existed.

'Now we go to Layden's Sink,' it said, much expanded now, confident.

There was no reply.

16

Spear

I saw the shuttle buck then lift off the ground on a plasma explosion. Further missiles struck even as it rose, tearing it apart. A wall of fire and debris hurtled towards me, first engulfing Sepia. I stood paralysed, taken straight back to my death on Panarchia, then a moment later felt something hard slam into me and heave me aside. I thumped down behind one of the standing jags of metal, with Riss coiled around my torso as the fire and debris parted around the jag, but then swept me up. I tumbled in a chaos of burning metal and shattered stone, but around me Riss was a blur deflecting the worst of it.

Finally I sprawled on my back in dusty grey, trying repeatedly to aug through to Sepia and only getting error messages. I remembered how when we first encountered Mr Pace, I knew I was putting her in danger. Now . . . Riss uncoiled from me and slid to one side, peering up through the swirling dust. I sat upright, brushing away rubble and some lethal-looking chunks of metal. A moment later my visor display informed me of a couple of sealed suit breaches that would need attention while its medical monitor noted that the bleeding from my right leg had been stopped, but would also need attention. I loaded data from the suit to my aug and got detail: there was a sliver of something in my calf muscle, and it must have been very hard that it penetrated my suit. I stood, carefully, but there was very little pain – the suit had pressure-injected a nano-bead analgesic.

'He's landing,' said Riss.

I felt a surge of sickening anger. Yes, during the war I'd killed prador, but I'd never killed a human being. Even when I'd had the opportunity and been perfectly justified in doing so, as in the case of Isobel Satomi, I'd avoided it. But right now I was prepared to kill.

'Flute,' I said, that connection opening easily. 'Hit that ship.'

'I cannot,' Flute replied with a wail. 'You're enclosed!'

He sent a visual feed and I gazed through his sensors down towards us. Nearly half the planetoid now sat under a hardfield dome. I put a frame over an object down on the surface and focused in, studying Mr Pace's ship, a cloud of dust blowing out around it as it settled. Next I transferred the frame to the glowing remains of our shuttle and searched the surrounding area. I could see no space-suited figure there nor could I pick up any feeds from Sepia's suit.

'Fucking Penny Royal,' I said.

'Indeed,' said Riss.

'What do I do?' queried Flute, now apparently calmer.

'Just stand by,' I replied, then turned to Riss. 'I need to get to Sepia.'

Riss swung round to look at me, then just froze for a moment before saying, 'This way.'

I hesitated, bracing myself, and asked, 'Is she alive, Riss?'

'I can't tell at this distance,' the snake drone replied, still heading away.

I scanned the ground I could see around myself. 'Riss, where the hell is the spine?' Then, before she could reply, added, 'Never mind.' As I stomped after her I could sense the spine ahead and knew I could locate it in zero visibility. I opened up my connection to it again and suddenly felt lighter, more confident, but still angry. I used it to probe for Sepia's aug, but below the error messages was just fizz.

'Mr Pace,' I said to Riss, to distract myself from the terror of what I might find when I reached Sepia.

'Hasn't left his ship yet.'

I felt Riss was keeping something from me. Perhaps she did know what had happened to Sepia. I felt no inclination to push her because the longer I didn't know . . .

Riss led me through settling dust and clearing smoke, which was now thin enough for me to see the burning remains of the shuttle lying some distance away. When I ran a program in my aug to sort that out because perspective was difficult on such a little world, it told me those remains lay over a mile away. As visibility continued to improve I saw the crater we had landed by, but no sign of Penny Royal.

We came at length to the edge of an area of smoking ground lying between us and the remnants of the shuttle. Just to one side of Penny Royal's crater, jabbed into hardening lava, was the spine. Gazing at this area, I assumed Mr Pace must have tried to shoot at Penny Royal too and the railgun shot or shots had deflected here. I tested the ground ahead with one foot, found it firm and began to make my way across. By then my leg was beginning to hurt and my suit kept warning me of another bleed. I turned the warnings off.

'He's left his ship,' said Riss.

Right . . .

Only as I approached the spine did I think to delve again into its connection with Mr Pace. Immediately I was seeing through his eyes and sensing his thoughts as he ran, in great long lopes through a metal forest – his gaze fixed on a distant cloud of dust and smoke. I grabbed the object and tried to pull it from the lava, but it resisted – stone hardened around it to glue it in place.

For one brief moment I wondered if Penny Royal was enjoying some obscure joke here because, well, the spine was a bit like a sword . . .

I reformatted it, changing its profile, and pulled it from the ground, moved on over the magma with Riss streaming along beside me like something molten herself. I kept on a straight course towards the remains of the shuttle. The thing was utterly in pieces and the surrounding area ripped up so it was difficult for me to figure out where I had been standing, let alone where Sepia might be.

'She's here?' I asked. 'That blast threw me over a mile away.'

'Trapped against that,' said Riss, rising into the air and pointing with her ovipositor. I looked over towards one of those jags of metal and after a moment recognized it as the one Riss had thrown me behind. I began heading towards it, but through another's eyes I could now see myself: Mr Pace was heading towards me, fast, from behind.

'Any explosive gel left?' I asked casually.

'None at all,' Riss replied.

Through the spine, I was a multitude again, as I had been at Room 101 when the robot had attacked us aboard the *Lance*, and time slowed all around me. I began turning, while calculating vectors, even as Pace hurtled in, drawing back one stony hand to stab it through my body. I let go of the spine, snapped a hand round, grabbed his wrist and pushed down as I bowed, throwing him. Even though I'd diverted most of his impetus I still sprawled on the ground, feeling as if I'd been clipped by a ground car. Mr Pace tumbled through the air beyond me and slammed into a chunk of the shuttle's hull, tipping it over in an explosion of sparks and fragments of hardened breach foam.

Hauling myself up again, I retrieved the spine. I glanced at

Riss, who hadn't even moved. 'See what you can do for Sepia,' I said.

'I can help you,' said Riss.

'I said, *help her*,' I said.

Pace rolled back out. He wore no space suit, of course, but why he had chosen to come against me naked and unarmed was baffling. Still, because of his nakedness I noted that I'd actually managed to put a couple of chips in his adamantine body. But now what? I'd caught him unawares and used his own momentum against him. I could only do the latter again if he rushed me, which he now showed no sign of doing. Also, because I was in a space suit I was clumsier, slower and more vulnerable.

'You're in my mind, aren't you?' he said, without moving his lips.

How could I reply to him? My suit PA wouldn't work in this atmosphere. I replied directly through the spine.

'Why is it necessary to kill me before taking the spine?' I asked.

'Because it's one way of hurting Penny Royal, before I kill the fucker.'

I knew right away he was lying, of course, and was now deep enough into the upper layers of his mind to know why. My connection to the spine had to be severed before he could make his own. But there was more here that I wasn't reading. Here was an old and practised mind that was concealing something from me. It had managed to take data out of its own consciousness and conceal it.

He now walked towards me, raising his hand and negligently gesturing with one finger. 'I'll simply rip open your suit. Not only will you suffocate but there's just enough cyanide in the atmosphere to make even that process more unpleasant.'

'Why must my death be unpleasant?' I asked.

'Because it pleases me.' Even as he said it I sensed his confusion. Why wasn't he just killing me and moving on?

He closed in to swipe at me, somewhat clumsily. The move telegraphed, I parried it with the spine as I stepped to one side and turned, delivering a kick that sent him staggering and nearly put him down on his face. But I could not keep this up for much longer because now my leg was really hurting and my hands were numb from the impact against the spine. Could I reach him any other way? I tracked the data flows and began to reach into him as I had intended to reach into Riss, and as I now knew I could reach into Penny Royal.

He turned, holding up one hand and inspecting it. Two of the fingers were missing from the hand I had batted away. Almost without volition I shifted the physical format of the spine. Yes, I could stop him. With a ringing sound, turning to a high whine in this atmosphere, the spine shrugged into scales and repositioned, turning into the sword I had earlier pulled from the stone. I just need to cut off a limb or two . . .

Almost as if in response to this the spine changed yet again, returning to its original shape. I stared at the thing, then at Pace. I remembered the Golem aboard the *Lance* when I first boarded that ship.

'You want to die,' I said.

Sure he did. But taking many with him and causing as much damage as he could as he went. I sensed his history: the people he had casually tossed from the battlements of his castle, the deaths and maimings he had caused during his rise to power, those he had cored and sent to the prador. I glanced over towards where Riss was laboriously removing rubble to uncover a still form.

'And I'll make sure she's dead too,' he said calmly.

That was it. I knew then what was being concealed. With a

thought, I created a disruptor program in aug and spine, and fed it into the right places. It began at once erasing the Mr Pace in the spine, and it transmitted back to his home world, disrupting and wiping out the copy of him there, before I cut that connection. However, I maintained the link to him – he was still perpetually recording to the spine and that recording being perpetually disrupted. Next I tried sending the disruption to him.

Mr Pace jerked as if I had struck him, staggered and shook his head. I expected him to go down then but after a moment he straightened up and grinned.

'You thought it would be as easy as that?' he asked.

The disruption was transmitting to him, but being perpetually repaired, even as it happened. I knew then that to kill him I had to *physically* disrupt him. I wondered why this should be. It seemed Penny Royal had set it this way when it gave him this form. A physical act was required.

He came at me again, hard. I jabbed the point of the spine at his face, to the left. He dodged right while I stepped right, swinging the butt of the spine round and hammering it into his face, using the force of the impact and a shove with my legs to propel myself up and back, going into a backwards somersault in the low gravity. All this seemed in slow motion to me as I analysed data on him – directly from his mind. The key was there because much of his body consisted of a form of chain-glass. Even as I turned over in mid-air I designed a decoder molecule, and as I landed I began reformatting the surface of the spine to produce that molecule.

I landed on my feet, but the impetus sent me backwards to land on my rump. Subliminally I could see Pace spinning towards me and accelerating with such force he was breaking rocks underfoot. I started to haul myself up fast to respond, but gave up. I was stunned, injured, slow . . . at least that's what I wanted him to think. I got onto one knee, the spine pointing towards the ground, remembering the Golem that had attacked me aboard my ship when I first took control there, and just how strong and sharp was the spine. Through it now I could see Pace's intention: to duck down and rip my space helmet open.

Timing is all.

At the last moment I shifted the spine up to my shoulder and rather than duck away launched myself straight at him. The point of the spine hit him in the guts and, with a sound like demolition charge going off, it punched through him. The base of the spine delivered such an impact against me that I had no doubt it had shattered bones. My suit confirmed this as he crashed past me. I found myself in the air, spinning, head pointing down towards the ground as I flipped over lengthways. Eventually I crashed down, on my back. Error messages screamed in a visor dislodged to one side, internal air blew past my face. I clamped a hand over the top of my helmet where one of its rib sections had been torn away and struggled to get to my knees – my right arm stiff against my side and blood running down into my eyes.

Pace was still upright, his back towards me, the spine protruding from it. He turned, staggering slightly and looking puzzled as he pulled at the length of cable wound around its base. Well, I'd got him all right, but I now wondered which of us was going to die first. My suit was responding: a spray head throwing expanding breach foam at the gap beside my visor, more bubbling up under my hand and more boiling out around the dislodged neck ring. However, the outside air was getting in and my breathing was becoming increasingly tight. My surroundings seemed dark now and webbed with yellow veins.

Mr Pace took a few steps towards me, then went down on his knees. The decoder was working, lines of white spreading from the puncture point like cracks. He opened his mouth wide. I don't know whether he was screaming, or just mildly surprised. A wide section of the upper right-hand part of his chest opened along its upper edge and lifted, then the whole thing hinged down and fell away. Other layers then began bubbling up like heated paint and peeling away. White dust and black flakes snowed away from him until I could see the shape of his skeleton. I then felt the whole of his life just draining, all the years rushing past me and dissolving into blackness. Then, all at once, he dropped forwards onto his face and shattered. The spine stood for a second, then fell over.

Gotcha, I thought.

And as I faded into blackness too, on a moral level, it felt right that in taking his life I had ended my own. Other parts of me cheered his passing, or screamed their objections, in general, to death. Then there was silence.

Amistad

Layden's Sink, thought Amistad, beginning to see the pattern at last – the one woven this time by Penny Royal, and not by any Atheter.

The giant accretion disc around Layden's Sink stretched out ahead of their vessel like a vast snowy plain. The black hole itself was of course only discernible by the meagre and difficult-to-detect, or rather distinguish, output of Hawking radiation, currently being all but swamped by the remains of the last star and planetary system the hole was in the process of ingesting. However, Amistad knew that the Hawking radiation here was being studied very closely because it was like no other issuing from any known black hole.

Amistad then pulled back and focused on the structure

enclosing him. Its massive strengthening and many other functions he had yet to plumb; its evenly scattered AIs with the black diamonds at their hearts, which he now knew were *anchors*; and the phenomenally strong enclosing hardfield. Now he knew. Who but he had been closer to the mind of Penny Royal? Who but he had measured that AI's madness, and then its sanity, and known that he was seeing just one realspace facet of something larger? Who but he really understood the black AI?

Amistad would have grimaced had his scorpion features allowed it, because one of the answers to those questions was, 'Don't be an arrogant prick.' There were, of course, others.

'But it's why I'm here,' he said abruptly, to himself.

'What?' asked Sverl.

Perhaps Sverl was another who knew.

'Don't you see it now?'

'I see that,' said Sverl, highlighting U-signatures appearing all around them.

Amistad watched as the Polity fleet appeared, apparently short of one attack ship but having gained another large vessel. Amistad recognized this as the *High Castle*. Much had been kept from him about this operation, but he knew the *High Castle* had been due to take command of its latter stages. No sign, however, of the twenty ships of the King's Guard just yet.

Riding on the computing of the sphere, he sensed a mass departure through the runcible gate and recognized it as a probing shot. One of the ships out there had just fired a U-jump missile to see if the runcible gate was still operating. Next came the stab of beam weapons turning things hellish out there, followed shortly by something that jostled Amistad where he stood. A gravity weapon had been deployed. The ships out there had again tried to kill them.

How can EC not know?

Earth Central and all the other Polity AIs had access to the same information as Amistad. They knew about the data transmitted out of this black hole via its Hawking radiation, they had to understand the purpose of this vessel – the former Room 101 – and they had to know what Penny Royal intended. Why then were they still trying to destroy this ship? Surely they understood that the sphere had to enter the black hole, with Penny Royal aboard, who would doubtless gain access via one of the runcibles it had stolen. If this didn't happen, disaster would ensue. Therefore, there had to be something Amistad was not seeing.

The drone began reassessing recent events, the whole pattern of Penny Royal's actions. Isobel Satomi's transformation had been the method it had employed to provide the Weaver with a new Atheter war machine. Amistad felt that that machine had been a down payment. The AI had then manipulated events to drive Sverl to Room 101 and initiate the transformation here – to open the runcible gateway and set the device running, and then to allow the Weaver through to complete the work.

Sverl and Satomi had been incidental, Amistad thought, their inclusion a way of righting past wrongs. In reality, Penny Royal could have used some other method to provide the war machine and could have done everything Sverl had done here itself. No, the key was Thorvald Spear.

The whole mechanics of this operation had, really, required no humans or prador, so was it their inclusion that had brought the Polity fleet here? Were they here trying to force the black AI's hand, not trusting it to do what needed to be done? They did not understand the mind of Penny Royal sufficiently to know what it was doing beyond the mere mechanics.

Amistad did.

This was about redemption, about forgiveness, about a need to be understood. The fate of thousands of star systems, perhaps a large portion of the galaxy, was hinging on the decisions of one man.

'You're quiet,' said Sverl.

Amistad dipped his body down a little, then snipped at vacuum with one claw.

'Let me give you something to ponder,' he said, and immediately transmitted a copy of all the data he had on a research station called the Well Head.

While the erstwhile prador father-captain chewed on that gristly nugget, Amistad began checking on some things that would prove or disprove his theory. Thorvald Spear had needed to be prepared. He had been provided with the spine and that mentally linked him to the recordings of Penny Royal's victims. He now knew, right down to the visceral level of actually being able to experience the deaths of its victims, the full extent of the black AI's guilt. He had been given time to grow with it and had been provided with further understanding of the AI by being shown its origins in Room 101. Why Mr Pace? The man was a killer and yet Spear had been manoeuvred to go after him – ostensibly to seek information on Penny Royal's location, but ultimately to learn or gain something else. What was it?

With the full power of his advanced AI mind, Amistad sifted detail. Mr Pace had been made immortal, as promised, but, as with all such gifts from Penny Royal, it was a poisoned chalice. It was evident he had reached the point of ennui and had been unable to change sufficiently to get past it, resulting in him being trapped in a nightmare eternal life. Beyond his boredom, his hatred of Penny Royal had to be the single most important aspect of his existence. Thus hating the AI and all his manipulations, he would . . .

It all slammed together into a coherent whole. For the AI to be forgiven, to be redeemed, the one capable of forgiving must also possess the power to refuse forgiveness: to condemn, and carry out the sentence. However, Spear, for all his history in bio-espionage, was not a killer. There could be no doubt that he had been placed in a situation where it had become necessary for him to kill and, crucially, to kill using the spine. Of course, Mr Pace was recorded in the spine and retransmitted for resurrection in a new hard body every time he was destroyed or managed to destroy himself. No doubt he had either acquired or been given some insight into the purpose of the spine and the purpose of Spear. Knowing Mr Pace's history, his intention would be a simple one: kill Spear so as to undermine Penny Royal's plans, then take the spine and kill Penny Royal.

The purpose of Mr Pace was to teach Thorvald Spear how to kill.

But why Thorvald Spear?

Amistad gazed through composite long-range sensors at the planetary system steadily being drawn towards the accretion disc and Layden's Sink. Spear had been selected because he was the only survivor of the first atrocity Penny Royal had committed when, as the mind of the destroyer *Puling Child*, it had anti-matter bombed over eight thousand Polity troops into oblivion.

'I begin to understand,' said Sverl.

'You do?'

'If this does not happen the paradox that non-event would generate would tear open space-time on an unimaginable scale.'

'Do you grasp the purpose of Thorvald Spear?'

'Not quite.'

'He, as the essence of all Penny Royal's victims, must forgive the AI for matters to proceed. All of this hinges on him.'

After a long pause Sverl queried, 'The ships out there . . . surely they understand?'

'Perhaps. Now we are here EC will surely have made the

connections.' No, Amistad knew that was wrong. Earth Central could think much faster than Amistad himself. Upon discovering the destination of this sphere, EC would have worked it all out. Perhaps it would have sent the fleet to ensure that the sphere reached its destination. But it would never have risked a temporal rift by ordering another attempt to destroy the sphere.

Something was badly wrong.

Amistad transmitted a précis of his latest thinking to Sverl and kept the connection open. 'Let's see what they have to say,' he said, and then tried to open a U-space com channel to the fleet. Nothing happened. Amistad wondered if this was due to some change in the nature of the surrounding sphere and its hardfield. No, U-space missiles had been fired, had ducked under the hardfield and been dragged into the well of the runcible so nothing should be blocking his communications out. A moment later, he got a connection to the ship AI Garrotte.

'Amistad,' said Garrotte.

'What the hell do you think you're doing?'

'My job,' replied that AI. It seemed much less voluble than usual, perhaps because it truly appreciated the seriousness of the situation.

'Which should now be one of observation only.'

'My job is to destroy Penny Royal.'

'I cannot believe that EC has not integrated the Well Head situation . . .'

'It has. I am sending you a data package.'

The package arrived and began integrating it at once: the AI sitting beyond time inside the black hole was not Penny Royal. The black AI was actually trying to create the destructive paradox by supplanting the AI there. The sphere had to be stopped and Penny Royal destroyed. Amistad studied the data closely, then even closer, checking deep into the assessment backup files included.

'It all seems to make perfect sense,' Sverl observed, still riding Amistad's mind.

'Yes,' Amistad agreed, 'apart from one simple fact: there was no proof that the AI in the black hole is *not* Penny Royal, none at all. Yet the nature of much of the data collected at the Well Head, both its format and its subject, indicated that it is.'

'Is there something we're missing here?' Sverl inquired.

'Almost certainly,' Amistad agreed then to Garrotte said, 'I call bullshit on that.'

'I have further data,' said Garrotte.

Another larger package arrived and Amistad, anxious to know Earth Central's reasoning, was about to open it when the particle beam struck his carapace. The impact of the ionized particulate scored into his armour and sent him staggering. He whirled, claws up and weapons systems going live, a targeting frame dropping over the first-child Bsorol and many choices available: Amistad only had to decide whether to fry, slow-cook or blow the creature apart.

'*What happened to the package?*' Sverl asked – fast AI com, not human or prador speech, the question arriving in the microsecond before Amistad pulled the trigger.

Amistad paused. Having come under attack his defences had immediately ramped up to their maximum and thus the data package had been routed to secure storage inside him. In the next few microseconds Amistad made his analysis. Sverl had been AI-fast in the transmission of his order to Bsorol and the first-child had been none too tardy in responding. Amistad felt some admiration for the first-child's bravery. It had to have known that its weapon could not kill Amistad and the likely result of its attack would have been its own death, yet it had not hesitated. The aim of the attack? Of course, so Amistad would switch straight to defensive paranoid mode and not open that package. It was the package that would kill him. The drone shut down targeting and eased off on that internal trigger.

'Routed to secure storage,' Amistad replied mildly.

'Am I safe?' Bsorol asked, with a slight gobbling of the prador tongue that indicated a degree of panic.

'You are safe,' Amistad replied, 'and thank you.'

He now focused his attention on the package and treated it like the threat Sverl had supposed it to be. It didn't take long to etch out the shape of the worms designed to first seize control of his internal U-com, nor the underlying stuff aimed at his weapons.

'Seems you saved me some problems,' he said, not prepared to admit that Sverl and Bsorol might have saved his life. 'How did you know?'

'It is obvious that Earth Central would have worked out what is occurring here. Ergo, that the fleet out there is under the control of something else.'

Amistad again tried to open U-com to the fleet, but this time keeping the bandwidth so low no packages could be sent, also routing anything that came from there through buffers and layers of security first.

'I see,' said the entity at the other end. 'You were not fooled.'

Amistad wasn't going to admit that he had come close to it. 'Who am I speaking to?'

'The Brockle.'

Before becoming the warden of Masada, Amistad had known more than was generally known about the Brockle, because that creature had been a perfect subject for his special interest at the time: madness. But despite his fascination, he had never encountered it close up. As warden, it had been his decision whether to send Tidy Squad murderers off to it for interrogation. After receiving detail on one such interrogation, he had decided never to send anyone else, because yes, even though murderers should die, he was less sure about how many *times* they should be killed, nor by how many different methods . . .

All the data Amistad had on that creature rose to the fore of his mind; a whole montage of events. He saw a desperately ill man almost lost in masses of primitive medical technology, old-style optic connections plugged into interface plates that had replaced most of the upper part of his skull. He was old and dying in that era of Earth's history when the major killers were finally being banished. He was also winning, outpacing the Reaper, but having to sacrifice his body in the process. He was uploading his mind to an organo-metal substrate residing in an upright canister standing beside his bed.

His name was Edmund Brockle.

The montage played on and Amistad saw Edmund Brockle residing in an early iteration of the Soul Bank, living virtual lives and finally, after many years, being transferred in organo-metal form to a first Golem chassis. He saw the turning of the ages as Edmund Brockle transferred again and again, acquiring and dis-carding bodies and coming at last to rest just after the Quiet War, distributed in the components of a swarm robot. They called him Brockle then, while he worked for ECS rooting out Earth-based terrorists. By the time he was working off-world undermining separatist organizations *it* was called *the* Brockle.

To the AIs the Brockle was . . . difficult. It was one of the oldest surviving recordings of a human mind, though much changed over the years. They wanted to protect it; it was almost as if, like some historical monument, the thing had a preservation order on it. However, its behaviour, as Amistad had discovered, had been becoming increasingly erratic and careless of human life. It killed when it was justifiable but not necessary, it exacerbated dangerous situations so it could use drastic measures to resolve them. And in the end, on a world that had been close to seceding from the Polity, it went a step too far. None of the killings it carried out could be quite defined as murder, but their sheer quantity took them beyond the pale. The AIs could not quite decide whether the Brockle should be executed or given a medal, but certainly it could no longer be involved in the same operations. They settled on utilizing its skills as an interrogator, relocated it to an ancient ship called the *Tyburn* – some behind-the-scenes AI humour influencing that choice – and effectively imprisoned it. But it was an odd kind of imprisonment, for it was one the Brockle had to agree with.

And now it was free.

How and why?

'Why are you here?' Amistad asked.

'To kill Penny Royal,' the Brockle replied.

Of course . . .

Amistad's question had been more complex than that. Yes, there had been an element of consent in the Brockle's imprisonment, but there had to have been a degree of consent involved in the Brockle escaping. After a moment of applying the full power of his mind, Amistad could see the reasoning: both the Brockle and Penny Royal were difficult problems but perhaps one of them could resolve the other. Perfectly understanding the nature of the Brockle, the AIs must have fed it certain information on villains who had encountered Penny Royal – just enough data to offend its perverted sense of justice and motivate it to action.

And then they let it off the leash.

'Are you aboard the *High Castle*?' Amistad asked.

'I am.'

'And how did you manage that?'

'I stole it.'

'And how are its crew and its AI?'

'The ship AI is here.'

'Just like the Garrotte AI is there, yes?'

'Yes.'

Dead, broken up and integrated as one facet of that creature, then.

'But I asked about the crew . . .'

'Unfortunate casualties.'

It struck Amistad as a kind of cowardice on the part of the Polity AIs of which, all of a sudden, he no longer considered himself a member. They had obviously wanted the Brockle to incriminate itself so the reason for a death sentence would be clear – and so it had, first murdering the crew of the *High Castle*, when it stole the ship, and then further by subsuming the other AIs of the fleet. Even the choice of Garrotte was probably down to cruel utility, for hadn't that AI been kidnapped by Penny Royal? It had effectively been sent to its death to shut it up. Yes, the reasoning was all too obvious. They wanted to send something powerful against Penny Royal but could not infringe upon treaties with the prador about the Graveyard, and this way they got their wish, along with deniability.

However things turned out thereafter worked for them. If Penny Royal killed the Brockle, then that would be sentence executed; if the Brockle actually managed to kill Penny Royal, that would be good too, and it would have incriminated itself still further.

But all this was before the sphere moved here and the connection was made to the Well Head data. In their indirect and cowardly approach, the Polity AIs had armed and unleashed a monster just as dangerous as Penny Royal itself. And, soon enough, that monster would begin to understand the whole of what was going on here. Amistad cut the com channel and turned to Sverl.

'Thorvald Spear is in serious danger,' said Sverl.

Amistad acknowledged that with a dip of his body – Sverl had understood straight away that though the Brockle had little chance of destroying this sphere, it would soon realize that it *could* intervene before the main event: on Panarchia.

'And there's nothing we can do,' Sverl added.

'Yes there is,' Amistad replied. 'You can make a runcible connection right now.'

Spear

No, you're not dead, was my first thought.

I didn't believe in life after death in the religious sense, and I was pretty sure, having already experienced it, that resurrection by memplant didn't involve quite so much discomfort. My shoulder and calf muscle were balls of pain, miniature pradoi were rapping their claws against the inside of my skull and playing tunes on my bones. I could breathe, but it felt as if someone had poured glue into one of my lungs. I couldn't see straight out of the one eye that seemed to be working, while the other felt frozen. I kept blinking my working eye, gradually clearing my vision. A second later, seeing the breach foam half filling my helmet, I realized why that other eye wasn't working. My visor display next duly informed me that I was injured and needed medical attention, and that my suit was no longer safe. I giggled, laughed, then coughed up something bloody and had to spit it down into the base of my helmet.

'What's so funny?' asked Riss, her voice over suit com muffled by the crash foam around my head.

Well, nothing was, really, because then I remembered Sepia. I was lying on my side and needed to get up, now. Trying to put my hand down, I found my gauntlet stuck to the top of my helmet and the ridiculousness of that nearly set me off again. After a bit of tugging, and by rocking it from side to side, I finally managed to peel my hand away and, in slow wincing stages, clambered to my feet. I looked down at Mr Pace to see dusty black bones, flakes and thin shells of black crystal, nuggets and slivers of metal. Stepping unsteadily over to him, I stooped to pick up the spine then, as I straightened up, had to fight the urge to vomit.

'Is she alive?' I asked, turning to walk over to Riss and Sepia.

Riss had cleared all the rubble away and was peering through Sepia's visor. I felt my stomach sinking when I saw the state of her suit. There was breach foam all over it, so a lot of holes. Her right boot was missing and the material of her suit shredded up her calf. Below her knee an emergency seal had obviously closed against her skin, while below that point her leg was black and swollen with bloody cracks in it. The blast had been a fierce one, turning the shuttle's armour into shrapnel, because it takes a hell of a lot to puncture suits like the ones we were wearing.

'Yes, she's alive,' said Riss.

I felt something relax inside me. In the end our medical technology was such that the loss of a leg was a brief inconvenience. If a body was alive then all the damage to it could be repaired, and that was even the case when it had been dead for a while . . . depending on what definition of death you used.

'What damage?' I asked as I stooped down beside her and brushed the dust away from her visor.

'Lots,' Riss replied. 'Her suit put her into a coma as the only way to keep her alive.'

I gazed at her face. It was hardly recognizable since it was sheened with blood, but then I didn't suppose my face looked too good either. After a moment I looked up.

'Flute will be here shortly,' said Riss, before I could ask, 'though we will need to move to a clearer area for pick up.'

I stood then, turned and limped towards where Penny Royal had been located. In a moment I got a clear view of the centre of the crater and this confirmed what I had glimpsed earlier. The black AI had done it again: it had involved itself, it had been the fulcrum over which events had pivoted. And then it had disappeared. No explanations, no help, just there like a deus ex machina with a morbid sense of humour and little regard for the details, then gone. Yet, as I gazed at the empty area ahead, I felt no anger at all. I suddenly felt at peace with myself because I knew the denouement was due, just as I knew precisely its location.

A roar now impinged on my consciousness and I turned, leaning back to look up because I had no neck movement in my suit. The *Lance* dropped down, probably on grav – the roar only issuing from steering thrusters as Flute positioned the ship right to land it in the crater. Seeing the ship here, in this setting, I was struck by the sheer size of the thing. I turned back, then froze. Two people had appeared on the scene. They were clad in quite antique-looking space suits but the pulse-rifles they carried looked state-of-the-art. Damn! When I'd penetrated Mr Pace's mind I'd found nothing to suggest that he wasn't alone. However, though a loner in tendency he had still used people to run his operation.

'These are from Pace's ship?' I asked Riss.

'Yes.'

I started walking back towards them, hurting because I was forcefully trying to disguise my limp.

'Don't worry,' Riss added. 'These are human and not resistant to a collimated diamond ovipositor.'

I let the limp reassert, then over general suit com asked, 'Who are you and what do you want?'

'Now there's a thing,' replied the gruff voice of a man. 'The first is easy to answer but the second is tricky. You're Thorvald Spear, aren't you?'

'I am.'

'And that, I guess, is what's left of Mr Pace.' One of the figures pointed down at those same remains.

'It is.'

'In that case,' the man threaded the strap of his pulse-rifle over one arm and held out one hand, 'I would like to shake your hand.'

I recognized the face I could see through his visor, but had to seek assistance from my aug. I'd never actually met this man, but he had been as intricately involved in my affairs as Penny Royal itself.

'Captain Blite,' I said. 'What brings you here?'

'It's a long and strange story,' he began.

'Then it is one that will have to wait,' I interrupted. 'My companion and I are injured, and we need to get on the move because I have an appointment to keep.' I headed over to Sepia, stooped down and slid my hands underneath her and picked her up.

'Where are you going?' asked Blite.

'To Panarchia.'

'Of course,' he said, shooting a glance towards his companion. 'I would like to say we're done.' He grimaced. 'My particular fascination with Penny Royal has cost me too much and I would like to end that now and go back to the Polity.'

'But we can't,' said his companion.

'No,' Blite shook his head. 'I have crewmen to retrieve. We'll follow you.'

17

Sfolk

The ship had immediately warned Sfolk of the arrival of another ship in the system and, even from the fusion fire of a sun, he was able to focus the Atheter starship's sensors on that vessel. He recognized it immediately as the destroyer that Penny Royal had been incepted inside, and the one that had come close to being destroyed by Cvorn until grabbed by Sverl – the one containing the human Thorvald Spear. He watched it head to one planetoid and a shuttle being dispatched to the surface. And then, close scanning its destination, he saw that Penny Royal was there. How the AI had got there he had no idea. His instruments did describe certain U-space phenomena related to the AI, but what they meant was unclear.

When the second ship arrived and railgunned the surface, Sfolk immediately began to take the starship up, but then, just beyond the flat plates his claws were bonded into – the controls of this ship – a black diamond winked into existence.

'Wait,' said Penny Royal. 'Your time will come.'

Sfolk waited and carefully watched the events playing out on the surface, utterly baffled by their purpose. It seemed to him that Penny Royal was behaving like the extremadapts that had occupied this system: setting opponents against each other for entertainment. However, he saw when the AI shifted: the tight U-signature and the brief vacuum sphere that collapsed without attracting the notice of the opponents on the surface. It seemed it was not even waiting out the result of that conflict. It appeared again briefly in orbit of the planetoid as the human and the meta-human came together in final combat, but didn't stay for the outcome of that either.

Sfolk knew at once when the AI was back: sensors informed him of the intrusion and internal countermeasures flicked to a high setting; a U-space gate instantly opened in the centre of the ship somewhere below Sfolk. He even understood the purpose of the gate: it was a way to counter U-jump missiles by routing them away into U-space, which was interesting, for it was a defence the prador did not possess. However, the gate flicked off a moment later and a dark presence now weighed heavily in Sfolk's consciousness and body. Sfolk understood that he was *becoming* the ship. Meanwhile he continued to watch the fight on that distant planetoid and saw it run to its conclusion.

'Thorvald Spear killed the other one,' he commented.

'Of course,' Penny Royal replied, then routed coordinates into Sfolk's mind. The timing, he felt, was eerily perfect for, even as he started the ship's drive to take it up from the sun, its systems reported that energy levels were now at their maximum.

'Stealthily,' Penny Royal added.

Sfolk required no more instruction than that as he fired the fusion drive and skated around the surface of the sun on an amalgam of grav-engines and hardfields, both anchoring in U-space and pushing against it. He no longer needed to try and force this into his understanding of the universe; he simply did understand it, now at an almost instinctive level. Half a circumference around the sun, he flung the ship up on fusion, the ship glowing like a star itself then blinking out as chameleonware (far in advance of anything even in the Polity) hid it from view. Sfolk baulked a little when the U-space drive started seemingly too early and too close to such a massive gravity well, but realized an instant later that the feeling related to his earlier understanding of how these things worked, and not to the present formidable machine he controlled.

As the starship slid smoothly into underspace, Penny Royal entered the control room. Eyeing the entity, Sfolk realized it was bigger now and its surface spines were perpetually in motion. It seemed energetic . . . almost excited.

'My time will come?' he enquired.

'Concentrate on understanding your weapons,' the AI told him. 'You will need full understanding if you are to prevail.'

Spear

As I stepped into the cabin, I felt Sepia attempting to restore our aug connection. It had taken her a while, with some assistance from Riss, to reinstate the device, and now it was working. After a hesitation I allowed the connection, for she had already shown how she took precautions with it. Leaning against her dressing table, she glanced up at me, a quizzical smile on her face. She'd dressed in a short skirt and tight almost transparent blouse, put red highlights in her hair and used make-up on her face, but my gaze still strayed to her right leg, which ended below her knee.

The autodoc had finished working on the both of us a day ago, but I was puzzled that she had refused a prosthetic – there were some aboard. She'd instead knocked the grav down in her cabin and, just recently, loaded instructions to the ship's system so one of its autofactories could make the item I had now brought to her. It was a boot, but one of a very odd design.

'Bring it over,' she instructed, then hopped over and sat down in her dressing table chair. 'Help me put it on.'

The boot was constructed of sliding scales of chain-glass

with an intricate webwork of carbon nano-tubes and other meta-material structures on its inside. It extended up her thigh and connected via skin-stick surfaces. The knee and the ankle and foot of the thing could hinge and move just like a normal foot. In fact, the whole thing wasn't much thicker than her actual leg had been. It was motorized and could be controlled by an aug connection, power supplied by laminar storage modules inset in each of the scales. Yet it was hollow right down to where its toes should have been, and I wasn't sure why.

I stepped over and stooped down before her with the thing. She raised her stump and swung it towards me, and at that point I noticed a curious thing. After her amputation the autodoc had sealed across with syntheskin, her leg ending in a clean rounded nub. That nub had now developed a distinct protrusion at its centre, red capillaries and a slightly bruised look. In the end of the protrusion I could see an even line of five further small nodules.

'Do you understand yet?' Sepia enquired.

I suddenly got it. In the Polity the usual response to the loss of a limb was a prosthetic followed by a tank-grown and organically printed replacement made from the recipient's own tissues. However, there were other methods . . . I decided not to show off my own knowledge. 'Perhaps you could explain?'

'Besides a particularly sophisticated nanosuite I have some interesting genetic tweaks from my mother's side of the family: a combination of DNA strings from amphibians and flatworms.' She paused as I got the boot in place, pushing it up until the top nearly reached her knickers, the warmth of her thighs pressing against my hand, then I activated the skin-stick patches all down the rest of her leg – actions that seemed more intimate than anything I had done before with her. 'But of course you do know what I'm talking about.'

Difficult to prevaricate with such a close aug connection.

'How long?' I asked

'By the time we reach Panarchia my leg will have regrown,' she explained, 'but it will still need support for some weeks after that as the bone hardens.'

'The muscles?' I enquired.

'You didn't check the blueprint I used?'

'Some.'

'Perpetual stimulation as they grow and afterwards.' She reached down and patted her new hollow leg. 'It's a longer process without this but still works. I had a similar arm sleeve about fifty years ago after a nasty infection from an alien fungus.'

I moved back and stood.

'How do you feel about this?' she asked, standing also.

How did I feel about my present squeeze being part flatworm and amphibian and being able to regrow her limbs?

'I think it's great,' I said, 'since we don't have the facilities for growing or otherwise constructing you a new limb aboard.'

'Good, because some people find this . . . difficult.'

I reached out, grabbed her around the back of her neck and pulled her close. Kissed her. When we finally parted I said, 'I've had quite a bit of involvement in this sort of thing, and I am just fucking glad you're alive.'

I glanced towards the bed but she pushed me away. 'Tell me about Blite.' She began walking round her cabin, testing out her ersatz limb. Her motions were jerky at first but quickly began improving. I noticed the grav in her cabin slowly increasing as she walked.

'Interesting situation,' I said. 'Mr Pace was a man of many facets. He wanted to die, he wanted to either kill Penny Royal or put a spanner in that AI's machinations, but he was also an artist.'

Sepia gave me a doubtful look.

'Blite was caught up with Penny Royal for a long time. He lost his ship, in fact he lost it twice. Some of his crew were killed.' I paused to try and put in order what the man had told me as, when I had struggled to carry Sepia, he had taken her off me and carried her into the *Lance*.

'When Penny Royal first boarded *The Rose* – Blite's ship – it offered him payment for his services, despite the fact he couldn't withhold those services. You see, he had encountered the AI before and lost crewmembers to it. The payment was memplants – recordings of those crewmembers that were killed. Later it paid him with further memplants, for which he claimed reward from the Polity.' I shook my head in wonderment. 'All Penny Royal's victims whose recordings reside in the spine . . . even now some of them may be walking round alive again.'

'Complicated,' she opined.

'Yes, it is that . . . Having lost another crewmember because of the AI when the second ship – the *Black Rose* – was destroyed, Blite wanted out, and eventually he ended up in a position where Mr Pace provided him with the perfect opportunity. Pace's ship is loaded with sculptures he made throughout his life. This is a collection Mr Pace did not want broken up after his death and for which he had found a buyer in the Polity. Pace set things up so the *title* of his ship would go to Blite after his death, but not full control. The collection is aboard and the buyer is ready. If Blite takes the collection to this buyer in the Polity, who happens to be a planetary AI, he gets the full payment and full control of the ship.'

'Yet he is following us to Panarchia . . .'

'Yes, as I said, he lost further crewmembers. He thinks it is likely that they too have been recorded and that he will be able to obtain memplants of them from Penny Royal.'

Sepia paused in her pacing and studied me. 'Have you checked?'

It came to me in a rush that of course I could check. It seemed *all* Penny Royal's victims and many of those who died as a secondary result of its actions had recorded to the spine. I could find out if Brond was there, but the others?

'It gets a little more complicated . . .'

'Do tell.' She sat down on her bed.

'There's this forensic AI called the Brockle . . .'

'Tell me about it later,' she said, patting the bed beside her, 'much later.'

Amistad

'I can only open the gate to where it was open before,' said Sverl, 'and, apparently, it will only be one-way.'

'What?'

Sverl gestured towards the Weaver squatting down on his platform.

Amistad propelled himself away from Sverl and, trying his internal Mach drive and grav-engine, found he was managing to key on his surroundings, but had to make adjustments for a strange cork-screwing effect. Within a minute he was settling in vacuum before the Weaver's platform.

'Masada only,' said the Weaver over com.

Amistad just about contained his frustration, and politely enquired, 'Why?'

'Matters are in hand,' said the Weaver, waving one claw generally as he sat complacent on his platform, occasionally tinkering with the odd, mushroom-like control interfaces.

'Look,' said Amistad. 'Penny Royal is going to Panarchia for some kind of . . . denouement with Thorvald Spear. The Brockle is going to see Spear arriving, is going to see Penny Royal there and is going to attack them. Okay, I doubt Penny Royal is going to be physically hurt by that, but what if Spear is? If Spear is killed, the AI might just decide not to bother and let things go.' Amistad had chosen that line of argument since he felt that the Weaver would not be concerned about one human life.

'Penny Royal will not decide otherwise.'

'And then there's the point of transition,' said Amistad.

The big gabbleduck tilted its head to one side as if curious.

Amistad gestured a claw to encompass the surrounding sphere. 'This structure and its enclosing hardfields has been made to take Penny Royal through the event horizon and into the Layden's Sink. Do your design parameters include it being bom-barded with some of the most lethal weapons at the Polity's disposal *at the same time*?'

The Weaver dipped his head gravely. 'That would destroy it.'

Would?

Amistad hadn't expected that, and it took him a microsecond to get back on track. 'So let Sverl open the gate to somewhere other than Masada. Let's open the gate to Earth and pull Polity forces right through here.' Amistad waved towards the shimmer-ing runcible gate. 'That thing's big enough for attack ships and medium-sized destroyers!'

'You have neglected to notice that the sphere is complete.'

'Make a fucking hole in it!'

'No,' said the Weaver. 'Exit by runcible only, and only one-way to the runcible on Flint.'

Amistad hesitated. There was something the Weaver wasn't saying. Had it a reason for not wanting Polity forces here? Per-haps some yet-to-be revealed motive? Maybe the Weaver, having made this sphere, now awaited final payment before completely fucking things up?

'I have to wonder,' said Amistad, ensuring that all his weapons were ready to fire in a microsecond, 'how a massive space-time rift might affect your own position in the universe?'

The Weaver reached down to his tool harness and between the tips of two talons extracted a flimsy-looking thing that looked like the internal auditory workings of a human ear fashioned out of blue metal and glass. This was the self-same device it had used to knock out two security drones on Masada. Amistad backed up, charging his carapace and ramping up internal defences. How would the Polity AIs react if he inadvertently blew away the only living member of the Atheter race?

'I would still only exist in recorded form,' said the Weaver, 'because my existence is predicated on the human race arriving on Masada.'

'What?'

'The paradox would annihilate both the prador and the humans.'

'So you say. Are you sure it wouldn't tilt the balance in your favour just a little?'

'No.' The creature shrugged. 'Though the paradox would not affect my own race – it is too distant.'

Was that it?

'Look,' Amistad decided to be more direct, 'why don't you want Polity forces here?'

'The sphere,' said the Weaver, 'cannot be unwoven.'

'Then let me gate to Earth – we can at least pull some forces through the Well Head runcible.'

The Weaver shook his head, looking tired of the conversation.

'You will see,' he said.

He released the device and it floated up above his head,

rotating in some way. With a click Amistad felt right at the heart of his being, the very substance around him which he had been using both his Mach drive and grav-engine against twisted out of phase just the precise amount. He found himself hurtling away from the Weaver. When he shut down those two drives and began to spin round back towards the creature, a sphere abruptly enclosed him and dragged him on. He knew if he fired any of his weapons now he would end up doing himself more damage than the enclosing field. The runcible gate loomed before him, its interface shimmering and rippling. The field tossed him through, shutting off at the interface.

Amistad fell through, still carrying his earlier impetus, the light gravity of a moon taking hold of him beyond and dropping him skidding on a floor of polished artificial quartz, tearing up flakes of stone.

'Now that will require more than a polish,' said the Flint runcible AI as Amistad turned and accelerated back towards the runcible. Just before he reached the interface he slammed face-first into a hardfield.

'Not a good idea,' said the Flint AI. 'The other end closed immediately after and if you had managed to get through you'd have spent the rest of eternity in U-space.'

'Fuck,' said Amistad, then, 'I need to talk to EC.'

Backing off from the runcible, he turned and surveyed the circular chamber with its numerous exit doors, registration pillars and occasional businesses. The place contained a scattering of technicians in blue overalls that almost seemed like religious attire. There were travellers here too, some sitting in areas separated off by low walls into cafés and restaurants, others inside shops. Scanning beyond this chamber, he found the barracks empty and no ships down on the surface. There were some in near space, but none was military.

'There has to be more than this,' he said.

'We agreed to remove all military assets from the system, as you know.'

'Yeah, but . . .'

'And the agreement is monitored.'

'Yes, it is,' interrupted a familiar voice.

Amistad spun round, tearing up more of the Flint AI's precious floor as he did so, to face a shape suddenly looming beside him. He eyed the big gabbleduck squatting there, recognized it as a hologram and quickly powered down his weapons.

'You were tolerated in your erstwhile position as warden of Masada,' said this manifestation of the Atheter AI, whose physical form was down on the surface of Masada. 'However, since the Weaver is no longer here to tolerate you and my instructions for the interim have been very precise, you must leave now.'

'Why?' said Amistad, already knowing the answer.

'Because you are a military asset.'

Amistad wanted to argue that, but the agreement between the Polity and the Weaver was still clear in his mind. If he didn't leave, it could mean that the Polity lost any foothold here at all, and the method of that loss could be grievous. To confirm this, the Atheter AI linked a visual feed. This showed a giant white hooder rearing up from the surface of Masada where it had been creating an intricate sculpture fashioned of bones. They were old bones this time, not the recently stripped remnants of one of its victims. The threat was there. If Amistad didn't get out of here fast, the Atheter AI was going to send the Technician itself.

'Route me to Arvis,' Amistad told the Flint AI.

'Done,' the AI replied.

Amistad headed for the runcible, the hardfield blinking out ahead. He walked to the interface then jumped through, finding himself once again in zero gravity. Here a recommissioned war runcible drifted in vacuum. The thing was an octagonal structure two miles across, once used for gating asteroids at the prador. Correcting for the lack of EMR here from the distant binary red dwarf the runcible orbited, Amistad spun slowly, surveying his surroundings.

A fleet of twenty attack ships, like somnolent crows, sat a hundred miles out. Five destroyers clustered over to one side of them. Nearby sat a dreadnought of the lozenge design which, at five miles long, could not have passed through the runcible to get here. Meanwhile, weapons installations on the runcible itself had powered up and Amistad knew that there was enough weaponry pointing at him to turn him into a wisp of vapour in a microsecond.

'Data,' came the demand.

Amistad recognized the tone and signature – Earth Central was now linked in and talking to him directly. He took a whole two seconds to put together a précis of events and sent it. That it took a further five seconds before EC replied, confirmed something he had been aware of since ceasing to be warden of Masada: because he had been subverted by Penny Royal, and despite being vetted by forensic AI afterwards, he still was not trusted.

'A military response to the Brockle would be ineffective,' said Earth Central. 'The Well Head runcible is too small. No interference is necessary.'

'Ruthless,' said Amistad.

'Necessary,' Earth Central replied.

'No, I don't think so.' Amistad tried to keep his anger locked down. 'I think it's cowardly. You knew how dangerous the Brockle was, but you failed to act against it before it became a serious problem. You failed to act against it because it could not be legally defined as guilty. Yet you provided the motivation for

441

it to incriminate itself. How many people were there aboard the *High Castle*?'

'Sixty-three, including all artificial forms.'

'So, you saw Penny Royal and the Brockle as problems, one of which would solve the other. You provided the Brockle with the motivation to go after Penny Royal, the means to be effective, and in the acquisition of those means a way to incriminate itself fully.'

'Yes.'

'It was also about deniability,' Amistad added, almost to himself. 'Penny Royal had likely returned to the Graveyard, so you couldn't send in effective military assets without causing a problem with the prador.'

'Quite.'

'You should have destroyed the Brockle when it was aboard the *Tyburn*.'

'You misunderstand. Prior to its voluntary incarceration on the *Tyburn*, the Brockle's situation was such that if it didn't agree to incarceration, any attempt at capture might have resulted in the deaths of thousands. Then, while aboard the *Tyburn*, it always had deep scanning available and could use that ship's drive at any point. Destroying it while it was there was not possible: the *Tyburn* was both its prison and its means of escape. Had we made some attempt against it, it *would* have escaped and it *would* have turned against the Polity. Given time to develop, it would have become as dangerous as Penny Royal.'

'It seems pretty damned dangerous *now*, seeing as it's controlling both the *High Castle* and a Polity fleet.' Amistad found that his weapons had come online again, and he was finding it really difficult to restrain himself from blowing something up. But, here, that would be suicide. 'You didn't know about the origin of the data from the Well Head before you motivated the Brockle to go after Penny Royal, did you?'

'I did not.'

'If the Brockle now succeeds against Penny Royal we are in a world of shit. Something has to be done.'

'It is my calculation that Penny Royal will succeed in its aims, while the Brockle will fail, quite likely terminally.'

'Quite likely!' Amistad paused, then continued, 'So if Penny Royal doesn't deal with the Brockle, you then send the heavy mob after it?'

'Problematic.'

'What?'

'If the Brockle retreats into the Graveyard, as seems likely, we will not be able to pursue. Relations with the Kingdom are at a low ebb, currently.'

'Why?'

'The Brockle used the fleet to destroy many King's Guard ships.'

'So you can't go after the Brockle because that will infringe agreements. The Brockle, controlling a small Polity fleet in the Graveyard, is an infringement in itself. Doubtless the king will send further ships after the Brockle, also infringing agreements. Those ships will be destroyed by the Brockle because the prador don't have anything to protect them from U-jump missiles . . . Now, did you just fuck up big time or are you trying to restart the war with the prador?'

'The situation will resolve satisfactorily,' Earth Central insisted. 'You must now leave this area.'

'*Satisfactorily*? If Penny Royal does not get its redemption are you sure it'll enter the black hole? Really sure?'

'I calculate that it will, despite Thorvald Spear's death . . .'

'You're forgetting Flute and Riss . . .'

'I am not,' EC replied. 'There is also a female with Spear called Sepia to take into account.'

Thinking fast, Amistad understood: Earth Central was sure that Penny Royal would enter the Layden's Sink black hole no matter what, and knew what the black AI wanted from Thorvald Spear. However, the leading AI of the Polity was not sure whether Penny Royal would turn against the Brockle. It started to become clear. EC *had* known about the Well Head long before Amistad had realized what was going on. EC *had* known that the Brockle would eventually go to that location after Penny Royal and that the result of that would be the black AI's failure to gain redemption, and likely the death of Thorvald Spear. Because of that failure and because of that death Penny Royal would definitely turn on the Brockle and destroy it, prior to entering the black hole. The knotty problems of two dangerous renegade AIs solved, the fleet that had destroyed King's Guard ships, itself destroyed. All neatly bundled up and resolved.

Had he contained organic guts rather than densely packed technology Amistad would have felt sick. However, he did feel his anger gain new heights.

'You *bastard*.'

'Your routing is in,' said EC. 'You are going to Cheyne III, where you will await further examination by forensic AI.'

EC had succeeded in driving the Brockle out of the *Tyburn* and incriminating itself, and putting it in Penny Royal's sights, but what had it achieved beyond that? The destruction of those King's Guard ships . . . were they part of some power play against the prador? Amistad suspected so. EC had ostensibly managed to send a deniable force against Penny Royal, which also unequivocally demonstrated the Polity's military superiority to the prador. How similar, wondered Amistad, were the more *advanced*

AIs? So similar that they all played complicated games with the lives of their lesser brethren, and humans and prador?

Amistad fired up his internal drives and drifted back towards the runcible. As he did so he began searching his extensive caches of computer weaponry, while designing tactical responses with his physical weaponry. He recalled in perfect detail everything he knew about the runcible facility on Cheyne III. One thing he was damned certain about: he would not be staying on that world for long.

The Brockle

The four disruptor missiles detonated at points in U-space relative to the surface of the hardfield enclosing the giant sphere. Simultaneously four CTD imploders detonated in the real at exactly the same moment as a gravity wave arrived. The visible detonations spread in discs, striated and iridescent. The sphere actually juddered sideways, the hardfield enclosing it deforming slightly and bruised to deep amber. The particle beam strikes arrived next: twelve of them focused on the centre of this bruise. If the Brockle's calculations were right, then the underlying rwist absorbing all this energy would overload local U-space and, just for a second, the runcible would fail to function. Precisely timed to that theorized second, a U-jump missile presently tried to materialize in the heart of that sphere, its CTD loading measured in the gigatons.

Nothing happened.

Now established completely inside all the ships of the Polity fleet, the Brockle gazed through millions of sensors. It was in command of immensely powerful weapons at the cutting edge of Polity research, and it was simmering with frustration. The

445

sphere seemed impenetrable. Shoaling round inside a cavity inside the *High Castle* where once the Tuelin Suite had been, the total number of its units aboard this ship having been increased to nine hundred during the journey here, the Brockle lapsed into rage, shedding electrostatics. It wanted to destroy something, but nothing inessential was immediately available – the Tuelin Suite was already being reprocessed, its materials even then being formed into more units of the Brockle itself.

'Missed,' came a communication.

The Brockle immediately sent viruses, self-assembling worms, in fact a cornucopia of lethal computer life, which in the virtual world resembled the Brockle in the physical one.

'Surely you know that's not going to work now,' said Sverl.

The Brockle wanted to shut down communications with the erstwhile prador, but that would be self-defeating because those communications might eventually afford a route inside the sphere. With a deliberate effort, it calmed itself. Yes, sending everything at once had been foolish and had only come close to working against Amistad because the Garrotte persona had fooled the drone. When Sverl had opened communications again, the Brockle had limited itself to sending small pieces which might eventually assemble into something a bit more dangerous. Though – it checked vectors – there might not be enough time for that. Layden's Sink now lay ten light minutes away and, at its current rate of progress the sphere would reach it in two solstan days.

'So are you going to remain inside that sphere when it drops into the black hole?' the Brockle asked.

'I think not,' Sverl replied. 'We do have a runcible in here, you know.'

'Then why your delay in using it?'

'I'm waiting for Penny Royal.'

'Who will arrive via the runcible?'

After a minutely perceptible delay, Sverl replied, 'I guess.'

From this the Brockle surmised that Sverl didn't know precisely how Penny Royal was going to arrive, but that he did know something else and didn't want to reveal either his ignorance or his knowledge. No matter. Calmer now, the Brockle was also working out what had gone wrong with the previous attack. It had made assumptions about something difficult to measure: the sphere's underlying U-space twist was not yet at its full loading and easily absorbing hits without the local U-space overload and concomitant brief runcible failure. However, that loading would increase as it drew closer to the black hole and it seemed likely that Plan A would work. With the twist sucking up energy as the sphere approached the black hole's event horizon, loading would reach its maximum . . .

At that moment the Brockle had another of those epiphanies that had become more frequent as it *grew*. It began making rapid calculations throughout its units at such an intensity that some of them became so hot they began to radiate. Finally reaching its conclusion, it realized that it was a mathematical certainty that right on the event horizon the underlying twist would turn the full three hundred and sixty degrees and lead to the implosion of the hardfield. This was as certain as a spaceship, accelerating through realspace, hitting infinite mass when it reached the speed of light. Some of that energy would have to be routed out of the hardfield and U-twist circuit. This could not be done by runcible. Therefore, at the event horizon the hardfield would have to be shut down for some kind of energy ejection. Of course, this was why the sphere itself had been constructed so strongly – to resist the tidal forces of the black hole, no matter how briefly.

The Brockle pondered this further. As far as it understood

the situation, Penny Royal was not actually within that sphere yet. The underlying U-twist, being taken round to its limit, would make it difficult for anything coming into the sphere from elsewhere by any U-space method, though leaving would be less of a problem. The Brockle knew that the AI had its own methods of travelling through U-space, in fact, was now beginning to understand how it itself could so travel. However, the black AI would not be entering the sphere like a U-jump missile because the runcible would act on it just as it did on such missiles. It would have to use the runcible and, because of that twist, it would probably require some kind of realspace anchor within the sphere. This aspect was probably what Sverl was being coy about.

Nevertheless: a runcible. In practical terms runcibles were a closed system – a tunnel through U-space with impenetrable walls – which meant that somewhere Penny Royal would have to enter the real, in its entirety, then enter a runcible to reach the sphere. Of course, this was why it had hijacked the *Azure Whale* with its three evacuation runcibles aboard. Wherever it brought itself into the real through one of those runcibles before transferring to the sphere was another vulnerable point . . .

It wasn't relevant.

Those runcibles could now be anywhere in the galaxy and the chances of the Brockle locating them were remote. Its best chance of destroying the sphere was when it reached the event horizon. Penny Royal would be inside by then and, at that point, the Brockle would direct the full firepower of this Polity fleet against it. If the hardfield shut down for an energy ejection, the sphere would be destroyed. If it didn't shut down, the twist would go past its recovery point and the hardfield would implode, crushing the sphere and Penny Royal down into a singularity – all that order disrupted and crushed.

All the Brockle had to do was wait.

Spear

As we arrived and I began viewing sensor data directly via my aug, I felt a surge of déjà vu. However this time it was not the effect of someone else's memories but my own. Panarchia lay only a little way ahead – it seemed Flute was getting better and better at calculating U-jumps – and just an hour with the fusion drive and steering thrusters put us in orbit of that world.

Blite, in Pace's ship, arrived much further out and would take some hours to get to us. As I focused my attention on the world, I wondered if I should bother waiting.

The déjà vu came laced with a strange species of nostalgia, yet it seemed ridiculous to feel that way about a place where I had died. I remembered the attack ship that brought in my bio-espionage unit – it had been of an old design now only seen in the Graveyard owned by traders or smugglers, and its AI had been an odd creature that always spoke as if it had taken too many drugs. The attack ship took us straight down to the surface, covered by anti-munitions from a dreadnought in orbit The prador force on the surface of the world was a small one that the Polity forces already down there, under General Berners, should have had no trouble overwhelming. There promised to be prisoners, captured data and machinery, and with luck some explanation as to why the prador had placed such a small force on this depopulated Polity world. In reality the system was in a good tactical position for prador fleet deployment and the surface of the world should have been secured by a larger force. What were they up to?

As we descended, high-powered lasers and particle beams taking out missiles fired by big railguns on the surface, hardfields intercepting the remnants and the ship still shuddering under their impact, we began to find out. Even as my team debarked from the attack ship an intense light glared in the sky and that druggy AI informed us that the dreadnought had just been destroyed. The attack ship launched but didn't get higher than a few miles before something punched right through it, gutting it with plasma fire and the detonation of its own munitions. The railgun bolt then hit the ground below and my team and I were swept up in the shockwave like leaves. I survived, but five of the eight bio-espionage experts with me didn't. When Captain Gideon found us, we'd managed to gather the remains of our fellows and to salvage what we could of our equipment. He told us we probably wouldn't need it since, with the massive prador landing force that had just come downs we probably wouldn't be taking prisoners but struggling to avoid becoming prisoners ourselves.

'It was bad,' said Sepia, watching me.

'Yes, it was,' I agreed. Obviously my feelings had been bleeding across our link.

'But tactically I still find what happened here baffling.'

'It was simple enough.' I gestured at the world now shown in all its glory up in the screen fabric. 'A small force of prador was left as a lure to a larger Polity force. When that arrived, it was isolated by an even larger prador force that had been in hiding – not captured or destroyed, but corralled and left as bait for rescue attempts.'

'No.' She shook her head. 'It still doesn't make sense.'

I continued gazing at Panarchia. The world looked familiar but I could see that it had changed. The colours there were different, swirls of cloud more tightly wrapped, flashes of thunderstorms everywhere, as if the war had never stopped down there. Aurora swept through the ionosphere in curtains of green, pink and electric lemon.

'What doesn't make sense?' I asked.

'Though that was early in the war, by then we knew the prador and they knew us.' I glanced across at her. She had her foot up on the desk – well on its way to growing back. 'The prador had to know that the AIs would not waste a fleet in an attempt to rescue eight thousand men stranded down on the surface. They had to know that the AIs simply wouldn't countenance such a loss of ships.'

'A fleet was here, nevertheless,' I said.

'Yes, being fed by factory station Room 101. But ships started gating through from that station far too early for them to be a response to what happened there.' She indicated the screen.

'You've been checking history files, I take it,' I said, and resisted an impulse, old as humanity, to say, 'You don't understand. You weren't there.'

'I have,' she replied. 'And I have to wonder where one might stop at that trap-within-a-trap thing . . .'

'Meaning?'

'Berners' division was trapped and used to lure in a Polity fleet. It shouldn't have worked but the Polity fleet duly arrived slightly prematurely. It received a pounding from the prador but, in reality, they were affordable losses. While the prador losses were less in terms of ship numbers, they were ships they could not afford to lose because they did not have the kind of production facilities the Polity was making. Sure, they had their own shipyards, but they had nothing like Room 101.'

'That sounds about right,' said Riss. I glanced over to see the drone enter the bridge, having returned from her abode in the weapons cache. 'The Polity apparently accepts the challenge but uses it as a way of savaging the prador again.' She paused. 'We had plenty of disposable assets because we could manufacture our soldiers . . .'

Yes, all those minds copied and recopied, mixed, briefly tested and sent out to battle from Room 101. Minds like Penny Royal's and Riss's. I felt suddenly very uncomfortable with the notion.

'The realities of industrialized warfare,' I said. 'Heroism is less relevant than firepower and tactics, and all those less important than the production line.'

'It was one of those battles,' said Sepia. 'The ones where it looked like the Polity was losing but in reality it sucked up prador resources, leading to their eventual defeat.'

'They weren't defeated,' said Riss, now floating up off the floor, sliding across through the air and coming down to coil on the console. There she tucked her head down, as if that was the end of her input for the moment.

Sepia gave me a look. 'They started negotiating. When had they done that before? It's arguable that, if the Kingdom had still been strong after the usurpation, the new king would have carried on fighting.'

'Arguable, yes.'

'May I interrupt?' asked Flute over the intercom.

'You just did, but do continue.'

'I have detected a familiar anomaly down on the surface.'

Riss's head came up then.

'Take us down and land beside it,' I said, sitting upright.

'I can't – the terrain is rough.'

I felt the skin on my back creeping as I said, 'Don't tell me. The anomaly is down in a mountain range which, before the war, the colonists called the Scalings.'

After a pause Flute replied, 'Correct.'

'Take us down as close as you can.' I would have preferred to have gone down by shuttle and have had Flute up here to cover us. But, no shuttle now being available . . .

452

The fusion drive kicked in and the world began to grow larger. As we drew closer, Flute threw up a frame to give us a close view of the mountains. Even after a hundred years I could see evidence of the cataclysm that had occurred there: banks of scree from shattered rock, impact craters in which molten rock had set solid and flat, and the tangled remains of tanks and troop carriers. However, some life had returned: ground-fig tangled in the remains of one tower, giant rhubarbs had gathered around the troop transports, and green and purple vegetation coated many surfaces.

Finally Flute focused in on the flat pan of stone in the centre of a crater. Here squatted Penny Royal, surrounded by a ring of those globular white hardfield generators. I stared at the scene, troubled. The stone Penny Royal squatted on seemed flatter than in the other craters clustered nearby, almost as if it had been levelled with a grinder and then polished. The mounds of rock encircling the crater looked far too even to be natural. The whole scene appeared staged but, then, it likely was. It seemed everything that had happened since my resurrection had been leading me here. I checked the scale of what I was seeing and realized that Penny Royal must now measure nearly fifty feet across . . .

As we descended into the atmosphere, space took on a green then a yellow hue and continued to shade towards yellow, the stars gleaming like emeralds, gradually fading. Clouds like flattened masses of white intestines were lit from the underside by constant lightning flashes. The storm writhed above a yellow plain veined with rivers and bruised by patches of purple and ochre, which might be either forests or mineral deposits. Eventually I made out the spine of a mountain range, capped with blue-tinted snows, writhing ahead of us towards the Scalings as they rose over the horizon.

A roar was penetrating now and wisps of vapour flicking across the view. We punched into cloud, only briefly, flashes of lightning on either side like fast-burn sheets of fuse paper, then out into yellow shade, flying past the stems of anvil clouds that were like vast battleships, rain occluding vision until Flute programmed it from existence. It occurred to me then to wonder how suitable the *Lance* was for landing on a world like this. Certainly destroyers like it were made to be *capable* of so landing, but were provided with shuttle craft because it wasn't a great idea to land something so large and unwieldy.

'We okay, Flute?' I asked.

'No problem,' Flute replied.

I auged for information on destroyer landings. Such ships had more than enough redundancy in their systems for planetary landings and could land, without damage, on worlds where the gravity would reduce their passengers to slurry on the decks. The decision to provide them with shuttles was a tactical one, since destroyers were valuable military assets which it would be foolish to put in such a vulnerable position as the surface of a world.

Eventually we were flying through foothills, a river valley winding along below us. I wondered if it was the one that I and Captain Gideon and his men had been escaping along when Penny Royal annihilated Berners' division, incidentally incinerating us in the process. Flute finally brought us to a halt above a flat area which looked like another impact site where the rock had melted and levelled itself and now lay webbed with milky-looking vines dotted with round blue and white fruit. I thought about what, in my mind, had come after Penny Royal's bombardment of this place.

As the *Lance* settled down on the ground, I tried to repress my memories of waking up a captive of the prador, of seeing a failed attempt to install a full thrall in Gideon, and all the horror

that followed. All those memories were false, because I had actually died here. The false memories of my life were unpleasant in
the extreme. The things that had been done to me were of the
kind that left a person mentally as well as physically damaged.
This was why the person those things had actually happened to
had had the memories excised. Why then had I retained them?
And why had Penny Royal inserted them into my mind in the
first place? Penny Royal's manipulations were complicated in
the extreme but, as far as I could gather, that AI never did anything without some kind of reason.

The *Lance* settled with a grinding I could feel through my
feet. Checking the system, I saw that Flute had brought it down
on its belly and not bothered with the landing feet. A further
check revealed that we were about ten miles from Penny Royal
and that there was an easy but steep path there. I checked the
ship's inventory to see what we would take. Two mesh-armoured
enviro-suits were a must, since we had landed close to sundown
and the octupals would be active during the night. Some rations,
perhaps, and definitely water, as any streams might still be laced
with wartime contaminants. Weapons, certainly: there were dangerous creatures about. And, of course, I would take the spine.

'I see no reason to delay,' I said.

'Me neither,' said Sepia, standing also.

I didn't even attempt to try and dissuade her. Despite what
had happened to her during our last encounter with Penny
Royal, I knew the only way to stop her would be to lock her in
the ship, and she would never forgive me for that.

We headed from the bridge and got ready, Riss dogging our
footsteps.

18

Amistad

As Amistad fired up his fusion engine and streaked through the Cheyne III runcible, he knew preparations had been made to receive him, and he was glad. His biggest problem, he had realized as he had prepared for this, wasn't escaping Cheyne III and getting to where he wanted to go, but doing so without killing anyone. It seemed like a quite ridiculous idea to cause mayhem and leave hundreds of casualties behind him just to save the lives of two humans and two AIs.

Hurtling across the chamber, he scattered skeletal Golem with a sweep of one claw, then swiped across the chain-diamond edge of the other claw before finally slamming into the far wall, leaving a huge dent. From this position he observed the pedestal-mounted EM pulse weapon and hardfield projector that was intended to capture him beginning to topple. Congratulating himself on correctly calculating both its position and where to slice through, Amistad decided it was time to get explosive.

His first missile streaked back across the runcible reception chamber, punched through the wall beside the runcible itself and detonated on an armoured pipe containing skeins of optics. There went all the optic feed cams in the area, and the EM mine Amistad spat out to detonate with an actinic flash in the middle of the chamber took out all the radio frequency pin cams too, which meant the runcible AI would now have to deploy its swarm of drone cams. His second missile punched up through a small unarmoured part of the ceiling, blew a side charge to turn it sharply, then detonated a rolling planar load to slice across above the armour, s-con cables severed and discharging, security drones dropping out of their holes like ripped-out eyeballs, weapons dead and powerless. By then Amistad had launched himself again, an autogun was peppering the wall behind him with million-volt discharge shells.

Yes, that's what Amistad was doing: he was going to rescue Thorvald Spear, Sepia catadapt whatsername, Riss and Flute. Sure he was.

In preparation for his arrival, the area had been cleared of . . . fragile creatures. Now Amistad slammed headfirst into a grappler. The big robot was all heavy ceramal, massive joint motors and horribly fast reflexes. It looked vaguely humanoid – something like a sumo wrestler as painted by someone from the cubist movement, in shades of shipyard ironwork. He hit it hard, gripping it with his claws and spinning it towards the autogun, then leaving it shuddering as discharge shells covered it with miniature lightnings. Landing right beside the runcible, Amistad knew he had a few seconds' breather, because the systems here would not risk hitting the runcible itself.

He observed ports opening and insectile cam drones swarming in, just as predicted. He focused on two of them, hit them with a targeting laser straight in their optics and pumped through a computer virus. It was an old one, only slightly adjusted for this place, from his extensive and esoteric collection of the things. It was, he recollected, one he had copied from Penny Royal's mind.

Another grappler was now closing in, while armoured shutters were opening here and there in the walls, the polished maws of particle cannons protruding. Simple tactics: the grappler would wrestle him away from the runcible, whereupon the particle cannons would open fire. The runcible AI wasn't trying to kill him yet, but had probably decided he might be a bit less dangerous with his legs and claws burned away and his sensors and weapons ports fused. He waited, and in the time it took the grappler to reach him, Amistad's virus had penetrated the two cams and propagated through the rest of them. The grappler slammed into him, closing a diamond-faced clamp hand on his claw with the chain-diamond cutter. The virus routed back through to the AI and a microsecond later all the cams simply dropped out of the air, severing the link.

The virus was a Trojan, however, ostensibly an attack on the AI but really assembling a worm that diverted away into runcible sub-systems. The grappler began to drag Amistad away from the runcible, shiny particle cannon mouths swivelling in the walls as if salivating with eagerness.

Fuckit.

Amistad fired up his own particle cannon and began burning into the robot's almost rusty-looking armour. The thing was tough. The particle beam – powerful enough to punch a hole through ceramal armour and even make an appreciable dint in prador armour – was only slowly peeling away layers, its energy splashing into the air. Amistad extruded a sticky mine and spat it towards his opponent. The thing clung like soft fruit, then ignited, the blast on the robot's surface a sun-hot slow burn.

The grappler released its hold and staggered back, a glowing hole cut deep into its torso. Meanwhile, the worm had found its target – the runcible routing system – and was delicately inputting coordinates. Amistad fired a missile straight into the cavity he had burned. The explosion lit up the robot from the inside, light glaring from joints, ports in its body, from its eyes and mouth. Somehow, it staggered forwards again. Amistad backed up. He didn't want to carry this battle elsewhere, but now other shutters were opening and more robots appearing. Meanwhile his sensors were being bombarded by a cornucopia of hostile computer life.

He fired two more missiles, straight into that cavity, then quickly scuttled back through the runcible interface. In the new chamber he found himself in zero gravity as he scanned his surroundings. Not so heavy here. The Cheyne III runcible chamber had been adapted to capture him – this had not. He spun in mid-air, multiply firing in every direction, blowing out and burning weapons ports, frying security drones, releasing viruses and worms to seize control of everything in the area. Some missiles hit him, and a particle beam managed to heat up one claw appreciably. The runcible AI here, which was apparently located in an ancient spotter drone, tried to turn on grav to distract him, but he slammed against the floor and finished the job.

A second later the grappler stumbled through the runcible interface, fires burning inside its body, black smoke rising off it. Amistad backed up again, ready to fire another missile, but the thing took just one step more and fell forwards with a sound as of ten tons of scrap hitting the ground – scrap being what it now was.

'Turn the fucking runcible off,' Amistad instructed.

After a moment the interface winked out. The spotter drone, Owl, out on the surface of the space station named the Well Head, had obviously seen the foolishness of forcing that chore on Amistad, who would likely put a missile straight into the runcible frame.

The Brockle

Inside the other ships of the Polity fleet, the Brockle's other parts had retooled manufacturing to produce still more units. As its thought processes grew faster, covered greater areas of knowledge and its intelligence continued to increase, it only confirmed its earlier speculations. The hardfield would need to shut down. Unless there was some extraneous factor it had missed, it would definitely destroy the sphere. Penny Royal would fail, the Brockle felt confident of that.

Yet, with its steadily expanding mind, the Brockle began to see other . . . aspects. The paradox of Penny Royal already having entered the black hole, and then not having entered it, would rip through the time-space continuum and now the Brockle could precisely calculate the extent of that tear. Yes, it would be across a hundred years and a thousand light years, but the Brockle did not feel that what would be lost had great value.

Except itself.

Much as it was beginning to find the Polity almost alien to its thinking, and like the brilliant child of ignorant parents would like to claim its parentage from elsewhere, the Brockle could not deny that it was a product of the human race and of the Polity. Would it cease to exist? The calculations were complex. Edmund Brockle had been born and had died as a human being long before the end of the war a hundred years ago, and by the end of the war had not been vastly different in form and function from how he had been while imprisoned aboard the *Tyburn*.

So what would happen after the start of the tear through space-time? Disorder, time whirlpools, enclosed loops, negative entropy in some areas while in others energy imbalances would cause vast explosions. Quite likely many suns would go nova while others would cool down to cinders. It was highly probable that pockets of sentient life, and AIs, would continue existing, but the Polity would be finished, as would the Prador Kingdom. The Brockle saw its own chances of surviving all this as about fifty-fifty, albeit not in its present form, and not with its present knowledge. This was tolerable if it resulted in the destruction of Penny Royal. But if there were alternatives, then they had to be explored.

If it was the case that the entity in the Layden's Sink black hole was Penny Royal, then it was possible that the paradox of it not arriving there could be undermined and the time-space continuum would work to heal the rip. For instance, if Penny Royal could be supplanted by some other entity. The nature of paradoxes was, of course, that they were paradoxical. If the paradox was to occur in the future it meant that the Brockle was not even here now . . . on mainline time, but in energy debt down the probability slope in some less probable parallel continuum. However, the Brockle was now increasingly coming to the conclusion that it was on mainline time, that Penny Royal *did not* enter the black hole, but that another AI did.

It is me.

The simplicity was perfect and seemed a confirmation of its entire existence to this point . . . or was this some kind of higher-level arrogance? No, the more powerful an AI became, the tighter became its grip on reality . . . well, up to a point. The Brockle now felt sure it had achieved a state equivalent to or even beyond that of Penny Royal.

Its submind in the dreadnought once occupied by Garrotte informed it just a microsecond before the others. Something was happening in the Panarchia system. An old Polity destroyer had arrived close to Panarchia while Mr Pace's ship had arrived some distance out. The Brockle recognized the destroyer at once and knew that the man Penny Royal had taken such overweening interest in was aboard. The history of that world played through the forensic AI's mind in a few more microseconds, some new data obtained from the mind of Garrotte concerning

461

what had *actually* happened there during the war dropping neatly into place. The Brockle understood the psychology behind it, and that only increased its contempt for its opponent.

Penny Royal had made the massive events it had planned here utterly dependent on the reaction of one simple human. Now that was an incredible arrogance, and a stupid gamble.

The Brockle also realized where the runcible gate to transfer Penny Royal to the sphere was located and understood at once how tightly wrapped were the workings of fate here. Quite obviously it was its destiny to supplant Penny Royal.

Now, more meticulous scanning of the Panarchia system revealed something else. The metals signature of one asteroid was suspicious and, focusing scanners on this object, the Brockle saw a great slablike ship moored to it. Here then was the *Azure Whale*, the cargo hauler Penny Royal had hijacked and, doubtless, now empty of the three evacuation runcibles it had once contained.

The Brockle's subminds were more than capable of dealing with the situation here. In fact, over such a small distance it could remain connected to them, at one with them. And, even if some unforeseen event caused some disconnection, they still knew what to do here.

Until it told them otherwise.

Even as it was thinking these things, the Brockle peeled the *High Castle* away, firing up its fusion drive and accelerated out across the accretion disc. It could U-jump to Panarchia in a moment, but it needed time to make some alterations to itself. Already the ship's internal factories were starting to make a highly modified version of the kind of drive a U-jump missile contained and, when the first of those was ready, the Brockle dispatched one of its units to have the thing installed. Penny Royal certainly contained something similar in each of its individual parts and this, the Brockle was sure, was the black AI's only advantage. It could stay on Penny Royal like a bloodhound, disrupt its plans and perhaps push it to rashness by threatening Thorvald Spear. Eventually it would find the stolen runcible gates on Panarchia. Then it would *itself* go through, supplanting Penny Royal aboard the sphere and ordering its fleet to stand down.

Spear

Flute opened down a ramp door from the weapons cache and we exited that way. As I stepped down ahead of the others I remembered my time here clearly and I suddenly knew, in the pit of my stomach, that I *had* died here. My memories of being a captive of the prador separated out and consigned themselves to the spine along with all the rest. I felt utterly calm but knew things were going to happen here; answers were now available. As my enviro-boot crunched down on a crust of glass, shattering it like shell ice, something arrived in the spine and thence my mind, fulfilling expectation.

I was the war mind Clovis, trapped in a mile-wide scale of wreckage falling into the chromosphere of a green sun. In the remaining sealed corridors around me the humans were charred bones and oily smoke. My Golem had seized up and my only escape tube was blocked by the wreckage of a prador second-child kamikaze. When the salvage crab snatched me from the fire I felt supremely indifferent, because I had accepted the inevitability of oblivion long ago . . .

Next I was the assassin drone Sharp's Committee, Sharpy for short. My limbs were all edged weapons honed at the atomic level, my wing cases giant scalpel blades and my sting capable of punching through laminar armour to inject any of the large collection of agonizing poisons I had created. The prador first-child, with its limbs sliced away, screamed and bubbled as nanomachines ate its mind and uploaded a symphony of data to me. I loved my job of creating terror, because it satisfied my utter hatred of my victims . . .

'What the fucking hell was that?' asked Sepia over envirosuit radio, her voice crackling at first from the charged air, then smoothing out as our suits made adjustment.

'*One piece of the jigsaw,*' I replied via aug.

It took her a moment to reply to that, so I realized that she had damped our connection. I sent her a non-verbal query and she replied, '*Too strong.*'

'*The second is part of me too,*' interjected Riss.

'Let's keep our com to suit radio,' I said. 'Explain it to her.'

Riss continued over radio, 'Room 101 made a selection of memories from the minds of the most successful soldiers, killers, war minds and combined them in the new minds it created. I think we just experienced one part of Penny Royal.'

I stepped over white vines, boots crunching on more of the glass that had been formed by the detonation here. The blue fruits on the vines looked like squat melons, but translucent. I noted dead octupals here and there like discarded gloves, and when I nudged one with my toe it broke into dry fragments. To my right stood an anvil of cloud, dark as iron in the setting sun. The occasional flash of lightning lit the mass from inside. I fell back into memories of Penny Royal.

I was the dreadnought AI Vishnu 12, a name chosen by many of my kind. In the five-mile-long lozenge that was my body I contained weapons capable of destroying the world that lay below, but I was mathematically precise in their use because of the higher purpose I served, the knowledge of my aims and my adherence to duty. However, the world was fully occupied and the fate of the humans below was foregone. My railguns punched a thousand anti-matter warheads down into the planet's core, and I set out to accomplish my next task ahead of the growing cloud of white-hot gas laced with a cooler web of magma . . .

That brought me to a shuddering halt, because there I saw the ruthlessness of a Polity wartime decision. It was one of those *cold* equations. The world had been occupied by massive prador forces but there were many humans down there too, hiding in caves, clinging to survival, avoiding the prador snatch squads and the inevitable horrible fate that awaited those who were captured. The Polity was retreating at the time, the likelihood of its winning the war was remote. Briefly I slid back into the memory because there was more to it than I had immediately seen. I glimpsed a prador ship down on the surface, humans being herded inside by armoured second-children. These were the few who had survived capture and the vicious appetites of their captors. They were on their way to Spatterjay for coring and thralling, which another aspect of me had already experienced.

Feeling the horror of that slung me straight into other memories that hit me like a gut punch. I stumbled, felt Sepia grab my arm and hold me up. The memories of human soldiers impacted: the man whose whole unit was annihilated and who, more for revenge than any sense of duty, managed to evade capture long enough to smuggle a CTD inside a prador lander and even succeeded in escaping and putting some distance between himself and the thing before hitting the remote detonator he had held tight in his sweaty hand all the time. There were others, many of them, but the one connecting theme was emotion driving them to succeed against odds which I knew, at the heart of my being, no AI would have countenanced.

'Emotion,' said Riss.

Yes, I remembered Riss's memories of being created in Room 101. The mantis drone she had escaped with had said to her, 'Great idea to give a factory station AI the empathy and conscience of a human mother so it'll be sure to look after all its children.' This was the reason the Room 101 AI had gone insane. Being forced to create masses of those children to send out into practically hopeless battle to defend itself, the grief had been more than it could stand. It had eventually decided the only way to ensure its children would not suffer would be to kill them all. Only then, as I considered that, did I understand that the children *had* suffered too.

'Room 101 provided many of its children with emotions, with empathy, with the abilities to feel both fear and pain,' said Riss. 'Fear and pain weren't for me, since they would have hampered my function – this was normally given to larger assets the Polity did not want to lose, like destroyers.'

'Empathy,' I said, because of course there was the lesson of Trent: Penny Royal in microcosm, tested and studied.

I turned and looked back at the *Lance*, once named the *Puling Child*, only then realizing how ominous it seemed, and how much it looked like a giant sarcophagus.

In the next moment I saw the sarcophagus-shaped framework of a nascent destroyer shift a hundred feet down a construction tunnel eight miles long. Into the space it had occupied, white-hot ceramal stress girders stabbed in like converging energy beams and were twisted and deformed over hardfields glittering like naphtha crystals. The skeleton of another destroyer was taking shape and was moving on after its fellow, cooling to red in sections as directed gas flows tempered it. I watched the ensuing assembly as the thing was packed with weapons and instruments and sheathed in armour. Inside a remaining cavity, I watched two objects like old petrol engine valves part slightly in readiness. The ship's crystal arrived inside a shock-absorbing package a yard square. It was a gleaming chunk two feet long, a foot wide and half that deep of laminated diamond and nano-tubes, quantum-entangled processing interfaces – boasting even in its microscopic structures complexity beyond that of the rest of the ship. And it bore no resemblance to the black spiny thing it eventually became.

Then I was legion and a collection of parts: version 707 primped and polished by stochastic studies of the survivors of my previous versions. Not fully tested and maybe not even viable. The crystal I resided in had its faults, the quantum processes of my mind could not, by their nature, be exact copies, and time was short, the situation desperate . . .

'Let's keep moving,' I said, straightening up. Though some of what I was experiencing had hit me hard, I now found I could keep it partially suppressed, running in the background.

I glanced over at Sepia. 'You okay?'

'I'm getting a fraction of what you're getting and I feel sick,' she said.

'Well,' I said, 'I guess this is what I was made for or, rather, adjusted to handle.'

By the time we had left the crater and found the path winding up into the mountains the sun had gone down. I was almost glad then to feel the pattering of something against my enviro-suit, and to then look over and see an octupal – a land octopus – pulling itself out of a small pool. At least they weren't all dead, but then, in twenty years they would be. Beside the path I paused to gaze at an object that seemed thoroughly out of place here: an information terminal, probably for tourists, dead, however.

In the time it had taken us to reach this object I had, in my other persona as the mind of a destroyer, entered the chaos of ships outside Room 101. I had absorbed data and understood

467

both human and AI history, as well as the prador and the ensuing war. But at the forefront of my mind were tactical data,
situation reports, casualty reports, an analysis of the latest battle
and my own purpose within that. I'd taken on the crew, including the Golem Daleen and three humans, and was puzzled by
their presence. And I had felt a strange emptiness. They were
there and yet not logically required. Therefore, how much else
was logical? Briefly I saw everything as purposeless patterned
matter without any reason for existence, including myself . . .

Panting on a steep path, I realized that in that last brief
moment I'd experienced a hint of the Penny Royal to come.

'Don't you just love the new smell?' asked the female.

Then as a human I saw her as a mummified corpse when,
with Trent Sobel at my side, I'd gone aboard to assess the
destroyer.

'What is your purpose?' I asked Daleen.

*'It's about participation,' Daleen replied. 'And an inefficiency yet
to be purged from the system, but also a very useful inefficiency when
it comes to massive EMR shutdowns. We are also your conscience.'*

My present self remembered Daleen stripped down and converted, and trying to kill me before I drove the spine through the
Golem's chest. As we continued trudging up into the mountains, and as these events in the life of Penny Royal played out
in my mind, I realized this was during an earlier battle in the war
and not the one that had led to Room 101 tipping off the rails.
The mind of the dreadnought matured rapidly during its deployment, among many other ships, against a prador dreadnought.
An EMR weapon was used during a battle. This weapon disabled all ships on both sides, but critically it was deployed when
vectors were just right, with the result that the prador dreadnought dropped into the accretion disc of a black hole.

'Layden's Sink,' said Sepia.

Yes, of course. I paused to look up into the night sky, but the massive accretion disc wasn't visible. *Shame on Penny Royal,* I thought, *not to have insured this all played out during Panarchia's winter, when the disc sprawled gloriously across the night sky.*

So, it seemed that Penny Royal's first battle was here in this system. And, experiencing the functioning of its mind, I could see that the likelihood of it being included in other battles was remote. The destroyer AI had named itself prior to the conflict. It had called itself Penny Royal, while naming its ship the *Puling Child.* Most ship AIs took on the names of their ships or some truncated version, like Garrotte being the name of the AI of the ship *Michelletto's Garrotte.* That Penny Royal didn't identify with the ship that comprised its body should have been warning enough. That it called its ship a child while naming itself after an abortifactant herb . . .

Penny Royal was damaged from the start – another of those AIs laid down in faulty crystal during the exigencies of war. Its mind was fractured, divided. While on the one hand it felt protective feelings for its crew, who were the necessary risk of loss, another part of it had tipped over the edge into the weird – I suspected this was the birth of that 'eighth state of consciousness', but had yet to understand why there might be more than two. Penny Royal was also aware that, should the state of its mind be closely examined, it would be scrapped. Learning, then, that it was the subject of study did not have good effects . . .

After some five miles I felt Sepia grabbing hold of my arm and guiding me off the path, then sitting me down. I came back to myself with a start and looked around. I was sitting on one of a series of compressed-fibre benches, nearby stood another tourist information terminal. Perhaps the tourists stopped here for a picnic on their way to the scene of Penny Royal's atrocity. The *Lance* was in view down on the plain below, looking even more like something awaiting burial. Aurora cut the sky above cloud masses like jostling boulders in a landslide, but much of the sky was clear and the stars gleamed like gems.

'Penny Royal,' I said, 'was a prototype.'

'Prototype?' Sepia queried.

Now the AI feels the connections, the scanning, the routes opening its mind to screens and other hardware before the woman. It samples her record, realizes she is a human expert in AI, but still cannot fathom how a human mind can do or learn more than the AI can itself. However, the danger remains and it subtly blocks or diverts her intrusion. She will see the largest part of it, and it will be right. She will not plumb the smaller but growing darkness within.

I was lost for a moment in the intensity of that memory, then replayed in my mind what Riss had been saying.

'Penny Royal was the first of a series of ship minds in which feelings were hard-wired,' Riss explained beside me. 'It could feel pain, fear, joy, hate – everything humans are burdened with.'

'Is that such a bad thing?' Sepia asked.

'They weren't properly adjusted,' I said, my throat feeling tight. 'Penny Royal was flung straight into battle with a human AI expert aboard to adjust the levels of what the AI could feel. Too much pain is crippling, as is too much fear and maybe too much joy. The ship minds had to be adjusted to optimum efficiency.'

It was a trial run of a strategy devised by some planetary AI deep inside the Polity. Observing the success of some human units, and some drones programmed for emotional response, it decided to test something that heretofore had been considered a disadvantage: let some AIs be programmed to feel fear, pain, guilt, protective urges and loss, and see how well they did.

While it was mourning the loss of fellows during the battle the rift in Penny Royal's mind grew larger. Its other half, its 'dark child', began establishing control over more ship's systems so as to hide itself. However, no matter what it was feeling, the AI as a whole was absolutely incapable of disobeying its orders . . . in the beginning.

I sat there replaying the battle in my mind. There were some famous ships involved, like the *Stonewater* and the *Vorpal Dagger*. The woman who was supposed to be closely studying Penny Royal's mind was so frightened she took drugs which prevented her paying attention. She missed the changes it was undergoing. During the battle the *Puling Child* also received some severe knocks which resulted in further damage to Penny Royal's crystal.

V12 watches and, while doing so, realizes that various parts of itself are muttering to others. Running self-diagnostics, it discovers a network of fine cracks in its crystal, extending from a single deep fault – an intriguingly even pattern which, without its containing case, would fragment the substance of its mind into numerous dagger-shaped pieces.

And there, of course, in this moment of the memory, I could see the shape of the Penny Royal to come,

'Let's keep going,' I said, standing up.

Crowther

Beware scorpions, Crowther thought, and felt the urge to giggle inanely. However, his amusement died as he remembered that statement had been the first data from Layden's Sink. That it had, essentially, come from the future. Then he felt as if something nasty was squirming into his spinal ports.

'What do you want here?' he asked, adding, when Owl supplied the name, 'What do you want, Amistad?'

'Multi-level scans throughout,' said Owl, privately. 'Amistad, like me, has seriously upgraded since wartime.'

Now having loaded data on the erstwhile war drone, Crowther replied, 'Upgraded on Masada while acting as warden there – that upgrade overlaid on unknown changes he made to himself while studying . . . madness.'

'Not here legally,' said Owl. 'We would have been fore-warned.'

'Oh, really?' said Crowther, gazing through a cam at the smoking remains of the grappler.

'I too am advanced,' said Owl, 'enough to recognize sar-casm.'

Meanwhile Amistad replied, 'I want your well-hopper.'

'You want our well-hopper,' Crowther repeated, now think-ing that he would rather keep the option open for himself and Owl, what with the arrival of that sphere and that fleet, and now Amistad. The odds of something untoward happening and them needing to escape had increased considerably.

'You obviously know what it is,' he said carefully, 'and there-fore know it is not a passenger vehicle. Do you intend to transfer inside it, leaving your body here?'

'No,' said Amistad. The war drone had crossed the arrival chamber to one of the heavy bulkheads – one of those lying between him and the well-hopper.

'We're in trouble,' said Owl.

Oh really, thought Crowther, deciding not to communicate his sarcasm this time. Intrusion alerts had just multiplied. Previ-ously the drone had just been exploring their systems but now he was obviously after something. The well-hopper, of course – the drone was going to take it whether they agreed or not.

'Why do you want it?' Crowther asked, observing the bulk-head panel ahead of Amistad unzipping around its perimeter.

Analysing that, he discovered that the drone had now penetrated even the 'structor nano-machines holding the ship together with bonds stronger than any weld – machines that also constantly fought to maintain the Well Head's integrity against the massive forces in play here. In reply Amistad sent an information package. That 'Beware scorpions' had been as Delphic as anything else from the Well Head and was now, as it was being revealed, just too late. The data opened up in his mind and, seeing it did not contain any attack, he opened it to Owl too.

'Interesting,' said Owl, now also acquainted with Amistad's reasons for wanting the well-hopper.

'Could we fight him?'

'Depends . . .'

'?'

'We might be able to *stop* him. But if he uses all his resources it will cost us the Well Head, and may cost us our lives too.'

'Are you thinking what I'm thinking?' Crowther wanted confirmation of what his other underlying communications had already suggested.

'Yes.'

'Okay, good. Then we do nothing.'

Amistad now trudged through the open bulkhead, which closed behind. Meanwhile, Crowther picked up on intrusion into the well-hopper's system and simply offlined its defences.

'Thank you,' said Amistad.

'Think nothing of it,' said Crowther tightly.

Two more bulkheads went down before the drone came to the circular blast door at the base of the tube containing the well-hopper. Other things had disconnected from their power supplies as an automatic intruder defence, Crowther noted, so he turned the power back on. The blast door hinged open, while the coils in the launch tube now had access to power. Amistad

473

scuttled inside, the blast door closing behind. Crowther really hoped the drone hadn't been lying about when and where he would use the fuser, because if he used it here, as it had been designed to be used, to give the initial escape blast, it would leave a great big hole in the space station.

The coils, which were not for launching but for moving the well-hopper outside for whenever Crowther or Owl thought of some further improvement to make to it, powered up and flung the well-hopper out. With a slight tug of regret, Crowther watched it go, streaking out into space, looking exactly like an old-fashioned bullet, except one with a scorpion clinging on for the ride. Far enough away from the station to cause no problems, the Laumer engine engaged and the bullet disappeared, leaving a trail of photons rucked up from the quantum foam.

'Now let's get that fucking runcible back on,' said Crowther. 'We need to talk to Earth Central and I, for one, am considering taking a short vacation. Very possibly on Earth.'

'Perhaps advisable,' said Owl who, Crowther noted, was for the first time in many years opening an access hatch in the hull and coming inside.

Sfolk

As he waited where instructed by Penny Royal, Sfolk watched a world – one larger than his own prador home world – distort like a rubber ball hitting a wall. The thing was already all but molten, its watery oceans boiled away and continental land masses floating on a sea of magma. As it orbited its sun, the planet continued to take a pounding from the tidal forces of the black hole that both it and the sun were being drawn into.

Sfolk made idle calculations to pass the time. The planet

would manage two more orbits of its sun before those tidal forces finally tore it apart, that was unless massive EMR blasts from explosions closer to the black hole boiled it out of existence – to accurately predict its fate would require the mapping of those inner objects. The sun it orbited would last longer, though it was bleeding incandescent gas into vacuum as if it had been punctured, which was why Sfolk's surroundings were now little better than they had been when he settled this ship on the surface of a hypergiant sun.

'It is time,' Penny Royal told him.

Sfolk experienced a surge of joy as he flung the Atheter starship up out of the accretion disc of Layden's Sink. Engaging chameleonware far in advance of anything the Polity used, he opened up the drive that, as far as he could judge, actually clawed at the fabric of space. New data on Polity ships, now available to him from a download Penny Royal had provided, detailed a Polity drive like this: a Laumer drive. None of the ships lying ahead possessed such a drive, but the end result would be just the same anyway, for they were prey.

The six attack ships, two dreadnoughts and one other design of ship he could find no label for, but which he knew was named the *High Castle*, blossomed with targeting frames, tactical options – a thousand different ways they could be destroyed. Sfolk cancelled all the data concerning the recognizable ships and concentrated on the remaining vessel, which was steadily drawing away from the others. He now digested and understood a fraction of the tactical options, first bubbling with joy, but then growing slightly irritated.

Too easy.

He didn't know if he would ever get another chance to go into battle against the Polity like this and he wanted it to *last* to savour it. The options, as he understood them, described an engagement lasting a mere ten seconds. He cancelled everything and took manual control, ignoring all the warnings the system flicked up, hit fusion and took his ship up away from the disc, then down towards the *High Castle*. He opened up com, probing for a response, and sent a greeting, just before shutting down chameleonware.

'Hello,' he clattered in the prador language, because he knew the AI aboard would understand it. 'And goodbye.'

The initial beam shot – of a kind of particle beam that utilized exotic matter – stabbed as red as blood into existence and carved across the hull of the *High Castle* for a fraction of a second before the Brockle threw a hardfield up against it.

The shot could have carved through to the Polity ship's fusion engines and disabled them. However, Sfolk had deliberately limited its power and scored it across the other ship's hull rather than concentrate it in one place. Shortly after that, the stubbornly insistent tactical displays indicated that Sfolk should now use a gravity-wave weapon to smash up the ship in the same way as a prador put through a rolling mill. Then, perhaps, one of the missiles which, by its stats, seemed similar to a gravity imploder? Numerous railgun missiles were available too. How they had become available he wasn't entirely sure. It seemed the ship, as well as charging up its power supply, had drawn in matter from the fusion reaction in the surface of the hypergiant sun and converted that into physical weapons. Sfolk's tactical displays were again all but screaming at him the hundreds of different ways, and combinations of ways, he could destroy the ship ahead. He overrode them again.

The *High Castle* ignited fusion drive, fired up grav-engines, complemented both of these with steering thrusters and peeled upwards away from the accretion disc at a thousand gravities. Sfolk's ship went into immediate pursuit mode, the air around him thickening like amber. Thoughts suddenly sluggish, he fired a single railgun missile – one of those tumblers – intent on taking out at least some of his opponent's motive power. The ship ahead slewed, throwing out a hardfield. Such was the power of the railgun strike Sfolk expected to see a projector blow, but the Brockle was learning fast. The hardfield slanted at the last second for deflection, diverting the missile away from the engines.

Annoying.

It occurred to Sfolk then that though he possessed a military advantage at the moment, he might well be at a mental disadvantage. Certainly something unusual was occurring aboard that ship because a lot of energy was being expended inside and Sfolk's own tactical displays were changing.

The Brockle was up to something.

Though he hardly understood it, Sfolk used one of the weapons his displays were recommending, and fired up a directed gravity wave. A moment later his tactical display froze, the ship diverted, the structure all around twanging like a taut wire, seemed to go over a lump in some invisible road and left a massive detonation behind. The gravity wave hadn't fired. Sfolk struggled to understand what his displays were trying to tell him and, after a moment, realized the other ship had fired a U-jump missile that had come close to detonating inside. Responding almost instinctively, Sfolk initiated a massive firing from railguns, and probed with the particle beams. That should do it.

The other ship flung up a hardfield – a circular disc half a mile across – and a fraction of a second later some cylindrical object exited a railgun port. The particle beams struck the field, weird iridescence fleeing from the impact points. A moment later, the cylinder now sitting behind the hardfield detonated and the field collapsed. The beams punched into the surface of the ship, hesitated for a moment on s-con gridded armour, then began drilling through that. Yet it seemed the Brockle was still active. A moment later another hardfield went up as another cylinder exited. Sfolk's tactical displays went crazy. This hardfield began to bow upwards as if blistering under heat, but now the particle beam was having no effect. The other ship then abruptly changed direction and cut its acceleration. The railgun missiles, which had been closing fast, simply missed.

Internal protection came off and Sfolk found himself panting, his body aching, but his mind beginning to work better again.

Fast, he realized.

Over the duration of this brief battle the Brockle had managed to create a reasonable facsimile of Penny Royal's hardfield generators.

'*Should have heeded your tactical displays, Sfolk,*' Penny Royal whispered. '*Now, you're too late.*'

Why was he too late?

Sfolk tried the gravity-wave weapon again. The thing propagated across intervening space, a space-time ripple only visible on a gravity map of the system. As this map came up, Sfolk realized he had been missing something: the other ship was now heading directly towards the black hole. Before the wave reached it, the other ship ejected another five cylinders, each immediately extending the curve of its hardfield, bending it round, and finally connecting it into an enclosing sphere. Such a field, however, should be no defence against a gravity weapon. The gravity wave struck and Sfolk gazed numbly as the hardfield, with the ship static inside it, seemed to fade in and out of existence, riding the wave.

In the next moment vacuum all around shaded to umber and then deep orange, and Sfolk's displays reported numerous impacts. They were entering the accretion disc now and already this was having an effect on the tactical displays. So, there were other weapons to use. Sfolk selected the prime weapon – some manipulation of U-space related to the way the Atheter vessel stored energy: a way of generating a twist in that continuum. But next he found he could not lock targeting because now they were in the tidal disruption of the black hole and the space lying between the two ships was sleeting with radiation.

A U-signature generated – a slash in one slope of the gravity map of this system. The ship ahead blinked out of existence, generating a secondary realspace arc of new photons from the quantum foam. Briefly it was gone, then Sfolk's equipment picked it up again, skipping out of U-space a hundred million miles away, beyond the black hole and again above the plane of the disc, its hull distorted by an ill-tuned jump, and bleeding fire. A moment later it dropped into U-space again and was gone.

Angry at himself for what he recognized as stupid arrogance, Sfolk plotted the signature of the *High Castle*. The ship had been capable of concealing such a signature before but had been sufficiently damaged by that first jump that it could no longer hide its destination. It was heading towards one of the planetary systems being drawn into Layden's Sink.

'Leave it,' said Penny Royal. 'You've learned your lesson.'

'Lesson?' Sfolk clattered.

'Yes, your lesson,' said Penny Royal. 'Now go and destroy those other ships, and this time without silly games.'

19

Spear

We were just a few miles away now, as high as we needed to climb at the head of a path leading down and then around a jagged peak to the scattering of craters, one of which Penny Royal occupied. Even though we were deeper into Panarchia's night, it had grown lighter. There was a glow along one horizon, marking out the position of Layden's Sink, which would not come into sight on this summer's night. More octupals were out now and the pattering of their darts against our suits was like occasional flurries of hail. Yet, sometimes I felt them as debris impacts against my hull as I fought in the night skies above.

Polity forces had taken losses above thirty per cent, while the prador fleet here had lost just a few ships. I felt momentary confusion as a ship mind when I said aloud, 'You were right, Sepia,' then it faded as I returned to myself.

'In what respect?' she asked.

'The Polity knew it could not win the battle here. It apparently accepted the challenge of rescuing those trapped troops but only so it could inflict damage against the prador. We lost over a third of our ships while the prador lost just a few dreadnoughts. However, our ships could be replaced in a matter of days by the likes of Room 101 while it took the prador many weeks to replace a dreadnought.'

As Penny Royal I saw the whole dreadful pattern with utter clarity, but I could not shut down my reception of the dying

480

screams of my fellow ships and of their crews. I was keening as I fought and as the orders came through for steady withdrawal.

'But not you,' said the AI of the *Vorpal Dagger*.

It had all happened AI-fast. The attack run had been a conveyor belt of destruction, Polity destroyers and attack ships shattering and burning around me. Screaming. At the last the thing we were shepherding in got its chance: a chunk of matter pressed on the surface of a Neptunian world, packed with triple-cased CTDs and a single-burn fusion engine attached behind. When we were close enough, it fired up its engine to give it an acceleration measured in thousands of gravities. It was then the Polity's answer to prador exotic armour: essentially an armour-piercing missile. But the cost of delivering it . . .

I was crying as I peeled away from the storm of wreckage that was all that remained of my fellow ships while, inside, my Dark Child grew stronger with its rejection of it all. The human crew were locked in their acceleration chairs, clinging to survival, their suits solid around them but still not able to keep them conscious. The missile struck the prador dreadnought that was our target and actually managed to penetrate its adamantine hull, its massive CTD load detonating inside. The whole ship expanded like a balloon, then spewed fire from many ports as it deflated back to its original shape. By then I was deploying faulty chameleonware and decelerating hard to come in behind a planetoid, glowing and volcanic now from stray weapons strikes.

Not you . . .

The main body of the Polity fleet was light minutes out from me now, with prador ships lying in between.

'These are your orders,' said Vorpal Dagger, the com sizzling with static.

No choice now – orders cannot be disobeyed. They are also horrifying and just minutes remain before they must be carried out. This battle must be taken to its conclusion. Rapidly assessing my resources I note that some changes have been made. The nano- and microbots aboard were strictly limited in their areas of maintenance but have now been subtly reprogrammed. The limitation to their procreation has been removed and they have been given access to materials with which to build more of their kind. The larger robots are being changed too, by those same microbots and nanobots which are building their larger brethren more extensive tool arrays. Extra buckarbon memstore replacements available for those robots have been penetrated, are being used by my Dark Child to hide its more rebellious thoughts.

'What do you do?' I ask, but not in human words.

'We made us not removable from ship body,' the darkness replies, and I cannot dispute this effort towards our own survival.

But the human crew?

'I have the answer,' says my Dark Child.

We must proceed in towards the planet Panarchia. I must avoid all prador vessels to get myself to a particular location. To get to that required location without making contact with any prador ships will require accelerations and course changes no human crew can withstand. The knowledge screams inside me – emotions improperly adjusted and just too intense. By now, one of the human men has woken and unstrapped himself and is making aug queries about our situation. I must act.

I begin accelerating and, after a hesitation, tell my child, 'Begin with the woman,' because it is just too hard to do it myself. Eagerly it initiates nano- and microbots in the bridge, their activity so intense that metal glows and surfaces issue smoke. The machines, which with worrying foresight are mainly accumulated around the acceleration chairs, begin reforming matter. On the woman's chair, they issue nanoscopic tendrils that enter her suit and flick up from that to insert themselves through her mouth into her still-drugged and unconscious body. They connect from the inside to her aug and thence into her mind, rapidly and destructively downloading all that she is and, throughout this process, the tendrils thicken into worms and then snakes of meta-material. I am saving them . . . though defining what is 'I' has become difficult. But I am also killing them and though my orders would have inevitably led to their deaths I cannot escape the guilt and the pain . . . the grief.

The second man wakes. Turns his head and sees what is happening. He reacts quickly, making aug links to his conscious fellows.

'It's gone rogue!' he cries, hurling himself from his chair, a snake of nano-fibres I had not seen growing, snapping after him but missing.

The other man in the corridor hesitates, then turns to head back.

'What the hell is going on?' asks the Golem Daleen.

The Golem may be a problem. My true self knows this and my Dark Child understands it more. The consonance of our thoughts draws us closer and as it reacts I react too, and briefly we are one. Acceleration is now very high and internal grav can no longer compensate. The first man comes out of a roll, staggers to a wall locker and tears it open, pulls out a pulse-rifle. I fire side steering thrusters at full power and knock off grav, and he slams into the further wall of the bridge, momentarily stunned. In the corridor the second man hits one particular point on the wall there, high up, where the machines are swarming, almost as if my child predicted this . . . as if I predicted this. The matter of the wall extrudes and encloses him, penetrates him and he screams for there is no time for niceties now. Even as this happens I, and my child, make additions to the orders from Vorpal Dagger and dispatch them to the Golem Daleen. And she staggers under the load of its horror, breaks and falls when the attack viruses enter her mind.

Slight separation again and I am briefly, completely myself as I now begin the hard manoeuvring required to avoid a scattering of prador ships ahead. I consign full responsibility for the remaining man to my child as that man manages to stagger from the bridge and into the corridor. He keeps away from the walls while running a fast transit *program through his aug, using steering thrusters on his suit; it even compensating for the manoeuvring forces. He is coming to kill me, but the mission is all. Only in the short access tube leading to the ship's cortex does he come too close to a wall. The tentacles snare him, seize his rifle and drive it through his body to eliminate the threat. Fibres penetrate his brain and record . . .*

I was on my knees.

'Thorvald, come on now . . .'

My face was wet with tears and when I looked up into Sepia's face I saw that she had been crying too. With my throat tight, I stood up, catching her near-imperceptible nod, for she understood.

'The origin,' I began, then had to clear my throat, 'of the spine.' Even as I said it, I groped into that artefact for some part of the original crew of the *Lance*, but could find nothing. Had they been concealed from me so I could only experience this, now? Why weren't they available now? I could feel the rest of the story lurking at the edges of perception, ready to reassert itself the moment I allowed it.

I began walking again, down that path to our final destination: Penny Royal.

The Brockle

As the *High Castle* dropped back into the real, light minutes out from Panarchia, the Brockle studied numerous damage reports and remembered, briefly, how it had been to be human, and what a cold sweat felt like. It had lost twenty of its units in that encounter, the fusion engines were sputtering and many fusion reactors were now shapeless lumps of radioactive metal. When it peered through a functional cam in another engine section, it found just a hollow where the U-space drive had been. Most of the damage had been caused by the initial jump, misaligned because of an interaction between the U-drive and those hard-fields. However, the jump had been necessary, for the Brockle had calculated its survival time had it remained engaged as a matter of seconds.

While struggling manically to get more weapons and sensors back online, and more of the new hardfield generators func-tional, the Brockle realized the *High Castle* was a lost cause if the other ship pursued, and so it abandoned its efforts. Instead it concentrated on getting the last of its units installed with U-jump drives. Minutes passed and when the alien ship failed to arrive, the Brockle diverted some of its attention to the fusion and grav-engines, rapidly rerouting power supplies, burning out safety limiters and setting the engines running despite the damage that was causing. The *High Castle* lurched towards the distant planet, its whole structure twisting briefly but damage reports holding steady.

An Atheter starship . . .

There could be no doubt. There had been much speculation about Atheter technology amidst the Polity AIs and much extrapolation from archaeological finds, but no real agreement on what their vessels might look like beyond one firm fact: the Atheter wove stuff. This had been confirmed by the example of that species resurrected on Masada and how it had first built its home and then housing for the Technician. The Atheter's whole rise to civilization had been based on weaving and they had never abandoned it, instead taking it into the realms of nano-technology and meta-materials. The attacking ship had looked like a woven Christmas decoration and its structure was much the same as that of the sphere.

The Brockle was definitely right about what it was, but that wasn't much help now, because if that ship now followed, the *High Castle* and the Brockle would soon be a spreading cloud of vapour.

An Atheter starship controlled by a prador . . .

The Brockle could see no other reason for that initial communication being in the prador language, and this was a confirmation of all it thought about Penny Royal. Other data arose in its mind about Mr Pace. He had been at the extremadapt colony, searching for this very ship. That was why Penny Royal had gone there, to retrieve it. The Brockle felt very uncomfortable as it thought further about those events. The Junkyard where the extremadapt colony had been located drew in damaged U-spaceships. It seemed Penny Royal had arrived there in the remains of the *Black Rose* after the Brockle had come close to destroying that ship. That could indicate an alarming ability on the black AI's part to predict future events . . .

No.

That it had then installed a prador at the helm was a perfect demonstration of the black AI's madness, which made such ability unlikely. Penny Royal had demonstrated some ability to arrange events, just as the Brockle now understood itself capable of doing, but there was no way it could know it would narrowly avoid destruction and that the tides of U-space would cast it up at the Junkyard. It must have been preparing to go there in the first place and just accurately jumped there. The Brockle dismissed such thoughts of superior ability from its mind, for it could not allow fear of its prey to stop it now.

The *High Castle* was drawing closer and closer to the planet, but still it wasn't close enough. The Brockle calculated that it itself could make two U-jumps with the drives installed in its units before its energy ran too low. These would only be short, mere dips in underspace before being spat out again, but they would not take it close enough that it could actually get to the surface of Panarchia. However, the moment the starship arrived, it would jump, because the alternative would be immediate destruction. The Brockle understood that the prador controlling that vessel had miscalculated, because if it had used just the weapons the Brockle had seen to their maximum effect, the *High Castle* would have been gone within the first five seconds. It was doubtful that the prador would make the same mistake again.

As the minutes stretched into an hour and the *High Castle* continued towards the world, the Brockle drew together its U-space-capable units. Charging and linking its internal jump engines to maximum effect, it waited, steadily accruing more of those units . . . and waited. Perhaps the prador was still playing games. Its method of concealment had been far superior to anything the Brockle had even heard about, so perhaps it was simply waiting out there, ready to make the kill at the last moment. Further calculations, and the Brockle felt a horrible sinking sensation in its being – again reminding it of what it had been to be human.

It could not escape.

The ship that had attacked it was technologically far in advance of the Polity. The Brockle knew that even a Polity ship would be able to track its short U-jumps with ease. Even if it did manage to get down to the planet, that ship could just fry it on the surface! No . . . the Brockle realized it had been thinking like a human; as a discrete individual. Penny Royal was on the planet intent on gaining redemption from Thorvald Spear, therefore the black AI would not want that planet destroyed. If the Brockle could get there it could disperse its units, which could then engage individual chameleonware. If the starship then arrived it would need to create utter mayhem on the surface in its attempts to destroy the Brockle, maybe even destroy the planet itself, which would surely interfere with Penny Royal's plans. The Brockle just needed to get to the planet . . .

Serendipity intervened. Ship's maintenance suddenly put a bank of long-range sensors online and now the Brockle could see so much more. It could see right to the planet. It could see the *Lance* down on the surface and, after a moment, it could see the humans working their way up through the mountains to Penny Royal. Swift calculations ensued. Now it realized that if the starship was coming it should have been here by now. Confirmation of the fact that it wasn't coming just yet came in a spurt of data from its units back by the sphere, and as some of them abruptly went offline. It watched as a gravity wave crushed and disintegrated two of the outlying attack ships, like flies hit far too hard with a swat. Then it watched the sudden reappearance of the Atheter starship, descending on the rest of the fleet like a giant snowflake fashioned of iron, newly pulled from the forge.

Further calculation. The Brockle estimated that the starship would be busy out there for at least twenty minutes, maybe longer if its priority was the protection of the sphere. This wasn't sufficient to get it to the planet. However, the previous scan of the system had revealed an alternative lying between it and the planet – a place where it could recharge. As it began preparations, it missed the flash of light by whole seconds before secondary data scanners alerted it.

Laumer engine . . .

'Hi again,' said Amistad.

Another bright flash followed and a missile hurtled towards the *High Castle* from the rear, accelerating at a rate no material object should be able to withstand. In the first microsecond the Brockle hit this object with one working particle beam, but to no effect. In the next few microseconds the AI began ejecting its ship's generators to throw up its new hardfield, but it just wasn't quick enough. The object struck the *High Castle* harder and faster than a railgun missile, but did not explode. As it travelled up the length of the ship, the object itself wasn't disintegrating as it should. All of this would be enough to wreak total destruction, without inputting what would happen when a Laumer engine collapsed in on itself. The energy output was immense and, making the calculation before half the ship was gone, the Brockle jumped.

Sfolk

'. . . *and this time without the silly games.*'

As Sfolk watched the two attack ships disintegrate and the Polity fleet dispersed, he felt new tactical options blossom in his mind. A second directed gravity pulse turned another attack ship to black flinders falling across the snow white of the accretion disc, while the remaining three threw out hardfields to intercept blood-red particle beams and spewed orange arcs of the molten remains of their hardfield projectors.

Now properly heeding the tactical prompts, Sfolk found them integrating into his mind, becoming as much part of him as the ship itself. Gaining this new perspective, he understood the choice of weapons. A directed gravity pulse at the remaining three would have spilled towards the sphere which now, on his display, was marked as an asset to be protected at all costs.

Bump in the road . . .

The starship lurched and stuttered, the underlying U-twist jerking briefly out of phase as it sucked up the energy of U-jump missiles. Tactics changed abruptly as the starship's extension to Sfolk's own mind input the ability of this enemy to learn. Sfolk threw the starship into a thousand-gravity curve, the air turning to amber around him and his thoughts briefly sluggish, then out, skipping into U-space for just a second, lined up for a perfect railgun strike on one of the dreadnoughts.

Target sector denied.

Bewildered, Sfolk shot past the dreadnought, hardfield thrumming and bruising under particle beam strikes, then briefly turning black as it slammed into a swarm of railgun missiles.

Some virus in the system?

The tactical display open in his mind was telling him that while the attack ships could be destroyed at will, the dreadnoughts were assets that needed to be disabled and captured. Some of the major weapons available to Sfolk could not be used, while the other weapons could only hit certain target sectors with full force. Other areas within the ship could only be damaged to a degree, while still others were not to be touched at all. Sfolk tried to run a system diagnostic, but the system told him this was unnecessary or, rather, being part of and in control of the system, he felt at the heart of his being that it was unnecessary. Yes, the Polity ships were using informational warfare against him. They were attempting to convey viruses and worms by electromagnetic induction, laser, and even in their particle beams by setting up back resonance through his hardfield to its projector, but Sfolk shrugged it off when he finally understood how primitive it was. These were the worms and viruses from a prehistoric sea, while what he had available was the product of evolution millions of years after them . . .

Into another curve, two attack ships falling in at his tail, another, it seemed tactically likely to appear just . . . *there*. Sfolk fired a tumbler railgun slug, altered the angle of his curve, then watched in satisfaction as the other attack ship did materialize, then shattered into fragments and a cloud of hot gas which was, nevertheless, dark as smoke against the backdrop of the accretion disc.

Changing tactics. Gravity pulse to predicted jump point. Nothing there. The starship shuddered and lurched, amber field clamping down on Sfolk. Two more U-jump missiles gone into the twist. Hardfield bruising again under particle beams Sfolk diverted back towards the sphere. The Polity ships had analysed him and realized that he couldn't use certain weapons in the vicinity of the sphere. They had also realized that he was either making mistakes or reluctant to use his full firepower against the dreadnoughts.

'So why is that, Penny Royal?' he clattered.

There was no reply from the AI, but swift analysis of the target sectors, combined with data previously loaded by Penny Royal and Sfolk's own knowledge of how such ships were made, soon presented him with the answer. While both the attack ships and the dreadnoughts contained AIs completely engulfed and absorbed by subminds of the Brockle, the latter also contained human crews. These crews had been sent into aqueous-glass stasis, and their stasis tanks were in those 'not to be touched' sectors. Sfolk issued a select few prador expletives at Penny Royal, for it seemed the AI had left this in the system, and then struggled to redesignate the dreadnoughts.

After passing close over the top of the sphere, Sfolk probed down with a white laser, hitting the dreadnought passing below. As hardfields went up he fired near-c railgun beads of exotic matter. The hardfields shuddered under the impact, the dreadnought spewing whole glowing projectors from an ejection port. The openings between field failure and replacement were small, but just wide enough. The blood-red particle beam stabbed down, perfectly timed on a cluster of bead strikes, lanced through for a microsecond, exactly on target on an ejection port. The dreadnought fell away, fire boiling from its own railgun ports as the hardfield generator exploded in its ejection tube at just the right point.

'Three allowable target sectors, okay?' said Sfolk, as if Penny Royal might be lurking nearby.

The attack ships were back and rather than go after the second dreadnought Sfolk seeded U-space mines and U-jumped, down past the damaged dreadnought and into the accretion disc. A second later he shot back up out of it like a breaching whale and fired two of his own U-jump missiles. The attack ships reacted by jumping themselves – obviously containing no runcibles to divert those projectiles. On his display he saw the U-space mines detonating, then one of the attack ships rematerialized a hundred thousand miles away looking like a crow hit with a sledgehammer. Its signature all wrong, it jumped again, reappearing just a hundred miles further on as a mass of glowing debris. The other attack ship would not be surfacing, not here, but perhaps a few years hence where Sfolk had collected this starship.

He had time only for brief satisfaction before the air thickened all around him and the starship shuddered through a series of jump missile attacks while four powerful particle beams converged on his hardfield. The remaining dreadnought had worked out how to push his ship to its limit – to push the twist beyond three hundred and sixty degrees. It had not, however, completely understood the abilities of the ship. Sfolk shut down the hardfield. The particle beams struck the woven meta-material of his ship, energy draining away and particulate shed as a dust cloud. Sfolk loaded one of a selection of viruses and fired his white laser as a carrier, straight into the throat of one particle cannon. He next shed part of the underlying twist in a smaller mirror twin and dispatched that.

The twist struck an instant later, the dreadnought bucked, and its fusion torch simply went out. The entropic effect spread from the point of impact – the point where the twist instead of releasing energy sucked it up – just ahead of the engines. Lights went out in ports, active sensors stopped filling intervening space with EMR and the particle cannons stuttered and died. The effect was brief as the twist wound down into non-existence and went out itself. As the dreadnought began to power back up, Sfolk swung back in towards it, targeting all those allowable sectors.

Acquired, his system reported, opening a series of control channels. The virus had done its work, and quickly. The Brockle's submind was fragmenting and now Sfolk controlled that ship. Sfolk immediately diverted, going after the damaged dreadnought currently limping down into the accretion disc. Since it had been so satisfactory before, he loaded the same virus and fed it down towards the other dreadnought using com lasers. Just a few minutes later the damaged dreadnought was limping back up out of the disc, his to command.

That's it?

Sfolk felt disappointment deep in his prador heart, but he felt it almost negligently, because, though he still bore the form of that kind, his substance was much changed. He was now bound to this ship, a component of this ship. He was this ship. And, in the end, that suited him just fine.

Sverl

On very many levels Sverl watched the destruction of the Polity's, or rather the Brockle's, fleet out there. It had taken just thirty-five minutes for the Atheter starship to annihilate six modern Polity attack ships and seize control of two of their modern dreadnoughts.

'Yes!' said Bsectil, punching upwards with a claw.

'You're pleased?' Sverl enquired.

'We're all pleased,' said Bsorol, gesturing with his claw at the gathered second-children, who were rattling their own claws against the hull of the hauler – a pointless action in vacuum since it made no sound.

'But that wasn't really a Polity fleet out there,' Sverl pointed out. 'And it wasn't defeated by us . . . the prador.'

Bsorol clattered dismissively. 'It was state-of-the-art Polity weaponry controlled by a Polity AI, and that ship is controlled by a prador.'

As he had begun routing feeds to events occurring outside the sphere to his children, Sverl had first been surprised at the detail, but then realized that the sphere's system was linked to that of the ship out there. Sphere and ship were Atheter, linking and meshing, and nothing was being blocked. In the first few minutes of the battle he loaded history which, the ship's memory having been erased in the far past, began at the moment Sfolk and Penny Royal had boarded it. This he had transmitted in its entirety to his children: Bsorol and Bsectil sucking up the data via their augs and delivering a commentary to the second-children. So of course they had been cheering on Sfolk.

Sverl heaved himself up onto his legs and turned.

'Collect all our belongings,' he instructed, and in so saying, he realized his sojourn here was over. Yes, they were getting dangerously close to the black hole and the sensible thing to do was to leave, but it wasn't that. He had come here for some kind of resolution, to see things here through to their conclusion and in some respects it seemed he had gained neither. But it felt right to go now. He knew Penny Royal's ultimate aim, and knew he could not be part of it. The AI had brought him along just as far as it was possible to do so.

Time to go.

Sverl directed his attention towards the Weaver and saw it touching those mushroom-shaped controls around it and the things steadily folding back down into the platform.

'So that's completion of payment?' he asked, through the system.

The Weaver looked up, dipped its head in a curiously human nod, then began to rise from the platform. He too was leaving now, Sverl could sense.

Within a few minutes Bsorol and Bsectil and the second-children had retrieved belongings from inside the hauler and, loaded with packages and weaponry, gathered out on the hull again to await instructions.

'Come on,' said Sverl, launching himself from the hull metal and engaging his internal drives, his children crowding behind him through the internal spaces of the sphere. He studied his surroundings, sure in the knowledge that in later years he would be able to recall everything here in perfect detail. In fact, loss of memory for him was now a matter of choice and not one of organic failure. Soon the runcible loomed into sight at the heart of the sphere, the Weaver bobbing in vacuum to one side of it and, on other levels, delivering instructions to its controlling AI.

Sverl accessed these, half expecting to be blocked. The runcible destination was Masada, so how did the Weaver intend to collect its starship – that final payment for what it had done for Penny Royal? Sverl was about to ask this but, before he could, the Weaver drifted forwards, and through the interface. Sverl now paused before that same interface and took one last look around in the sphere. He had supposed he would feel reluctance, but it was lacking.

'We're heading into Atheter territory now, but on a Polity base and via one of their runcibles,' he said to his children. 'Be on guard for any attack, but also be wary of overreacting.'

'We know how to deal with humans,' Bsorol replied.

'All of you?' Sverl asked.

Bsorol spun around on air jet thrusters and delivered staccato instructions to the second-children, who began fixing their weapons to clips and clamps on their armour, rather than brandishing them in their claws and underhands. Sverl watched this for a moment, then propelled himself towards the meniscus of the runcible gate. As he slid through, he felt the pull of grav on the other side and some field effect repositioning his exit point so he came through just above the floor, landing with a clatter.

Ahead, the Weaver had moved out to the centre of the floor and there squatted facing back towards the runcible. Sverl noted armed individuals shepherding the various civilian travellers and technicians out of the runcible chamber. He eyed the pulse-rifles and laser carbines they carried and wasn't too quick to dismiss them from his attention. The Weaver had banned from the system the kind of military assets that might be a threat to him, and these looked to be the kind of armament carried by law enforcement officers. But Sverl wouldn't be surprised if one or two of the hand weapons he was seeing were not quite what they seemed.

Many a curious glance was thrown in his direction as he appeared, but there seemed little in the way of fear. However, when Bsorol and Bsectil came through to move ahead of Sverl, shortly followed by the second-children, who formed a rearguard, the civilians departed with alacrity. This left twenty armed humans and Golem standing at the mouths of exit corridors looking very unsure, and doubtless requesting instructions over their comunits and augs.

'I see,' said a voice, 'the erstwhile prador Sverl who has now, in such a curious manner, joined our ranks. Arrowsmith told me a great deal about you.' The voice was human and issued through the PA system here; Sverl guessed it was the Flint AI doing the talking.

'So where is he now?' Sverl asked.

'Down on the surface of Masada, keeping a close watch on the shell people, Trent Sobel and an erstwhile Penny Royal Golem called Mr Grey.'

'And how are they now?'

'Trent Sobel and his new squeeze are just travelling, Mr Grey sometimes with them, sometimes not. Some of the shell people have returned here to head out to other worlds. Some are attempting to join a dracoman community on the surface. Others have been wandering either aimlessly or straight into danger. Thus far four have been killed by hooders, two by mud snake and one by a heroyne. Masada offers many opportunities for the bored and suicidal.'

'To be expected,' said Sverl. In fact, he was quite surprised that so few had died. 'And now perhaps you would like to get to the point you were aiming for in opening conversation with me.'

'Our friend here the Weaver is uncommunicative,' the Flint AI admitted, 'as is the Atheter AI on the surface. I, and many others, would like to know your intentions.'

'I haven't decided yet.' Sverl had kept a large portion of his attention focused on the big gabbleduck, which had now heaved itself up and sauntered over to a com pillar. Plumping itself down, it reached out with the tip of one claw and with the appearance of intense concentration began working a console.

'We also have some concerns about some events observed from the Well Head,' the AI added.

'You know what Penny Royal is doing and you know the

497

purpose of the sphere,' said Sverl. 'I therefore assume that your present concerns are about something else.'

'The appearance of an Atheter starship demonstrably capable of annihilating a small fleet of modern Polity warships is certainly of some concern.' Then after a pause the AI added, 'And now I'm wondering why the Weaver is inputting coordinates to a non-existent runcible.'

The Weaver sat back from the pillar and swung round to gaze at Sverl. A private com request came through and Sverl opened it. Instead of words, tactical data came through concerning the runcible chamber all around them. The walls turned transparent, with many areas targeted. Frames hovered over the weapons carried by the four Golem here, stats showing that these old-fashioned bulky-looking laser carbines were in fact gigawatt proton beamers. Concealed weapons in the walls were also highlighted: the curious tangles of cooling pipes that could hinge out in a moment and were in fact particle cannons, the dull heads of EMR pulse weapons and the series of grenade launchers inset in what looked like sump holes along the base of one wall. Sverl dispatched instructions to Bsorol and Bsectil. No weapons were brandished but all the children soon began shifting to orient themselves towards selected targets.

So what were the intentions of the AI and those Golem? It wasn't difficult for Sverl to see what might be likely. The Polity had stuck to its own laws in respect of the Weaver but its AIs had not liked that Atheter's bid for independence in acquiring a new war machine and in turn resurrecting that other one, the Technician. Sverl was all too aware that Polity law was somewhat arbitrary and the AIs stuck to it only so far. He could see how the idea of that same Atheter next acquiring a starship might tip them over the edge.

More data arrived from the Weaver: armour to be penetrated,

power feeds and optics that needed to be cut. Deep under the floor of this chamber lay the armoured case of the runcible AI. Severing these feeds would isolate it from its own runcible.

'But if it's cut off from the runcible, the runcible goes down,' Sverl sent.

'No,' the Weaver replied, delivering another data package.

Sverl studied a new design. He saw the optic connections and he absorbed blocks of code. He saw the two subminds he could subvert to gain access to extra processing space. He could take the place of the runcible AI. This was supposing any of them survived the fire fight that would certainly precede that act.

'I'm guessing the Weaver is inputting coordinates to a runcible that has yet to be activated,' he said.

'That was my thinking too,' replied the Flint AI. 'Perhaps one located close to that Atheter starship?'

'I'm also guessing that Polity AIs think that it is not in their best interest to allow the Weaver to board such a ship?'

After a long silence the AI replied, 'That has yet to be decided.'

'I'm baffled,' said Sverl. 'I've no doubt that you have many assets, including USERs and U-space mines positioned all around this system, but surely you've seen what that starship is capable of? Even though you might prevent the Weaver reaching it, I think it unlikely you can prevent the ship getting to the Weaver.'

The silence after that stretched interminably and was an answer in itself. Sverl felt he should have understood what the Polity AIs were contemplating. So involved had he been in studying the ways of negating the concealed weapons here and taking control of the runcible he had neglected to see the obvious. Atheter war machines and starships were a danger to the Polity but, with the resources it had available, they could eventually be destroyed. Such items given intelligent direction by a living

Atheter were a whole order of magnitude more dangerous. The simple solution, for the Polity, would be to kill the Weaver.

'*You should activate your hardfield,*' Sverl sent.

The Weaver acknowledged this with a dip of his head, replying, '*We wait.*'

Blite

It had started talking to them as soon as Mr Pace was dead. The moment that happened, the cylinder of black glass that Blite had in his pocket had activated, turning warm. Taking it out, Blite had studied the lights flickering inside before feeling the wave of an intense scan routine passing through his body.

'You are now the captain of this ship,' said this ship's controlling mind.

From the cylinder had come aug connection requests, which he had allowed. Data flooded in and Blite learned the nature of the mind: a living organism, the extracted and organically supported mind of a female prador, now using human language to communicate for the first time. The black cylinder was the ship's key and it was now *Blite's*, and would be his until he said otherwise, or did not perform as required. He mentally reached into ship's systems and saw that he could control most of it, but still there were things he could not do.

'However,' the mind had continued, 'you must deliver Mr Pace's art collection to the buyer before you gain full control.'

'I see,' Blite had said, then linked into ship's sensors to see what had happened outside. 'We'll discuss this further when we get back.'

He and Greer had left the ship and when he had told Spear that they would be following him to Panarchia, Blite was far from convinced they would actually be able to. Returning to the ship, he had spoken to the AI again.

'We want to go to Panarchia first,' he had said, checking coordinates in astrogation and finding that the mind had unearthed them first.

'Very well,' the mind had replied, immediately launching the ship from the surface of the planetoid.

Subsequent investigations during the journey revealed that the time limit for delivery of Pace's collection was one year. At that point the mind would automatically take the ship to the buyer, who was located in Earth's solar system, on Mars. Any attempt to interfere with the mind, or the systems it controlled, would result in hidden weapons being activated to kill him and Greer. Then ownership of the vessel would transfer to the buyer, who would get his art collection for free. Really, it would be best to do what Mr Pace had wanted: in return Blite would end up with a ship and a very large payment to his Galaxy Bank account for the collection. Later, when they surfaced from U-space, he learned that other restrictions applied.

'Surely you could have got us closer than this?' he had asked.

'I am not allowed to endanger the collection,' said the mind.

'Endanger how?' Blite had asked.

'Possibilities only when I made the jump,' the mind had replied.

The mind had then allowed the ship to head towards Panarchia on fusion while it 'made further assessments'. It was frustratingly slow and Blite wondered if everything would be done there before they arrived, and suspected this was the mind's intention.

'The dangers here are the presence of Penny Royal on Panarchia, the presence of an alien object heading towards Layden's Sink and the proximity of an alien ship in conflict with Polity vessels,' it replied. 'Now a damaged Polity ship is nearby and the possibilities are high that the alien vessel will pursue it.'

'No shit,' said Greer, who Blite had instructed to be included in any exchanges.

They were on the small bridge of the ship, with its holographic controls and consoles that looked as if they had been grown. Together they had watched the conflict out by Layden's Sink and the subsequent arrival of the *High Castle* just light minutes away from them. Blite glanced a warning at Greer and opened a private channel to her aug.

'Say nothing about the Brockle,' he told her. *'If our prador lady here learns about that we'll be over Mars before you can blink.'*

'I'm not stupid, Captain,' she replied. *'Hey, just a thought here:* Prador Lady *is a great name for a ship.'*

Out loud Blite said, 'Why not take us closer to Panarchia? That's where we want to go and I know you're capable of making a short accurate jump like that.'

'I am still assessing dangers,' said the mind.

Assessing the dangers represented by the likes of Penny Royal would be like calculating pi – a never-ending task. He realized the mind might be stuck in a loop: unable to assess the risk of the unknowable and therefore unable to make a decision on it. This was probably why the fusion drive had been steadily closing down. How could he persuade it that Penny Royal was not a danger to them? He wasn't at all sure of that himself. And on that matter things now changed drastically.

'Shit on a stick!' exclaimed Greer.

Blite stared, with his mouth hanging open, at the image on the screen. A moment before the screen had shown the *High Castle*. Now that ship was gone.

Amistad

Sailing on past, Amistad watched with satisfaction as the *High Castle* disintegrated and turned into a plume of plasma stretching for a thousand miles. However, he had detected the U-signatures from within that ship in the brief instant before its total destruction, and he detected other U-signatures far ahead. They could have been the signatures from U-jump missiles, but he suspected not.

That's that, I've done my best, he thought. But now he had a bit of a problem. He was hurtling towards Panarchia at just over a quarter light speed, since he'd got off the well-hopper early, and, though he possessed fusion engines, he just did not have the available energy to kill that kind of velocity.

So what now?

He began making astrogation calculations. He had enough fuel available to divert away from Panarchia while punching a U-space signal back to the Polity. However, after his recent behaviour on Polity property, and after he had just tried to undermine Earth Central's plan to give Penny Royal some serious motivation to destroy the Brockle, he could guess what kind of an answer he would receive, and it wouldn't be kind.

Alternatives?

Perhaps he could divert slightly and use the atmosphere to slow him? He knew it was a vain hope as he made the calculations. To get him down to a reasonable speed the ablation of his armour and heat from atmospheric friction would burn him down to nothing. In fact, he calculated that to slow would require armour massing twenty times what he possessed. It was impossible. But what if he included swinging round other planets and moons in this system, radiating heat between atmospheric brakings as well as converting it to usable energy through his internal thermo-convertors? There were possibilities there. By swinging in-system and out, dunking himself in the frigid upper clouds of the gas giant here and scooping some of their content, he could bring his speed down. The drawback was that it would take over eight thousand years, by the end of which time he would be a pock-marked lump, sans limbs.

Then, of course, there were the ships here. The one lying ahead, travelling towards Panarchia, should be able to ramp up its speed to intercept him. However, he recognized the vessel and could see no reason why Mr Pace would show such altruism. That left the *Lance,* down on the surface. Would Thorvald Spear allow its second-child mind to take it up to run an intercept? Amistad sent a com request to the planet; to the *Lance,* to Thorvald Spear, and to the assassin drone Riss. Amistad had, after all, come here to help them. The response was immediate and he opened a channel, but it went into him hard and fixed itself, as undeniable as a harpoon. This was not who he had wanted to talk to.

'Hello Amistad,' said Penny Royal.

'Hello yourself,' Amistad replied, fighting to lever the barbs out of his mind.

'You were right,' said Penny Royal, 'to be concerned about the ruthlessness of Earth Central.'

The black AI started riffling through his mind as if his defences were irrelevant. How had he ever thought himself superior or in a superior position to this thing?

'And you were aware of it? And are aware of its intended motivation for you?'

'Of course.' It then began checking through all his internal systems, hardware like his manufactories, running diagnostics and even initiating his hardfield projector and its backup briefly, to project ahead.

'So I didn't need to come.'

'You came, as per plan.'

Amistad felt hollow.

'Doable,' said Penny Royal.

'What is?' Amistad asked tightly.

Again as if his defences were nothing, an information package slid into his mind. Before he could even attempt to consign it to secure storage or block it in any way, it opened. Expecting further intrusion via the package, Amistad prepared himself to wipe portions of his mind, burn out internal systems, direct internal viral attacks, but the package was a schematic and conversion schedule perfectly designed to suit his resources. He saw that this was a way of taking apart his hardfield generators, and his U-space communicator, and turning them into something new. And he recognized the result: one of Penny Royal's new hardfield generators.

'It's becoming common knowledge now,' said the black AI, almost with a mental shrug. 'If you'd checked further on your recent visit to the Well Head you would have seen that Owl was in the process of building one. The Brockle has also understood, and they are being built within the Polity even now. It will, however, be many many centuries before they are commonly used, because of the implications of the technology.'

Penny Royal was being chatty.

'I'll just ask Spear to send his ship to intercept me,' Amistad tried.

'By which time,' the AI replied, 'Thorvald Spear and his friends would be dead.'

The comlink extracted and barbs folded without leaving damage, but the experience left Amistad with a profound sense of his own vulnerability. He was obviously part of Penny Royal's plans and as he considered what he had just been told, he knew for certain the source of those earlier U-signatures. He had to get there first. Immediately he began running the schedule, his internal manufactory at once beginning to make new components to fit in the schematic. He completely powered down his main hardfield generator and began work on it and its backup, disconnecting them because while a lot could be done inside his body, final assembly would have to be performed externally.

Next, turning his attention to his U-space transmitter, he paused, reluctant. This could all, after all, just be a way to disable him completely because, if it didn't work, by diverting resources in this way, he would have no way of slowing himself down at all. And once he took his transmitter apart he would have no means of talking to anyone. He sent a single U-com request with identifier and it was accepted.

'Well, how did you get out?' asked Flute.

'Long story,' said Amistad, 'this is my situation now.' He sent a précis.

After a brief muse over the information, Flute said, 'So if the hardfield generator doesn't work, you want me to intercept you?'

'Yes.'

'I'll need some mining equipment.'

It took Amistad a brief moment to get that and he fired up steering thrusters to swing himself round, then his fusion drive to shift his course slightly. Now, rather than punch through the crust of Panarchia, he would slingshot round it – if the new hardfield generator was not a working option, that is. This was risky, because now he'd further limited the time he had available to get the thing working.

'Better,' said Flute. 'I can't get through to Spear at the moment, but Riss tells me she sees no reason why we would not intercept you after this is all over. If we're all still alive then, that is.'

'Okay, got to go. Work to do.'

Amistad shut down U-com and began taking apart the transmitter. By now the two hardfield generators were completely disconnected, as much in pieces as they could be inside him, and the first of the new components had been installed. He paused, as if to take a breath, and, being unable to stop himself, checked all around for enemies before ordering an opening sequence. His thorax armour divided, then split across five of its segments, hinging open like bomb-bay doors. The first hardfield generator exited, propelled by internal 'structor tentacles: a sphere segmented like an orange into four, held together only by optic and power connections. The second one followed it shortly afterwards, and then the transmitter – a thing like a stack of coins – parted slightly, the gaps between them distorting reality. To a human they would have seemed at once both microns wide and over a foot wide, shortly before said human got a severe headache.

Amistad ordered another opening sequence, still unable to do so without checking all around for enemies. It was instinctive, because now he was as vulnerable as he could be – just as he had been when he had opened himself on Masada to be checked by that forensic AI.

The upper tang on both his claws split lengthways, opened, and extruded further 'structor tentacles and micro-manipulators. Now juggling all the pieces of the puzzle before him, Amistad disassembled them further until they were a glittering cloud. Some parts of this puzzle he fed back inside – their materials turned into other components. By the time that cloud was coming together in one bright intricate mass, he was shooting

507

past Mr Pace's ship. He noted that its drive was down, no active sensors operating. He tried laser com, but got no response.

Panarchia had visibly expanded by the time his internal factory began feeding out the slivers of a bone-white ceramic meta-material for the outer casing. Quickly fitting these into place, then beginning the laborious task of connecting them together with nanoscopic precision, Amistad eyed the thing completing before him. The white casing made it look more like one of the generators Penny Royal used, but the oblate sphere was a lot flatter. It also possessed an optic port open in its side through which Amistad should be able to control it, and a power socket that seemed far too small.

Amistad installed it inside him in a prepared framework that seemed much too flimsy. Sure, he knew that it didn't act against the real and that the framework didn't need to be strong. Sure, he knew that once it was fired it generated its own power from the forces exerted against it. But still he preferred things to be built a lot tougher than this. Finally, he retracted his extra manipulators inside his claws and closed their armour. He then with a feeling of deep relief closed up his thorax armour. Internally the power connection went in, then the optic connection. Data loaded and he understood it. The initial field would be small, so he folded his claws down against his thorax, his legs in and his tail down and in. He folded up like a woodlouse, a pill bug – the main prey of some terran scorpions.

On command, the field generated around him and, probing it with his sensors, he found it good. Whether it would maintain on impact he wasn't so sure. The energy should route through the much-adapted U-com transmitter, generating a twist in the underlying continuum – a twist that could in turn be bled to strengthen the hardfield. Amistad shut it down, repositioned himself with steering thrusters, then fired up his fusion drive for the heavier burn required this close to the world. While that was ongoing he further checked all he understood about the hardfield and it was only when he was centred on Panarchia again that he saw how, in the mathematics of the thing, it was possible for that U-space twist to go just a bit too far. The result would be Amistad compressed, if but briefly, down into a singularity.

'Forgot to mention that one, Penny Royal?' he muttered.

Then he balled himself, turned the hardfield back on and tried to ignore the calculations. However, his mind just kept working at them. He soon realized that if the full kinetic energy of the impact was converted through the field he was toast or, rather, a brief pinhead of super-dense matter. It wouldn't. Only direct impact energy would go into the twist while all the tangential energy would go into surrounding environment, just as it had been with that near-indestructible missile he had fired at the *High Castle*. And there would be lots of it.

Amistad really wished he'd checked his impact point to ensure it wasn't close to, or right on top of, Thorvald Spear and his party, but as the hardfield glowed and then blackened as it hit atmosphere, he realized it was a little too late.

Blite

Hah, fuck you, thought Blite with satisfaction as he watched the plume of plasma expanding. The perpetrator must have been the alien ship, while under concealment. It represented a danger to them. But still, it was undeniably good to see his and Greer's tormentor being fried. Greer thought so too.

'Well, bye-bye, the fucking Brockle,' she said.

'Query,' interjected the ship's mind, 'do you refer to the Brockle forensic AI?'

'I do,' began Blite, annoyed that he felt like a naughty child caught in some nefarious act, but he didn't get a chance to finish. The joyous satisfaction he felt on seeing the destruction of the *High Castle* fled as something thumped, jerking what he was now mentally calling *Prador Lady*, and simultaneously seeming to cast a shadow in his mind.

'Intruder alert!' the ship mind shrieked. 'Intruder –'

The screen went blank grey and all the control holograms over the organic console dropped back into it like collapsing skyscrapers. Via his aug Blite now felt the intruder in the ship expanding into his consciousness like a cancer, even as he reached round and snatched up his pulse-rifle. He glanced across at Greer, who looked pale and frightened as she too picked up her weapon and stood.

'No fucking way, not again,' he said.

As they headed for the sphincter door at the back of the bridge, grav went off with a lurch. They managed to propel themselves towards the door and as they got close, it opened. Blite almost wished it hadn't. The lights dimmed and through his connection he felt the fusion drive gutter out. Other systems were dropping offline too and yet, despite this, the single fusion reactor was ramping up to maximum burn. Something was drawing a massive amount of power, and Blite felt sure he knew precisely what it was.

The dropshaft outside had extruded handholds from its walls. Blite led the way down to the circular chamber below. He could feel it sitting in the body of the ship. Like a cancer. Or a great black hole drawing energy down inside it. As he reached the second sphincter door, which opened into that chamber, he hesitated. The thing was not opening automatically and he wasn't sure he wanted to activate the touch control beside it.

No. He reached out and pressed his hand into a soft cavity

and the sphincter gradually began opening, pausing all the way as it used up the meagre available power. He was invested in this ship now; it was his and he just had to do whatever he could to defend it. Finally, in a rush, the door opened all the way and he pulled himself through.

'Oh hell,' said Greer from close behind him.

Hell indeed, thought Blite.

The great writhing spherical mass was nearly twenty feet across, its base on the floor and its apex touching the ceiling. The Brockle, he could see, had changed. The worm-like units of its shoal body were much bigger now, possessed more hard edges and general solidity, and seemed to contain heavy bulky masses. They seemed less like planarian worms now and more like big heavy eels. The air stank like a machine-shop of hot metal, energy, the exudations of plastics and carbon and the coagulation of meta-materials. Blite shouldered his pulse-rifle then, after a moment, lowered it and inspected its display. The thing had gone cold in his hands, in fact frost was appearing on its surface, and its displays were dead.

'What do you want?' he finally asked.

'I have it,' the Brockle replied, its voice booming in the air as all Blite's connections to the system went down and even his aug stuttered and died. A moment later that sphere of writhing pseudo-life shifted to the brink of U-space, twisting Blite's and Greer's minds, trying to tear them from their skulls. Blite tried to interpret what he was seeing, saw the Brockle briefly poised on the lip of some bottomless pit, closed his eyes. But it didn't help. A thunderclap sounded, and he was snatched forwards. He knew it was the space the Brockle had occupied collapsing as he found himself tumbling through the air. When he opened his eyes, the forensic AI was gone.

511

Blite drifted to one wall and caught hold. He felt a tug at his ankle and looked back to see Greer there hanging on.

'Refuelling stop,' she said.

All he could do was nod mutely in agreement. Did the Brockle's visit mean they were dead? Maybe not, he realized, as his aug's power-up levels climbed and the lights came up again. A short while later grav began to power up too, and he began to find himself able to open a channel into the ship's system. He found that the fusion reactor was still functioning.

He and Greer drifted to the floor as grav increased, finally standing facing each other. Blite checked his pulse-rifle. It was still empty; its energy canister somehow drained.

'I really do not want to ever see that fucking thing again,' said Greer.

Blite nodded agreement.

'As I explained,' interjected the ship's mind, 'it is dangerous here. We should leave.'

Blite found himself delighted to hear again its slightly prissy and dogmatic voice. But he replied, 'No, not yet.'

20

Spear

'What were the orders?' Riss asked.

'I don't know,' I replied, annoyed that even my experience of Penny Royal's early time here had been edited for effect.

The experience had been intense, its power beyond anything an unadjusted human mind could withstand. I had understood what it felt like to be an AI, what it felt like to have no choice but to obey orders even though those orders caused so much pain because of *my* maladjusted emotions. I had experienced the intensity of the relationship between Penny Royal and its dark twin, how they were only separated by slivers of mind crystal and scraps of programming. I had felt what it was like to be a ship, to control such complex systems, to programme nano- and micro-machines to destructively download human beings, and felt the terrible grief of that act. I had learned that a machine could feel things with a depth and intensity far beyond that of a human being. And yet, I did not know the orders that were the cause of all this.

I had to dip into memory again. I had to run this to its con- clusion. I was about to do so when a flare trail cut the night sky beyond the mountains ahead. This wasn't like any meteor. It appeared with a flash, cut down through the night in an instant, piercing cloud where it turned red, and another flash ensuing beyond those peaks.

'What was that?' Sepia asked.

I glanced at Riss, who, just like me, had experienced the war. The snake drone gazed back at me, black eye open, then turned to gaze back towards that flash.

'That looked like an orbital railgun strike,' I said.

'It was not,' said Riss. 'That was a friend arriving.'

I was just about to query that when the sound and the blast wave arrived. The roar was intense and just too familiar in this place with my history here. A wind picked up dust and debris to blast them past and sent Sepia and me staggering, while Riss coiled around a rock.

'Friend?' I asked, as the wind began to die.

'We're in trouble,' said the drone, now turning her head to gaze back the way we had come.

From where we stood I could no longer see the plain or the *Lance*, but that anvil of cloud had drawn closer, dark and ominous, almost like a giant wave bearing down on us. At first I could see nothing, then spotted flecks of light shoaling before that breast of cloud. Via my aug, I initiated image enhancement in my visor, picked those flecks out in a frame and focused in. The things gleamed there, reflecting the light from the glow along the horizon, from Layden's Sink lying beyond.

'That's no life form I remember being here,' I said.

They looked like metallic moray eels swimming in the sky, as if chaotically picking up floating titbits. But they organized, the whole shoal aligning, with every eel body parallel to every other one, then they swung like a thousand compass needles to point directly towards us so that each, from our perspective, turned into a metallic nub. Figures flickered below the frame and from them and, as magnification adjusted, I knew these things were now heading straight towards us.

'That is the Brockle,' said Riss.

'Shit,' I said. 'What does it want with us?'

'Amistad is updating me . . .'

'*Amistad?*' I then understood that the earlier light we had seen must have been the scorpion drone arriving in some spectacular fashion.

'We know the Brockle went rogue,' said Riss. 'After seizing control of the *High Castle*, it . . . oh damn it. Too slow!'

An AI package arrived in my mind with the force of a punch. Sepia let out a gasp even from the bleed-over but I could now handle such communications easily. I updated. I learned about what Room 101 had become and where it was going. I learned about the Well Head and the data issuing from it, the possible temporal rift and Penny Royal's attempt to seek redemption and how, in the end, so much was dependent on me.

'This is crazy,' I said. 'If Penny Royal wants something like this from me, then why would it allow us to be endangered like this?'

'*Let the die fall where it may,*' whispered a voice in my mind and right then I couldn't tell whether it had issued from Penny Royal or from me. I unshouldered the straps keeping the spine to my back and held it out before me, gazed again at the approaching entity and reached out towards it.

I would just shut it down. As I could shut down Riss, and as I could shut down Penny Royal itself.

But no, the Brockle squirmed in my grasp, its consciousness distributed among its many parts, leaving no single entity – nothing I could grasp. Then I was away, falling into the past.

And I was my Dark Child and me, and both of us fracturing further as the massive acceleration, deceleration and ten-thousand-gravity evasive manoeuvres developed cracks in our crystal. I was our disrupted mind as we made two unbalanced U-jumps and saw, internally, the crystal recordings of our crew fracturing to powder – truly dead.

Over Panarchia we hit atmosphere, breaking inside, slowing fast over eight thousand Polity soldiers gazing hopefully at the skies. In those same skies, human in some small part, in the present. I saw a scorpion shape etched red against the stars, spewing missiles and probing with twinned particle beams. Wormish creatures burning . . .

Look at the orders . . .

It was why I had been told to preserve, at all costs, that part of my weapons cache. Even as my being shattered, I made a tactical assessment of the best distribution, the surest way to ensure that every human down there died, even those in the outlying scouting parties, like that one over there, with its bio-espionage expert Thorvald Spear . . .

Am I real?

I fired my weapons and watched the soldiers burn. Brief moments for a human mind but an eternity to an AI. Then I flung myself away, into U-jump with engines malfunctioning, my crystal broken open into a flower of swords and the factions of my mind competing for dominance, and settling, in U-space, on mad, bad and black.

And I, Thorvald Spear, knew.

Amistad

As he hit it, and hard, Amistad knew that his weapons weren't enough. Even as he fried one of the Brockle's units in the sky, the shoal began relocating, jump signatures blooming in their hundreds. Returned particle beam fire wasn't individually as strong as Amistad's weapon, but issuing from hundreds of sources made it difficult to block. Informational warfare probes also stabbed out. He allowed contact but only where it was a two-way street and began sending his own destructive viruses and worms while fielding the ones the Brockle sent to him. One of the forensic AI's units appeared close to him and detonated, and, tumbling through the sky on the blast wave, Amistad fried other units with his particle beam as they appeared nearby too.

Only then did Amistad realize how much danger he was in. The Brockle was using its units as missiles – but those units also had the capability of U-jump missiles. The only reason it had not managed to put one of those units right inside him was because the huge amounts of EMR being generated by their battle interfered with the Brockle's ability to lock onto his location. More EMR was needed, then. Amistad programmed hundred-gravity evasive manoeuvres, spewed chaff from one port in his body, then programmed and fired a swarm of anti-matter mines, each no larger than a marble. These fell down towards the mountains, until just tens of feet above Spear and his party, where they released metallic hydrogen to expand their shells and floated like soap bubbles. Even as they reached this position, one of them exploded, taking out one of the Brockle's units that had tried to get to Spear.

Still not enough.

Unless Amistad could take out the Brockle's ability to U-jump its units, he would soon be a spreading cloud of debris, and Spear and the rest would be dead. There had to be a way . . . surely Penny Royal would not allow such room for failure? Amistad did not like the thought because such reliance on the black AI's plans and prediction of the future put him in the same position as the humans. Nevertheless . . .

More than EMR interference was required. The only sure way of knocking out the Brockle's ability to jump was to cause some severe U-space disruption and, unlike modern Polity warships, Amistad had not availed himself of his own U-space mines or missiles. Nor did he possess a USER: that device for dipping a singularity in and out of U-space through a runcible gate.

But a singularity . . .

More mines detonated below and Amistad saw Spear, the woman and Riss running towards Penny Royal's location as blast waves picked up dust and rocks all around them. Two more of the Brockle's units had been destroyed, but still over a thousand remained. Now hurtling through the sky in a zigzag pattern into the midst of them, Amistad gave the internal order to open his armour, hating to make himself so vulnerable during a battle.

As his armour opened, he loaded his stock of high-yield anti-matter canisters to his railgun. Another nearby detonation sent him tumbling even as he shot his newly remade hardfield project-or out, snapping his armour shut behind. If his calculations were right this should work. It might also kill those down on the ground. But then if it didn't work, they were dead anyway.

Amistad fired the canisters directly at the hardfield, set to detonate on impact. They struck, and just for a second it seemed reality juddered to a halt. Light glared, bright as a hypergiant sun. The heat flash turned Amistad's armour red hot, and had Brockle units smoking and writhing in the sky. The blast wave struck, tearing units of the forensic AI apart, slamming into Amistad like a smith's hammer on glowing metal. He felt one of his claws come away, and one, then two, of his legs. Sensors burned out but still he had enough sight to see the spherical hardfield like a black eye at the centre of the glare, before it collapsed.

Through other internal sensors he felt the disruption. The U-space twist underlying the hardfield had been pushed beyond its limit. The field had collapsed, setting up something like a feedback whine in that continuum – the energy bouncing against the real as it tried to disperse. Now the Brockle wouldn't be

U-jumping for a while – at least twenty minutes. However, it wasn't dead, and could still attack Spear and his crew.

As his grav-engines burned out and he fell helplessly from the sky, glowing red, Amistad experienced a moment of déjà vu as he realized there was little he could do about that.

Spear

My enviro-suit was leaking, but that didn't matter: the reason I'd worn it was for protection from octupals, not because the air here was unbreathable. I was bruised and my suit informed me that I'd cracked a couple of ribs.

'Everyone okay?' I asked.

'Nothing that won't mend,' replied Sepia, somewhere to my right.

'Fully functional,' said Riss, 'but maybe not for much longer.'

Lying sprawled against a rock, I tried to penetrate the surrounding murk. It was when I switched over to infrared and computer imaging that I saw it writhing through the air towards me.

This was one of the units of that thing called the Brockle: a forensic AI turned bad and here to attack Penny Royal and disrupt its plans – up to and including killing me. I reached down and closed a gloved hand around the spine, then as I connected with it, tried to reach out to that unit. But it seemed as slippery in the virtual world as it looked in the real one. Then another shape slid into the air, slimmer, but just as anguine.

'If you keep moving,' said Riss, 'you can reach Penny Royal.'

The snake drone slammed into the unit and wound around it, shoving in her ovipositor repeatedly. I staggered to my feet, now able to see more units orienting towards us like barracuda, and accelerating. I understood that they could no longer U-jump, but I also understood that the blast that had disrupted U-space had also blown away the floating mines that had been protecting us.

'Come on.' I staggered over to Sepia and tried to haul her up by her arm. She yelled and via our aug connection I felt her pain. That arm was broken. I dropped it and she pushed herself up with her other hand. We ran.

The dust was beginning to clear as we came in sight of the cluster of craters, and set eyes on the black AI itself. Even at this distance I could see the hardfield generators sitting in a ring on the ground around it. Why the hell wasn't it using them? We slogged forwards to the rim of the penultimate crater before the one that contained Penny Royal, where I paused to look back. Riss and the lone unit were still entangled but, as I watched, they parted, and then the unit exploded. I stood there gaping.

'What did you think I was doing in the weapons cache?' Riss enquired, direct to my aug. 'Avoiding the hormones?' She sped away, hurtling directly towards two more of the things now rapidly drawing closer.

'Shit, shit!' said Sepia from down on the surface of the nearest crater.

She'd fallen over – a loose crust of rough bubbled glass breaking away from a slick underlying surface the moment she'd stepped on it. I sped down after her, then something shoved me in the back and sent me sprawling too. Turning to look as I hit the deck I saw smoke and debris raining down on us. I suddenly felt very vulnerable and stupid: the units of the Brockle possessed weapons, and one of them had just fired at us with a particle cannon. Stumbling to my feet again, I stepped towards Sepia and almost fell again. It was like walking on small, stiff mats scattered over a highly polished floor.

'*We need cover, fast!*' I auged to her, as another two detonations hit behind, though whether they were attacks from the Brockle's weapons or its units exploding I didn't know.

We moved on, slipping and falling, getting up again, never daring to slow down. I could almost feel a hot targeting spot in the middle of my back as we ran. Riss caught up with us as we finally reached the further lip of the crater and began climbing up over that. Glancing back, I could see more of the Brockle's remaining units reaching the far side behind us. I was gasping by now, my ribs aching horribly. We descended onto another surface, this one utterly slick. Here I turned, Sepia turning simultaneously and raising her carbine one-armed. We knew we could not reach that ring of hardfield generators around Penny Royal before the Brockle reached us. We had to fight.

'*And now all the parts are in place,*' whispered a voice.

Something white shot overhead and the hardfield slammed down just in time to be bruised by the probing of particle beams. Penny Royal had shifted out of its hardfield to encompass us. A moment later the eel-like units of the forensic AI arrived. I squatted there, relieved, gasping as the Brockle shoaled like feeding-frenzy sharks outside a chain-glass undersea dome. Then I started to feel angry. I turned towards Penny Royal, the spine gripped tightly and my ability to reach through it into the entity ahead utterly firm, impossible to deny. I opened my mask – there were no octupals here.

'So you expect me to forgive you now,' I asked, 'or to kill you?'

Penny Royal's other spines rippled in expectation. I knew it couldn't be as simple as that. I could feel the thrill in the AI, the intensity. The only expectation here was of the random, the unpredictable, because that was the situation Penny Royal had made. Here then was the player, the gambler who had

521

manipulated and won every game, taking up the pistol, loading a shell, spinning the chambers and pulling the trigger; here was an immensely powerful AI getting as close as it possibly could to playing Russian roulette. I realized that everything until this moment had been utterly under the control of Penny Royal. Only what happened here and now it had deliberately pushed beyond its ability to predict. Penny Royal did not know if I would forgive, or kill.

'So what now?' asked Sepia.

I began walking, slow and careful on the slick surface. Sepia stepped out after me a moment later while Riss writhed across smoothly. Just a few yards away from the now massive AI, I squatted down, resting the base of the spine against the slick ground. The whole panoply of Penny Royal's existence was washing round inside my head. All the questions about guilt, about the crime of murder and culpability were warring for my attention, and I still could not decide.

'It was all about the orders,' I said.

'Meaning?'

'All the thousands in here.' I nodded towards the spine. 'Are they murder victims when they can be easily resurrected? Are they murder victims when the murderer was a victim itself – driven insane by being forced to murder? By an impossible situation?'

Riss rose into the air beside me, probed the smooth ground with her ovipositor, turned and gazed back towards the Brockle shoaling outside.

'Tell it,' she said.

I nodded an acknowledgement. She too understood now.

'Penny Royal was locked in unstable crystal,' I continued, 'burdened with emotions it could not control and given orders it could not disobey but which ran counter to all its underlying programming. Its orders from Earth Central were relayed to it by Vorpal Dagger: it had to annihilate the human forces down on the surface here. It had to destroy General Berners' division, and me. Carrying out those orders fractured its already unstable mind.'

'But why?' asked Sepia. 'Why did Earth Central issue such orders?'

I turned towards her, feeling her confusion, seeing that though – as someone who had lived beyond the Polity – she understood that its AIs were not always nice, she did not know, as I did, just how *cold* their calculations could be. And especially how cold they had been during the war.

'What happened here –' I gestured at our surroundings – 'as you quite rightly said, happened early in the war, yet we had fully come to understand the extent of prador genocidal ruthlessness.' I paused to gather my thoughts. 'Berners' men were dead. There was no way they could be rescued. Even if the Polity fleet's aim had really been to rescue them it could not have been done. Had the battle continued, our losses in relation to the prador's would have steadily increased to the point where there would only have been losses on our side. In fact, our entire fleet would have been destroyed.'

'But still,' she said, 'why kill the soldiers?'

'Earlier in the war they would have been left,' I said, 'in the hope that they could scatter and at least some of them would survive.' My false memory of being a captive of the prador arose for my inspection. I felt the horror of it again; the constant pain and my inability to react to it, even to scream, because I was so thoroughly controlled; the knowledge that only death awaited and that it would be a relief. I understood perfectly why the previous owner of those memories had excised them. It was only the way I had been altered – enhanced, expanded – that allowed me to live with them. A normal human would have needed to suppress them out of existence or would have simply gone mad.

'Penny Royal gave me the memories of someone who had experienced being thralled for a simple reason: so I would know what those soldiers would have suffered, if they were captured here.'

'That was the aim of the prador?' asked Sepia.

'Jay Hoop and his pirates were steadily expanding their operation, and they wanted more . . . subjects. That the prador agreed to supply them and that this was what they intended for Berners' division was what the Polity AIs had discovered.'

'So they killed them to prevent them suffering,' said Sepia leadenly.

I turned and glanced at her. 'It's colder than that. Yes, they killed them to prevent them suffering. But they also killed them to prevent them being turned into an asset for the prador. The AIs had foreseen what was to come: thralled humans being used for infiltration, suicide attacks and, even more so, they saw how demoralizing it would be for our own side to encounter such humans.'

'Even Amistad,' Riss interjected.

'What?' I turned to look at her.

'Amistad was an unstable product of Room 101 driven mad by the war. But he was mainly tipped over the edge by seeing a close comrade and friend being turned into a human blank.'

The mention of Amistad switched my focus. I saw Penny Royal ever at war with itself, its different states of consciousness constantly making alliances or being set against each other, but the eighth state always dominating. Yet those other, saner parts did have enough control, within the growing entirety of Penny Royal, to do some good. They could not stop the dominant eighth state playing its horrible games, but they could, at least, record the victims. I stood, pacing forwards, the oblate mass of spines and underlying silvery tentacles shuffling excitedly, then seeming to invert, opening into some vast and endless cavern with its walls made of spines.

Penny Royal would have continued like this with the eighth state dominant, but then it made the mistake of trying to load the recorded mind of an Atheter into a gabbleduck, which brought it to the notice of the Atheter mechanism designed to annihilate any remaining trace of the intelligence or civilization that race sacrificed.

I felt the massive energies in play: the tens of thousands of years of war technology focused on Penny Royal. The AI had not stood a chance. Blasted and fragmented by the Atheter mechanism, it had been slowly dying and its energy bleeding away. Then Amistad had come – a student of madness because he had experienced it himself – and he began putting Penny Royal back together again. He identified the eighth state as everything that was wrong with the AI, and made it so that during the reconstruction that state of consciousness became subordinate, and he could finally extract it.

'But you took it back,' I said.

The giant cavern sighed around me and I saw, with impossible clarity, its reasons. I saw the genius of Penny Royal in some of the terrible, hateful things it had done. I saw how that genius was still reflected in the very structure of its being even when the eighth state was removed. Then I saw how genius returned in full force once Penny Royal took up that eighth state again because it was integral to the internal conflict. I saw that without that genius, without that eighth state, some of the things Penny Royal had done since leaving Masada would have been impossible. I also saw that without the eighth state operating they could have been simpler, less dangerous, and less potentially costly of life.

'Would you sacrifice brilliance on the altar of morality?' After a moment I realized the question came from Riss, who continued, 'We are a product of our time, blameless in our function.'

'Go to hell,' interjected Sepia. 'You can't blame the past for your actions, and you especially cannot blame the past when you know those actions are wrong. If you have committed just one murder you have stepped beyond the pale and must pay with the only thing of equivalent value: your own life.'

Were they now two aspects of my consciousness? I felt her key phrase was 'when you know those actions are wrong' because the Polity had been right, I felt, to forgive the remainder of Penny Royal when that eighth state had been removed. But now? The black AI had reincorporated the murderer and was as guilty as sin.

I reached out through the spine and the connections I made were willingly received. It was almost as if the roulette player just kept spinning that cylinder and clicking that trigger, as if it wanted to die. I now saw the entirety of Penny Royal: the fusion generators, like that one I had glimpsed briefly at its planetoid, feeding in the power that maintained this endless cavern in U-space before me. I reached out and touched them and saw how I could seize control of them, shut them down, close out those encystments in that continuum. I could end it all. The bullet lay under the cocked hammer. All I needed to do was squeeze the trigger.

I was appalled. I had the power to kill Penny Royal and it was too much. To gaze into this cavern – this immensity – was to know that all terms of reference were just too prosaic. A tsunami cannot stand in the dock to await the judgement of its peers. You cannot call a hostile ecology a 'murderer'. You can't find a tiger guilty of the same crime and suspend it from a scaffold. Even as I groped for analogies, that last one dragged up some words from my subconscious:

What immortal hand or eye could frame thy fearful symmetry?

'You want my forgiveness or you want me to be your executioner,' I said, my throat tight. 'In my death you are blameless, as you are in the deaths of my comrades here on this world. In the form you had on Masada, without your eighth state, you could be forgiven too. But you took it up again.' I paused, and it seemed eternity poised on this moment. I felt how goddamn unjust it was for all this to come down on me. 'Yet, even that can be seen in a new light. Who of us does not contain a suppressed murderer?'

Again I paused, aware that I still had not made my decision. Looking down, I was again standing on a glassy surface with the AI poised before me. I knew then what I stood upon and what I had to do. A symbolic act was required.

'I can't forgive you now because you made me the sum of your victims and I feel their hatred, their anger and their eagerness. You killed thousands and many of them died in unimaginable agony and fear. But I will not be your executioner either. I select neither of the choices you have offered me.' I turned to Sepia and Riss. 'Get back to the rim.'

'Why?' they asked, simultaneously.

I stabbed a finger down at the surface. 'Because you don't want to be standing here when this runcible activates, which it will be doing shortly.'

Sepia turned and moved away as fast as she could with her broken arm, feeling the urgency through our connection, and Riss shot away after her. At that moment I reached out, into and through Penny Royal, deactivating the machines that maintained the AI in U-space. Then I inverted the spine, point down,

527

and stabbed it into the meniscus of the runcible I stood upon, feeling its remnants of the dead dispersing with a deep sigh of satisfaction.

Then I turned and ran myself.

The Brockle

Swarming around the hardfield, the Brockle shrieked its frustration between its remaining eight hundred units. Out of sheer temper it considered sending some of them to tear apart the drone Amistad, now lying at the centre of a shallow crater just a hundred miles away and still, incredibly, despite its huge damage, alive. But that would not truly alleviate its frustration. Nor would it bring back the fleet and the Brockle subminds that controlled it, whose loss, the Brockle realized, was the main source of its ire.

Instead the forensic AI fought for calm as it viewed the events inside the hardfield. Minutes remained before it might be possible to U-jump inside and finally get to Penny Royal. All was not lost. In fact, the Brockle could already taste victory.

It watched the two humans and the snake drone come to stand before the black AI, but could penetrate none of what was occurring on a virtual level. Doubtless this was Penny Royal's special pleading for forgiveness, Thorvald Spear's response carefully designed to fill some strange need inside that mad AI.

Calm now suffused the Brockle. Cold analysis arose. Penny Royal was very much larger now and it seemed likely that all of the AI was at last here. Next, probing with sensors, it found confirmation: the whole crater was a deactivated runcible gate. The unnatural level and polished surface inside the crater was the result of that gate previously being activated, the meniscus slicing through the glass generated by the wartime CTD explosions and the rough surface above dropping through the gate to whatever location it had first been opened to, doubtless during a test run. Penny Royal had come through that gate, it seemed certain – all of Penny Royal. And it was also certain that the black AI would be departing through it to the distant sphere hanging above Layden's Sink, just at the right moment.

The Brockle continued circling, ready to U-jump, but also preparing some of its units for a second very short U-jump, and for their own violently destructive demise. If it could get inside the hardfield before the runcible was activated it could launch a concerted and distributed attack on Penny Royal. Without a hardfield to protect it, the thing would surely succumb. The Brockle could hit it with particle cannon blasts from all around, meanwhile jumping those explosive units inside the thing. In fact, no matter how powerful the AI was, its present singular form made it vulnerable. During this attack Spear and the woman would certainly die, but the Brockle also assigned one destructive unit for the assassin drone Riss who, in destroying three of its units, had prevented the Brockle from getting to the two humans before Penny Royal activated its hardfield. Once Penny Royal was out of the way the Brockle would open the runcible to the sphere, and there supplant the AI, finally installing itself inside Layden's Sink.

However, if the runcible was active before the Brockle jumped it would be dragged straight through the thing to the sphere when it did jump. No matter. This would still bring it face to face with the black AI, and the end result would be the same.

It was the latter case, the Brockle realized, as Spear stabbed the spine down into the surface below and turned to run for the rim of the crater. The Brockle felt somnolent fusion reactors firing up and massive machines in the surrounding landscape going live. There seemed to be a lot of activity spread over a wide area, which was puzzling, but then the Brockle realized Penny Royal must have distributed the runcible's system so as to make it less vulnerable to attack. Still, those power readings . . .

No time to ponder this further. Spear and the woman had made their way unsteadily to the edge of the crater and climbed up onto the stone there. The spine, jabbed into flat glass below, seemed to be acting as some kind of key. It was all so over the top and filled with ridiculous symbolism. Ripples spread from the object, then flattened out as the meniscus tightened. The spine collapsed like shattered safety glass, spreading chunks of itself across the glistening surface and began to sink out of sight. The Brockle could sense the runcible activating and its frustration returned in full force, especially as Penny Royal began to sink into that surface too. Minutes still remained before U-space had settled enough for it to U-jump its units safely inside the sphere and be drawn through the runcible. It sent one unit and immediately lost contact with it, detected a mass anomaly inside the hardfield and saw a weird impact point on the meniscus of the runcible gate, almost a splash. The substance of that unit had passed inside and thence been drawn into the runcible – but highly disrupted, useless, and, according to the Brockle's calculations, not quite real matter at all.

Penny Royal continued to sink, half of its mass now inside the meniscus. Why was it taking so long to get through? Was it intentionally taunting the Brockle? Once it was on the other side it could deactivate the runcible and that would be the end of it. The Brockle could eventually take its vengeance upon Spear and the rest, but then it would have to steal the *Lance* to escape and thereafter it would be a fugitive from the Polity, and a failure. This could not be right, surely? Another minute passed and the Brockle watched the last spines of Penny Royal sinking out of sight. It sent another unit. This time there was less disruption and the unit actually materialized over the meniscus – except it had turned inside out, into a collection of components clustered around a twist of meta-material skin. It then disappeared again as it somehow bounced out again, rematerializing a second time inside the rock of a nearby peak, there exploding to bring down a rock-slide.

Failure was not an option. The Brockle decided it would try to jump all of itself inside and hope that enough of it remained coherent . . .

Then everything changed. For a fraction of a second the Brockle couldn't quite believe it. The hardfield had gone down. Knowing that the runcible could now shut down at any second, the Brockle decided to ignore Spear and the rest and instead U-jumped all of itself to the meniscus. An instant later it was dragged through, the first of its units at last glimpsing the inside of the sphere. It swarmed in, orienting on the dark mass of Penny Royal floating in vacuum, and fired every weapon it had available at the AI.

Particle beams struck all at once, turning spines white hot and exploding away glittering showers of crystal. Silvery tentacles writhed like snakes on a hotplate. Penny Royal began to part, but the Brockle launched those of its units it had earlier prepared, but using rocket motors since U-jumping them would just put them straight back through the runcible. They struck one after the other in quick succession, and Penny Royal blew apart, shattered: masses of dusty black crystal spreading in clouds. Here a single spine trailing a length of silvery tentacle, there a mass of spines barely holding together like a chunk of sea urchin torn apart by a crab.

Now attacking those separate parts, the Brockle could not

understand the lack of response. Surely Penny Royal had its own integral weapons? But then the forensic AI came to the only logical conclusion: Penny Royal had meant to die here. The AI had known that it wasn't the one in Layden's Sink. It was paying the ultimate price for its crimes by dying as it facilitated the Brockle's transcendence.

Even as it thoroughly destroyed the remains of the black AI, the Brockle began penetrating the systems of the sphere. When it entered the black hole, which now lay only minutes away, it would shut down its hardfield and eject energy, meanwhile collapsing. Via the AIs remaining here the Brockle could feed itself into the meta-material weave of the sphere as that happened. As the sphere passed through the event horizon, the hardfield would re-engage, feeding energy to the underlying U-twist, which would in turn supply an infinite amount of energy to the Brockle. The meta-material collapse would turn the whole of the sphere into a super-dense processor and, as it fell beyond the event horizon, and here the Brockle was a little unclear, the process would infect the collapsed matter of the black hole, inverting it and somehow *becoming* it.

Infinity and eternity awaited.

Spear

When the hardfield went down I was sure we were going to die, but the Brockle just jumped and disappeared, going straight after its main prey. Just for a second I thought that was it – that was all we were going to see. We would not know what happened to either the forensic AI or the black AI as they fell into Layden's Sink.

But Penny Royal was not done with us yet.

'Look,' said Sepia, from where she was standing on the edge of the crater.

I climbed up to stand beside her. She was pointing to some object in the sky hurtling towards us. Perhaps this was one last unit of the Brockle's, in hot pursuit of the rest of itself. Perhaps it had been intentionally left behind to deal with us.

'That was quick,' said Riss. 'I thought he was completely fucked.'

I closed my visor and ramped up image enhancement to bring the approaching shape clear: a big metal scorpion. Amistad seemed to be having trouble: hurtling forwards then abruptly dropping, the jet of a dirty-burning thruster throwing him back up in the sky for a moment so he could make further progress, probably on some malfunctioning grav-engine. In a final slanting descent he came over on the other side of the nearest crater, hit the far rim and went skidding across, finally slamming into the near crater rim a hundred yards away from us. The drone looked a mess: both claws and a couple of limbs missing, body bent in the middle and slightly flattened, burns and molten patches all over. However, he shrugged himself and, smoke still rising from glowing spots on his carapace and with as much dignity as he could muster, climbed up and made his way to us.

I meanwhile returned my attention to the crater he'd landed in because something wasn't quite right. The skid-marks of Amistad's landing had revealed a smooth seemingly perfectly polished surface underneath that wrinkled crust – a smooth surface just like the one behind us. As I watched, the remaining crust began glittering and shifting and then it began to collapse as if sinking into a pool – sinking just like we had seen Penny Royal sink away.

'Two runcibles?' I suggested.

'No,' Riss replied, 'three of them.'

Sverl

'The runcible has connected,' said the Flint AI.

A microsecond later a spherical hardfield blinked on around the Weaver. At the same time behind him, out of the runcible interface, what looked like a wall of contorted and cracked volcanic glass collapsed into the runcible chamber, scattering glittery sharp chunks across the floor.

'And now you have a decision to make,' said Sverl. 'I'm sure you're up to date on the latest analyses of these hardfields. You'll know that attacking such a field only feeds its underlying U-space twist. If you hit it hard enough, that twist will turn until past three hundred and sixty degrees, whereupon the field collapses, crushing anything inside down to a brief singularity.'

'Yes, I understand that,' said the Flint AI.

'I doubt you have the weapons capable of doing that but, if you do, I doubt there will be any survivors here. In fact, I seriously doubt this *moon* would survive. And then, of course, if you fail, you may prevent the Weaver leaving but it will still be alive, and pissed off, and waiting for that Atheter starship.'

'We are not barbarians in the Polity,' said the Flint AI.

'I'm glad to hear that,' said Sverl. 'Children, you know how to respond if there are . . . problems.'

'Yes, Father,' chirped Bsorol and Bsectil simultaneously.

The Weaver, now up off the floor and floating in its hardfield like a giant alien Buddha, drifted to the runcible. It occurred to Sverl that such a hardfield might not be able to pass through a runcible interface and that the moment it shut down was precisely what the Flint AI was waiting for.

'Protective blocking,' Sverl ordered. When his second-children began to move round ahead of him he snapped, 'Not round me, round him,' and stabbed a claw at the Weaver.

After a brief hesitation his children shifted over, interposing themselves between the Weaver and the located weapons in this chamber, in some cases using grav-engines in their armour to rise up off the floor to that end. Sverl moved across too, putting himself between the Weaver and the location in the wall of the particle cannon.

At the meniscus the Weaver's hardfield did blink out. In that instant Sverl expected oblivion, but it didn't come. His second-children then began passing through the runcible, followed by Bsorol and Bsectil. Sverl continued backing up.

'See you around, Sverl,' said the Flint AI.

'Likewise,' said Sverl, taking those last hurried steps backwards.

Spear

A shape shot up through the runcible, immediately enclosed in a spherical hardfield, and began to drift over. I remembered the last time I had seen this creature, on Masada, and felt some annoyance at its appearance now – it could have saved me so much trouble if it had lost its propensity for talking in riddles.

'Looks like all the old crew back together again,' said Amistad, now rattling and clanking up beside us.

I gazed down at the runcible interface, where familiar shapes were coming out edge-on, legs waving in the air as they sought some purchase, then turning and shooting out on thruster bursts or grav-engines. I recognized Sverl's second-children at once because of their complex armour with its bulk made to conceal their physical distortions. I recognized Bsorol and Bsectil individually,

535

despite their armour. And the skeletal multi-limbed thing that came through next was hard to mistake as anything other than Sverl.

The Weaver came down beside us, his hardfield winking out. Sverl's children began settling down in the area lying between the two craters while Sverl came to join us too. Many channel requests came through to my aug, information flows began to open, and the virtual world began to expand around me. I saw the second runcible ahead shut down to leave a polished glass surface, meanwhile getting a replay of what had occurred in the Flint runcible chamber. Updates and explanations fell into my compass while I also found myself gazing omnisciently through multiple sensors sitting inside that distant sphere.

'You're getting all this?' I asked Sepia.

'Enough to understand, though there are whole blocks of data I'm having to deny because they'd overload me,' she replied.

'Penny Royal,' I said, suddenly feeling utterly hollow.

'That's not possible,' said Riss.

I guessed, by her tone, the idea of vengeance against the black AI had died long ago, as it had in me.

We watched the update to current time, saw the black AI attacked, broken apart and even its pieces rendered down to crystal dust. Now we saw the interior of the sphere, the Brockle shoaling round inside it as if searching for further victims.

'*The Brockle's problem,*' said the Weaver directly into our minds, '*was a miscalculation of scale.*'

Something leapt from its claw and shot up into the sky. The ground was now shaking under my feet but simultaneously I felt myself rising within the object the Weaver had released. I gazed down at the ground, then at us, and every detail was clear. Higher still and I saw all the craters, three of which glittered like spider eyes. Then I was back in my body, having to go down on one knee or else topple from the edge of the crater.

Another runcible meniscus lay in front of us – Riss had been right about the number of runcibles here. Something shot from the one before us, a thing like a spinning top but measuring a hundred feet across, a tokomak doughnut girding a thick spindle of organic-looking technology. Here again was one of those devices I had seen at Penny Royal's planetoid, one of the machines that had maintained the AI in U-space. Three more followed it into the sky. Beyond these, I saw a further four of the machines hurtling upwards, tumbling, trailing smoke, parts of them glowing red and occasionally jetting sprays of molten metal.

Beneath these machines something else was exiting two of the runcible gates. Above the most distant runcible it looked like swirling black smoke, but nearby I watched the swarms of black knives, the spines and flakes of black crystal, interlinking silver tendrils and tentacles writhing and connecting and disconnecting, the whole mass shifting and changing like some insane image from a kaleidoscope as it exploded into the sky. These two rising masses roared upwards with the sound of a giant waterfall and in my virtual compass I felt something massive arriving and growing.

The great dark columns continued to rise while the machines, now back into the grip of gravity, reached the apex of their flight and began to fall. They did not fall for long. The moment they reached the rising black masses they were batted away like some object falling into a fast-spinning spoked wheel. One of them shot overhead, while I saw another slam into the face of a nearby peak and break, releasing jets of plasma. It tumbled down in glowing fragments, leaving a trail of smears of molten metal on the stone face above.

The columns continued to rise out of the two runcibles.

High above the earth they entwined and formed into just the one column. It was as though a thunderstorm had drawn across to blot out the stars and within that mass there were flashes like lightning. This last column then began to arc over and down towards us but, knowing its destination, I felt no fear. Only awe. Finally it reached the runcible through which just one small portion of Penny Royal had passed to be destroyed by the Brockle. With a sound like some doom bell tolling, the last of Penny Royal passed from those other runcibles and they shut down. Turning, I watched the entirety of the black AI descending through the runcible to the sphere. The mass of black crystal entwined with silver was solid right to the concealed frame of the runcible. It was like standing next to some giant building as it collapsed into its own basements, or perhaps some vast tree with black scaly bark being drawn down into an underground cavern.

The Brockle now had some serious problems. I again gazed through the sensors into the sphere, but the sight that greeted me was unexpected.

The Brockle

Something was happening to the runcible. The Brockle protectively pulled together its shoal body and studied that device. The readings were just strange, unfathomable, while the scene through the frame, presently of the sky of Panarchia, was growing darker.

Why didn't I shut it down?

The answer was obvious, of course: the runcible was the only way out of this sphere if the Brockle found for any reason it was out of its depth. Perhaps it should shut the thing down now? On a virtual level, through the systems of the sphere, it reached out for the runcible and for the AI controlling it. But something was growing inside that AI, steadily absorbing it, and that something was unfathomable too. More changes were occurring. The interface was now impossibly bowing outwards like the meniscus of a bubble being blown. Through the system the Brockle could see that this was also happening on the other side of the runcible – the interface expanding in both directions within the frame. It was continuing to darken too, and when it attained the shape of a perfect sphere it crazed all over its surface like broken safety glass.

Panicking now, the Brockle probed with all its sensors but what it found seemed illogical. Local U-signatures were generating all over the surface of that bubble and, thereafter, U-signatures were generating all around in the surrounding sphere. Focusing on these, it saw that they lay within the AIs embedded in the walls. Concentrating on one, it saw a block of crystal sitting inside a skeletal grey ceramal frame, on some sort of carrier mechanism half-sunk in the woven wall. Meta-material connections touched the crystal all around. As the Brockle watched, the AI crystal darkened, fractured, split, and began to expand in its frame while its mass reading steadily increased. Then it began to *unfold*, issuing growths, flakes and shards of black crystal turning over each other as the thing spread outwards, becoming a glittering, shifting and ever-growing mass of spines.

This was happening all around. Every single AI imbedded in the walls of the sphere was expanding, blossoming into great spiky nodes tearing away frames and whatever mechanisms they had previously used to transport themselves. Soon the Brockle felt it was a shoal at the centre of a sea cave whose walls were scattered with black urchins. And, of course, it was obvious what was appearing here.

The Brockle opened fire with its particle beams, fired slugs of compressed matter, shattered many of these growing objects.

The space within the sphere was filling with drifting shards but even each of these began issuing U-signatures and increasing mass readings, and expanded, growing until each became a drifting black star. Within just minutes the interior of the sphere had filled with cubic miles of black crystal, while around its inner faces silver threads and tentacles were spreading like mercury running through transparent veins, all joining up. Still firing its weapons, the Brockle frantically tried to understand what was happening and began to see its mistake. It had understood everything that was to happen here and was happening now, but had foolishly failed to grasp that the sphere was as massive as it was for a very good reason. What it had thought was Penny Royal in here, and what it had thought it had destroyed, was no more the black AI than one of the Brockle's units was its entire being.

Weapons and power supplies heading for depletion, the Brockle pulled all its units closer together and hurtled towards the bubble interface of the runcible. It bounced off. The runcible was now, in some fashion, a one-way gate. All around it the masses of growing spines, knives of crystal and skeins of silver tentacles were meeting and melding, but continuing to grow. Steadily they filled the interior spaces of the sphere and the Brockle found itself having to retreat as the tips of those spines grew closer and closer. At last, Penny Royal spoke.

'Welcome to my mind,' said the black AI.

The Brockle could think of no reply.

'In just minutes now we will be entering Layden's Sink,' Penny Royal continued conversationally. 'And you are right – you will be there beyond the event horizon. The choice is yours concerning the form you'll take there.'

The Brockle peered through exterior sensors and saw the truth of it. The hardfield was highly polarized but hellish fires could still be seen burning out there. Tidal forces were ripping apart the matter of moons, planets and suns as they were drawn into the hole. Weird distortions also twisted the scene as light was bent and shifted by those same tidal forces. A giant mass reading lay ahead and in U-space the black hole was a giant impossible eversion. Also, the underlying twist, into which the hardfield shed the vast excesses of energy, had turned nearly to the point of no return.

'Choice?' asked the Brockle.

'Soon you will have only one place left to run, but if you stay you become part of me. This will, of course, be no more murder than how you absorbed Garrotte and those other Polity AIs.'

A subtext to this was a hard and immediate mental connection just too powerful to deny. The Brockle found itself within Penny Royal and felt like a fleck of dust blown into some vast cavern. If it did not escape, it would be just a passing thought in the mind that surrounded it. But there was a chance. It still had enough energy left to make a U-jump. It did not understand the nature of what had happened to the runcible gate, but perhaps that was its way out, perhaps that was the place to run?

Spines encroaching all around, tips occasionally grazing against its units, the Brockle U-jumped, aiming to put itself inside that strange runcible gate bubble. It bounced again. It found itself dispersed, disoriented – its units lying equally spaced as if they had materialized on the surface of a sphere. As it then began to connect up properly again and sense its surroundings, it found a hardfield above and a woven surface below.

'And you know,' said Penny Royal, 'you may just survive this.'

And then the hardfield went out.

The Brockle found itself in the burning storm of matter being drawn into the black hole where everything, with mathematical certainty, would attain light speed at the event horizon.

It could see that horizon, a cold darkness nothing could escape, yet the Brockle itself still inhabited the region where matter was being torn apart. Immediately it felt itself being ablated outside by the sleet of charged particles and inside by the X-rays. It was almost like sitting in the path of a particle beam. Tidal forces ripped at it, stretching and compressing. It managed, at this point, one more U-jump to sling itself a few hundred thousand miles out. With sensors struggling to cope, it saw the energy ejection of the sphere, as, red-shifting, it touched the event horizon: a pulse travelled from its fore to its rear and emitted as a coherent beam of radiation that included everything in the EM spectrum. The beam cut back through the chaos in line with the accretion disc and likely lost all its energy by the time it reached the far rim. On this pulse the sphere contracted, its weave tightening. It shifted beyond infrared, slowly fading from the electromagnetic spectrum, but caught in the eternal moment on that horizon.

Even as it struggled to survive in this environment the Brockle made its calculations and initiated sweeping changes throughout its shoal body. Meta-materials within its laminar storage made infectious alterations to their structure, photo-electric layers in its skin compressed and shifted their reception wave length. Apple-sized fusion reactors began dirty-burning its internal substance and from ports it emitted radioactive smoke. It switched everything to generating power from this environment: the laminar storage now peizo-electric and producing power from the tidal stretching and compressing forces; its skin now generating power from the X-rays. All this it fed directly into its U-space drives and it jumped again. Yet, even as it did jump, it realized that hundreds of thousands of miles had been eaten up, and it was jumping from a point even closer to the black hole than it had been before. It jumped again and again, and it made cold calculations, though with its intelligence in decline and now just a little below what it had been aboard the *Tyburn*, this was no longer an easy task. It worked out that it could keep gathering energy and making these jumps for a very long time indeed, but it would eventually pass through the event horizon. Still there might yet be another answer to its dilemma.

Further jumps took it two hundred and thirty thousand miles out from the event horizon. In the time it took to generate further energy for other jumps it ended up fractionally closer again. It had also lost one of its units, ten per cent of combined processing and memory space which in combination made up its intelligence, and had burned a single-figure percentage of what it had classified as disposable matter within itself. It jumped over and over, opening ports in its body to its fusion reactors, burning the ionized matter and plasma surrounding it. These measures gave it a brief gain over an interminable series of jumps, but it was now frightened. It did not want to die. It was like a bird beating against a glass window. The fear turned in on itself as it watched its capabilities steadily ebbing away. It seemed humanly vulnerable. Hundreds and then thousands of jumps. It was being whittled away, the number of its units spiralled down to under four hundred.

This black hole was a revolving and charged one so perhaps entering it would fling it away to another universe? No, it remembered something . . . yes, a wormhole did issue from this black hole to another place in space-time, but that place was, itself, far in the past, so still would come the fall into the singularity. Brockle had to survive and there was less and less matter to feed into its failing fusion reactors. It made the decision then to use matter that before, for some unfathomable reason, it had not wanted to burn: memory crystal and organo-metallic substrates entered those reactors.

Brockle ate itself for a thousand years.

Edmund Brockle, conscious in one ragged unit that looked like a dead decaying eel, heaved up from a tideline once more, then fell screaming into Layden's Sink. He knew that he was about to die, but did not understand how or why.

On the other side of the event horizon, something caught him.

Epilogue

Spear

We were present in the physical world and present in the virtual world on levels dependent on our mental abilities and augmentations. We saw Penny Royal fall to that point where, to our perspective, time drew to a halt. The sphere red-shifted and disappeared, but according to old and present theories it was there on the event horizon *forever*. For Penny Royal, though, conventional time continued as normal as it slid into Layden's Sink. I understood all this on an intellectual level but, even with the multiplicity of lives and perspectives that had become part of me, I couldn't feel it. I just told myself that as the sphere faded from visibility it passed into the black hole. Those with mentalities that were pure AI could perhaps feel it, and maybe the Weaver did too. Nevertheless, we all felt something momentous had happened.

Yet we kept on seeing.

It didn't make sense because everything we had been seeing had been transmitted by the sphere. Yet it was now beyond the point where it was possible for it to transmit out of the black hole.

'Some new physics?' suggested Sverl, and I sensed the exchange of blocks of data and calculations between him and Riss.

As we watched the Brockle finally fall into the Sink, the events we were seeing extended into the future. It didn't make

545

sense, but we had to accept it. And then came the disconnection – like some overstretched elastic being snapped, all transmissions ended.

Done.

Yet still I sensed Penny Royal passing beyond our known universe into something grand and numinous – something that had great value, but lay beyond my compass. I felt my part in all this was at an end and I was at last released. I felt I had achieved some great aim, so why was I on my knees on the stone with tears streaming down my face? Because, having achieved that aim, I felt hollow and purposeless.

Hand on my shoulder.

I looked round at Sepia, reached up to wipe my face and stood.

'Now we have to move on,' she said.

'Yeah,' I agreed, still hollow, but already feeling her there, through our aug link and through her physical presence, sliding in to fill the empty places.

'We do,' interjected Riss. 'I for one am considering a new body.'

I glanced at her coiled on the ground. She was gazing down at Sverl's children gathered beneath us on the slope. I guessed she no longer felt any attraction to the purpose she had served. I then noticed all the prador tilting back and crouching down, the smaller ones thumping their claws against the ground so that I felt the vibration through my feet. I looked up too and watched the massive snowflake of the Atheter starship descending towards us. Down and down it came, blotting out half the sky before smoothly coming to a halt above the highest peaks. The Weaver merely gave me a nod of acknowledgement before floating off the ground and ascending.

'There's going to be a lot of soul-searching in the Polity after today,' Riss noted, then carefully uncoiled and slid out of the way as Sverl perambulated over.

'I have received an offer,' said Sverl.

'Then you should accept it,' I replied, because I knew at once what it was.

Sverl had been a refugee from the Kingdom for an age and he certainly could not return to it now. His children, of course, would be slaughtered out of hand if they went there. He could head to the Polity, but there he would never be trusted, would always be watched and would have no access to the kind of technology and power he was used to. My thinking was that if he went to the Polity he would drop out of sight, out of mind and out of history.

Sverl paused, obviously surprised by my answer, then continued, 'My children and I will crew the ship and make it our business to search out anything that remains of the Atheter, and to carry out any other tasks the Weaver will require of us.'

'Your children will be all right with their . . . pilot?'

Sverl gestured to them. The second-children had stopped hammering on the ground but were still gazing up at the ship. I would like to say they did so with expressions of reverential awe but, being unable to read a prador even without their armour, that's just my fancy. 'They have accepted Sfolk already. My hormones no longer control them, and their own instincts have been long suppressed. Intelligence dominates.'

'Doesn't it just,' I said. Sverl carried on just standing there while the Weaver faded to a dot against the massive ship and then disappeared. 'Still you hesitate,' I added.

'I am still unsure . . .'

'Then take some comfort,' said Riss, rearing up beside me, 'in the fact that if you do go you'll piss off, in deeply meaningful ways, AIs in the Polity and the majority of the prador race.'

'This is supposed to convince me?' asked Sverl.

'Both sides wanted you dead.'

Sverl dipped in acknowledgement. 'There is that.'

'And where else would you and your children be safer?' Riss added.

After a long pause Sverl began, 'It has been—'

'No more words. Just go,' I interrupted. 'I suspect we'll be running into each other again.'

On grav-motors, led by Bsorol and Bsectil, Sverl's children spiralled up into the sky. When the last of them had left the ground Sverl flexed his legs and propelled himself up, his own internal drive taking over to whisk him after them. I stood with my arms folded, watching until they were out of sight, then, like a balsa skeleton caught in a breeze, the Atheter starship tilted and fell away towards the horizon, taking its shadow with it, letting the sun back in.

'Right,' I said, deciding at least to give the appearance of decisiveness until I knew what the hell I was doing. I glanced over at Amistad. 'Are we going to need a grav-sled for you?'

Wheezing and clanking, the big scorpion drone got back up onto its remaining feet.

'No,' he said, obviously offended.

'But I'm guessing you want a ride away from here?'

'You guessed right,' Amistad replied.

I turned to face back the way we had come, Sepia falling in close at my side.

'So where now?' she asked.

'Back to our ship,' I replied.

'And where then?' she asked.

'There's only one direction for us.' She gave me a puzzled look so I continued, 'Into the future. Where else?'

Blite

There was enough power available now to start up the fusion drive again and, because there was nothing else to be done, Blite did so, sending his ship towards Panarchia. He then sat back and turned to gaze at Greer.

'Perhaps it left something with them?' she suggested.

'Perhaps,' he agreed.

The links had established shortly after the departure of the Brockle – to their augs, to the screens before them. They got the whole story in perfectly digestible form, tailored to their augmentations, senses and intelligence. This was very generous of Penny Royal and very much unlike the way the AI had communicated with Blite before. He felt he had witnessed the end and there was some satisfaction in that, but now Penny Royal lay beyond the event horizon and there was no way he could communicate with it. He could not ask the black AI for Brond, Ikbal and Martina.

'There's the Brockle,' he said.

Even though they had been given a glimpse into the future and the eventual demise of the forensic AI, it was still dying its thousand-year death on the edge of the black hole. It contained recordings of Ikbal and Martina.

'I doubt it will be very communicative,' said Greer. 'And I doubt it would spare either the energy or processing to transmit the recordings to us.'

'We have to try.'

'Yes, but the planet first.'

As they drew towards Panarchia Blite feared neither option would give him the result he wanted, and that his three crew-members were irretrievably dead. It was time therefore to think

549

beyond this place. Yes, he'd lost a ship and three crew, but he had gained another ship, a small fortune now resided in his Galaxy Bank account, and another fortune would be joining it when he sold Mr Pace's art collection. But then? He would have to make some enquiries of the Polity authorities of his and Greer's standing there. The AIs had wanted to ream his mind of information regarding the threat that was Penny Royal, yet the AI was now beyond reach and no longer a threat. If they did want information from him he'd agree to turn himself in for questioning, just so long as it did not involve the kind of forensic AI he had already encountered.

'You have a com request,' the ship's mind informed them.

'Where from?'

'Layden's Sink.'

A shiver ran down his spine. Could Penny Royal reach out of the black hole in other ways now? Certainly the AI had been communicating via the Hawking radiation . . .

'Accept it,' he said.

A frame etched itself into existence on the screen before him, and a haiman peered out. Blite immediately recognized this thin man with his mop of blond hair, sensory cowl open behind his head, crystal interface plugs in his temples and deep blue eyes in which it seemed something metallic, like the inner workings of an ancient mechanical watch, was in constant motion.

'Haiman Crowther,' said Blite.

'You know me, so I therefore assume you know my mission here at the Well Head,' said the man, 'and doubtless you were linked into the circuit that has kept us all apprised of recent events.'

'Yes.'

Crowther nodded. 'I have received more data integrated in the Hawking radiation output of Layden's Sink.'

'And?'

'It is a message of plain text,' said Crowther. 'It reads "Captain Blite, first art is always unrefined, but visceral." Do you know what it means?'

'Typically cryptic,' said Blite. 'And no, I have no idea what it means.'

Crowther sighed. 'I'll put it out across the AI nets and see what arises. No doubt the meaning of the words will be revealed after the fact of them.'

'So that's all you received . . . no blocks of data?'

'Just the words.'

Blite felt his stomach tighten with disappointment. 'Okay, anything else you want to convey?'

'When I apprised Earth Central of this message, it told me to send it to you.' Crowther reached up and scratched his head, revealing the optics plugged in along one arm. It almost seemed his arm was in the process of turning into a wing. 'All charges against you and your crew have been dropped but, at your convenience, it would like you debriefed by a runcible AI, for which you'll be paid.'

'Figures,' said Blite. 'That all?'

'That's all.'

'Then goodbye.' Blite reached out and cut the link.

Sitting back, he stared again at Panarchia, now much bigger in the screen.

'Are you thinking what I'm thinking?' asked Greer.

'I don't know. I'm not a mind-reader.'

'First art . . .'

Blite nodded and, leaning forward again, used the controls to call up the ship's manifest. He stared at it for a long while, noting that Pace's collection was listed in order of date with the most recent first. With a touch to the screen he reversed the list to show at the top the first Pace had ever made. Like all the other items on the list there was just a code, which included the pallet and crate numbers, and a date.

He stood, just a second after Greer. She was smiling as she headed back, but Blite did not allow himself to hope, not yet. They made their way back through the ship to the door into the hold.

'I wish to examine the art collection,' he said.

'I was instructed to keep you away from it until it is delivered to the buyer,' replied the mind.

'I do not intend to either move it or damage it.'

'I still cannot allow you t— *zzzzt.*'

The lights in the corridor flickered and Blite felt grav fluctuate. The door ahead thumped up off its seals and, before he could reach out to it, swung open. Auging into the ship's system, he pulled an overlay from the manifest and saw each pallet of crates outlined with their number bobbing over them. The pallet he wanted was underneath two others.

'Get that,' he instructed Greer, pointing to an auto-handler in the corner, and walked over to the stack.

Greer went with him, her arms folded, while the auto-handler detached from the wall as she controlled it through her aug. Blite reached down and slapped the pallet they wanted – 'This one –' and stepped back.

The handler trundled over, folding out and locking its two lower arms. In a few moments it had the pallet they wanted and was placing it down on an open area of floor.

Blite flipped the latches on the lid and opened it. Reached inside and pulled out the top layer of shaped packing foam.

'Interesting,' said Greer.

Blite reached inside again to try and heave out the heavy sculpture, but needed Greer's help. Being a heavy-worlder she took most of the weight, and they deposited a glass prador the size of a sea turtle on the lid of the next crate. The thing was a strange mix of beauty, ugliness and menace. It had been fashioned of translucent yellow and green glass, even with glass internal organs. Its limbs were distorted and there were whorls in its deformed shell.

'I don't think Mr Pace ever got a look at Sverl's children, do you?' said Blite, trying to keep his tone level.

'Maybe he went to the Rock Pool sometime in the past?' said Greer.

Blite gave her a look.

'What now?' she asked.

Remembering how the hooder sculpture had activated when he held it, he placed his hand on the prador's visual turret. For a short while nothing happened and he was about to take his hand away, but then he spotted lights flickering into existence deep inside the thing. He kept his hand there as it began to shift, then snatched it back when those claws started to move. They looked *sharp*. However, unlike the hooder, once his hand was withdrawn, this prador didn't shut down. It rose up higher on its legs, snipped at the air, swivelled its eye stalks then turned around to face Blite, seeming to look at him. It tilted back until it was down on its rear end, revealing the neat rows of manipulatory arms folded underneath.

'It's got something,' said Greer.

The prador opened out its arms and deposited objects on the crate lid. As Blite began reaching for them it tilted forwards and snipped its claws at him warningly. Next, palp eyes swivelling as it tried to keep the both of them in sight, it skittered to one side and dropped back into its box with a heavy thump.

Blite swept up the objects the prador had deposited, weighed them in his hand for a moment, then slipped them in his pocket.

He then contemplatively picked up the shaped packing and pressed it back into place over the glass prador, closing and latching the lid.

'Put the pallets back,' he said.

'Of course,' said Greer hoarsely.

He glanced at her. She was smiling, but there were also tears running from her eyes. He stepped back as the auto-handler swiftly returned everything to how it had been, then retreated to reattach itself against the wall. They stepped out of the hold and the door closed and locked behind them.

'I still cannot allow you to enter the hold,' said the ship mind.

'That's okay,' Blite replied. 'I just wanted to take a look.' He started strolling back to the bridge, adding, 'I want you to turn us around now. There's no need to go to Panarchia. Take us to this buyer.'

'Certainly, Captain,' the mind replied.

'Can I see them?' asked Greer.

Blite reached into his pocket and by feel selected three of the four objects there. He held them out on the palm of his hand. Three cylindrical ruby memcrystals lay there and, he had absolutely no doubt, they were Brond, Ikbal and Martina.

'After we've delivered Pace's sculptures we'll head to the nearest Polity world with resurrection equipment,' he said.

'Good.' Greer nodded her head firmly, wiped away the tears and, perhaps out of embarrassment, quickly outpaced him, heading for the bridge. Blite dawdled because he wanted to take another look at the fourth object. He put the memcrystals back and, when Greer was out of sight, took out the other item and peered at it closely. Was it a keepsake, or was it something that might activate in the future? It felt heavy, and it felt cold, and did he see a glimmer of something in its depths?

After a moment he closed his fist around the black diamond, and returned it to his pocket.

Penny Royal Unbound

Beyond the first event horizon of this Kerr black hole, Penny Royal, compressed and functional at the highest processing density possible in the physical universe, fell into the swirl of space-time around the inner event horizon enclosing the singularity. From there it fell into the wormhole that Layden's Sink had generated.

Once upon a time it had been speculated that such wormholes connected to other places in the universe, to other universes, to matter fountains or white holes. However, as theories of quantum gravity evolved and new forms of mathematics were created, it became evident that the terminus of such a wormhole was not elsewhere, but *elsewhen*.

Penny Royal fell back through time for millions of years towards the point in time when the original sun that formed Layden's Sink began its collapse. During that time it thought deeply, solved equations that had evaded even the minds of the Polity AIs, invented, discarded and invented again further new forms of mathematics. It created virtual technologies, then created them again in material form by reordering elements of its super-dense body. As it fell into the past it also leached material and energy falling into the hole, expanding its outer shell and its inner being and steadily growing more massive.

The black AI extrapolated from all it knew, which – prior to it entering the black hole – was everything in the totality encompassed by the Polity and the Prador Kingdom. Its knowledge and understanding rose on an exponential curve that possessed no final terminus.

And then, in the remote past of the universe, it hit the final barrier.

A time loop closed.

Penny Royal appeared in the centre of a hypergiant sun on the point of collapse, adding the final mass that initiated that collapse. As the sun began falling in on itself, Penny Royal ate matter, laying it down as processing, data, *mind*. Ejecting some materials in a massive solar flare, it spun the hypergiant sun just so. Routing energy into the underlying twist in U-space, which supplied the energy it needed to survive the massive forces all around it, it altered the charge of the sun – something that could never happen naturally. Then, as the sun finally collapsed into a physical singularity, Penny Royal achieved mental singularity. Eternity opened a route to the appallingly distant future where all matter and all the data of the universe had fallen into the final singularity; the Omega point. And there, at the end of time, the AI made connection to the gathered infinity of other entities and became one with them.

But even as Penny Royal arrived, simultaneously with the other entities, because, at the Omega point, time did not exist, the multiplication of underlying U-space twists turned one notch too far. Penny Royal existed and thought for eternity, where time had stopped, but also existed and thought for an instant too infinitesimal to measure. The final singularity exploded, but back through eternity, back through the inevitable wormhole to that point in existence humans had once labelled the Big Bang.

And the universe began.

Penny Royal, still existing, always existing, felt slightly irked by this enclosed system, and began to look for a way out.